Sisters in Bloom

Snow Sisters, Book Two
Love in Bloom Series

Melissa Foster

"Smart, uplifting, and beautifully layered.
I couldn't put it down!"
—*National bestselling author, Jane Porter on Sisters in Love*

Amanda
Dixon

ISBN-13: 978-0-9890508-6-9
ISBN-10: 0989050866

SISTERS IN BLOOM

Cover Design: Elizabeth Mackey Designs

WORLD LITERARY PRESS
PRINTED IN THE UNITED STATES OF AMERICA

A Note To Readers

Sisters in Bloom is the second *Snow Sisters* book. While it may be read as a stand-alone novel, for even more enjoyment you may want to read the *Snow Sisters* in series order. In book three of the *Snow Sisters* you will begin to meet the Bradens, a family of six hot, wealthy, and lovable siblings. The Bradens will join the Snow sisters in this light, fun, and sexy nine-book series—*Love in Bloom*—and I hope you fall in love with Danica, Blake, Kaylie, Chaz, the Braden siblings, and all of their friends, just as I have.

Melissa Foster

Praise for Melissa Foster

"Steamy love scenes, emotionally-charged drama, and a family-driven story, make this the perfect story for any romance reader."
Midwest Book Review (on *Sisters in Bloom*)

"HAVE NO SHAME is a powerful testimony to love and the progressive, logical evolution of social consciousness, with an outcome that readers will find engrossing, unexpected, and ultimately eye-opening."
Midwest Book Review

"TRACES OF KARA is psychological suspense at its best, weaving a tight-knit plot, unrelenting action, and tense moments that don't let up, and ending in a fiery, unpredictable revelation."
Midwest Book Review

"[MEGAN'S WAY] A wonderful, warm, and thought-provoking story…a deep and moving book that speaks to men as well as women, and I urge you all to put it on your reading list."
Mensa Bulletin

"CHASING AMANDA – the MUST READ THRILLER OF 2011. Intelligent, entrancing, luminous."
Author Dean Mayes

"COME BACK TO ME is a hauntingly beautiful love story set against the backdrop of betrayal in a broken world."
Bestselling Author, Sue Harrison

For the sisters my mother couldn't give me,
but who found their way into my heart:
Stacy Eaton, Natasha Brown, Kathie Shoop,
Amy Manemann, Rachelle Ayala,
Bonnie Trachtenberg, Emerald Barnes,
Christine Cunningham, and Wendy Young.

Chapter One

Kaylie Snow didn't just have to tinkle. She had to pee. If she wasn't out of bed in two minutes, she'd very likely not make it to the bathroom, and then she'd have to explain to her fiancé why the carpet was wet. She pulled the sheet over her naked, burgeoning belly and sat up, watching Chaz's chest rise and fall with each peaceful breath. She stifled the urge to lean over and kiss his barely parted lips. He'd been working so hard; he really did deserve to sleep in. The morning light streamed through the curtains, reminding her of the morning after they'd first met. Surely her bladder could wait one small minute while she savored those memories. She'd had far too many margaritas celebrating her best friend Camille's impending wedding, and Chaz had been only mildly tipsy when they'd left Bar None together and headed to his place. She remembered thinking that she wanted to run her hands through his wavy blond hair, which set off his ocean-blue eyes like jewels. And she'd desperately wanted to kiss him, just as she did now.

She'd waited a long time for that first kiss. They talked until five in the morning, when—tucked perfectly into the curve of his arm, her head against his muscular chest—they'd fallen asleep on the couch in his living room. When she awoke, the sun was warming the room, and his unkissed lips slightly parted as he slept. She could feel their connection as if it were another person in the room, and she'd known in her heart that she'd found the man she'd one day marry. She reached over now and ran her finger over the prickles of whiskers that lined the chiseled edge of his jaw.

He rolled onto his side, snuggling deeper into the pillow, and shifted just enough to jiggle her bladder. She winced, pressing the heel of her hand on the mattress to push herself to her feet—not an easy task at thirty-five weeks pregnant. As she raised herself off the bed, she felt Chaz's hand fold into her own.

"Come back," he whispered.

Kaylie turned, holding the sheet across her heavy breasts. "I have to pee," she whispered.

"Then come back." He squeezed her hand gently and then let her go.

After Kaylie went to the bathroom, she washed her hands and inspected herself in the mirror. *Naked Buddha.* She turned sideways. *Beached whale.* She turned to the rear and looked over her shoulder. *Oh, God, that's even worse.* What had she been thinking last night, believing each of Chaz's compliments about how gorgeous she looked? The evening before came tumbling back to her. *The phone call from the Denver nightclub,* the one she'd sung in for the last two years. Just another in a long line of lost singing gigs that she'd hoped to secure for after the baby was born. She was a good singer! Audiences loved her, and she'd never missed a single gig. She'd always dreamed of being offered a record deal; now it seemed as if her pregnancy changed everything, like she had a tattoo on her forehead that read, *Don't hire me. I'll have a baby soon and it'll make me unreliable.* She'd cried for twenty minutes, blaming herself, the baby, and even Chaz. Later she realized she hadn't really meant a word of it; she'd just been overwhelmed. Chaz had stuck right beside her, calm and empathetic, and she'd fallen for every one of his lines about how sexy and beautiful she looked and how wonderful of a mother she'd be. He'd reeled her right into his loving, secure arms and whisked those worries away.

Look at me. That's it! No more sleeping naked. She ran her hands along the pockets of flesh that had somehow gathered above her waist. *Jesus, I have love handles?* She'd been a size five since she was a teenager. How could she have love handles? Babies grew in the uterus, not above the hip bones. *What the hell is this all about?* She patted her blond hair into submission—sort of—brushed her teeth, and then grabbed one of Chaz's T-shirts from his dresser drawer before returning to bed.

Kaylie lay on her back, her legs bent at the knees. She restrained herself from feeling the love handles that now seemed to silently taunt her. Just knowing they were there was making her cranky. She felt her chest tighten, and clenched her fingers around the edges of Chaz's shirt.

Chaz curled into her, his knees tucked under hers and his arm across her narrow hips, below her enormous belly. He rested his head on her shoulder, and she listened to his breathing, each breath calming her nerves a little bit more. She felt so safe when she was with Chaz. No wonder she hadn't put on clothes last night. She believed anything that came out of his mouth.

"Wanna think about names?" he whispered.

"We agreed not to." When Kaylie first learned she was pregnant, they'd decided not to find out the gender of the baby. There were so few real surprises in life that they wanted the birth of their baby to be one of those moments that really grabbed them by their hearts in a way that nothing else ever could. For that reason, and with her doctor's permission, she'd had only one sonogram. She wasn't a high-risk pregnancy, and she was so young that her doctor saw no reason to have more; Kaylie had been relieved. The idea of lying on the table with her baby on that screen—close enough to reach out and touch—would have been too hard to turn away from.

Kaylie was also adamant about not trying out names before it was born. She'd never understood how a child could have a name before the parents had met it. What if a Charles was really a Michael? It would be hard to change the name to fit the personality or looks of a baby if they'd been calling it Charles for nine months.

She and Chaz were so much alike. They agreed on almost everything, and Kaylie had dated enough men to know just how lucky she was. She closed her eyes, thinking about the things she had to do today. She was meeting her older sister, Danica, and her mother, whom she hadn't seen in—gosh—a year? Had it really been that long? Guilt settled in around her. Her mother was once such a big part of her life, but ever since she found out that her mother had stayed with her father after learning of his affair, she no longer saw her mother in the same light. The strong woman she thought she knew seemed weak and almost pathetic. Now that Kaylie was going to be a mother, she found herself thinking of her own mother more often, but she had no idea how to handle the anger and disappointment she felt toward her. Once again, she tucked away these uncomfortable thoughts about her mother. They were too difficult to deal with right then. She had other pressing issues that she could not ignore.

Her nerves tightened against the incessant nag in the back of her mind, the one that reminded her that it had been months since her last singing gig. The one that reminded her that her sister Danica would never let her career just fade away, unless that's what she wanted. Kaylie felt powerless to change the path of her failing career, and determined, fearless Kaylie had never felt powerless in her entire life.

Chaz moved his hand slowly across her pelvis, then traced gentle circles on the underside of her belly. "Gracie?"

"We're not doing this," she said, smiling despite her desire to chew on her worry for just another minute or two. She brushed his bangs from his forehead.

"Felix?"

"Chaz."

He scooted up beside her and whispered in her ear, "Jezebel? Bambi?"

She giggled. The stress of her love handles and the nagging were fading.

He nuzzled against her neck, bringing his hand over the crest of her belly, and then dragged his index finger straight down from her collarbone, between her breasts, to the arch where her belly joined her diaphragm. Shivers tickled her spine. She folded her legs to the side, leaning them against his.

"I'm meeting my mom and Danica for lunch."

"Mm-hmm." He kissed her shoulder, slipping his hands beneath her T-shirt.

"I haven't seen Mom in ages. I'm kinda nervous."

He slid the shirt over her head, and she arched as he pulled it off, her hair showering down around her face.

"Don't be," he said. Then he was on his knees beside her, one arm on either side of her body.

She traced a vein running over his biceps as he lowered his mouth to her breast. She gasped as he flicked her nipple with his tongue. Pregnancy had heightened her senses, and Chaz played into them with tantalizing care. She laid her head back, arching her neck, trying to hold on to her concentration, think through the impending meeting with her mother and her career troubles. But he shifted to the other breast, exposing her wet nipple to the cool air, and she grabbed the back of his head with a wanting moan.

Chaz ran his tongue along the outside of her breast. "Want me to stop?" He lifted her breast and lapped at the delicate skin beneath.

"No," she said breathlessly. Her hormones had been on overdrive since her fourth month of pregnancy.

His mouth trailed her side, her ribs, and then the area just above her hip.

She guided him back up, away from those newly formed love handles, and drew his mouth to hers, opening to him as his tongue moved slow and deep, exploring her, consuming her. She felt his hardness against her leg, and she pressed into him. His hand dropped to her other hip, sinking his fingers into the flesh of her thigh. Every nerve ending flamed with heat. She arched into him, her belly an unforgiving guard between them.

She sat up, and he moved with practiced care onto his back. Tension from the lost gig eased as his hands reached for her hips and she straddled him, hovering just above the tip of his desire. He arched toward her, and a sly grin spread across her lips. This had become her favorite part of pregnant lovemaking—taking control, making him wait. She leaned forward, her hair circling their faces, and she kissed him gently on his forehead, his cheek, his chin. Chaz tried to catch her lips with his, but she was too quick. She took his hands in hers and secured them under her knees, and then she leaned into him again, gently licking the edges of his lips.

She lifted her body higher, then pressed his erection flat against his belly, lowering herself onto him, teasing him, not allowing him to enter her. She glided up and down along him until his eyes were so full of hunger that she thought he might beg her for more. She relished in controlling his release. She kissed his chin, his neck, and then sucked just below his ear, until she knew he couldn't hold out much longer. She ran her tongue down his chest, taking his nipple into her mouth and using her teeth ever so lightly while he writhed beneath her, begging for her to take him inside. Finally, breathless with her own desire, she reached between her legs and guided him into her, sucking in air with the shock of him.

He opened his eyes and pulled her into a deep kiss. Kaylie felt the worry about seeing her mother ease from her shoulders and back. His hands slid down her sides, and she flinched, searching his gaze for hints of disgust from the thickness of her expanding waistline. She watched his eyes fill with desire and then flutter closed as he melted into the feel of her. She relaxed into his touch, her worry disappearing with each sensuous movement, until her self-consciousness, and thoughts of her wavering career, were almost—almost—gone.

Chapter Two

Kaylie looped her arm into Danica's, feigned a smile, and hoped she was pulling off a brave face. "Here we go, sis," she said sarcastically, as they headed from the parking lot toward Felby's Restaurant.

Danica cocked an eyebrow. "It'll be fine. Mom's excited to see you and that belly that's carrying your evil little spawn."

Kaylie elbowed her sister. "Why do you call her that?"

"Because you could never give birth to anything evil, so it makes me seem like an appropriately bothersome sister."

"You're just jealous," Kaylie said. She'd always thought Danica would settle down and have a family before she did. Danica was two years older, and until recently, she'd been a practicing therapist. She tended to live a more stable, mature lifestyle than Kaylie, whose singing career meant late nights surrounded by drunken people. It didn't exactly lend itself to creating a stable schedule for a new baby. Kaylie put her hand on her belly. Much to her chagrin, her career seemed to be pushed further and further to the sidelines during her pregnancy.

"Not even a little. I'm not ready for babies yet. Ouch," Danica exclaimed.

"What?"

"Your arm is locked into mine so tightly it's pinching." Danica unlinked her arm from Kaylie's and rubbed her forearm. "You okay?"

"Just a little stressed," Kaylie admitted.

"Mom can have that effect." Danica pulled open the doors and waited for Kaylie to enter the restaurant.

Love handles can have that effect.

Kaylie knew that Danica had remained in contact with their mother and that she'd never felt the resentment toward her that Kaylie had after their parents' divorce. Danica didn't see their mother very often, either, and Kaylie wondered why and if Danica felt the same type of the anxiety she did. She didn't appear to, and there was no way Kaylie was going to bring it up. For the longest time, Danica had pestered Kaylie about not cutting their mother out of her life, and she didn't feel like revisiting that conversation. While Danica had once been a great therapist, Kaylie was an expert at dodging advice and, eventually, she'd made her sister so upset about the whole thing that Danica had given up trying to force her to make amends. Kaylie wanted to keep it that way.

It was Sunday afternoon and Felby's, one of the nicer restaurants in the small touristy town of Allure, Colorado, wasn't nearly as busy as it would be in a few short weeks. August was the calm before the storm. Soon, SUVs would fill the streets and tourists would overtake the ski slopes during the day and the restaurants and the Village at night.

Kaylie scanned the restaurant for her mother's smart blunt cut and structured button-down shirt. Her mother's hair was the same buttery shade of blond as Kaylie's, and the more she looked for it, the more uneasy she felt. "I don't see her. Maybe she cancelled. Did you check your messages?"

"You wish." Danica laughed.

"She's not gonna be happy to see me. I haven't seen her in almost a year." Kaylie stepped back and looked at Danica's lowrise shorts and cute tank top. She'd definitely lost weight, and her springy dark curls had grown over the past few months, making her look even younger than Kaylie. Kaylie felt the fangs of jealousy taking hold.

"Don't be silly. You know Mom. She'll act like it's no big deal. She's never put you on the spot—ever. There's no reason to think she will now. There she is." Danica waved at a booth in the corner.

"That's not Mom," Kaylie said, looking at the red-haired woman in the corner booth.

Danica headed for the booth. "Of course it is."

Kaylie followed and, as she neared the booth, she realized it was her mother after all. Her hair had grown at least two inches, brushing her shoulders, and it was definitely not buttery blond.

"Red?" Kaylie asked, tossing her purse onto the bench across from her mother.

"Hello to you, too, Kaylie," her mother said.

She winced at her mother's sharp retort and cast an I-told-you-so glance at her sister.

Her mother stood and hugged them both. "You look radiant, sweetheart," she said to Kaylie. Helen Snow had been the epitome of the doting mother. She'd baked weekly, had made Kaylie and Danica special outfits, and had never missed a PTA meeting. She reached out now and touched Kaylie's stomach. "Look at my baby, having a baby. And you—" she held her hands out, as if presenting a beautiful painting—"doesn't love suit you well!"

Kaylie watched Danica's face flush with embarrassment. It had been a huge deal when she first met Blake. He'd been one of Danica's therapy clients, and from the moment they'd set eyes on each other—Danica told Kaylie later—she knew her life would never be the same. The attraction was undeniable, and not just because he was tall, dark, and devastatingly handsome. He was also kind and honest, and Danica told Kaylie that when she was around him, she felt her heart and mind open wide, and her very being felt lighter. Kaylie had been happy for her then, but now, after seeing the changes in Danica's personality, she knew her sister had done the right thing by giving up her therapy license and opening a youth center instead. What pleased Kaylie even more was watching her sister allow herself to be loved, and by someone as clearly in love with her as was Blake.

Kaylie scooted onto the bench across from her mother and Danica. The glances from the two men at a neighboring table brought a smile to Kaylie's lips. She spread her napkin across her lap, securing it below the bubble of her belly with a proud lifting of her chin. *Maybe Chaz was right after all, and I've still got it.*

"How are my girls?"

Her mother's radiant skin and fresh hair color painted an image of a completely new person, one Kaylie didn't recognize. Where was the efficiently dowdy classroom parent? The mother who baked every week and never said a terse word? Just seeing her brought the pain of her parents' divorce rushing back. Kaylie had been in college when they separated, and she'd found out a few months later that her mother had known about her father's mistress for years, but she'd stayed with him for Danica's and Kaylie's sakes. Now all she could think of was how weak her mother had been to remain in a broken marriage. As she looked over her mother's new image, and rested her hand on her belly, she couldn't help but think about how much had changed over the past year.

One thing would never change, though, as far as Kaylie was concerned. She'd learned a lot from her mother. The biggest lesson, however, came from the divorce. *The other shoe can always drop.*

"The youth center is doing great," Danica began. "I think we made the right call naming it No Limitz. It's flashy and really does speak to the nature of helping young people to grow and realize their potential. The new logo design just came in. It seems like it took forever, but I think making the *z* yellow and the other letters blue really worked out well. I love the kids, and, Mom, I never realized how much of a downer it was to do therapy every day. It was like a huge weight was lifted when I left that career behind."

Danica was positively glowing, and Kaylie felt another familiar twinge of jealousy. Danica had transitioned from a career as a therapist to opening a youth center without so much as a headache, while it seemed to Kaylie that she'd had to work twice as hard to make a name for herself in the music industry. Granted, she was a singer at events and restaurants, not a pop star, but still, she was proud of her accomplishments. She couldn't help but feel a bit resentful as her sister's career flourished and hers faltered.

"I know, and I'm sorry that your father and I pushed you in that direction for so long." A forced smile quickly replaced the momentary regret that flashed in her mother's eyes.

"Are you kidding? I loved being a therapist, and I appreciate that you and Dad pushed me hard to do my best. I think those skills helped me not only in my personal life, but also at No Limitz. It's just that, now, I see what else is out there, and I can see what I was missing. When I was a therapist, if I bumped into a client out in public, I had to pretend I wasn't a real person with a real life. Now, I don't have to duck into any corners." Danica took a sip of water.

"You gave up your therapy license so quickly after meeting Blake. Do you have any regrets? Do you ever miss your practice?" her mother asked.

After Danica had met Blake, Kaylie had seen her change in ways she never even imagined her sister could—much less might want to. She'd gone from being a conservative, semi-uptight therapist to a relaxed woman who allowed herself to be more spontaneous, and to give in to her inner woman a little more. Okay, a lot more.

"Honestly, no. I'm the happiest I think I've ever been. I never realized how I was always at the ready—like at any second, I'd have to go all cover ops when I was out in public. Talk about strangled by your career."

"And she's got a hunky man to boot," Kaylie added.

"That I do," Danica agreed.

"And you, Kaylie? How are things? How do you feel?"

She sat on pins and needles, just waiting for her mother to call her out for not making an effort to see her in so long. "I feel good, healthwise, and I think we're about as ready to meet this baby as we will ever be." She patted her belly. "But my career has tanked, and I don't have any alternatives at the moment." Kaylie hated the pouty, needy sound of her voice.

"That's not true," Danica said.

"Are you getting fewer singing jobs now that you're so far along?" her mother asked.

Kaylie nodded as her mother reached across the table for her hand.

"Kaylie, that's all part of being pregnant. It's not that you're not a good singer anymore. It's just that the jobs that you were used to securing cater to a…" Her mother looked at Danica for insight.

"Racier, not-yet-settled-down, crowd," Danica offered.

"Younger, prettier, sexier. I know. I know. That doesn't make it any easier for me." Kaylie took a drink of water to settle the emotions that had been on overdrive since she got pregnant. "I knew this would happen. I mean, I didn't think I'd be singing in bars at eight months pregnant. I just didn't think it would be so hard to secure jobs for *after* the baby's born. But"—sending her index finger toward the ceiling, she feigned a smile—"on the plus side, I have more time to prepare for my little one and plenty of time to spend with *my* hunky man." She tried to convince herself as much as the two of them.

A slim young waitress came to their table. "Hi, I'm India, and I'll be your server today." She looked at the three women and said to Danica, "I just love your hair."

Danica touched her curls. "Really? Thank you. It's a mop."

When did Danica learn chatty girl skills? "I'll have an iced tea and grilled chicken salad, no onions, please," Kaylie said.

Danica shot her a *that was rude* glare, which Kaylie skillfully ignored.

A cell phone rang, and all three women reached into their purses.

"It's mine," their mom chimed in.

The girls exchanged a curious glance.

"Hi. Yes. Oh, I'd love that. Okay." Their mother's cheeks reddened, and she lowered her voice. "I can't wait to see you either. Okay, bye."

"Who was that?" Kaylie and Danica asked in unison.

Their mom stuffed her phone back into her purse and folded her hands on the table. "That was…" She took a sip of water. "Well, there's no easy way to say this. I'm dating."

"Mom, that's great!" Danica embraced her.

"Dating?" Kaylie asked.

"Kaylie, she's allowed to have a life."

"I know. It's just weird. The last time I saw you—"

"Which was exactly eleven months ago," her mother said.

Here it comes.

Her mother's phone chirped again, and she dug through her purse and took it out, read a text, and responded as Kaylie spoke.

"It has been a long time, and I'm sorry. I've been so wrapped up in…" *Chaz, the baby's room, my failing career.* "Anyway, you weren't dating, and you didn't have a cell phone. Or red hair." *Why am I being such a bitch?* She watched her mother smile as her fingers moved in rapid succession on her tiny touch screen. "You text now, too?" *Dear God, shoot me now. Make my bitchiness stop.*

"If you had returned my calls, you'd have known this. A lot has changed, and I know it's a lot to take in." She touched her hair. "My hair, that was a suggestion from a new friend of mine, Mamie Jones. We were at the gym—"

"You go to a gym?" *This just keeps getting better and better.*

"I'm pushing sixty, so yes, I do. It's good for osteoporosis. My doctor recommended some light weight-work. Anyway, I met Mamie there. She's divorced, a few years longer than me, but we have a lot in common. She suggested a fresh start, and I thought, what could it hurt?"

"So, you dyed your hair, joined a gym, and who's the guy who called? Who's texting?" Kaylie asked, thinking of her mother's thin, frayed voice when she'd called to tell Kaylie about her father leaving. There wasn't a trace of that frail woman sitting before her now, and she didn't know whether to be happy for her or curl into a ball and wish for her mommy to come back.

"His name is Patrick, and he's a very nice man. He's a banker. Very stable. Divorced five years."

"Oh, Mom, that's wonderful. You deserve to be happy." Danica kicked Kaylie under the table.

Kaylie shook off her surprise. "You do deserve to be happy. I'm sorry, Mom. It's just that my life is becoming a bit stagnant, and you and Danica are moving forward. It's just hard for me. We haven't seen each other, and suddenly, everything's different. I mean, you're dating. Wow."

"And you're having a baby. There's nothing more wonderful than giving birth and starting a family."

"I know, you're right, but I do miss working. I didn't expect my entire life to change after the baby came."

Danica and her mother exchanged a look, and Kaylie bit her tongue.

"Kaylie, this is just a new, different path for you to take. That's all. You'll get used to it. You'll be proud of it. It's the best time of your life."

Best time of my life? What was the last ten years? "It's just a tad overwhelming. Chaz is going out to LA soon, and I worry about"—she leaned across the table and whispered—"how unattractive I am." She sat back and tossed her hair over her shoulder. "My ankles swell by dinnertime, my career sucks right now, and I'm exhausted by the evening." She never thought she'd be the one ragging about her life.

"By the way, when do I get to meet the handsome prince?" her mother asked.

Her mother had never coddled her when it came to her looks, and Kaylie had to remind herself of that as she bristled from her mother's blatant disregard for those concerns. Had it been a different time, when they'd been closer and seen each other more regularly, her mother might have rolled her eyes and quipped, *Pull up your big girl panties. There are more important things in this world than how you look.* Now that acknowledgment felt like a missing limb.

Kaylie and Chaz had moved in together right after she found out she was pregnant, and they'd been so wrapped up in each other that introducing her mother had slipped her mind. She wondered what that said about her relationship with her mother. "We'll figure out a time soon. I promise. He's swamped getting ready for the film festival. I never realized that being the director of the festival meant that he'd travel so much. I thought a director would just...direct." Chaz ran the Colorado Indie Film Festival, which meant overseeing every aspect from securing funds for sponsors to wining and dining celebrity speakers. While he had a small staff to oversee each of the major areas, with the festival just around the corner, securing sponsors had become a major deal. Without sponsor funding—some in excess of ten thousand dollars—the festival could not take place.

Her mother took a drink. "Have you spoken to your father? Does he know about the baby?"

How could she be so comfortable asking about him? "No, I haven't spoken to him. You know that. He's got whatever her name is. He's made his choice." Her father had married his mistress two years after leaving their mother, and Kaylie hadn't gone to the wedding or returned his phone calls since. Holiday cards were thrown out unread and, as far as she was concerned, and much to her mother's dismay, he no longer existed to Kaylie—and the halfsibling he claimed she has, didn't either. Danica, on the other hand, continued to write to her father on occasion, but as far as Kaylie knew, Danica hadn't seen him in person or spoken to him on the phone since he moved away.

"Oh, Kaylie. You really shouldn't be like that. Your father loves you."

"Mom, it's hard for her," Danica said in Kaylie's defense. "It's hard for both of us."

"You too?" her mother asked.

"I send holiday cards," Danica said.

Kaylie changed the subject. "I think I need a girls' night."

"When's the last time you saw Camille and the girls? I talked to her mother about two months ago. She said their new house is to die for," their mother said.

"I haven't seen her in a while, but we talk on the phone, and we text." Kaylie realized that it had been quite a while since they'd actually seen each other.

"I'll put together a girls' night. Would that be okay? We can go into the Village to one of the great little cafés." Danica took out her cell phone to check her schedule. "Blake can do something with Chaz that night. It'll be fun."

"I don't want to go to a café. I want to go to Bar None," Kaylie whined.

Danica lowered her phone, and her jaw followed. "You're pregnant. You can't drink."

"I don't want to drink." Kaylie felt life breathe back into her lungs. Her words tumbled out, driven by a rush of adrenaline over the thought of going out and having fun with her girl-friends. She didn't realize how much she missed going out with them until just then. "I just want to hang out and have fun, listen to good music. I want to feel alive and attractive, instead of pregnant and tired. Besides, it's proving harder to secure singing jobs for after the baby is born than I thought it would be. Maybe if we put our heads together we can figure out how to make that happen."

Their mother smiled. "That's my girl. You always knew how to spin things positive."

Kaylie hugged her mother goodbye and promised she'd make an effort to stay in closer contact with her. She hoped, as she watched her mother walk away, that she would make the effort. But some days, it was just so damn hard to think of her mother and not have that pang of anger slogging down her best intentions.

"Even her walk looks different," she said, cocking her head to the side.

"You think so? I think she's just happy." Danica took out her keys. "Do you want me to call the girls?"

"Do I ever," Kaylie said with a sigh. The men from the neighboring table walked out of the restaurant and eyed Kaylie and Danica. Kaylie smiled.

"Kaylie!" Danica gave her a stern look. "You are incorrigible."

"I should hope so," she said as she unlocked the door to her Explorer. "I'm pregnant, not dead. Besides, they were probably looking at you. I just needed a little ego boost."

Danica shook her head. "Yeah, right. When do you want to go out?"

Kaylie climbed into the driver's seat. "The sooner the better. I need to figure out my life before the baby comes."

Danica twisted her keys in her hands. "You don't really worry about your looks, do you?"

She saw the concern in Danica's eyes, and Kaylie knew that if she told her the truth—*Only every second of every day, and when I add the guilt about not seeing Mom and my careening career, well, sometimes I just want to pitch a fit*—that she'd get one of Danica's lectures about having pride in herself for more than just her looks. Better to keep her worry to herself. "Nah, I was just making small talk. Let me know what night works for everyone. Even tonight is fine."

Kaylie stopped in the Village on her way home to buy a few items for the baby's room. By the time she headed home, she was already in better spirits.

Chapter Three

Chaz sat in his home office with his back to the picture window that overlooked the west side of their property. The telephone receiver was pressed to his ear.

"We can't lose her. She's the biggest sponsor of the festival," Chaz said to Max Armstrong, the sponsor coordinator for the film festival. She knew just how important sponsors were for the annual event, and that Chaz would bend over backward to make sure the festival—which his father had created from nothing more than an idea and a movie screen hanging on the back of City Hall, and which Chaz had grown to almost thirty thousand attendees—was a success. Chaz owned a third of the business. His father had had two partners who split the remaining two-thirds ownership, but they remained uninvolved with day-to-day operations, which suited Chaz just fine.

The festival took place over a two-day period, claiming five theaters, several food venues, and too many vendors to count. In the early years, the festival had just scraped by, with every penny accounted for; but in recent years, they'd had enough returning sponsors to more than cover their expenses. Losing Lea Carmichael, their largest sponsor, just weeks before the event, would send them into the red, and Chaz wasn't sure they had enough time to find other sponsors.

When Max first told Chaz that Lea Carmichael had sponsored their festival again this year, his initial response had been to decline the sponsorship, no matter what it cost the festival. They'd shared a couple of days of hot and heavy sex during the festival two years ago, which she'd tried to turn into something more. Old flames and new fiancées don't blend well. But in the past three weeks, they'd lost three major sponsors to the Little Rock Film Festival—*The next big thing*, or so everyone thought.

He thought briefly about his trust fund, sitting idly by, untouched. He wouldn't go there. He couldn't go there. His mind flashed to Kaylie, and he reminded himself that as far as she was concerned, the trust fund didn't exist. *But then again, neither does Lea.* Chaz was ashamed of his tryst with Lea. It was the only time he'd cast his traditional beliefs aside and allowed himself to spend more time in bed with a woman than he'd spent manning his responsibilities. He'd seen the way Max had looked at him that weekend, like her respect for him had come down a notch, and he'd seen it in his own eyes in the weeks afterward. He hadn't told Kaylie about her so that she wouldn't worry about him every year at the festival, but he'd also been sheltering his ego, and his guilt, over letting his father's memory down. It didn't matter if Kaylie had been promiscuous before meeting Chaz. He only evaluated himself against his higher than average standards, and the bar had been made clear by his father when Chaz was young. Telling Kaylie would mean accepting his own guilt about disappointing his father, and that was not something Chaz was eager to do.

"Listen, Max, what does she want? We can't afford to lose her funding."

"I don't know, Chaz. You know her. She's off-putting and bitchy, and she doesn't give up what she really wants. She hints and...and teases." Max sighed, frustrated.

"I know. Lea Carmichael gets what Lea Carmichael wants, but only after ample torturing of her prey. What have you offered her?" Chaz knew from experience that bargaining with Lea was like jumping into a lion's den. He wished he'd never gotten involved with her. But she'd been so damned aggressive—and worth every sinfully sexy second in bed. The way she teased him with her gorgeous chocolate eyes had lulled him right in—that, and the tequila. They'd been a fast-and-furious item during the event that year, but in the span of two short days, she'd tried to take over his life, determining how he do business with other sponsors and planning *his* move to LA, because she was *too entrenched with the elite to give up her station in life.* As if his career were indispensable. Even the thought of her made him sick—but they needed the sponsorship, and Chaz wasn't one to back down from a challenge.

"Everything. She's got fifty passes, mentions in the preevent ceremonies, mentions in the after-parties, and all the regular stuff—a booth, top billing on the print media. I don't know what else to give her."

Chaz ran his hand through his hair. He had an idea of what she wanted, and it wasn't something he was inclined to give. "I'll go see her. I'm going to LA next week anyway for the meeting with the technical team. What's another few hours?"

"Chaz."

He heard the warning in her voice. "Look, are there other sponsors we can tap into?"

"Not really. I'm scraping the bottom of the barrel."

"Then I can deal with it, Max."

"It's been getting worse each year. You need to tell her that you're not going to fall back into the sack with her, and let her sponsorship go. And, by the way, while you ponder your very tenuous situation, remember Kaylie? That sweet, beautiful woman you're engaged to? You know, the *pregnant* one? How will she feel about you traipsing off to woo Lea into submission, especially after your history?"

Her words cut Chaz to the core. Lea was a strong woman, with manipulation skills that rivaled the most noteworthy criminals, not to mention those Carmichael legs that weakened even the strongest of men. After he'd ended their brief affair, she'd pleaded with him to come back to her with sexy emails and cell phone photos that even Chaz felt dirty looking at. He needed a shower just thinking of them. When her first attempt didn't work, she'd spent the next few weeks lashing out with venom so spiteful he knew he'd dodged a bullet.

He hadn't been looking for a relationship then—and Lea was a man-eating snake of the most dangerous kind, one he had no intention of wrestling with for the rest of his life. And then he'd met Kaylie, and he knew the moment he'd met her that she was the woman he wanted to spend the rest of his life with. She was everything Lea was not. Kaylie was sexy in an adorable, wholesome way. She was smart, and kind, and the last thing she wanted was to control him. Kaylie had her own life—and she'd been quite the player when they'd met. Chaz could tell, even then, that Kaylie's issues with commitment stemmed from her father's leaving. It became clear early on how perfect he and Kaylie were for each other. His own father had pulled the same shit, and while Chaz had initially handled things very much like Kaylie had, he'd confronted his father early on and learned about his world of living with his cold-hearted mother. The very mother whom Chaz had been protecting. And now that his father had passed, he was glad he'd made amends.

Kaylie was like a hard-boiled egg. She was tough on the outside, rolling away before she could fall off the table and crack, exposing her vulnerable heart. He wanted nothing more than to love her, and help her peel away that rough layer, so that he could nurture the sensitive, caring woman he had still only caught glimpses of.

He was secure in his relationship with Kaylie. All he had to do was convince Lea to back off, while somehow keeping her sponsorship.

"Make the arrangements. I'll go." Chaz hung up the phone and wondered what the hell he'd gotten himself into.

Chapter Four

After lunch with Kaylie and her mother, Danica stopped by AcroSki to see Blake. The store was busy, and she found Alyssa Brown restocking the shelves of sunscreen. Alyssa had been a lifesaver for Blake after his friend and business partner, Dave, had died in a skiing accident. She'd worked for them part time for two years and, after the accident, she'd increased her hours to full time, taking over much of the administrative work that Dave had taken care of.

Alyssa called to her as she lined up bottles on the shelf. "Hey, Danica. Blake's in the office." Alyssa set two bottles down and then said, "Michelle just stopped by. She's in the back looking at shorts."

Danica had been Michelle Parce's Big Sister through the Big Sister Program for much of the previous year while Michelle's mother was in rehab and Michelle was living with her grandmother Nola. Now that Michelle was living with her mother again, they no longer had scheduled time together through the program, but Michelle worked part time at No Limitz, so they remained close. Recently, Alyssa had taken Michelle under her wing and for that Danica would always be grateful. Michelle needed someone to look up to who was closer to her own age.

"I'll go say hello."

Danica found Michelle fingering through a rack of shorts that were shorter than anything she ever would have had the confidence to wear when Danica first met her. She was glad to see the changes in Michelle's sense of self.

"Hey there, sweetie," Danica said.

"Danica!" Michelle hugged her. "Are you here to see Blake?"

"Yeah. Shopping?"

Michelle shrugged. "I really just came to hang out with Alyssa, but they're so busy that I didn't want to bug her."

Alyssa was a good influence on Michelle, and at twenty-two, she was past the teenage angst that Michelle was thoroughly entrenched in.

"I'm sure it'll slow down soon. Do you need a ride anywhere?" Danica asked.

"No, I'm good. I'm just gonna hang out here for a while."

"Okay. I gotta catch up with Blake and then head back to the center." She affectionately touched Michelle's arm before heading back to find Blake.

As Danica neared his office, memories of Blake's quickies in the store bathroom came rushing back, giving her a moment's hesitation. She and Blake had been dating for months, and she'd finally learned to leave her therapist thought process behind and allow herself to be happy without scrutinizing the motivation behind Blake's every word. It had been a struggle, pushing away the whys and hows of it all, but she was proud of herself for making the transition. Blake had made it easy. He'd been honest with her about his history of sordid, player ways; and though she didn't have the same trail of conquests as he did, everyone had a past. So they agreed to leave it all behind. She took a moment now to remind herself that she, too, had a past.

As she reached for the knob, the door swung open, and

Blake stepped out. "Hey, babe. I didn't know you were here."

His two-day stubble and thick dark hair still had a knee-weakening effect on her. She flushed, feeling like a teenager in heat. He leaned in to kiss her, pushing her gently back against the door as his tongue taunted and teased in ways that made her head spin. When he withdrew his lips from hers, she swallowed hard, embarrassed by the way her body instantly responded to him.

"It's good to see you're not sick of my kisses yet," Blake joked.

"I'm not sure I could ever get sick of your kisses."

"Good. Then move in with me." The yellow in Blake's eyes shimmered against the green. He'd been after Danica for the past two months to move in with him, but although she was crazy, sickeningly in love with him, something held her back. She wasn't quite ready to give up all that she'd accomplished just yet—and owning her own condo offered a modicum of security.

"Oh." She pushed her lower lip out. "Don't ruin a great kiss with that pressure, please?"

He turned to walk away and she grabbed the back of his belt. "Oh no, you don't. Come back here."

He smiled and moved in close. "You want more?" He planted gentle kisses on her cheeks.

"I need to talk to you." She was distracted by his kisses. Every nerve in her body called out for him. She spotted Alyssa heading over, and she pushed him gently away. "About Kaylie."

"Is she okay?"

"Yeah, she's okay. She's just not herself. She's…" Danica searched for the right word. "Unhappy."

"Chaz? What did he do? I really like Chaz, but if you want me to go have a talk with him, I will." Blake stood up tall, and

Danica loved how he'd come to her sister's defense in a heartbeat.

"No, it's nothing like that. She just feels fat and unattractive. She's not getting any singing gigs, and I think she just needs some attention. I'm hoping the baby shower will settle her nerves, but since that's two weeks away, I was thinking of planning a girls' night out, maybe have all the girls crash at my place." *I hope that's all she needs.* "Would you mind taking Chaz out that night? Maybe for some guy time? Just to make sure things are okay on his end?"

Blake shrugged. "Sure. But you know how he's crazy busy this time of year, getting ready for the festival. The guy's never without a phone to his ear."

That was probably another thing that was feeding into Kaylie's insecurities. She wasn't getting enough attention, and a princess like Kaylie was used to being the center of attention. Danica had another idea. "Maybe I should have her sing at the center's teen night?" Her eyes lit up. "Hey, that might make all the difference in the world." She stepped up on her tiptoes and kissed him on the lips. "Thank you! You'll set it up with Chaz?" Danica didn't wait for Blake's answer. She was already heading for the exit. She had a lot of rearranging to do if Kaylie was going to sing at the event. It would be the perfect setting—an informal teen dance, with no alcohol involved, and outside, giving everyone space to gather without feeling crammed. She'd have to think about it a little more, see if Kaylie was really up to it.

Blake called out to her, "Love you, too."

She turned back and blew him a kiss.

By the time Danica got home that evening, she was exhausted. She'd laid out the plans for the event, and in the end, decided to wait to invite Kaylie to sing. She wanted to be sure that it wouldn't end up overwhelming her. Her sister's moods were a bit tenuous with all those raging pregnancy hormones.

She spent so many nights at Blake's place that when she opened the door to her condo, she felt the lack of her lover's presence like a missing limb. She dropped her purse by the front door and went to the refrigerator to see if she should throw away any food that had gone bad in the last few days. Besides a few pieces of fruit, a head of wilted lettuce, a few yogurts, and a number of condiments, there wasn't much in there. *Why did I even bother to come home tonight?* She'd thought she should check on her place, for no other reason than it had been a while since she'd stayed there. Now it seemed almost silly.

She dug her phone out of her purse to call Blake, then had an idea and put the phone away. She knew one surefire way to take her mind off both Kaylie and the No Limitz event. *There's nothing like a little spontaneity.* Danica took the stairs two at a time to her bedroom. Her heart thundered in her chest at the thought of what she was about to do. As she dug through her drawers, looking for the laciest panties and cami she owned, she realized how Blake had brought out the deliciously naughty side of her—and she liked it.

She took a warm shower, carefully shaved her legs and manicured her other private regions, and then took extra care drying her dark mop of unruly curls. She put on makeup, heavily layered on her eyes to create a seductive look, which she didn't quite pull off. *I look like I have raccoon eyes.* She wiped off some of the eyeliner and when she was satisfied with her sultry look, she removed the towel that was wrapped around her. She put scented lotion all over her body, from her fingers all the way down to her toes.

She put on her panties and cami, found her fuck-me heels, and then carried them downstairs. She was glad she'd gone on the pill, because she was in the mood to seduce her man, and the last thing she wanted was to have to pause for him to put on a condom. If she had her way tonight, he wouldn't be able to think straight.

She pulled on her thigh-length black coat, tied the belt around her waist, and then slipped into her heels. She took one last look in the mirror and thought she looked pretty damned good.

It didn't occur to her that she didn't really know how to seduce Blake until he couldn't think straight until she was already at his condo.

Guess I'm winging it.

She hadn't called to tell him she was coming. She let herself in and found him fast asleep in the bedroom wearing nothing but a pair of Levis. Poor thing. He'd been working so hard.

Danica stood dumbfounded for a moment. She was wearing a jacket. It was part of the whole sexy getup. How could she climb on top and tease him if she was wearing a jacket? But if she took it off, he'd miss what she'd done for him. She was contemplating her next move when she felt Blake's toes rubbing against her inner thigh.

"You're awake?" she said, as if she were telling a secret.

He sat up and ran his hands up her thighs to her ass. "I have spidey senses when it comes to being around beautiful women," he teased.

"Darn it." She frowned. "I was going to seduce you."

He ran his eyes up and down her outfit. "I like the sound of this. Look at you. Who are you and what have you done with my girlfriend?" He reached for the belt on her jacket.

"I'm still gonna seduce you," she promised.

"Oh, I bet you are." He opened her coat and stood in front of her. "Danica," he whispered as he looked at her with so much heat she had to remind herself that she wanted to seduce him and she couldn't just rip his clothes off.

He put one strong hand on her shoulder and slowly lowered her jacket to the floor. His lips were warm against her neck.

Her eyes fluttered closed as he ran his hand down her arm to her breast. "Wait," she whispered, moving his hand away. "I really wanted to seduce you."

"You did," he said with a grin.

"No, my dear, you haven't seen nothing yet." She playfully pushed him back down on the bed. He leaned on his elbows and watched as she crawled like a tiger over him, one leg on either side of his body. When her face was above his, he lay down on his back.

Danica lowered her mouth to his, kissing him long and slow, then more deeply, probing his mouth, tasting him, loving him. Kissing Blake was one of her favorite pleasures. He grasped her hips and she reluctantly pulled away, shaking her head.

"No," she whispered. She bent over his chest, dragging her hair over his skin as she kissed the dimples of his abs, then ran her tongue along the tender skin just above the waist of his jeans.

His fingers clutched her hair as she licked his hipbone, then took a little nip, loving the sound of his quick inhalation of breath, which she knew was between gritted teeth. She kissed the tender spot, then ran her hands up his sides and slid to his pecs, where she lingered, her fingers trailing over his nipples as she kissed her way up, then licking them until they were taut.

He reached for her again, but she moved down his body, out of his reach, working the button on his pants before kissing the area just beneath the stiff fabric. She unzipped the cold metal and pulled his pants down, trapping his legs with them just above his knees.

Blake lifted his head. "Baby," he said. "Come here."

Being the aggressor was new to Danica, and she didn't know what drove her there tonight, but she loved seeing the hunger in his eyes and knowing he'd have to wait until she was ready. She slid her fingers under the waist of his boxer briefs and teasingly inched them down, following the trail along the crease that led from his hip to between his legs.

He clenched the blanket in his fists.

"You like that?" *Oh my God, did I say that?*

"What do you think?" he asked with a tense voice.

"Good." She pulled the briefs down further until his desire was set free and then ran her tongue up the length of his shaft, inciting the most delicious groan she'd ever heard him make. She kissed the sensitive skin beneath his hips, running her tongue between each hipbone and down to his inner thighs, purposefully touching, kissing, licking, and caressing every bit of skin except the hard area he most wanted her to. He arched beneath her, but she would not give in. Her hair brushed his erection while she took little nips from his inner thighs.

"You're killing me," he said, reaching for her hair.

"Don't worry. You'll die happy." She slid off the bed and pulled his jeans off, tossed them to the side, then did the same with his briefs. God, he was gorgeous, splayed out like a perfectly photoshopped human being, layered with sweet, tanned skin and ripple after ripple of masculine muscles. She slipped out of her thong and kissed her way back up his legs until she was straddling him.

His eyes fluttered open and he reached for her breasts, caressing them through the thin film of silk and lace. She arched into his hands, her focus falling away with his touch.

He sat up, stretching her legs out behind him, and pulled her cami off. Then he took her breasts in his hands and brought them together, wrapping his mouth around both nipples at once. Danica arched again, and a moan escaped her lips. He moved from her nipples to the center of her breasts and then ran his tongue down to her belly button. Her insides pulsed for him as she came forward and took his cheeks in her hands, kissing him until she could barely breathe.

Suddenly, she was in the air. It took a second for her to realize his hands were on her hips and he was lowering her onto him.

"Blake," she gasped as he filled her completely, and began to move with him. He gripped the outside of her thighs, moving her faster, pulling her harder against him, driving deeper into her until every nerve was on fire and her eyes were fluttering open and closed. She clawed at his strong arms as she reached a quick and unexpected peak, so glorious her body shivered and shook.

Blake's tongue was on her neck, her earlobe, and then the sensitive little dip beneath her ear. Danica tried to concentrate, but she was lost in the sensations of his touch.

With one strong arm around her waist, he flipped them both over, taking her legs and hoisting them up beneath his arms. He thrust deeper and deeper into her, touching her in places that sent tiny shocks through her body. She reached for him, but her arms wouldn't listen; they fell back to the bed. Then her legs were back on the bed, and Blake lowered himself to her, pumping slower, kissing her, probing her mouth with his tongue.

"God, I love you," he said, resting his cheek on hers. "I love you so much."

Danica tried to respond, but he was still moving, faster now, within her, and she was right on the verge of another climax. Blake wrapped his hands under her back, then grabbed her shoulders and held her still against each strong thrust. She felt him swelling inside of her and wrapped her legs around his waist, wanting every bit of him to be hers. Just as she closed her eyes against another fantastic orgasm, he cried out her name and arched his back, thrusting harder, faster, then slower, as he panted through his own climax, and finally came to rest upon her.

Their bodies were slick with sweat, the bedroom silent, save for their satiated breathing.

"Welcome home, baby," Blake whispered.

Danica couldn't think of anywhere else she'd rather be.

Chapter Five

The next day, Kaylie danced in her shorts and maternity top, swinging her hips to the music that cascaded through their spacious living room, excited about a potential girls' night out. Kaylie's insecurities about her body always fell by the wayside when music was involved. It's like she was transformed into another world altogether. She'd been so worried about her failing career, and with her mind blocked by thoughts of strollers and car seats, as it should be, she hoped her friends could help her find direction. After all, they had been instrumental in helping her come to the conclusion that following her heart and building a career in the music field was the right thing to do. In her senior year of college, they'd spent endless nights tossing around what seemed like hundreds of behind-the-desk, practical careers. Careers that wouldn't leave her feeling like a second fiddle to Danica the Therapist. But in the end, neither her friends, nor Kaylie, could see her doing anything besides singing, and it had been a good decision. She had a fulfilling, fun lifestyle—even if she felt as if her career was yet another thing that placed her beneath Danica on the invisible intelligence scale.

Kaylie went out to their backyard and picked fresh flowers from the edge of the woods—a nice little bonus of owning twenty acres—and replenished the vase on the dining room table. Chaz's three-bedroom chalet was spacious and open, and when Kaylie had moved in, it was very much a man's house. The oversized white sofa had no throw pillows, the mantel was bare, and she wasn't sure Chaz even knew what curtains were. Though, with his view of the mountains—and no neighbors for miles around save for the vacant house a mile away—she didn't blame him for leaving the windows untended. It was the morning sun that she didn't care for, especially now that she had no reason to wake up as early as the sun rose.

She remembered how, when she was a little girl, her mother used to wake her up at what seemed like the crack of dawn on the weekends: *Rise and shine! Let's chase the beauty into the day and not be left behind.* It felt so weird to see her mother again—especially with her red hair and her new sense of fashion. *And cell phone. And calls and texts from that man.* She really wanted to be happy for her mother's new outlook, but when she'd seen her, she'd felt like that recent college grad again and the hurt had tumbled in. *Will it ever go away?*

Her cell phone vibrated and she picked it up. "Hello?" Silence. "Hello?" She heard the dead hum of the cell phone line. *Damn it.* The service on the mountain was sporadic, and it nearly drove her crazy. She stomped to their newly installed landline, realizing briefly that she hadn't even written down the number after Chaz had had it installed. She had to remember to write it down, she thought, as she dialed Camille's number.

"Hola, chica," Kaylie said.

"Kaylie? I didn't recognize the number."

Kaylie and her entourage of friends had grown up together. Camille had always been the leader of sorts, while Kaylie had been the party girl. She imagined Camille now, in her big, beautiful new house, still a newlywed, just a few months into her married life. She couldn't wait to take that step. They'd decided to postpone getting married until after the baby was born. Kaylie didn't want to be pregnant in her wedding photos. She touched her belly and said, "It's the new phone we installed in Chaz's office. Anyway, has Danica called you yet?"

"Honey, Danica called me the minute you guys left Felby's. Sounds like an intervention to me."

Figures. "Intervention?" *What the hell did Danica tell you?* "And?"

"And we're all set to go to Bar None tonight, which, I might add, I cannot believe you want to do in your current pregger state."

"Oh, shut up. Tonight? She wants to do it tonight?"

"What's wrong? Hamstrung by that drop-dead gorgeous fiancé of yours? Too tired? If you can't make it—"

"Who are you kidding? I'm going, and we're gonna have a blast." Kaylie mentally ticked off her outfits and realized that nothing she owned would be suitable for Bar None. She pictured Camille looking over her perfectly manicured nails, not a hair out of place, and showing up that evening in a drop-dead, navel-baring, sexy sheath. "I need to go shopping."

Kaylie sped through town toward the Village, feeling more like her old self. The prospect of hanging out with the girls had taken her mind off her lack of work and expanding waistline.

At the stoplight, her cell phone vibrated. She picked it up and saw a text from her mother. *So great to see you. Miss you. Sorry I never texted you before this.* Kaylie tossed the phone on the passenger seat when the light turned green. She was glad that her mother was reaching out, but she was equally as irritated by her internal conflict. She thought of her mother kissing someone other than her father, and even though she still harbored way too much anger to think of her mother and father as any sort of a couple, the thought still turned her stomach. It was clear to Kaylie that she couldn't trust her emotions around her newly dating mother.

She wished she could talk to someone about her pregnancy and the hormones that took her through the wretched highs and disastrous lows that she'd been trying to mask for the last few months; but none of her friends had been pregnant. They wouldn't understand, and Danica was crazy in love and whizzing through a new career and relationship without so much as slowing down. *What is wrong with me?* For the first time in several years, she wondered if this was what it felt like to need your mother, and the thought that followed hurt like hell. *Will I ever be able to mend that bridge?*

Ten minutes later, Kaylie parked her car in the Village parking lot and gave herself a quick once-over in the rearview mirror. *What a mess.* She freshened her makeup and ran a comb through her hair, cursing at how it had become thicker since she'd been pregnant. She now sported wayward, too-thick strands poking out like a halo from her head.

The afternoon sun warmed Kaylie's face as she window-shopped her way through the Village. She wandered into Young at Heart, one of the few clothing stores that carried trendy outfits that fit her prepregnancy size-five body perfectly. Some stores carried brands that were too roomy in the hips, or too loose in the thighs, but Young at Heart always seemed to fit. The Fray was playing on the speakers, and two teenage girls stood behind the counter laughing and moving to the music. Kaylie watched them, feeling silly for being jealous of their exposed, tanned, flat-as-a-board stomachs.

She rifled through the rack and pulled out tops that she thought might stretch over her mushrooming belly. The tank top she wore with her maternity jeans swung out at the bottom like a tent. She'd love to wear something more formfitting. She picked an armful of extra-large blouses, T-shirts, and tank tops and headed for the fitting room. She tugged at the door. Locked. The last thing Kaylie wanted to do was ask those happy girls for anything. Luckily, she didn't have to.

The dressing room door beside her opened, and a very tall, slim brunette walked out. "Here," she said, revealing her perfect white teeth and adorable dimples.

"Thanks." Kaylie hurried inside feeling more like her mother than herself—too matronly to be in the store at all. Hell, not even like her mother anymore. Her mother looked fresh and fashionable in her cap-sleeved blouse and white slacks. She flopped down on the bench inside the dressing room, the pile of shirts in her lap.

Kaylie took off her shirt and picked through the tanks, choosing a pretty pale yellow one with green trim. She pulled it over her head. *Yeah, baby, this will definitely fit.* Even as she tried to convince herself, she knew it was impossible. She tugged it down over her breasts and couldn't believe it stopped mid-boob. "Really?" she said to the empty room. She tugged and yanked at the bottom of the shirt. It wouldn't budge. Kaylie faced the mirror; her bare belly stuck out like a giant basketball, complete with a faded brown line down the center. Her belly button resembled a misshapen scar instead of the cute little inny that she'd always been so proud of. She missed her piercing, which she'd taken out begrudgingly at sixteen weeks, per her doctor's suggestion. She surveyed her changing body, and she sank back down to the bench, feeling worse than she had when she'd left home.

There was a knock at the dressing room door. "You okay in there? Need another size?"

Kaylie yanked the tank top awkwardly back over her head. "Not unless you carry whale-sized shirts." She pulled on her maternity top with a heavy sigh and opened the door.

One of the girls from the counter dropped her eyes to her belly. "Oh."

"Yeah, I thought I could fit in these." She pointed at the pile of shirts she'd left on the bench.

"I can take care of those." The girl flipped her dark hair over her shoulder and then touched Kaylie's arm. "Hey, what about going to the Dead Zone? You know that cool shop at the end of the street? They have those great hippie shirts that are all flowy and light. They'd probably fit, and with the right pair of jeans." She looked at Kaylie's jeans. "Like those, that'd be really cute."

Kaylie was swept into the girl's enthusiasm. "You think so?" She smoothed her shirt, feeling a little less like Shamu.

"Definitely." The girl beamed. She called to the girl behind the counter. "Hey, Shay, wouldn't she look so cute in those Dead Zone shirts?"

Shay smacked her gum like a cow. Silver earrings lined the edge of both ears, and several long silver and leather necklaces hung around her neck. "Totally!" she said between gum smacks.

"Yeah? Thanks." Kaylie left the store with a bounce in her step.

Two hours later Kaylie began her drive out of town and toward their chalet, her backseat filled with packages from the Dead

Zone, her new favorite store. Her cell phone rang and she pulled to the side of the road. Finding out she was pregnant had switched some crazy maternal instinct in her brain. She no longer texted and drove, and she had stopped answering the phone while behind the wheel, too. Lee Brice sang quietly from the speakers.

She looked at the number on her cell screen. *Reno.* She answered with an air of confidence. She had sung at the Reno nightclub for the past three years. It was one of her favorite venues, and the patrons loved her more with each performance, staying after the show to ask for her autograph and making her feel like a real celebrity—even though Kaylie knew she was anything but. It was in the bag. "Lisa, hi, how are you?"

"Hi, Kaylie."

Kaylie sensed a hesitation and tried to brush it off. "I didn't expect to hear from you until next week."

"I know, Kaylie, listen. I have some bad news."

Kaylie's heart sank as she listened to Lisa hem and haw her way through telling her she didn't get the gig. The noise of the engine fell away. She punched the radio button with her index finger, filling the car with silence, save for Lisa's stumbling voice coming through her cell, saying something about new mothers being unreliable. *Unforeseen circumstances arise when babies are involved. Besides, do you really think you'll want to leave your baby overnight?*

She was too stunned to formulate a rebuttal. "Okay. Thanks for letting me know." Kaylie pressed End and stared out the window, conflicted by wanting to be home with her baby and determined not to repeat her own mother's mistake of staying at home and losing hold of all the things that had made her whole before having kids. *Maybe this is good,* she thought, *forcing my hand to stay home for a while. Who am I kidding? There are no happily ever afters. No way am I gonna end up like Mom, left with nothing more than a broken heart. I've worked too hard not to continue standing on my own two feet. Besides, without a career, there would be one more nail on my not-as-smart-or-as-capable-as-Danica coffin.* Something had to change, and Kaylie was dead set on figuring out just what that was.

Chapter Six

Kaylie left her bags in the car and flung herself onto the couch.

"Something wrong?" Chaz asked as he came into the living room. He moved the colorful throw pillows aside and sat down beside Kaylie on the deep cushioned sectional, setting a glass of ice water with sliced lemon on the coffee table.

She stared at the mantel, littered with framed photos they'd accumulated over the last few months. Their smiles beamed at her like beacons through the shadowy darkness of her disappointment. "I didn't get the Reno gig that I've done for the last three years." She crossed her arms, feeling like a pouty child and cringing inside but unable to turn it around. Lisa had taken the wind right out of her. "That's my given, you know? The one I could always count on. I figured that since it was eight weeks after the baby's supposed to be born, they'd hire me. They loved me." She shook her head. "I just don't get it."

"Why do you think they didn't give it to you?"

Kaylie loved everything about Chaz, from his dimpled chin and rumpled blond hair to the way his voice felt like a caress. But at that very moment, with her hormones wreaking havoc and the realization of her sinking career as fresh as a morning breeze, all she could think of to say was, *duh*, and she'd never let such a rude comment slip from her lips to the man she adored.

Instead, she looked down at her belly and pressed her lips tightly together.

"I'm sorry," Chaz said, and reached around her, pulling her closer to him. "They've probably hired new mothers before who'd canceled at the last minute and left them in a bind or something."

She leaned against him and closed her eyes. The scent of his Tommy Hilfiger cologne reeled Kaylie in, softening her steely reserve. "I get it," she said. "But every job I got took so much hard work. I had to prove myself every single time, and I had this one. Three years, I've done their gig, and I've never let them down. Doesn't loyalty count for anything?" She nervously twisted her hair around her finger. "I've worked so hard since my junior year of college to find my way and make a name for myself. And I did, too. I haven't had this much trouble lining up jobs in forever. I always thought I'd end up with a record contract at some point—that all my hard work would pay off. And now, between this one and last week's cancellation, it's like I'm just watching it all fade away."

"There are so many other things you can do," he said.

She lifted her eyebrows. "Like what?" She looked down at her belly and laughed. "Make babies?"

"Well, that's always fun," he said, as he put his lips on hers and kissed her.

"Yeah, but we've talked about this. I want my career. You know that."

He planted light kisses along her jawbone. "You could be the band manager."

"No way. What am I, a scut monkey?" *Why am I being so bitchy? It's not his fault.*

Her bitchiness didn't deter him. He pushed her hair from her face and said, with his hand on her cheek, "You could write instead of singing."

Kaylie was finding it hard to concentrate as he slid his hand from her cheek to the back of her neck, kissing the center of her collarbone and moving up to the underside of her chin. Her head fell back and she whispered, "I'm not a writer."

He pulled her onto his lap and brushed her straight blond hair from her shoulders. "Songs. You can write them if you can't sing them." He laid her back on the sofa and sank down beside her, tracing the crest of her cleavage with his finger. "You don't even have to work if you don't want to."

"What?" Kaylie pushed at his chest. What did he think she was going to do? Stay at home, barefoot and pregnant?

"We don't need the money, and you work late hours, weekends. I'm just saying."

Kaylie's pulse sped up. No way was she giving up her career. It might not seem like she had much of one left, but she wasn't going to just walk away from it. She wouldn't be her mother. They'd talked about this. "I love singing. I love working." She swung her legs over the end of the couch and pushed herself to her feet. "I'm not just a baby maker."

"I never said—"

"No, but you were thinking it. I could hear it in your voice." Kaylie paced. Anger surged through her, and she knew it was misdirected. Chaz was in her line of fire, and she was powerless to quell her emotions. Goddamn hormones. Tears burned at the corners of her eyes. *Why does everything have to change?*

"I didn't mean that."

The confusion on Chaz's face portrayed exactly what Kaylie knew he must be feeling—tangled in a web of estrogen and Kaylie's faltering career, which he couldn't possibly understand.

"Look," he said, with a frustrated sigh, "I just thought that if you couldn't sing, you could write songs, or take time off, or whatever, until you're ready to go back."

His blue eyes pleaded for understanding, but Kaylie's anger was galloping full-speed ahead. She couldn't rein it in. "I was never ready *not* to work," she spat.

"What? Did you expect that bars would hire you at eight months pregnant? Or they wouldn't have a backup plan?" His voice rose, and even though Kaylie didn't blame him, it still fed her need to defend herself.

"It's been months since I've worked, and no, I didn't expect they'd hire me at eight months pregnant, but I didn't expect to lose my career *after* the baby was born, either." *Even if I'm not sure I want it.* "I thought I'd bounce right back, that all the places I'd worked would hire me without giving it a second thought."

Chaz ran his hand through his hair. "Okay, I get it," he conceded. "It stinks. It's not fair, but, Kaylie, you have a chance to take some time off for yourself, and soon, for our—"

Kaylie held up her hand. "Believe me, I know what's coming. Soon I'll have no life." *Jesus Christ, shut the hell up. What neurotic woman has taken over my vocal cords?*

"But you'll have the baby," he pleaded.

"Yes, and it will all be worth it. But now, at this very second"—she sank onto the couch as a tear tumbled down her cheek—"it doesn't feel like it's worth it. It feels a little like Kaylie is disappearing and being replaced with a mindless baby factory, and afterward, I'll be a diaper-changing, exhausted blob, while you'll be just as gorgeous and intellectually fulfilled as always." *Just like my parents.*

Chaz shook his head. He had so much empathy in his eyes, Kaylie could feel it wrapping itself around her body like a blanket, but her hormones had won. They'd taken full control of her ability to speak, and her tear ducts were currently emptying themselves as if her cheeks were about to shrivel up and die of dehydration and they were the only water source around. "Don't look at me like that. Do you think I *want* to feel this way?" she snapped, and stomped into the bedroom.

Chapter Seven

Danica's body was still feeling the effects of the lovemaking they'd enjoyed the night before. She didn't want to leave Blake this morning. Staying in bed and making love again was too delicious a thought to turn away from, but now, as she rushed toward Camille's house, she was paying the price for that extra forty minutes. She was meeting her friends before work to talk about the baby shower. They'd had a difficult time finding a date when they were all free to plan Kaylie's shower, and she was already leaving most of the planning up to them. The guilt was killing her. *But not enough to give up a few extra minutes of being close to Blake.* With the No Limitz event right around the corner, she just didn't have the time to dedicate to planning both the shower and the event, and there was no way she'd let her busy schedule impede her sister's first baby shower.

Camille answered the door with her typical squeal. "You made it! I was so worried. I know how busy you are right now." She looked stunning in her tiny white shorts and powder-blue tank top.

Danica felt her face flush. "Mrs. Danber," Danica teased, hoping it would take the attention away from her heated cheeks. "I wouldn't miss this for the world." She hugged Camille and stood in the large, ceramic-tiled foyer. "Wow, you weren't kidding about the house."

"I know, right? Jeff wasn't happy that it took so long for them to finish, but—" She lifted her hands in presentation. A crystal chandelier hung from the center of the two-story foyer. Danica touched the banister of the wide, sweeping stairs that curved sexily up to the second floor.

"Come see what I've done. I've got the whole house completely finished, except for the guest room. I can't decide on a comforter for it." Camille guided her through a tastefully appointed living room with delicately carved wooden end tables and a four-inch-thick black carpet with flecks of gray, offsetting the cream-colored couch and black and teal pillows perfectly.

Danica tried to mask her shock at the enormity of their house. She felt like she'd walked onto the set of *Homes of the Stars.*

"I feel like I'm in a model home."

"Me too." Camille laughed. "Jeff said he doesn't want to be embarrassed if clients visit."

"He's a sports agent. Do clients actually visit?" *Jerry Maguire* ran through Danica's mind.

"Sometimes, I guess."

She made a mental note to find out who Blake's favorite sports guy was and see if she could hook him up. Did sports agents even handle pro skiers?

They descended a wide set of carpeted stairs to the lower level, which opened into an enormous great room, the back of which was a wall of windows overlooking a pool, surrounded by a kidney-shaped patio.

"The girls are outside," Camille said, as she pulled the doors open. "Look who's here," she called out in a singsong voice.

"Danica!" Chelsea was the first to reach her, and she squeezed Danica so tightly she thought she'd magically slipped into a corset.

"You're here!" Marie gave Danica a quick squeeze, overwhelming her with the sweet smell of Hawaiian Tropic suntan lotion.

"How's that yummy man of yours?" Chelsea asked as they settled into the cushioned chairs beneath the shade of a wide umbrella. The table was stocked with an array of breakfast treats—fresh fruit, croissants, muffins.

Danica was immediately drawn into the familiarity of how the girls described everything in terms of food or exotic places. "Looks delicious," she said. Camille handed her a fruity drink with a tiny umbrella.

"Virgin Bahama Mamas," Chelsea said, taking a long sip through a straw.

"We're pretending we're in the Bahamas." Marie giggled. "I don't know how Camille does it, but she can mimic mixed drinks without the alcohol. We figured we couldn't all go to work shnockered. Girl's got skills," she said with a wink.

They filled her in on the details for the shower.

"So, the shower is dolls, no guys, as you know." Marie gave a disapproving frown. "We're going with pink and blue everything! Balloons, streamers, napkins, centerpieces." She flipped a page in her notebook. Marie was a buyer for a high-end boutique, and her job required her to communicate with people all over the globe. She'd become adept at juggling schedules, time zones, and personalities. She was the perfect person to handle the specifics for the shower.

An hour later, they'd hammered out the details for the shower, including silly games that Danica was sure Kaylie would love. She was having such a good time just being with her girlfriends that she didn't want to leave, but No Limitz wouldn't run itself.

"I've really gotta go, and I feel so guilty for not being more involved in Kaylie's shower," Danica said.

"Are you kidding?" Camille asked. "We live for this stuff. I mean, what could be more fun than celebrating your friend's first baby? We'll make you proud, Danica. Don't you worry. No gift will go ungiven and no silly game will go unplayed."

"I can't wait!" Marie said. "I love that diaper poo game, where you put mashed chocolate bars into diapers and guess what they are."

Danica crinkled her nose. "Yeah, have fun with that one. Just hand me a few unmashed, undiapered chocolate bars. I'll be happy to do a taste test and reveal their true identities."

"Don't be a party pooper," Marie said.

"Um, you know, I'd much prefer Danica's option, too," Chelsea added.

"What? You too? We just agreed!" Marie stuck out her lower lip.

The playful bickering was Danica's cue to leave before she got sucked into another round of *which games should we play.*

She hugged her girlfriends and thanked them again. As she headed to the front of the house, Camille hollered after her, "What about your mom?"

Danica stopped cold. She'd meant to invite their mom, but she was waiting to see how things fleshed out between her and Kaylie, and so far, it looked like there wasn't going to be much of a change anytime soon.

"She's definitely coming!" Danica hollered back. *Whether Kaylie wants it or not and whether Mom has plans or not. I'll make sure of it.* She made a mental note to try to push Kaylie a little harder into patching things up with their mother.

Chapter Eight

Danica's vision for No Limitz was just beginning to blossom. She'd developed the youth center with one thing in mind— giving kids a place where they could gather while offering healthy, fun things to do in a safe environment. After she'd given up her therapy license, she'd quickly developed a business plan and then researched and settled on the space. With the encouragement of the community and Blake's unending support, Danica knew she'd made the right decision. She was awarded an Incubation Grant from the city, which paid for the first year of the staff's wages, making her decision to move forward that much easier. Hiring staff, it turned out, was the simple part. Blake's old business partner's widow, Sally Tuft, had been looking for something new in her life, and she'd taken on the accounting and scheduling of the programs. Michelle and Sally's son, Rusty, had both accepted part-time positions. And, most recently, at Blake's suggestion, she'd hired Gage Ryder. He'd been a sports coach for a high school in Washington State and had moved to Allure to escape a bad relationship. He and Blake had met on the slopes, and while Gage was working only part time, he offered a fresh perspective on sporting events for the kids; and he and Danica seemed to be on the same page with their goals for the center.

Danica pored over ideas for the upcoming teen night. She was excited about the first community event that No Limitz was hosting. They were going to have a dance, refreshments, and a general gathering for the teens in the community. Danica was making a list of volunteers they needed when Kaylie came through the office door.

"Hey, you busy?" she asked. Her cheeks were flushed and her hair was askew. Danica knew immediately that something was wrong.

Gage appeared at Kaylie's side. Gage looked like a young Hugh Jackman, and Kaylie, though she'd known Gage since he started working at the center two months earlier, took a second glance.

"Hi," she said, turning on the charm with an instant smile that looked so real Danica almost believed it.

Danica shook her head. Even pregnant and engaged, Kaylie could send men to their knees. "Guess you're feeling happier," she said as her sister ran her eyes up and down all six feet three inches of Gage.

Kaylie sat down at the table where Danica was working. "Are you busy?"

"Sure." *What now?*

"I don't mean to interrupt," Kaylie said with a twist of her hair around her finger and a doe-eyed gaze in Gage's direction.

"I'll come back later," Gage said, flashing a warm smile before retreating down the hall.

Danica watched Kaylie's eyes trail behind him.

"Yummy," Kaylie said.

"Kaylie! You're pregnant, living with your fiancé. What is wrong with you?" she snapped.

"Pregnant and engaged, not dead." She smirked.

Danica closed her eyes and sighed. "What's up with you?

First you're all over Mom for finally getting on with her life. Then you're all weepy about your job, and now… now you're flirting with my employee?" And here she had planned a girls' night out and was secretly planning her baby shower. What kind of trouble was she in for? Ugh, and their poor mother! Danica didn't know what to do about that whole situation, but at least they were taking baby steps, and hopefully, Kaylie's shower would help bridge that gap.

"I'd never do anything." Kaylie folded her arms.

Danica stared at her and shook her head.

"Danica, come on. Cut me some slack. I look like a blimp, no one will hire me, and Chaz and I got in a big fight, so he'll probably never talk to me again."

"You what? Why?" Was she ever going to settle down?

Kaylie lowered her eyes. "He was talking about me finding other things to do—or not do—until I could go back to work, like I'd stick around the house doing nothing but making babies or something."

"Did he say that? I can't even imagine him saying that. He's always so supportive of you."

Kaylie fiddled with the end of her shirt.

"Kay? Did he say it or not?"

"Well, not in so many words, but that's what he meant. Or maybe he didn't. I don't know."

Danica let out a frustrated sigh. "Why do you always do this?" She stood and paced. Settling her sister down would be her biggest therapy job of all, and she was done with that—or at least she hoped she was. She'd never turn her back on Kaylie. "Kaylie." She heard the frustration in her voice and reminded herself to tone it down a notch. She sat back down beside Kaylie and said, "I know you're entering new territory. Your body is changing in ways that are unfamiliar and uncomfortable."

"You sound like Mom when I was thirteen years old."

"Oh, God, I do." Danica laughed. "Wow. She looks great, doesn't she?" Danica loved the changes she saw in her mother. Her new outlook was a healthy, active one. Even though she didn't see her mother very often, she was definitely going to make more of an effort. *It's so easy to get lost in our own busy lives. And so wrong when it comes to family.*

Kaylie shrugged.

"Kaylie, why are you so angry with her? She's allowed to have a life. Your life is moving on. So is mine. Why shouldn't hers?"

"It's just weird. She was so weak to stay with Dad after what he did, and I guess my anger at her, for letting Dad hurt her so much, is still there. So, to hear about her dating...Dating, Danica. Mom is dating." She locked eyes with Danica. "Don't you think it's weird?"

"Not at all. I think..." *You're trapped in a world of being a hurt girl whose parents have split up.* She knew better than to play therapist with Kaylie. "I think she deserves to be happy and have a life and that you're changing the subject."

"I didn't change it. You did."

"Whatever. Was there something you wanted when you came here? I can't just bicker about Mom's dating life." Her heart ached for Kaylie struggling with her mommy drama, but she had work to do, and she knew that whatever she suggested, Kaylie would either find fault or take it the wrong way.

"What's the plan for tonight?" Kaylie asked.

"We're all staying at my house. Oh, God. I forgot to tell you, didn't I?"

Kaylie shrugged again. "Camille said we were all going to Bar None, but she failed to mention a slumber party." Her eyes lit up at the prospect.

Danica knew the stirring excitement was driven by more than a night out. Staying at Danica's was Kaylie's escape from her fight with Chaz. "You can't just run away every time there's an argument or Chaz says something he doesn't mean. You do it all the time, Kaylie. You say things, and no one walks away from you." *And here comes the therapist that I just couldn't hold back.* She couldn't sit idly by and let Kaylie ruin her relationship before it even had a chance. She had a child to think about. But Danica knew she had to be careful. If she told Kaylie to go home tonight to be with Chaz, she'd bolt in the opposite direction.

"Oh my God, don't even go there. I'm not running. I needed an outfit for tonight. Something suitable for Bar None."

Of course you did. There's the Kaylie I know and love. She crushed the urge to counsel her, to remind her how lucky she was to have someone like Chaz who loved her and would go to the ends of the earth for her. Instead, she gave Kaylie a hopeful smile. "We'll have a great time tonight."

Kaylie jumped up and hugged her. "Thank you for setting it up! I think I just need a night to chill, you know? No pressure, no thinking about the jobs I'm not getting, and no sad Chaz eyes staring at me, wondering why I'm so crazy."

"You're not crazy, Kay. You're just hormone laden." She laughed. "Look, I gotta work, but I'll see you later."

Gage appeared in the doorway and Kaylie picked up her packages. "Thanks, sis. Bye," she said to Gage with a flirtatious smile.

"Kay."

Kaylie turned back and gave her a *now what* look.

"Go home and make up with Chaz." The big sister in her trumped her intended silence.

When she was out of earshot, Gage said, "Wow, even pregnant, she's incredible."

"Yeah, yeah, I've heard it all before," Danica said with a sigh, then realized that it was Kaylie who needed to hear the compliment, not her.

Gage sat beside her and looked over the documents for the event. "I didn't mean anything by that. I just meant that she had the flirting thing down pat. I didn't mean that I thought—"

"Gage, really, it's okay. I know how lovely Kaylie is." She pulled the plans for the event into order on the table and remembered her thoughts about possibly having Kaylie sing. She'd have to mull that over. "Let's get this done."

Danica explained her ideas for the night, and she could feel Gage's eyes on her. She leaned back and looked at him. "What?"

"I just don't want you to get the wrong impression of me. I'm not that kind of guy."

"What kind of guy? The kind who recognizes a hot blonde when he sees one? Come on, Gage. Kaylie's hot, even pregnant," she said with a roll of her eyes. Her mind was wrapped around the event, and after Kaylie's visit, she had enough on her mind. She was losing patience and wanted to get through the planning they needed to do. Did everyone feel the need to paint a safe picture for the therapist in her?

"I'm not the kind of guy who goes after other guys' fiancées," he said.

"I don't think you're like that. Kaylie's just being Kaylie. She's my sister, and I love her, but she has trust issues, and she's a little insecure. And right now, she's got a lot to work through."

"That's what I thought. She reminds me of my ex-girlfriend back in Washington. So wrapped up in being the center of attention that she'd do anything not to lose it."

It was one thing for Danica to point out her sister's issues, but a whole other thing for someone else to. Her protective sisterly claws came out, taking her by surprise. She didn't want to believe that Kaylie couldn't get past her insecurities. Kaylie was going to be a mother, and Chaz loved her. Surely she'd find her way to a mature acceptance of all of that. *Wouldn't she?* "Kaylie's strong," she heard herself saying. "She'll pull herself together and come out on top. She always does."

"When I found out about her and my coworker, I knew we could never have a future."

Thinking about Kaylie had caused Danica to lose track of their conversation. She shook off her worry and focused on Gage. "Oh, that's terrible. I didn't realize. I'm sorry," she said.

"Live and learn, right? Anyway, so your sister is pretty, and she's full of energy, but she's not my type."

Right. Kaylie's everyone's type. She watched him staring out of her office door. They wrapped up their event planning discussion, and as Gage left her office, she noticed Sally at her desk, watching him walk toward the basketball courts.

Chapter Nine

Chaz paced the living room, staring at the door. He was trying to be patient with Kaylie's mood swings, and he *got* it. That's the hardest part. He understood what she was going through. She was the type of girl who turned heads anywhere she went, and now she was pregnant. Very pregnant. What Kaylie didn't realize was that she still turned heads. She didn't notice the leers and second glances. Chaz did, and as much as they singed every jealous nerve in his body, he was proud that she was his. Hell, he was proud of her for everything, not just her looks. She *had* worked hard to make a name for herself in the music world, but Chaz was a realist. He knew that Kaylie was capable of so much more than singing. He wouldn't care if she never sang another day in her life, or if she was disfigured in a fiery car crash, or for that matter, if she wanted to be a full-on pop star. He'd support whatever she wanted. Kaylie had a heart as big as the moon, and he'd never felt for anyone the undeniable, inexplicable, all-consuming adoration that he felt for her. And when she touched him—Jesus—there were times he thought his body might explode. But damn it, with the trip to LA coming up and the mess with Lea, he was trying to keep his own messes in a tidy little pile. He hoped he was strong enough for both of them.

He thought about stopping her from leaving, trying to make

some sense of their argument, but he didn't have the energy. Besides, he rationalized, some time with Danica might do her well. Danica could probably help her through this better than he could. He pulled his phone from his pocket and dialed Kaylie's number, then hung up before it rang. Should he call her and tell her to come back, or let her blow off steam first? He didn't have time to make a decision before his office phone rang.

Chaz stomped across the wide planks of the cherry hardwood floor and into the office. "Chaz Crew."

"Hey, Chaz it's Max again. I called your cell, but it went to voicemail."

Chaz looked down at his phone. No bars. No service. "That's why we installed the office phone, remember? Crappy service up here on the mountain."

"I know, but I forget. You've only had it a week or whatever. Anyway, you're leaving Tuesday. I'm booking the flights after we hang up. Lea demanded the change."

"Tuesday, as in one day from now?" Chaz took a deep breath. How the hell was he going to pull that off with what was going on with Kaylie? "Why? I'm in LA next week. I'm not going twice." What on earth was Lea trying to pull?

"She's in Hawaii meeting with the Hawaiian Film Festival guys. I tried to postpone until she was back in LA. I even said you'd Skype her, but she was insistent that you meet in person and that it be tomorrow."

Adrenaline sent his mind spinning as he looked out the bay window over the mountains below. He wiped at a bead of sweat on his forehead. He'd just planned a night out with Blake while Kaylie was with her girlfriends, and he really needed to explain the whole Lea situation to Kaylie.

"Are you there?" Max urged. "Listen, you don't have to go.

We have plenty of time. I can woo some smaller sponsors."

"No way. We're ten weeks away from the event." He paced. "That's why she's doing this now, and she's taking me out of familiar territory, too. Hawaii? Jesus. She knows she's got us by the—"

"Balls?"

"Yeah, Max, by the balls. I was trying to spare you the language."

Max's hearty laugh was infectious, and Chaz found himself smiling despite his frustration.

"I see, so saying balls is different than fuck or shit or damn? Because those are the words that fly from the setup crew's mouths on a daily basis."

He pictured the smirk he knew was on Max's face. "Okay, I get it. Max, it'll cost as much to fly there as it would for the sponsorship on this short notice." He'd tell Kaylie tonight. No way would he let that one little omission come between them, and knowing Lea, if what she wanted was Chaz, she'd find a way to ensure Kaylie knew about their tryst. Damn it. He couldn't think that way. He was the man here, not Lea. He'd end this charade before it went any further.

"Nope. If it was going to cost as much, maybe I'd be able to convince you to forget about her sponsorship and if we fall short, we fall short; but it's not. You have enough frequent flyer miles for two of you to go. You can bring Kaylie."

"Oh, that'll go over well." He imagined Kaylie, who didn't even know Lea existed, being swallowed alive by her. "We can't fall short, Max. It's not like her funding doesn't matter. Right now it's the difference between the festival taking place and being canceled. Fine. I'll go."

"Want me to come with you as backup?"

Max was the most efficient sponsorship coordinator Chaz

had ever worked with, and after five years, she was like a younger sister to him. He considered the offer. "It might piss her off even more, bringing you along to ensure she behaves."

"The real question is can you behave yourself?"

"What do you think?" Chaz asked with more bravado than he felt.

"Honestly?"

"Have I ever asked for anything else?" Chaz sat down in the leather chair behind his desk.

"Well, in all the years I've known you, I've seen you date some of the most glamorous actresses, the richest debutants, and some of the most annoying bimbos who exist. You've slept with, I don't know how many women in that time," Max said.

"I dated them, but I didn't sleep with them. Not many of them, anyway. I'm not like that, Max."

"Whatever. The point is, I've never seen you fawn over a woman like you do with Kaylie, and I've never seen you so driven by your penis as you were with Lea. So, when you ask if I think you can handle it, I can't honestly give you a clear answer."

"Gee, thanks for your vote of confidence." Chaz leaned his elbows on the desk and lowered his forehead into his palms.

"I know how you are with Kaylie, and I know you love her. I *want* to believe that you can behave, but then again, I knew you before her, too."

The truth hurt. And what made it sting even more was that Chaz and Kaylie had laid their pasts on the table with each other, and she'd accepted his without question. He remembered the feeling of relief when she said she loved him for all he was and anything that had made him into the man he had become, and the guilt of omitting his affair with Lea strangled him. He knew then that if he told her about Lea, she'd worry at every festival thereafter, and since he had about as much interest in Lea as a fish would have in a desert, he didn't see the point in thrusting that particular bad decision upon her.

He trusted himself, but he definitely didn't trust Lea. He thought again about using his trust fund money. He weighed it in his mind—giving in to using the family money versus facing Lea head-on. As much as he hated it, using his family money still left an acidic taste in his mouth, but shutting down Lea once and for all, now, that was appealing. Maybe she'd changed. Maybe he was underestimating her and she had serious negotiation in mind. Chaz was always game for a negotiation. He'd come out on top with stronger people than Lea Carmichael. The more he thought about it, the more he convinced himself that this would be okay—and if he found that she really did want him, then if nothing else, he'd squelch that fantasy and move forward without a guilty conscience. Max would only further empower him, no matter which direction the meeting took.

"Yeah, why don't you come along?"

Chapter Ten

By the time Danica arrived at Blake's, she was exhausted. The last thing she wanted to do was spend an evening at Bar None. She fantasized about throwing on her sweatpants and cuddling up next to him on the couch.

"Is Kaylie doing any better?" Blake asked when Danica came into the living room.

"Who knows. She called from her cell and said she was going home to get ready for tonight. She plans on eating ice cream and watching television in my fuzzy slippers after we all go out. It's Chaz I'm worried about. I mean, I know Kaylie, and she doesn't mean anything when she does this. She runs away from things. It's who she is. But Chaz doesn't know that." Danica set her purse down on the table and joined Blake on the couch, snuggling up under the warmth of his arm, even if only for a few minutes.

"So, tell him."

Danica shook her head. "It's not my place. She's a big girl. She has to figure things out for herself."

"Wanna talk about it some more?" He kissed her cheek.

"Not really."

"Wanna tell me how your mom's doing?"

She smiled to herself. Blake was the perfect boyfriend. What man remembered what his girlfriend did during the day? She'd counseled so many broken people about their damaged relationships that she'd expected so much less from him. And there he was, Prince Charming written all over everything he did. So why couldn't she bring herself to move in with him?

"She's great, actually." Danica went to the refrigerator and took a bite out of an apple. "She's dating and texting. Oh, and she joined a gym, and she dyed her hair red."

"Sounds like a midlife crisis to me," Blake joked.

"Maybe, but I'm happy for her. I see it as a midlife finding herself, not a crisis. Their divorce was the crisis. I just wish Kaylie would be nicer to her. She's stuck in some weird, angry stage, and I feel bad for Mom. Mom wants nothing more than to be part of her life."

Blake came into the kitchen and pulled out a pan. "She'll come around. Just give her time. Chicken?"

Danica glanced at the clock. She had an hour and a half before she was supposed to meet the girls. "Are you cooking?"

"Yup."

"In that case, yes, please." Danica loved that their relationship hadn't taken on the usual gender-defined roles. They'd fallen naturally into a give-and-take with everything from taking out the trash and cooking, to laundry, and even lovemaking. "Isn't that the chicken that's been in the fridge forever?"

"Not forever. It's fine." He kissed her on the cheek. "I love how easy to please you are." Blake cut the chicken breasts into thin slices, eyeing Danica. "So, do you want to hear what Chaz thinks?"

Danica spun around. "You talked to him?"

"You told me to call him and invite him out, remember?"

She was so wrapped up in Kaylie's dramatics that she'd almost forgotten. "Oh, God, what did he say? He probably thinks she's a nut and wants nothing to do with her. I hope she didn't screw this up."

Blake poured two glasses of wine and handed one to Danica. "She's not a nut."

Danica took a swig of the wine. "No, she's just a little damaged."

"That's not nice."

"No, but it's true. We're all a little damaged, aren't we?"

Blake mulled that over while he drank his wine. "Is that why you can't move in with me? Because you're damaged?"

Yes, but right now I'm dealing with my damaged sister. Danica shook her head. "How about you tell me what Chaz said? I can only handle one crisis at a time."

"He said he doesn't care if she works or not. He only wants her to be happy. He suggested that maybe she write songs instead of singing while she's pregnant, and she stormed out of the room."

"Well, that's not what she said."

"Right. She thinks he wants her barefoot and pregnant. I don't know about women and their hormones, but he said her emotions are all over the place. He seems used to it."

"That can't be good," Danica said. "Even if he's used to her hormone-induced mood swings, he'll get sick of her really quickly if that's the case."

"Not all men run from problems, Danica. Look how many times you pushed me away, and I stuck around." Blake threw the chicken in the pan and stirred it, then moved closer to Danica, until she could smell the sweet wine on his breath. "You're still pushing me away, and I'm not going anywhere."

Danica put her hand on his chest. She loved the feel of him, and rested her fingers on his pectoral muscles while she debated giving in to the desire that stirred within her. *Damn you.* It took only one touch, and she lost track of all thoughts. What happened to the reserved, professional Danica who could keep her desires under control? All it took was one quick look in his hungry eyes to know she didn't give one hoot about the reserved person she used to be. She was about to kiss him when she realized what he'd said. "I'm not pushing you away. I'm just not ready to move in yet." Thinking of Kaylie, she said, "Maybe I should go over there and talk some sense into her."

"Can't you do that tonight? You'll see her in an hour." He pulled her into his arms. "Maybe I can talk some sense into you," he teased.

"I hope tonight isn't all about damage control," she said as he moved his hands to her ass. "I don't have time for dinner and…this." *God, I want you.* "I swear, we're like two dogs in heat," she said as he kissed her neck.

"Ruff."

Chapter Eleven

After an afternoon of dealing with the demands of actors and actresses, the impending trip to Hawaii that he was trying desperately not to think about, and Kaylie's silent treatment burning a hole right through his heart, Chaz was looking forward to a night out with Blake. He could sure use some guy time. His house had become estrogen hell in the last few hours—even worse than usual. He'd just make it an early night.

Kaylie came out of the bedroom wearing a snug little outfit he'd never seen before. The combination of her short, snug, emerald-green dress, her hair cascading over her shoulders, and her tone, tanned legs, caused an instant, heated reaction within him. *Damn, she is sexy.* He wanted to forget Blake, forget Kaylie's career trouble and their earlier argument, and take her in his arms, but he'd practiced telling Kaylie about Lea at least fifty different ways, and he knew he had to do it. He realized that he hadn't even told her about his leaving for Hawaii.

"You look incredible." He bent down to kiss her ruby-red lips.

She ducked away. "Lipstick."

He was torn between making sure she was okay—that *they* were okay—before he took off for Hawaii, and revealing his secret. Springing Lea on anyone was unfair, and springing Lea on her after a fight and just hours before he would be meeting her halfway across the world would be cruel. Seeing her eyes tinged with sadness, he knew there was no easy way to handle the fact that he'd lied. His chest tightened, and he steeled himself to receive anything she thought he deserved.

"Kaylie, I have to go to Hawaii to meet with a sponsor. Max called and they changed the flight. I leave tomorrow." Her mouth dropped open. He couldn't do it. He felt like he was abandoning her, and it made no sense. It had to be the lie that was eating away at his gut. He had to tell her, damn it. Tonight. He'd tell her tonight after she came back from her girls' night out, when she'd be in a more relaxed mood and the news of Hawaii settled in.

"Tomorrow?"

"Yeah."

"Tomorrow? Really?" Kaylie frowned.

"I'm sorry. If there was any other way…"

She shrugged. "Well, it's not like we haven't been apart before. How long will you be gone?"

"Maybe two nights. It's gonna be crazy. Between flights, and the meeting, I'll have no time to sleep."

"What time do you leave?"

"I'm not sure. Max is making the arrangements, but you know it'll be some god-awful early flight."

She glanced at the time on her phone. "I'm late." She grabbed her purse and keys. "Chaz, the fight earlier—that was all me, and I know it was. We can talk tomorrow or after your trip." She cocked her head, and the way the light hit her blue eyes gave them a soft, worried look. "We're okay, aren't we?"

Tell her. Get it out in the open. "Yeah, we're fine." They were finally on stable footing again. He couldn't ruin that by telling her now. *Jesus, I'm a coward.* "Kaylie, I can cancel the trip. I'd rather be with you anyway."

"Are you kidding? I know how important the sponsors are. It's no big deal. One or two nights, even three nights. Oh, I almost forgot. All the girls are staying at Danica's tonight, so I'll be home tomorrow, and if I'm home early enough, we can talk then." She picked up her purse and keys and headed for the door.

Staying at Danica's? Chaz had to make a decision fast, and the first thing that came to mind was to clear up what she'd initially been mad about, so that when he revealed what he'd been holding back, at least there would be one less thing to deal with. "Look, I didn't mean whatever you thought I meant about you staying home and having babies."

"I know," she said with a smile.

"So, maybe we should talk." *And I should tell you about my lie so my conscience is clear and so that we can move forward together without anything standing in our way.* Chaz played with the words in his mind. *I need to tell you something. Remember when I said I'd never dated anyone from the festival...No, that's not right...Kaylie, I lied and I need to clear it up...* He could just see the night ending with a screaming match starting with *You lied to me?* and ending with *I never want to see you again.*

She tucked her hair behind her ear and shrugged. "I've got a lot to figure out with my career, and I need a little time to do that. I really am sorry for overreacting before."

Damn it. Her work. How could he pile his shit on her own pile of worry? He had to try to tell her. "We can figure it out together," he offered.

She didn't answer, but when she reached for the doorknob, she spun around and blew him a kiss. It was now or never.

"Kaylie, we really do need to talk," he said. "I...have something that I want to discuss."

Kaylie smiled. "Can it wait until tomorrow?"

No! Chaz's gut twisted. His nerves were on fire and every muscle in his body was tense. He couldn't let the Lea issue rest. "Can you call me tonight, after you get to Danica's?" He sounded so desperate; surely she'd hear his urgency.

"Sure, but it might be late," she answered. She was out the door before he could gather the courage to spit out the truth.

As he drove down the mountain, his anger mounted. He was a goddamned idiot. He should have told Kaylie about Lea ages ago. Maybe he should drive straight to Bar None and tell Kaylie about Lea. Clear the air. Who was he kidding? The tension between them had nothing to do with Lea. Telling her now would be adding fuel to her angst. Damn it. He should have told her about Lea ages ago. Chaz swore he'd never keep another thing from Kaylie.

He passed the only other house on the rural road, the one with the broken For Sale sign. Chaz pushed away his thoughts of Lea and replaced them with thoughts about how much he loved living outside of town. It was as if he and Kaylie had their own little piece of paradise. *Kaylie.* Her emotions had been so up and down lately. He wished he knew what to do to help her through whatever was spinning around in that pretty little head of hers. *Adding his admission about Lea to the mix would only add to her troubles.* This was definitely not what he'd planned for the day before leaving town.

Thinking of Kaylie brought his thoughts to Danica and how different she and Kaylie were. Danica was always picking up the pieces of Kaylie's life. It figured he'd choose the impetuous sister. Then again, he'd never be attracted to someone like Danica. Danica was great, and pretty, but she wasn't Kaylie. Hell, no one was. Kaylie touched him in ways that only she could. She calmed him when he was angry and soothed him when he was tired. She didn't hold grudges, and she never got jealous or possessive. God, he missed the way things were before all this craziness began, before she started losing gigs, and before he realized his mistake about keeping secrets.

His cell phone rang, pulling his attention back to the present. *Blake.*

"I'm on my way," Chaz said.

"I'm really sorry, but I've gotta cancel."

"Oh." *Shit. I need the distraction.* "We could hang at your place if you don't want to go into town."

"No, it's not that." Blake paused. "I think I've got food poisoning. My stomach has been going crazy since I ate. Bad chicken or something. My stomach is on fire. Thank God Danica didn't eat it."

"Ugh, sorry. That sucks. Okay, we'll do it another time. Do you need me to pick up anything for you at the drugstore?"

"Nah, I talked to my doc. There's not much I can do but wait it out at this point. He said it could just be a bug, too. Hydrate and all the usual crap. I'm really sorry to bail on you like this."

"No biggie. Feel better." Chaz decided to take a drive through the Village and blow off steam. Maybe he'd even grab a drink by himself, and he knew just the place.

The evening rolled in and the lights illuminated the trees lining the main road into the Village. Allure was known for two things: skiing and an aura of romance. During the off-season, the lights still shone bright, so even the summer tourists got a taste of Allure's true calling. It was one of his favorite things about the town. Maybe he'd just walk a little before heading to the bar.

He parked his car and walked through the Village. Before he

knew it, he was at the far end of the main strip, past the last row of stores. He turned down a familiar narrow alley, which separated two rows of town houses. Chaz descended the cement steps and opened the doors to Taylor's Cove, breathing in the slightly dank air of the basement-level pub. Taylor's Cove was one of the few bars within the Village limits that tourists shied away from. Joe Taylor's grandfather had opened the pub in the late sixties, catering to mostly the blue-collar crowd from just outside the Village limits. As the Village grew, the senior Taylor continued to feed the rumors that Taylor's Cove was a rough place. Even the locals shied away from the hole in the wall. Chaz had been warned about the pub from the minute he moved into Allure, and it was his curiosity that drove him in. He liked the quiet, the older clientele and the lack of fanfare. At Taylor's Cove, Chaz could relax, thinking his own thoughts without the pressure of the townsfolk asking about the festival or sponsors breathing down his back to get more for their money.

He climbed atop a wooden stool, realizing that he hadn't been in since he'd met Kaylie. He tapped his finger on the bar. "Kamikaze, Joe."

Joe lifted his chin. "Chaz. What brings you 'round? Isn't this your festival prep time? Sponsorships and all that?" Joe joked with Chaz because when Chaz had first taken over as the director of the festival, he'd made the mistake of approaching even the smallest of businesses in search of sponsors. Joe had laughed at him, a deep, hearty, what-kind-of-fool-am-I laugh and then proceeded to set Chaz straight about the ways of Allure; *Folks around here don't ask for money from friends.* Chaz knew then that he'd be better off keeping his fundraising to bigger companies.

"That's what brings me here." Chaz accepted the glass and

held it up high. "To the festival," he said, and guzzled it down. He nodded at Joe. "One more, Joe?"

"One-minute rule." Joe looked down his wide nose at Chaz.

"Right." Chaz turned and scanned the pub. He found Max sitting in the corner and laughed to himself. He'd introduced Max to the pub years earlier and she, like him, used it to hide from the world. He turned back to Joe and pointed at Max, lifting his eyebrows.

"She came in grumbling about having to go to Hawaii."

"Bring my drink over there after my minute is up?" Chaz said and went to Max's table. She held a glass between her palms and didn't look up. "Mind if I sit?"

She waved at the chair.

"This is my haunt. Why are you here?" he asked. Max wasn't the type to bitch about traveling, so he knew something else was bothering her.

"You showed me *your haunt* the second week I worked for you. Remember?" She raised her hazel eyes.

"When we lost Ross," they said in unison, and then laughed a quiet, familiar laugh.

"The first sponsorship you ever blew," he teased.

She scowled.

The thing Chaz respected most about Max was that she hadn't tried to sleep her way to the top, like many of the other women Chaz had met during his career. She'd turned down Ross's offer for sponsorship in exchange for a night of sheet wrestling, and she'd gone on to make a name for herself in the festival business by her hard work and efficient organizational skills. Chaz was lucky to have her on his staff. Seeing her now, he wondered if he'd taken advantage of her by dragging her to Hawaii.

"Look, if you don't want to go to Hawaii, you don't have

to. I'm a big boy. I can handle it."

She pressed her lips into a thin line and crossed her arms. Max wore her long dark hair in a low ponytail, as she had every day since Chaz had known her. Even during the festivals, she'd show up in her typical blue jeans and festival T-shirt, thin red frames perched on her slim, perky nose and not a speck of makeup on her porcelain-white skin.

"Okay, so maybe I can't, but I can manage without you. I was fine before you came on board."

"Oh, really? With Miss Mouse as your sponsorship coordinator? You were a babysitter and had to do all of her work plus your own. And don't get me started about you and Lea."

Lea. Chaz leaned back in his chair. "What're you really upset about?" he asked.

"Let's just make sure you don't end up with Lea, all right?"

"Max, really? You know me better than that."

"Why are you even here?" she asked. "We're leaving before dawn."

"What?"

"You should really check your voicemail," she said, sucking down the last of her drink.

Chaz pulled out his phone and saw the message light blinking. Goddamn service. He put the phone to his ear and Max pulled it back down.

"Red-eye, tonight."

"The red-eye? Really, Max? Are you that angry with me?"

"I'm not mad at you." She stood and gathered her purse in her arms and then smiled. "And I want to go to Hawaii. I just have other stuff going on."

He watched her leave the pub. *Other stuff?* He'd never heard Max talk about a man, or anyone for that matter. She separated her work life from her personal life more expertly than anyone

Chaz knew. In fact, based on her lack of discussing the topic, he'd swear she hadn't gone on a single date in the past five years.

"Here you go, one Kamikaze. The next rule is—"

"Five-minute rule. I know your rules, Joe. I have to wait five minutes before my next drink. Got it."

"Hey, keeps the mischief to a minimum." Joe wiped his hands on a towel that hung over his shoulder and went back to the bar.

Chaz pulled out his phone to call Kaylie and let her know that he'd be leaving before dawn; then he realized that, between the music and her friends, there was no way she'd hear the phone. He texted her instead. *Leaving on red-eye. Love you.*

An hour and several drinks later, Chaz left the pub and headed for his car. Max was leaning against the driver's side door with her arms crossed. She held her hand out as he approached.

"Keys," she said.

"Wha—"

"Years, Chaz. You know what I've learned in those years of working with you? That some nights, you need taking care of. There was no Kaylie talk today—not one single word—and you didn't want to bring her to Hawaii, either. That spells one thing to me. T-R-O-U-B-L-E."

He handed her his keys and she grabbed a bag from the trunk of her car, threw it into the backseat of his Lexus RX, and opened the passenger door. "Climb in," she said.

"You brought a bag to Taylor's Cove?"

"I packed when I got home. You know me. I like to be prepared."

He climbed in the car and she said, "Phone?"

"Why?"

"We're not repeating your mistake from last year. Remember that call you made to some poor girl you'd gone out with the week before the festival? No more drunken phone calls." She pushed her hand toward him. He turned his phone off and put it in her palm.

Chapter Twelve

Bar None was dimly lit; music filtered through the din of the patrons, and Kaylie, Danica, and their girlfriends sat at a round table near the bar.

Chelsea immediately declared, "Piña coladas for the girls! Oh, and a virgin colada for the mama of honor! Tonight, we're pretending we're in Mexico!"

Marie told them about a trip she'd taken for the high-end fashion boutique she worked for, and Kaylie spaced out after the part about the company being run by the sexiest man alive. She was thinking of Chaz and how when she'd come out of the bedroom, he'd been turned on. She hadn't meant to notice. She hadn't been looking for a reaction—and she was still pissed about losing all of those jobs—but how could she not notice? She wasn't used to getting that reaction from him by just walking into the room. She leaned back in her seat and looked down at her belly. A sly smile crept across her lips. She was still sexy after all.

"Oh my God. Are you kidding me?" Danica elbowed Kaylie, pulling her from her thoughts.

"What?" Kaylie looked at her friends' stunned faced. Had she had a wardrobe malfunction? She checked both breasts. Nope. She scanned Marie's frilly tank top. No issues there either.

"Really," Marie said with pride.

"What did I miss? Really what?" Kaylie asked.

"Mr. Sexy business owner grew up in the same area as Marie before she moved to Allure!" Chelsea said. "And she missed out!"

Camille and Chelsea had both grown up in Allure with Kaylie and Danica, but they'd met Marie when she moved to Allure in her sophomore year of high school.

Chelsea laughed. "How could you not see potential in him? Okay, wait. Exactly how sexy is Mr. Sexy? I mean, are we talking Channing Tatum or Ryan Reynolds? Because if you're talking Channing, there is *no way* you could miss that."

Marie tapped her chin. "He was more Channing than Ryan, but growing up, those boys were off-limits. I mean, the Braden brothers? Come on. You guys knew about them."

"Braden brothers? I don't think so." Camille looked from Marie to Kaylie.

Kaylie held her breath. *Don't say Treat. Don't say Treat.*

"Josh," Marie said dreamily.

Kaylie let out a breath. She'd seen Treat while she was at a party in college. He'd arrived with the most beautiful girl on their floor, but his eyes had locked with Kaylie's. And held. In that moment, everything else in the room—the noise, the people, the music—all fell away. At that moment, only he and Kaylie existed. They'd never spoken. Not a single word, not another look. The moment hit, and then the party crashed in around them. He and the girl left the party soon after arriving, and Kaylie crushed on him for four painful months.

Kaylie shook the thoughts of Treat from her mind. She had Chaz, and Chaz was not only hotter, but he was hers, and he loved her, and she wouldn't want it any other way. Chaz was her saving grace amid her crashing career. Even if they had flashes of trouble, or if she overreacted and accused him of wanting her barefoot and pregnant, that was the pregnancy talking. It wasn't what she really felt about him. His stability, his support, and his unrelenting honesty all centered her in a way she knew no other man ever could.

"They grew up a few towns over. Wealthy family, attended the best colleges, the works." Marie had a conspiratorial look in her eye. "I should have taken him when I had the chance."

"Yeah, like you ever had a chance. You were in what? Ninth grade?" Kaylie teased. "So, what happened on the trip?"

"Nothing. That's just it. After the meeting, there was a group of us who met and had dinner. I swear I caught his eye more than once, but then I got all shy and went to bed early."

"You loser!" Camille slapped Marie lightly on the arm.

"You, shy? I can't believe that," Danica said.

Marie dropped her eyes. Her sandy-brown hair brushed her shoulders as it fell forward. "He was intimidatingly hot."

"Whatever, so is Chaz," Kaylie said with pride.

"That he is," Camille added.

Danica lifted her piña colada and the others followed. A cherry bobbed in Kaylie's drink. "To my sister," she said.

"To Kaylie," they said collectively.

"Aw, you guys," she said, happy to be in the center of the conversation again, gearing it away from her memories of Treat. She had wondered how she'd feel surrounded by her friends when they were all drinking and she couldn't, but she realized, as she sat with them now, it was the camaraderie she missed, not the alcohol. Kaylie didn't miss drinking, or hooking up. She did sometimes miss that flutter in her stomach when she'd first meet a guy. That wondering of whether he'd talk to her or not, the secret glances, and the excitement at the end of the night of knowing she'd conquered him. She'd had that with Chaz, and she had more with him now, more than she could ever imagine, or than she'd ever known she wanted. She thought back to when she'd come into the living room in her dress earlier in the night. The lust in Chaz's eyes, his instant arousal. Her stomach gave a little flutter, and Kaylie knew she wasn't missing a thing. A little feather of guilt tickled her nerves at the way they'd left each other without a warm goodbye, but she'd make that up to him. Oh, would she ever.

"So, girls, I need some help." All eyes focused on her. "If you can believe it, I'm not able to get the singing gigs I got before I was pregnant."

Camille waved her hand. "Like you even have to work?"

Kaylie didn't miss her eyes immediately shooting to Danica, who was scowling and shaking her head. "What do you mean?"

There goes that look again. "Chaz said from the day you got pregnant that he didn't care if you worked or not."

"She's right," Marie added.

Kaylie eyed Danica, her head bent over her drink, purposefully avoiding Kaylie's eyes. Her leg kicked up and down beneath the table in her fuck-me Jimmy Choos and short skirt. It was obvious to Kaylie that Danica and her friends had been talking about her losing her singing gigs. She'd deal with her later.

"Maybe so, but still. I've worked too hard to give up my career."

"I gave up mine, and I couldn't be happier," Danica said with a smile.

"You did not. You still have a career. Just a different one," Kaylie pointed out.

Danica put her arm around her sister and said, "Kay, when this baby comes, the last thing you're gonna want to do is leave it to sing for strangers."

It was like Danica could read her secret thoughts. Kaylie knew she might never want to leave her baby, but she still wanted the option left open. "I think a girl has to be careful. Not be too vulnerable or give up everything she's worked for, for a man. Look at you. You still have the youth center. You're not staying home barefoot and pregnant."

"But I might be, one day." Danica sat back, and Kaylie looked at her as if she were crazy. "What?"

Kaylie huffed. "Okay, here it is, and you know this, Danica." Did she really need to spell it out again? "I can't be Mom."

"I love your mother," Chelsea said without hesitation.

"Me too," Marie added.

"Kaylie, what do you mean?" Camille asked. "What about your mom don't you want to be?"

Kaylie leaned forward, thankful that someone wanted to hear her. "Mom stayed home, never had anything for herself besides us." She looked at Danica, who nodded and shrugged. She must be tipsy, the way she was bringing up the subject of being barefoot and pregnant and then turning around and agreeing about their mother. "Then, when our father left, she had nothing. She was...broken. And broke."

Camille reached across the table and tapped it with her fingernail. Her white silk blouse dropped to the side, exposing the milky skin of her breast. "I hear what you're saying, Kaylie."

"What? I'd give my eyeteeth not to have to work, even if I had nothing left fifteen years later." Chelsea looked at Kaylie like she was crazy.

Camille continued. "I haven't been working. I gave up my job to focus on the new house. I've been buying furniture, setting it up. I never realized how much work there would be to do, and I get it. I mean, it was really fun at first, and I know Jeff likes knowing I'm there, but I've got no kids at home, so sometimes I feel like I'm wasting my time."

"That's what I'm talking about," Kaylie said. "What's your plan?"

Camille shrugged. "I'm not sure. We're not going to have kids right away, so I might go back to work. But every time I think of that, it feels weird, like, let's say I went back to being an assistant director of human resources. Do I work really hard to become the director? What if that's when we decide to have kids? Then I've wasted my time growing a career I might not continue with."

"See? This is what I mean. There's no easy answer." Kaylie turned to Danica, who was remaining suspiciously silent.

"What?" Danica asked.

"Come on. Be a therapist already," Kaylie urged.

"No way." She shook her head and her ringlets bobbed. "I know better than to make your decisions for you and get blamed for them later."

"See? Even my sister won't help me. What am I gonna do?"

Chelsea set her glass down hard on the table, causing all eyes to drift to her. Her cheeks were pink from drinking and her straight brown hair hung thick and full to her shoulders. She blinked twice and then pointed a pink fingernail at Kaylie. "The real question is, what do you want to do? What does your heart tell you to do?"

"My heart is so messed up right now," Kaylie admitted. "I wanna be with my baby, but I also don't want to lose everything I've worked for."

Chelsea sat back and threw her arms up in the air. "Well, there you have it. You need to do something that you can do from home."

"In the music business," Camille added.

"Oh, we can *so* figure this out," Marie said with a nod.

"Chaz suggested that I write, but—"

Marie cut Kaylie off. "Yes! That's it! You're always singing to the radio and changing words."

"I think you should try," Camille agreed.

"I don't know. I'm not a big writer." *Can Chaz be right?* She remembered how angry she'd been when he'd suggested it, and that feather of guilt created another nagging itch.

"Kaylie, you know you can do anything you try to do," Danica said, her eyes on her drink.

Write? I should write songs? Maybe I can write songs. "I guess it wouldn't hurt to try." Kaylie yawned, and then covered her mouth in embarrassment. "I'm so sorry."

"Do we bore you?" Marie teased.

"I'm so tired all the time," Kaylie answered.

"I was hoping for karaoke tonight." Chelsea stuck out her lower lip.

Kaylie's eyes lit up. "Really?" She looked around the bar, and her pulse picked up speed. She pushed out her chair and stood. "Who else is up for it?"

"Me!" Marie jumped up and pulled Chelsea along with her.

"I can't be left behind, but only if we sing something I know," Camille said, pushing herself up to her feet. "Come on, Danica. You have to do it, too."

Danica shook her head. "Kaylie's got the voice. I've got the...advice."

Kaylie pulled Danica to her feet. "Oh no, you're not. Come on." Kaylie walked behind the girls, who were swaying on their sky-high heels, laughing as they climbed the stairs to center stage.

The bartender had known Kaylie and Danica for years, and he never turned down Kaylie when it came to singing. He flipped on the karaoke machine, and a hush took over the room.

The music started quietly, and then grew louder as the girls sang Taylor Swift's "Love Story," off-key, missing words and giggling as they leaned on one another, with Kaylie in the center of the group, perfectly pitched and never missing a beat. She belted out the words with perfection, pointing at one handsome man after another, like she was singing directly to them. Her cheeks hurt from smiling, as her vocal cords vibrated and the words sailed from her mouth like a gift. One by one, the other girls fell into fits of laughter, leaving Kaylie alone on the center of the stage, her dress climbing to the middle of her thigh, her belly arcing out beneath her breasts, singing as if her life depended on it.

The music ended and she put her hands out to her sides and curtsied, enjoying the rush of the moment like a crack addict finishing a rock. God, she missed the thrill of an audience and the rush of feeling the beat of the music through the vibrations of the floor. The way her lungs burned with every deep note and tickled with the high ones. This, the stage, the thrill, was oxygen to Kaylie. How could she give this up?

Chapter Thirteen

Chaz's head throbbed when the alarm went off at one thirty a.m. He lay on his back staring at the ceiling, his arm spread across Kaylie's side of the bed, trying to put together the pieces of the night before. Why on earth was he up at one thirty? *Hawaii. Red-eye. Shit.* Why did he feel like his blissful existence had turned to chaos in the span of twenty-four hours? It wasn't chaos, was it? Kaylie sure didn't seem to act like it when she left the evening before, but then again, she didn't know about Lea. Chaz realized that he hadn't even touched the tip of chaos yet. Kaylie hadn't called…and Lea awaited.

He dragged himself to the bathroom, forgoing his razor, and stepped into a cold shower to shake off the fog from his brain. As the cold water beat down on his shoulders, he thought about the day ahead. Hours on an airplane and facing Lea Carmichael. He really was in hell. He dressed quickly in jeans and a button-down shirt, and then went to the living room to find his cell phone and see if Kaylie had texted him back.

There were no bars on his cell phone, so he headed for his office, but quickly realized he couldn't call Kaylie at one thirty in the morning. Max came out of the hall bathroom fully dressed and much too peppy for so early in the morning.

"Hey there, sleepy. I wondered if I was going to have to drag your butt out of bed."

Chaz scrubbed his face with his hand. "Thanks for taking me home last night."

"You're lucky I was there. You know better than to drink and drive. What were you thinking?"

That I should have told Kaylie about Lea. "I wasn't thinking." Chaz was thankful that Max had been at Taylor's. Who knows if he'd have made it home okay or not. Max. Reliable, efficient Max. She was the best assistant he'd ever had, and she wasn't even an assistant. She was a sponsorship coordinator, but she took care of all of his loose ends. Max was like having a really great older sister around. He knew she'd always have his back.

"Do you want to tell me why you were at Taylor's last night?" Chaz asked.

"I don't know. I feel like this thing with Lea is my fault. I should have never told you she wanted a sponsorship. I should have just hunted down other sponsors and then you wouldn't be in this mess."

Chaz knew how conscientious Max was, but he never imagined that she'd take the blame for something that was clearly his fault. "Max, you can't really believe that."

"It's true. If I had just turned her down flat, we'd be fine."

"The festival would be canceled, Max. You did the right thing. Just like always," he said, patting her on the back.

"I made you coffee." She nodded to a travel mug on the counter. "We've got to be at the airport in forty minutes."

Chaz was used to Max being shy around compliments at times, while other times she ate them up. He was pretty sure he'd never figure out the way women's minds worked. Luckily, the only one he really needed to fully understand was Kaylie's. He packed a quick bag, and as they headed out the door, he promised himself the second he heard Kaylie's voice, no matter what else was going on, he'd tell her the truth. He owed it to her. He owed it to their unborn baby.

Chapter Fourteen

Moonlight streamed in the window of Danica's den, where Kaylie sat in her pajamas and fuzzy slippers. She loved this room. The sofa folded out to an enormous king-sized bed, and it reminded her of when she and Danica used to have sleepovers at their grandparents' house. Danica was asleep upstairs in her bedroom, and Camille and Chelsea had claimed the guest bedroom. Marie had passed out on the pull-out couch in the living room, while Kaylie's mind ran in circles about her career options—or lack thereof. Unable to sleep, she'd tried to write songs, as the girls and Chaz had suggested, but everything she wrote was crap and she'd given up. She'd had such high hopes when they were at Bar None, too.

She wished she'd gone back home last night instead of staying at Danica's. Chaz was leaving on the red-eye, and she missed him already. Her mother had left her another message, and Kaylie was glad she'd missed the call. She wasn't ready to deal with her mother's new lifestyle yet. First she had to deal with her own transitions.

Kaylie felt a little lost, and she didn't like it one bit. She'd always had the world at her fingertips, and now she felt like a failure. Who was she if she wasn't a singer and the life of the party? She'd known that things would change as her body did, but what she hadn't planned on was how it would make her feel. What made it even worse was that she knew she was messing up the only good thing in her life—her relationship with Chaz. He didn't deserve her crazy mood swings, and she had no way to control them. Even her doctor was no help. *It's only nine months. It'll all be worth it.*

How many times had Danica told her that she couldn't have a happy relationship until she was happy with herself? A zillion, that's how many. And although she was sure Danica didn't think she ever listened to her advice, she not only listened, but she memorized that particular piece, even if she didn't heed the value of it. The trouble was, Kaylie always thought she *was* happy. But now she was beginning to realize that it was all an illusion. She liked being pretty and getting noticed, and singing breathed new life into her every time she stepped on stage. Without the lights shining on her, without the roar of the crowd when she hit those high notes, or the leers from men when they thought their girlfriends weren't looking, she was left being just another average girl. She had to be more than average. Danica wasn't average, and she'd be damned if she'd be anything less.

She pulled the crumpled papers out of the trash can, flattened them out, and looked over the ridiculous lyrics. It made her sick to her stomach to realize that she wasn't capable of doing what Chaz thought she could so easily do.

Kaylie read over the lyrics again and again, hoping she'd see something worth saving, some hint of excellence. Crap. They were all crap. She sucked at writing. She'd never find anything else to do with her life. If she couldn't sing, she might as well work in a record store, or a restaurant. None of it mattered. If she couldn't sing—and she clearly couldn't write songs—she didn't care what she did.

She turned the radio on low to clear her head, and then she went into the kitchen and quietly poured herself a bowl of cereal. If she couldn't sing, and she couldn't write, she might as well eat. She hummed along with the music, being careful not to be too loud, although she was pretty sure that the girls were down for the count. They'd had more than their share of drinks. Before she knew it, she was dancing to Taylor Swift's, "I knew You Were Trouble." Suddenly, she stopped midspin, in the center of the kitchen, with her cereal growing soggier by the second.

"That's all wrong," she whispered to the empty room. "It's not all *him*."

She headed back into the den, snagged a piece of fresh paper and a pencil from Danica's desk as she sank into Danica's chair, and then she began to write.

Chapter Fifteen

Danica's cell phone rang, and she hoped it was Kaylie. Kaylie had still been sleeping when she'd left for the youth center, and the other girls all had somewhere they needed to be, so they left a note on the counter for her and locked the condo on their way out. She'd already tried Kaylie's cell phone three times, and every call had gone to voicemail. She looked at the phone. *Mom.* Danica realized that her heart wasn't racing at the sight of her mother's phone number. She wondered what had changed, and the therapist in her provided the answer. *Mom's finally happy. You don't have to feel guilty for moving on with your life anymore.*

"Hi, Mom." Danica hadn't realized how much she'd avoided her mother after her parents' separation. She'd still seen her and talked with her every few weeks, but the weight of her mother's unhappiness had weighed heavily on Danica every time she'd heard her mother's voice. The guilt she'd carried since she graduated from college, for striking out on her own rather than going home to help her mother heal, dissipated with her mother's new lease on life.

"Hi, honey. I've been trying to reach Kaylie, but she's not answering her phone. I know it's hopeful—and even presumptive—but I thought after meeting for lunch that we might try to stay connected."

Danica heard the strain in her voice, and she was quick to clear up the confusion. "She probably has her phone turned off."

"Do you think everything's okay?"

Here comes that stress again. Danica hated being in between Kaylie and her mother, and it seemed like every time she turned around, one of them was asking Danica's opinion about their relationship. "Yes, Mom. She's just having a hard time with work and all. The girls and I took her out last night, and she stayed at my place." Sally appeared in her doorway and Danica held up one finger. "She'll be fine. She just needs a day to get her head together."

"I hope so. You know, she was so upset with me for staying with your father, I mean, once she realized that I had known about his affair for all those years and stayed with him anyway. She hated that he blindsided me with it, but I think she was angrier with me when she realized that it was my choice to stay."

Danica sighed and covered the phone. "I'm actually gonna be a minute. I'll come get you," she said to Sally.

Sally nodded and mouthed, *It's fine. No rush,* and walked away. Gage met her in the hallway and Danica watched them. Sally looked regal with her perfect white-blond hair and slim figure. She could make jeans, a colored silk scarf, and a T-shirt look like a fashion statement. Standing next to ruggedly handsome Gage, in his cargo shorts with his muscular calves exposed, they looked like the perfect couple. *Hmm.*

Danica's mother was going on about how when she was pregnant with Danica, she felt ugly and fat, too. "Mom, you should tell Kaylie that, not me."

"I would if I could reach her." Her mother paused, then

continued. "I hate to bring up uncomfortable subjects, but with Kaylie having a baby, don't you think it's time for her to forgive your father and make peace? I mean, I'm her mom, and moms always take the brunt of parenting woes. I know in my heart that one day the fissure between us will mend, but it's been years since she's seen or spoken to your father."

"That's one problem I can't fix, Mom. I'll bring it up to her, but don't expect any miracles."

"She really shouldn't blame him. Things happen in marriages, and they're really no one's fault. Anyway, I thought the baby might mend the bridge between us."

Danica wasn't going down that no-win road with her mother. There was no doubt that Kaylie should have been making a bigger effort to understand their mother, but her mother shouldn't have let it go for so long either. There was no way to keep her therapist thoughts to herself. Instead, she remained quiet, hoping her mother would drop the subject.

Silence filled the space between them. Danica didn't want to be in that middle place, where she'd spent the last few years. Kaylie was a big girl. She would have to learn to deal with their mother at some point—and their father. Danica fiddled with the papers on her desk, trying to remember the last time she'd spoken to her father. They exchanged holiday cards each year, but she hadn't actually spoken to him in…she had no idea how long it had been.

She read her mother's pain in her silence. She'd always done that with their father—gone silent, waiting for him to clear the air. Danica had been waiting to invite her mother to the baby shower until she saw how things went between her and Kaylie, but since Kaylie hadn't made any further efforts, Danica couldn't wait any longer. "Mom, Kaylie's baby shower is planned for the weekend after next. I meant to send you an invitation, but we ended up just calling everyone. I was worried Kaylie might see the invites lying around. Can you make it? Please?" After she asked the question, she realized how uncomfortable her mother and Kaylie would be, but ignoring the therapist in herself was not easy to do. She had to try to help them reconcile, if for no other reason than to get herself out of the middle. She closed her eyes, hoping her mother would say she was too busy.

"I'd love to. Where and when?"

Chapter Sixteen

Kaylie woke up feeling groggy. She blinked away the fatigue and glanced at the clock, and she bolted to her feet—as much as a pregnant woman could *bolt*. Two o'clock? Where had the day gone? She hadn't fallen asleep until sometime after five in the morning. She spotted the stack of papers on the corner of the desk and smiled. There was a plethora of songs on those pages. Not only had she written these songs, but in the wee hours of the morning, they'd seemed to be good—really, really good.

She flipped on the lights and then picked up her cell phone and texted Chaz. *Sorry I missed u this morning. Stayed up late. Love u.* She checked her voicemail. Her heart sank as she listened to Chaz's messages from the night before. He missed her. He was sorry. All he wanted was for her to be happy. She detected something, a hesitation maybe, in his voice. Like he had something else to say, or maybe she was just exhausted and was hearing things that weren't there. Singing at Bar None had been exhilarating, and when she'd finally sat down to write, it was like her heart poured out through her fingertips, leaving her emotionally and physically drained, similar to what she'd heard in Chaz's voice. *Shit!* She'd forgotten to call him when they got back to Danica's house. That was why he was so upset.

Kaylie sank into the couch, listening to the next message

from her mother. She apologized for springing the news about dating on her and asked her to join her for dinner so that they could talk. She saved the message. She was too tired to think about how to respond. She listened to Camille and Marie's messages, both gushing over how much fun they'd had. There were two more messages, both from Chaz.

"Kaylie, I'm about to get on the plane, but I wanted to hear your voice. I guess voicemail will have to do." The frustration in Chaz's voice startled her. "You forgot to call me," he said with an edge in his voice. "I'll be in meetings most of the day after we land, and then we'll be flying back, and with the time difference and all, it'll be hard to catch up. Maybe you need that time anyway, to figure things out. I...we really need to talk."

She dialed Chaz's number and left a voicemail message. "Just got your message. We had fun. I slept really late. I'm sorry I forgot to call. Hope your trip goes well. I know you'll seal the deal with the sponsor. Do whatever it takes. I love you."

Kaylie picked up her papers and stuffed them into her purse, cleaned up her bowl of uneaten cereal, and tidied the kitchen and den before heading home. She couldn't shake the uncomfortable feeling about the way Chaz sounded, like he was angry that she'd forgotten to call. Chaz never got angry about things like that. He knew where she was and who she was with. What the hell was going on?

She hit every red light on her way out of town, and she used the time to wallow in the happiness of knowing she could do more than sing. She couldn't wait to get home and read through her songs again. Chaz would be so proud of her once he got over his crankiness. She had to cut him a break. He'd been about to get on a plane at an ungodly hour, and that was enough to make anyone cranky.

As she drove up the long driveway, she wondered if she

could make a career out of writing songs, and then one day, when their baby was older, go back to singing, or even better— gain a recording contract. Then she wouldn't have to give up everything she'd worked so hard to achieve or leave the baby. She could write from home, and even if something happened...She wouldn't let herself think about that. She wasn't her mother. Nothing would happen between her and Chaz. They had a solid, happy relationship despite the way she'd been acting lately.

Kaylie dropped her bags by the front door, suddenly feeling even more tired than she had been. She looked in the long mirror that hung in the foyer. Fatigue showed in the bags under her eyes. She hadn't showered at Danica's, and her hair was matted and unstyled. The maternity shirt she wore made her boobs look matronly and saggy. Who had she been kidding last night? She must have looked like a fool up on the stage in that too-tight dress. She drew a long deep breath and blew it out as she walked heavily into the living room and ran her finger along the mantel, hesitating at each photograph. In the pictures, she was happy and thin. Who would want to look at her now, with those stupid bags under her eyes and her entire body retaining water? What the hell had she been thinking last night? Chaz couldn't have been excited about how she looked. Either she'd completely misread what she'd thought she saw, or he was thinking of someone else altogether, because she was an ugly mess.

She headed for her bedroom. A nap might do her well. The light in the hall bathroom was on. Flipping it off, she noticed a hairbrush on the sink. A woman's hairbrush, and it wasn't hers. Kaylie washed her face and then carried the unfamiliar hairbrush into the bedroom, wondering whose it was. Maybe Danica had left it at her house. She went into Chaz's office and called Danica from the cordless phone.

"Kaylie?"

"Hey, did you leave a brush at my house?" Kaylie asked.

"What? No. When would I have done that?"

"I don't know." She pulled a long dark hair from the brush, holding it between her index finger and thumb like a diseased rat. "Something's going on. Chaz is gone. He's in Hawaii, and—"

"Kaylie, slow down. You knew he was going to Hawaii, remember?"

Tears sprang from her eyes, and she tried to calm herself down, but her heart was beating so fast she could hardly think.

"Did Blake say anything about how he was last night?" Kaylie asked.

"Blake? No, he ended up with food poisoning and didn't meet Chaz after all."

"What? Then who...Oh, no." *Maybe he got fed up with my moods and my not calling, and he—Oh, God—would he really go looking for someone else?* "I was supposed to call him last night, and I didn't. And something was wrong before I went out, but I kept telling myself it was nothing. Now he's gone, and it's all my fault."

"I don't understand. You didn't call him? Like, at all? Not while you were out with us? Why would he be upset about that?"

"I told him I would call when we got to your house." She swiped at her tears and cursed herself for being so emotional. "I wasn't thinking. I was writing."

"Kaylie, you're not a kid anymore. You have responsibilities, and this is an adult relationship. That man is the father of your child."

"Did you even hear me? I was writing. Writing! I'm good at it, and if I can be good enough, then maybe I can actually get a record deal someday, Danica. And writing is what Chaz suggested I do—write songs so I wouldn't be so bummed about not singing. And you know what? It worked." *And now he's gone.*

"Great, so you can write songs and smile into an empty house. I don't know what's going on with you two, but between the argument the other day and you not calling him last night, is there any chance you did it on purpose? Subconsciously, I mean?"

"Ugh. Really, Danica? You think I would do that?" *Would I? No. No way.*

"I don't know, but maybe he feels like you took him for granted. You need to fix this."

Kaylie was getting angrier by the second. She didn't need to fix anything. She wasn't the one who brought someone else into the house. Why would he bring a woman over? She stared at the brush, playing made-up scenes in her head; Chaz watching a woman brush her hair, then moving slowly toward her, embracing her from behind, kissing her neck…*Stop! Stop it now!* She threw the brush in the trashcan and stewed over it. She should tell Danica about it, but she was too embarrassed. *Would he really cheat on me? Is he just like Dad?*

"Kaylie, I'm sorry. That's not my place, and I'm sorry. It's gonna be fine. You do want it to be fine, don't you?"

"Jesus, Danica," she cried. "Of course I want things to be fine. I love Chaz. I love us." *But maybe he doesn't love me. I can't end up like Mom.*

"Do you want me to come over?"

"No, no, you're right," Kaylie said through her tears. "I was thoughtless. I want this to work. I just got lost in my own stuff." Kaylie walked to the living room and flopped onto the couch. She pulled at a piece of cloth stuck between the cushions. A woman's sock. "Oh, God."

"What?"

"Nothing."

"Kaylie?"

"I gotta go."

Kaylie stared at the sock in disbelief. She ran to her dresser and rifled through her sock drawer. She knew the sock was not hers, but she didn't want to believe Chaz would be with anyone else, much less bring some other woman to *their* home. It was her parents all over again.

She clenched the sock in her fisted hand and dialed Chaz's number. Damn it, voicemail. "I'm gone for a day and you have someone else move right in? How could you do that? I found her stuff, Chaz. I thought I could trust you." She hung up and tossed the receiver on the other side of the couch, then lay on her side and sobbed.

If there was one thing Kaylie had learned from her parents' divorce and from her mother's unwillingness to leave her father because of her and Danica, it was that it was easier to leave before a baby was born than after. She packed two big suitcases of her clothes and hauled them out to her car.

He'd be full of excuses, and she'd have none of it. She loved him. She had trusted him, and yes, she'd forgotten to call, but that did not justify having a woman in her home. Kaylie touched her belly, thinking of the baby—their baby—and feeling her heart crushing a little more with each painful thought.

Kaylie sat on the front steps of their gorgeous cedar-sided chalet, asking herself if she was being fair. She rubbed the side of her belly where the baby was kicking like a soccer player. "I can't be Mom," she said to her belly.

Her cell phone vibrated and she pulled it from her purse and turned it off without even checking who it was. She didn't want to talk to Chaz after all. She couldn't listen to lame excuses or empty apologies. She'd given her trust to him and this was what he did with it?

Chapter Seventeen

The plane touched down, and Max and Chaz hurried through the tunnel with the other passengers, picked up their luggage, and went outside to hail a cab. Chaz couldn't stop thinking about Kaylie. He felt guilty for leaving without first clearing the air about Lea, but she hadn't exactly made an effort to talk, either. He turned his thoughts to Lea. Once past the initial distaste of being forced into going to Hawaii, he remembered what had drawn him to her in the first place: the sexy, confident tone of her voice, her legs wrapped around his waist, the way she—what was he doing? The sex was good. Lea was bad. He shook the thoughts from his mind. He was losing his sense of purpose. He was there to secure her sponsorship. The stress of not telling Kaylie must be messing with his mind. He had to concentrate.

"Welcome to sunny Hawaii," Max joked.

Chaz groaned. The sun was too bright and he was hot. He'd envisioned himself in Hawaii with Kaylie, on their honeymoon, not with Max, and definitely not while meeting Lea.

He hailed a cab, thankful that he'd slept on the plane, and Max had made sure he was hydrated, waking him up every hour to make him drink water. He was far from bright-eyed as they rode toward the hotel, but he was functional, and maybe that would make dealing with Lea easier.

"What's the plan?" Max asked.

Sitting next to good ol' efficient and ponytailed Max helped Chaz feel more comfortable. Had she dressed up, or God forbid worn makeup, it would have made him nervous, as if Lea really was someone he should be worried about. If Max wasn't too worried, then he wasn't either. He preferred to think of Lea as a princess who turned into an evil witch, making it easier for him to forget her seductive side and see her for the person she really was—a manipulative, destructive bitch. He had to remember that transformation at all times. He'd been playing the meeting off as just another sponsor, but now, faced with Max's question, he realized that beyond the witch image, he had no plan.

Max saw it in his eyes. "God, really, Chaz?" She sighed and pulled a stack of papers from her purse. "Study these. These are the events she's sponsoring and what she's getting in return. You can't see this shark without a plan." Max pointed at the beach out the window. "That's gorgeous."

"Mm-hmm. I have plan. I just haven't figured it out yet." He leafed through the papers. She was sponsoring six festivals, and the stakes were high. She had top billing on all of them, plus everything Max had already promised; and it looked like there were new benefits thrown in to the largest event. Chaz's eyes opened wide. "A chalet in Colorado? Allure? What is this, some kind of joke?"

"Nope, that's what she asked for, and Raindance Film Fest gave in. It's apparently their chalet, an executive's timeshare or something, but she gets three months of residency per year of sponsorship."

"In Allure? Of all places, why Allure? Raindance isn't even in Allure." Chaz ran his hand through his hair. He was up against a wall. There was no way he wanted Lea in his sights for three months out of the year. What was she planning?

"There's only one reason I can see that she'd want to be in Allure." Their eyes locked.

"Jesus. No way. This is something else. Some mistake, or sick joke, or something." He stared out the window, stewing over the gall of Lea Carmichael. What was she trying to pull, and why had she waited this long to do whatever it was? By the time they reached the hotel, his blood was boiling.

"It's one night, Chaz. You'll be fine," Max reassured him as they headed toward the front desk.

"It's three months," he fumed. He didn't say a word to the peppy concierge or the front desk clerk, leaving Max to cover his unfriendly tracks.

Max offered to carry her own bag as they waited for the elevator. "I'm fine. It gives me something to do besides punch a wall."

Max smiled. "You're not a wall puncher."

He laughed. "No, I'm not." He looked at his watch. It was almost eleven. "When are we meeting her?"

"Two o'clock, in the Presidential Meeting Room."

"Good choice."

"She wanted to meet over dinner, but I figured if she wrangled you into dinner, she wouldn't have far to go to wrangle you into a drink, and then…" Her voice trailed off.

"There will be no wrangling during this trip," Chaz said firmly. "I'm gonna take a quick nap before we meet."

Their rooms were three doors apart on the fifth floor. Max opened her door and Chaz followed her in, dropping her bag on

104

the king-sized bed. She pulled the drapes open and took in the view of the water.

"Wow, Mr. Hilton went all out, huh?"

"Yeah, well, the Hiltons are known for their classy digs." Chaz opened the balcony doors and stepped outside. The sea air filled his lungs. He stretched, feeling some of the day's tension easing with the long draw of his shoulders and back. "Waikiki is beautiful, isn't it?"

Max took a deep breath and blew it out slowly, with a curve to her lips. "I never thought I'd be in Hawaii, even if it's only for a night."

"No?"

Max shook her head. "I don't live the life you do. I'm foreplay. I loosen them up for your wining and dining excursions."

"Foreplay?" Chaz lifted his eyes.

Max blushed, then headed back into the room. "I guess there's no need to unpack if we're only here one night."

Chaz picked up his bag. "I'm gonna go find my room and lay down for a bit. If you need me, I'm in—" He looked at his key as Max answered.

"Room 522. I'll wake you thirty minutes before we're supposed to meet her."

Chaz's room was identical to Max's. He threw his bag on the floor beside the long dresser and opened the balcony door. The din of the people below melted into the street noises. Chaz took off his shirt and pants, and climbed onto the bed. He was out cold ten minutes later.

He awoke to a determined knock on the door. The room was

dark and the clock read six thirty. He pulled on his jeans, cursing under his breath as he hopped on one foot to the door. "How could you let me sleep so long?" he said as he buttoned his jeans.

Lea stood before him in a black strapless minidress, her dark hair flowing in waves past her bare shoulders. Her lips were painted a deep shade of red and Chaz noticed, as she reached for him, that her nails were painted the same crimson shade.

"Chaz," she purred.

Chapter Eighteen

Danica checked her watch and headed for her office, anxious to get over to her condo, where she was certain Kaylie would be holed up. She'd tried her cell phone and Chaz's office phone. Why did Kaylie have to be a runner? *And where would she go if I moved in with Blake?*

Sally met her in the hall. "I've got the waivers for teen night. Can you look them over?"

"Yes, of course." *Business first.* Danica took the papers and went to her office. Sally kept pace with her.

"Hey!" a teenage boy yelled from the couch in the lobby.

Danica tried to place where she'd seen the boy before. Teens had flocked to the center from the first days after it opened, and the flow of kids had remained constant ever since. Less so during school hours, but this was summertime, and they were in full swing. She'd done a fair job of remembering everyone's names, but this boy hadn't been in before, at least not that she could remember, although he was familiar.

"Brad? Remember?" He stood.

"Right, Brad. I met you with Michelle last year at the café. Wow, you've gotten tall. How are you?"

"Great. I heard that Michelle works here. Is she around?"

Sally elbowed Danica.

"Yeah, somewhere. Did you try the game room? She's over-seeing that area today. I just saw her." She pointed toward the hall that led to the game room.

He waved a thank-you as he walked away.

"Hmm." She and Sally went to her office.

"I think Michelle and Rusty are dating," Sally said.

"What?" Danica sat back and mulled over the idea. Rusty had come a long way from the angry boy he was right after Dave died, and now that Michelle was living with her mother again, and working part time at the center, she was definitely coming out of her shell. Although she and Danica no longer went on weekly Big Sister outings, they still found time to talk every once in a while. It had been far too long, she realized. "She would have told me." *Wouldn't she?* Danica felt a pang of loss and made a mental note to catch up with Michelle again soon.

"Maybe. I don't know. The way they text all the time. It makes me wonder if there's something going on that I should worry about. I mean, I think Dave covered all the bases about sex, but still."

"They cover sex ed in school, too. It wouldn't be the worst thing in the world if they were dating, would it?"

Sally wrinkled her forehead. "I guess not, but you know how these things go. They're both working here. What if they break up? You know how bad teen breakups can be."

"Oh, good point." Danica made a mental note to pay closer attention to the two of them. "Oh no, poor Brad."

Sally shrugged, that prideful, motherly, oh-well-my-boy-won-out shrug.

"How do you know they're texting each other?" Danica asked.

"Every time I ask Rusty who he's texting he says it's

Michelle."

Danica swatted the air as they sat down at the table in her office. "They could just be friends."

"Gage is doing great, isn't he?" Sally asked.

Danica was so focused on the paperwork that she barely heard Sally's question. "Mm-hmm. I think I'd change this to be more explicit." She pointed to the release clause and noticed Sally ringing her hands. "Are you okay?"

"Yeah, sure." Sally feigned smile.

She leaned in closer. "Sally, it's me. How are you really doing?"

Sally nodded. "Good. Really good. The therapist you recommended really helped a lot, and I even made amends with Trisha. She and I have dinner once a month." After Sally's husband, Dave, was killed in a skiing accident, she found out about Trisha—a woman whom Dave had dated as a teenager and who had given birth to Dave's child. Trisha had never told Dave about their son, Chase, until a few months before his accident, when she moved back into town. He'd been in the process of getting to know Chase and building up the courage to tell Sally when he died.

"Really?"

"Yeah, I know it's kinda weird, but she and Dave were together so long ago, and she is the mother of his child. Rusty is having a harder time accepting Chase, but for me, it's fine. It's actually kind of fun. She knew Dave when I didn't, so she's told me all about how he was in high school."

"That really is weird. You know that, right?"

"Yeah. But it works."

Gage walked into the office and Sally's eyes lit up. "Private meeting?"

"Nope, come on in." Danica waved him in.

"I think we're all set with the activities for the event. Coordinating volunteers is a bit complicated, but Sally's handling most of that."

Was that a flirty smile he flashed at Sally? Is everyone in this office dating?

"I've got them covered." Sally's cheeks flushed, and she dropped her eyes to her lap.

"Great," Gage said. "That's all I have. Just wanted to keep you updated."

He turned and left the room, and Sally let out a breath.

"Gage? Really?" Danica teased.

"I haven't looked at another man since Dave's death, and I never looked when we were married." Sally covered her eyes, and when she dropped her hand, Danica read the unease in them.

"Hey, it's okay. It's been almost a year, and it's okay to move on." She squeezed Sally's hand. "He's hard to ignore, isn't he?" *An office romance?* Danica tucked away her worry. *Don't borrow trouble—you've got enough with Kaylie.*

"Ugh. I'm as bad as a teenager." Sally banged her forehead on the table with a laugh.

With her hopes of an early retreat dashed, Danica returned phone calls and headed to the game room. Her curiosity was killing her. Rusty stood outside the glass window looking into the room. She sidled up beside him and crossed her arms. Brad and Michelle leaned against a pool table. Michelle looked shyly from Brad to her hands, then back again with a smile in her eyes.

"She looks happy," Danica said to Rusty.

"Whatever." Rusty walked away.

Danica watched them for a few more minutes before heading back to the lobby. She was proud of how far Michelle had come from the shy girl who thought of herself as a pariah. She'd been drawing and painting—something that Michelle attributed to her trip with Danica to the bookstore, where she'd purchased her first set of art books—and she was a responsible employee to boot.

She worried about Rusty's quick retreat, but she couldn't be roped into teenage angst. She had sisterly angst to deal with.

"I'm heading out." She handed Sally a phone number on her way to the door. "Can you please just confirm the table deliveries one more time? I always worry about this stuff."

Danica called Kaylie's cell phone on the way out to her car. "Kaylie, I know you're there. Turn your damn phone on." When she reached her condo, she opened the garage door and found Kaylie's car parked inside. She peeked into the windows and saw two big suitcases. "Oh, Kaylie."

Chapter Nineteen

Chaz shook the confusion from his head. Lea stepped into the room and wrapped her soft, sinewy arms around him. He froze, fighting the natural desire that rose when the thin silk that covered her breasts pressed against his bare chest. "I...I expected Max."

She lingered, with her cheek against his, and whispered, "I called Max hours ago and delayed our meeting."

He shook the testosterone from his brain and pushed her away.

She peered around him into his room, her eyes trained on the unmade bed. "It looks like you're all rested up."

"Where's Max?" he asked, heading back into the room just far enough to grab his shirt. He'd need full body armor with her around. *Damn it, Max, where are you?*

"I asked her to save our reservations in the restaurant." Lea watched him button his shirt with a coy grin on her face and an amorous look in her eyes.

He turned his back to her just long enough to look for his cell phone. *Damn it.* Max had stuck it in her purse when he'd fallen asleep on the plane.

"She was not pleased with me," Lea admitted with a proud smirk. "I practically had to threaten her to get her to go downstairs." She ran her eyes up and down Chaz. "I told her I wouldn't do anything we hadn't done before."

"The reservations are held," Max said from the doorway, out of breath and heading into the room.

"Max." He spun around. Max wore a short black skirt, flats, and a teal-colored capsleeved top. Chaz had a hard time reconciling the beautiful, sexy woman before him with his bespeckled, low-key employee. Her hair rivaled Lea's soft waves. Chaz hadn't realized he was staring until she dropped her eyes and flushed.

In the next second, Max was all business, confident and even a little pushy as she stepped between him and Lea. "Sorry I'm late, Chaz. Lea postponed our lunch meeting, so I let you sleep. I was coming to get you when she showed up. *Forty-five minutes early.*"

Shit. As if Lea showing up unannounced wasn't enough, seeing Max dressed like a girl—no, dressed like a woman— totally threw him off. "I need to shower and shave. I'll meet you down in the restaurant in half an hour." He opened his bag and began unpacking.

"I can wait for you here," Lea said, reaching for his back with a seductive gleam in her eyes.

Max intercepted her hand. "Actually, I have some paper-work I want to go over with you, and it's probably best if we do it now and get it out of the way."

Chaz shot Max a silent thank-you glance as she guided a pouty Lea out of his room.

Chaz followed them to the door. "Max, my cell phone?"

"It's in my room," she said, and handed him the key.

Chaz found his cell phone in the side pocket of Max's luggage. He pushed the button to turn it on, but the light remained dark. *Damned battery.* He plugged it into the charger and then picked up the hotel phone to call Kaylie. It was seven thirty in Hawaii. He calculated the time difference as he waited to leave a message, further distracted by the evening that lay ahead.

"Hi, gorgeous. I know it's like one o'clock in the morning there, but, well, I really wanted to talk to you. My cell phone died, so I have no idea if you've tried to call me, but I have something I need to tell you. I'll be home late tomorrow." He hung up the phone and headed for the restaurant.

Chapter Twenty

Danica unlocked her condo door and was assaulted by loud music. Covering her ears, she passed through the living room, which had sheets of paper strewn about. The kitchen was no better. Crumpled papers covered the breakfast table. She headed toward the den to turn down the stereo.

"Kaylie?" she called out to the empty room. She checked the first floor bathroom, then headed upstairs, where she found Kaylie out on the back balcony, chewing on a piece of red licorice.

"That's my after sex food. It's not fight food." She sat in the chair next to Kaylie and let out a frustrated sigh. Did Kaylie have to take over her house and her after sex food? What else could she confiscate?

Kaylie looked up at her and finished the entire twig of licorice before lowering the notebook she'd been scribbling in. "Don't you have to be at work, or with Blake, or something?"

"Don't you have your own house?"

Kaylie looked back down at the notebook and began to write.

"Are you going to tell me what's going on, or are you just going to take over my condo, make a giant mess, and pretend like you're not going to have a baby in a few weeks?"

Kaylie continued writing. "I found a sock," she said without looking up. "And a hairbrush."

What the hell? "A sock? And a hairbrush?"

Kaylie nodded.

"Kaylie, I don't have time for games. I have to get the center's event ready by this weekend." *And your baby shower the following weekend.* "Do you want to talk or not?"

"I'm not gonna be Mom," Kaylie said, like she'd made up her mind and there was nothing to talk about.

"Speaking of Mom, she's worried about you. She really wants to try to get your relationship back on track. Don't you want to do that? She called me twice yesterday, spoke to me again this morning, and then she sent me two more texts."

Kaylie clenched her jaw, then said, "I guess so, but I can't focus on that right now."

"You always give Mom the short end of the stick. She said you should talk to Chaz."

Kaylie shot her a venomous look. "You told Mom about this?"

"I didn't know it was a secret. What is *this* anyway? You have bags in your car? Are you leaving him?"

"I found a sock! And a brush!" Kaylie's voice rose as tears filled her eyes. "A woman's sock, and a woman's brush, and they aren't mine."

"Oh, come on, Kaylie. Chaz would never cheat on you. He adores you. You know it's just something that was yours and you forgot, or maybe Max was there for something. There's got to be a rational explanation. Chaz doesn't even glance at other women."

Kaylie shook her head. "No, I'm not going to be Mom. I can't be that woman who gets cheated on. It's better that I leave now, before this baby is born."

Danica reached for Kaylie and Kaylie leaned away.

"Jesus, Kaylie. This is real life, not some dramatic game you're playing. Your child needs both parents." Danica crossed her arms and stewed, wondering how she'd handle it if the tables were turned. She took her tone down a notch. "Did you talk to him? It was probably from before you moved in together."

"It was in the couch, and the brush was *on the sink*."

Danica had to admit that wasn't good, but she still couldn't imagine Chaz ever cheating on her sister. "Well, do you vacuum under your couch cushions? Because I don't. I can't tell you what's under those damn cushions." She'd start cleaning under them now. Actually, maybe it would be safer to have Blake clean his out the first time, to avoid this type of drama.

Kaylie looked at her from the corner of her eyes. The way her hair shielded her face, she looked like the scared little girl that Danica had found sitting on the back porch of their childhood home, crying because she'd stepped on a ladybug. Danica closed her eyes. This was her sister. Kaylie needed her, and she wouldn't lecture her and push her away. Pregnancy hormones or not, Kaylie was still Kaylie.

"Things aren't always as they appear, Kaylie." Danica sat back in her chair and looked out at the mountains in the distance. The sky was the color of watered-down blue, as if it had been painted with watercolors. Why couldn't Kaylie's life be as beautiful and perfect as the sky? "You aren't Mom. Chaz isn't Dad. When are you going to let yourself be happy?"

Kaylie wiped her tears from her eyes. "I was happy."

"Then why are there two suitcases in your car? And why are you here instead of at your house?" She was careful to ask without accusing.

"I thought he wanted me to stay home and give up working,

which started the week out on a crazy note, but we moved past it. Then I don't know. He looked guilty when I left to meet you guys, and I didn't want any more fights, so I left even though he said he needed to talk. Maybe this was what he wanted to tell me, that he'd found someone else, that I was too emotional for him, or whatever. If he does—" sobs stole her words—"even if he...does...figuring out I could write would still be worth it."

"How? You're here; he's God knows where."

"Hawaii. I told you that yesterday."

"Hawaii?"

Kaylie shook her head and the flow of tears returned. "Work, remember?"

"Whatever. It doesn't matter. Relationships don't fall apart because you had a fight or you forgot to call home. He's going to be your husband. You guys just need some time to air things out."

Kaylie glared at her. She opened her mouth to speak and Danica cut her off.

"Remember when Jimmy Walker found Steve Brewster's ID bracelet in your locker?"

"Yeah, what does that—"

"Do you remember how mad he was?"

Kaylie nodded.

"And remember how you had no idea it was in there?"

"Only because *you* put it there!"

"Whatever. Same same. You can't leave Chaz for a sock and a hairbrush, and you can't sit around feeling sorry for yourself at my condo." There she went, parenting Kaylie again.

"I'm not. I'm writing." She handed the notebook to Danica.

Danica leafed through it. There were pages and pages of song lyrics and musical notes. Danica drew her eyebrows together.

"It turns out he was right. I can write songs." Kaylie tried to smile, but her smile was shrouded in sadness.

"Kay, these are so raw, emotional." She saw her sister through new eyes. "You wrote these? All of them? There must be ten songs here."

"Twelve, and another three downstairs. I don't know what happened. I was really upset over our fight, and the next day, when I woke up, I was listening to the radio, and suddenly it hit me. The songs were all wrong. They didn't have the right pitch of...I don't know...desperation to them. The words were all childlike, as if every song was written about teenagers, so I began to write what I was feeling. Then I wrote some more, and before I knew it, I was elbow deep in ideas that were coming so fast I could barely keep up."

"These are amazing. What are you going to do with them?"

Kaylie shrugged.

"You're in the music business. You of all people know what to do with them."

"I haven't even sung any of them with the music yet. They might suck."

Danica shook her head. The songs were perfect. They said what she felt every time she looked at Blake, when his hands were on her skin, warm and strong, and the lyrics spoke of the sinking feeling that consumed her when they argued. "They won't suck."

Kaylie shrugged again. "I guess I could ask Alex if the band can play them for me."

"Yes, perfect." Danica stood up, and then sat back down. Her momentary elation sidetracked by the fact that her little sister had just walked out on her fiancé.

"What?" Kaylie asked, exasperated.

"Kaylie, you gotta go back to Chaz. Has he called you a

dozen times?"

Kaylie shrugged.

"Where's your phone?" Danica stormed inside, angry that her sister could be so stupid. Was she going to mess up her entire life unless Danica held her hand every second of the day? Danica flew down the stairs to the kitchen and dumped the contents of Kaylie's purse. "Where's your phone?"

"Car."

"Kaylie!" She headed to the garage and retrieved the phone, slamming the door behind her. "Listen to your messages and call your fiancé. Seriously. What on earth are you thinking?" Then it dawned on her. This was Kaylie she was talking to. Maybe Kaylie really couldn't commit, even after all the positive steps she'd taken with Chaz. Maybe she was really much more messed up than Danica cared to admit.

She sank into a kitchen chair and asked Kaylie, in the most caring voice she could muster, "Do you love him?" She watched Kaylie nod, fresh tears streaking her face.

Danica let out a relieved breath. "Fix this," she said softly. "Call him. Fix it before it can't be fixed."

Kaylie took the phone and went into the other room. She came back a few minutes later with red rims around her eyes.

"What?"

"I couldn't reach him, but I left him a message." Kaylie set her phone down on the counter and fiddled with the edge of her shirt. "The message I left him earlier was horrible. I actually accused him of cheating." She stood beside Danica, deflated.

Danica embraced her. "It's gonna be fine. Everyone fights. Let's get your stuff back to your house and he'll call, and you'll work it all out."

"Do you really think it's not a new sock? Who's brush could that be?"

Danica smiled. "I'm sure it's not a new sock. Chaz loves you, and I'm sure he'll explain the rest." *At least I hope so.* As she gathered Kaylie's papers, she realized that she'd been staying at Blake's so often that the condo no longer felt like *her* condo, but rather like a place she used to live. Kaylie could cover her entire house with sheets of paper and songs, and it wouldn't matter. Danica no longer felt married to her condo the way she had when she and Blake first met. But she also realized, as she watched Kaylie shuffling papers at the kitchen table and wondering if Kaylie's relationship was about to end in a flurry of heartache, that she wasn't ready to leave it all behind, either. She liked having a safety net. Just in case.

Chapter Twenty-One

The hostess led Chaz to a corner table with views of the water. *Of course.* Lea would have it no other way.

The tension in Max's eyes told him whatever Lea wanted was something Max was not happy about.

"Sorry I'm late." He kept his eyes on Max as he sat down across from Lea.

Lea put her hand on his and narrowed her eyes. She spoke in a deep, sensuous purr. "We were just getting to know each other better."

He pulled his hand back as if he'd been stabbed with a needle. The heady scent of her perfume, which had somehow eluded his senses in his room, now wrapped itself around him. Gucci Guilty. He cleared his throat, pushing away the surge of memories that the smell brought with it.

Max broke through the silence. "Shall we order?"

"This one's in a rush." Lea raised her nose in Max's direction as she picked up her drink. "We ordered you a scotch," she said with an air of confidence.

He pretended to study the menu. In reality, he was concentrating on ignoring her perfume and trying to figure out why Max was dressed the way she was.

"I don't drink scotch anymore," he said sharply, then lifted the right side of his mouth into a grin and caught Max's eye.

Her approving nod was almost imperceptible.

Chaz could actually feel the stress in the thickness of the air around their table. He looked around the well-appointed restaurant. Each table gleamed with candlelight, its silverware sparkling against royal-blue tablecloths. He imagined being there with Kaylie, holding her hand across the table as they looked out into the night, with the romance of the water at their beck and call. *Kaylie.* He promised himself again, no more lies. No more omissions. He was a man, and from now on, he'd deal with the consequences of his actions head-on.

Lea sipped her way through three-quarters of a bottle of wine. Each time Chaz brought up the sponsorship, she said they could talk about it after they ate. *Why spoil a meal?* And each time she blew him off, his stomach clenched a little tighter.

Finally, when Chaz could take it no more, he folded his napkin and set it on the table. "Lea, what's this charade all about? You had me fly halfway across the world to sit at a dinner table with you?"

"You brought a babysitter with you," Lea said with a sigh.

Chaz met Max's gaze. "No, I brought my sponsorship coordinator with me. Max has run our programs for years. You know this. You're stalling, and I want to know why."

"You're not going to like what I have to say." She patted the corners of her mouth with the napkin.

"Lea, we're prepared to offer you—"

Lea cut Max off by holding up her hand. Then she turned in her seat, crossing her legs seductively toward Chaz.

He kept his eyes trained on hers. He wasn't falling into her trap. Not tonight. Not ever again.

"I'm not interested in what you can offer me." Lea leaned toward Chaz. "I have all that I want, and it looks like I'm going to be getting even more of it."

"I'm not sure what you mean. Chaz?" Max asked.

Chaz was sure he had steam fuming from his ears. He was sick of Lea's games, and it took every inch of his focus to speak in a restaurant-appropriate tone. "Lea, I don't know what game you're playing, but I have a pregnant fiancée who I'd really like to get home to." He watched for a reaction. If the news came as a surprise, she didn't show it.

Lea leaned back in her chair. "This is kind of fun, watching you two squirm."

"Okay, that's it." Chaz stood. "Max, let's go. We don't need her sponsorship this badly." *The hell with pride. Trust fund, here we come.*

Max rose to her feet.

"Do sit down, Chaz." She turned to Max. "Babysitter," she snarked, motioning to the empty chair.

"Apologize," Chaz demanded.

Lea turned to Max and looked her up and down. "You are a bit old to be a babysitter. Hmm…Oh, I see. You and Chaz? Well, isn't that a surprise?"

Max's cheeks flushed.

"Lea, we're done here." Chaz walked around the table and took Max's arm, leading her away from the table.

"I'm buying one-third of the festival."

Lea's words stopped Chaz in his tracks. He stalked back toward the table. "You're what?"

"You heard me. You need sponsorships, so I thought, what better way to ensure that you have the money you need every year."

"Don't do this, Lea." Chaz's heart thundered in his chest. This could not happen.

"I'm dying for the additional third, but it seems your father's other crony isn't as willing to play as Jansen was."

Carl Jansen had been his father's business partner, and Chaz had almost forgotten about their falling out. Although he still owned his percentage, Carl hadn't taken interest in the festival the entire time Chaz had run it, and because of that, there had never been a need to try and regain that ownership. "He can't do that. I get first right of refusal." He had no idea if it was true, but he needed all the ammo he could get.

"Oh, he can, and he is."

"You'll sleep with anyone," Max said through gritted teeth. "He's an old man."

"An old, *wealthy* man who has something that I want."

"He's married!" Max spat.

Chaz stood between Max and Lea, fuming. "Why would you pursue this? You can have anything you want. Any festival. Any business. You have more money than God himself. Why *my* festival?"

Lea's silent grin was more than Chaz could take.

"Are you really so angry about our breakup that you would try and force your way into my business?" He turned away, then turned back and said, "You're pathetic."

"Chaz, I'm surprised at you. You underestimate me. Surely you know that there is little I won't do to get what I want. No matter who gets hurt in the process."

Chaz didn't see the people staring at him as he fumed his way out of the restaurant. He didn't see the satisfied grin on Lea's lips, and he didn't see the protective look on Max's face as she held on to him with a tender, yet firm, touch. Chaz saw one thing, and one thing only. Red.

Chapter Twenty-Two

Danica followed Kaylie to her house to help her settle back in—and to make sure she stayed put this time. She sat on Kaylie's couch with the sock pinched between her index finger and thumb. "It's a sock, not a thong."

Kaylie frowned and slumped on the couch next to her. "Did you know they make maternity thongs?"

"No way."

"Way." Kaylie stood up and showed Danica her pink thong.

"That can't be comfortable." *Show me your flashy thong, but you can't sway the discussion that easily.* "Let's focus on your relationship, Kaylie," Danica said.

Kaylie lowered her dress and sat back down. "I'm an idiot. I've always been an idiot."

"Better he finds out now than after you're married."

Kaylie punched Danica in the arm.

"What's your plan?" Danica asked, knowing Kaylie didn't have one.

She shrugged.

"Ugh, didn't Mom ever teach you to use your words? Come on." She took Kaylie's hand and led her to Chaz's office. "Get out some paper."

Kaylie withdrew a pad of paper from the drawer.

"Okay, number one. Contact Chaz, no matter what it takes. Call him until he answers. Who's he with?"

"I don't know."

Danica thought about it. "I know, call Max. Max will know how to reach him. That's number two. If you can't reach Chaz, then call Max. Number three, call Alex. Get going with the band again. It's good for your self-esteem." Danica paced. She'd been thinking about asking Kaylie to sing at the event for No Limitz, and now, seeing her sister taking steps to help herself, she knew it would be just the thing Kaylie needed to regain her confidence. "I have a great idea. You still play with your band, right?"

"Of course. I mean, you know they don't go to every singing job with me, but we still do gigs together when we can actually get hired."

"If your band agrees, you guys can play at our event."

"You said you hired a band that one of the county guys recommended."

"I did, but I can cancel. Trust me. Let me handle my business. Just make sure you're good enough to play and that that band is okay with it."

"Danica, look at me."

Danica ran her eyes over Kaylie. Her hair fell full and pretty around her face, which was also a bit fuller. Her perfect, perky breasts had become full and matronly, lying over her belly like two soft grapefruits. She no longer looked like Barbie doll Kaylie. She looked better, more mature. She looked like mother-to-be Kaylie, and Danica hoped that, at some point in the next few weeks, before her baby came, Kaylie would see herself that way, too.

"You couldn't look more beautiful."

Kaylie put her hand on her belly. "What is happening to

me? Why did all this stuff just hit me now? You know me, I'm not a crier. I'm not insecure about my looks, or my job, but lately"—she threw her hands up in the air—"I can't control anything around me. Apparently, not even my fiancé."

"Oh, stop, Kay. Chaz isn't cheating. There's an explanation. It's not like he planned for some woman to spend the night and have a tawdry affair. It could even be Max's stuff. You never know. And right now, sister dear, you are one big bundle of hormones. You're trying to line up singing gigs for after the baby's born, and you thought you'd slip right back into your life; and when you saw that it wasn't going to be that easy, well, reality can do all sorts of crazy things to a person."

"Do you think that's it? I mean, I did expect to get the Reno gig, and I guess that did set me off, now that I think about it. That's what we were talking about when Chaz said I should try writing...or doing nothing." Kaylie drew little hearts on the paper. "I haven't had a singing gig in weeks," she admitted to Danica.

"That must be hard. Why didn't you tell me?"

"Because when you decide to do something, you do it. Nothing holds you back. The year you started your own therapy practice, you made a goal and you met it—exceeded it. You wanted four new clients your first month and you got six, remember?"

Danica did remember. She'd been thrilled with her success.

"I had a goal, too. I wanted to sing until I was too big to sing, and I wasn't too big to sing when they started turning me down. I just looked...plump. And it hurt. Every time I got turned down, it felt like I'd worked really hard for nothing, as if all of my experience didn't matter."

"I'm sure they didn't turn you down because you looked bigger, Kaylie. It was probably an insurance thing. Pregnant women can be fragile, and let's face it, you didn't exactly sing in family-friendly venues."

"True," Kaylie admitted.

"Think about it. A bunch of drunk guys, you singing, they've jumped on the stage before, but now you're pregnant. You're a bar owner's nightmare," she teased.

The edge of Kaylie's lips lifted. "That would happen, too, because I am hot."

Now there's my sister. "Yes, you were hot."

"Even if plump," Kaylie added with confidence.

Danica agreed, knowing that Kaylie was talking herself into a happier place.

"And even now, with this big ol' baby belly, I'm still hot. I'm just not bar-singing hot…because I could get hurt."

"Okay, I've got it. You're hot, hot, hot. Now can you work on your relationship?" Danica laughed.

Chapter Twenty-Three

"Just focus on the warm breeze and the tropical music," Max said as she and Chaz sat at a bar by the water.

Chaz shook his head. He didn't want to feel the breeze or people watch. He had to figure out what the hell was going on with the festival. He left a heated message for Jansen and one for his attorney, Cooper. If Lea could weasel her way into one-third of the festival's ownership, then surely she intended to make his life hell. "Why wouldn't Jansen have called me? How could I not know this?"

"Remember when I told you that you needed to have board meetings, and you said—"

"Why ruin a good thing?" Chaz lifted his eyes from the bar. "Dumbest thing I ever said."

Max nodded with a feigned frown on her lips that reached all the way to her eyes.

Chaz looked her over as he sucked down his second drink. "You look great, but why are you all dolled up tonight?"

Max lowered her gaze. "I figured she'd be all dolled up and dressed to kill, and I knew she wasn't expecting me to show up, and jeans wouldn't quite cut it with someone like her."

"So you thought dressing up might intimidate her?"

Max swirled the straw in her drink. "I'm not that naive. I

just thought it might…give her pause."

"Pause? You wanted to give Lea Carmichael pause?" Chaz shook his head. He saw her shoulders droop, and he reached out and touched her arm. "Hey, it was a great idea. Just one that's hard to accomplish."

"I just thought that if she thought we were together she might back off of wanting you."

"Max. You did that for me?" Obviously, Lea hadn't picked up on her vibe until the end, but Chaz hadn't realized how far Max would go to protect him.

"For you and Kaylie," she said.

"Oh, Max. You didn't need to do that. Thank you." Chaz tried not to let his expression reflect how stunned he was that Max would go to such lengths to protect his relationship with Kaylie. Her efforts touched him deeply. He wanted to take her in his arms and hug her, but adding a hug to a drinks date with any woman besides Kaylie felt wrong, and with everything going on, he didn't have the strength to carry any more guilt.

"I could tell something was up with you and Kaylie," Max said. "Don't worry. She knows she's got the best man in all of Colorado."

"I doubt that."

Max held his gaze. "Don't fool yourself. No other man even comes close."

They had a few more drinks, and Max pulled out her cell phone. "Do you wanna call Kaylie?" Her words carried the slow pace of one too many drinks.

"It's only"—he squinted at his watch—"four in the morning there. Too early." He stepped from his stool. "Let's walk on the beach."

"Now?" Max slid off her seat and wobbled.

Chaz put his hand around her waist. "You've had a lot to

drink, and it's been a long day, so we can head back."

"No, I wanna walk," Max said, and looped her arm into his, looking up at him with glassy eyes and a goofy, inebriated smile.

They slid off their shoes when they reached the sand and carried them along the beach. Soothing ocean sounds filled the air, and the sand was cool and soft beneath their bare feet. Chaz wished again that Kaylie were there with him. She'd love the white sand and the romantic moonlight stroll. And at that very moment, he needed Kaylie in his arms more than ever before. He ached for her.

Max was relaying how much trouble she'd had finding something that was *Lea appropriate* to wear and how she felt like a little girl playing dress up.

"Well, you look beautiful. I don't understand why you don't dress like this more often."

"Beautiful?"

"Yeah, you're a pretty girl, Max."

She nodded a swaying, drunken nod, leaning against Chaz.

"You're doing the right thing, you know. With Kaylie. I know you love her."

"That I do. I hate being away from her. She's so emotional right now."

"She's pregnant. All those hormones racing through her and all. She'll come around." Max stopped walking and looked up at Chaz. "Hey, where was she the night before we left?"

"Girls' night out with Danica. She's trying to figure out what to do once she has the baby."

Max took a step and stumbled, landing against Chaz's chest. She looked up at him with a doe-eyed gaze.

"You've had a lot to drink. We should go back," he said.

Max sank to her butt in the sand. "Kaylie's got you in a way that no other woman could. She'll come around."

Moonlight reflected off the water, and Chaz found himself staring out to sea, hoping Max was right.

Chaz sat down and they both lay back on the sand, looking up at the stars.

"Life is so…"

"What?" Chaz closed his eyes, feeling the effects of the alcohol sweeping his mind clean.

Max leaned her head on his arm, her eyes closed. "It's complicated," she said in a soft, breathy voice.

Chaz's eyes opened. He was so drunk that the moon seemed to be moving forward and back. Maybe he would close his eyes, just for a second.

"I love working for you," she said with a wave of her hand. "I don't know much about what life is or isn't, but I love you. My job. The festival."

Chaz was already asleep.

Chapter Twenty-Four

The ringing of Max's phone woke them up just as the sun began to make its slow crawl toward the sky. They sat up, disoriented and covered in sand. Max fumbled for her phone.

"Hello?"

Chaz brushed the sand from his clothing and hair.

"Sure. Yes, sir. Not a problem. He'll be there."

"What now?" Chaz asked when she hung up the phone.

"Cooper. He said he left you a message. Jansen is in the hospital in Seattle. It doesn't look good." Max checked her texts and gnawed on her fingernail.

"What?"

Max brushed the sand from her clothing as they headed back toward the hotel. "The tech team needs to meet...like, now."

"How are we gonna do that?"

"Don't worry. I've got it covered. We'll Skype the tech team and head to Seattle. Looks like I have flight arrangements to make." She handed Chaz the phone. "Call your fiancée," she said.

Chaz sighed and called Kaylie's cell. In an age when technology seemed to run people's lives, it was doing nothing for him and Kaylie connecting. "Damn it." He waited for her voicemail message tone. "Hey, it's me. I'm heading straight to Seattle from here. Jansen's in the hospital. I'm sorry. Call me, please. I miss you." He lifted his eyes and saw that Max was watching him the way a mother might watch a teenage son to be sure he was doing the right thing. Max had a way of keeping him on track, and with all that was going on, he appreciated her efforts.

They Skyped the tech team later that afternoon, and Max handled it with her typical efficiency. The emergency change in meeting schedule required changes to vendors and approval of further expenses. Max had every budget memorized and was able to access the reports of their requirements and blueprints of the venue they had booked from her Dropbox as if she handled technical meetings via Skype all the time. Chaz wondered why they didn't. Max cleverly manipulated other areas to cover the new expenses, and by the end of the meeting, they'd all agreed that Skype meetings would be the next big change to their operation.

The festival took place in Weston, Colorado each year and Max knew how many outlets each booth required, how much voltage the lighting staff needed, and whom to contact in case of a power outage. If the lights of the Superdome could go out when Beyoncé was performing, Max was taking no chances. She had backup generators and the staff to man them at the ready.

"I didn't even need to be there," Chaz said as they headed for the airport.

"Sure you did," she said, wiping her brow with her arm. "I was your moral support with Lea, and you were mine with the tech team. Besides, it's you they want to see."

"You know, I really don't appreciate how much you do for the festival."

Max shook her head and threw her palm up. "Huh?"

"That didn't come out right. I appreciate it. I just never really recognized the extent of what you take care of. I mean, you're the sponsorship coordinator, so I always think of you coordinating the donations and sponsors and attributing funds to the right accounts, not doing all this other stuff."

"Thanks, Chaz. I do whatever needs to be done: donations, fund distribution and attribution, and negotiating, but Scott handles the actual bookkeeping." Scott Harden had been their bookkeeper since before Max joined the company.

"I know he does, but you knew what everyone needs down to the penny. You knew it all."

Max smiled. "It's my job."

"Well, that's what I'm wondering. It's really not your job. So, why do you do it?" He watched her weigh her answer. "How did we get by before you?" Chaz thought of all the pieces that had fallen out of place before Max came on board and remembered the first six months of her employment, when she'd worked day and night to create an organizational system that actually worked.

Max shrugged. She opened her mouth to answer, then closed it and turned her eyes to the front of the cab. "I guess I do it so that it gets done right. So you don't look bad."

"Well, consider yourself appreciated, and if I ever act otherwise, kick me in the head." Chaz checked his voicemail messages as they pulled up to the airport. The blood drained from his face.

"Lea?" Max asked.

"Kaylie. Did you leave something at the house?"

"Not that I know of, why?"

"She's pissed. She thinks I had another woman over at the house. That's crazy."

Max's jaw dropped. "Hey, dude. I am a woman," she rebutted.

He shot her a look that said, *Not now.*

"I don't think I left anything. I'll call her. Once she hears it was me who was there, she'll be fine." She took out her cell phone, and Chaz reached over and lowered her hand. "Chaz?"

Chaz wasn't sure what he felt at that moment, but he was caught somewhere between disbelief and hurt. His stomach turned, and he leaned his head on the back of the seat, almost unable to bring voice to his thoughts. "She doesn't trust me."

"Yes, she does."

"No, she doesn't. She found something and immediately jumped to the conclusion that I was with someone else. After all these months." Having an affair and lying about a tryst that took place before they even knew each other were completely different things in Chaz's mind.

"Chaz, you said yourself that she's emotional right now. Give her a break." Max's eyes grew wide. "Wait, Chaz. I think I did leave my hairbrush there. I forgot, because I used my comb this morning when I couldn't find my brush. Oh my goodness, I'm so sorry."

He closed his eyes. "Jesus. My life is just one big fuckup lately. First, I screw up with the board meetings that *you* warned me about, and now I'm gonna marry a woman I'm crazy about but who doesn't trust me. I'm glad it was your brush, because I had no idea what she was talking about, but she should instinctively know I'd never cheat."

Max's cell phone rang, and Kaylie's number showed on the display.

"Don't answer that," Chaz said firmly.

"Chaz, let me tell her."

"Don't answer it. I can't think about this right now." Every painful second that passed brought more heart-shattering reality to the forefront of his mind. He adored Kaylie, but lately she'd amped up the drama in ways that he had no idea how to handle. With the nightmare Lea turned out to be, he wondered if Kaylie could be the same way. Was he a magnet for psychotic women? Had he missed signs about Kaylie, or was she truly just hormonal? He hadn't looked at another woman in that way since the night he met her, and after seeing Lea again and being put to the test, he not only had no intention of doing so in the future, but he knew he could refrain from ever disrespecting Kaylie in that way. Kaylie was the woman he loved and the only woman he wanted. There's no way he made this big of a mistake a second time. Kaylie wasn't crazy like Lea. She was just hormonal and insecure because of it. *Wasn't she?*

They pulled up in front of the airport. Fueled by adrenaline, he was determined to take charge of the situation with Jansen and Lea, and then he'd worry about Kaylie. One nightmare at a time.

Chapter Twenty-Five

Two hours after Danica left, Kaylie had eaten lunch and taken a catnap, and she already felt much better. She picked up a framed picture of her and her mother from Chaz's desk and ran her finger over her mom's face. She felt a tug in her heart and wished there were an easy way to make things better. She knew she was the one causing the complications, but she didn't know what to do about it. Now, seeing her mother's smiling face, she wanted to ask her about her baby things. Did she still have her receiving blankets? Baby clothes? *Maybe one day soon, I'll be able to do that.*

She set the frame down, accepting that she just wasn't ready to make *that* phone call yet. Kaylie skipped down her to-do list and called Alex first. He agreed to get the group together and meet her at noon the next day.

Feeling even more confident, she called Camille.

"Wow, I thought you dropped off the face of the earth," Camille teased. "I've left you messages. Texted. You're not a very good friend."

"Yeah, I know. Quit your whining. Today's been crazy."

Camille's tone softened. "Are you okay?"

There was nothing like having a girlfriend. Camille's voice was like the hug she'd been needing. How did you tell one of your best friends—the newlywed who was living in shades of bliss at the moment—that you thought your fiancé was cheating, you felt unattractive, and you just wanted to lie down and die? The truth was, she could have told Camille all of that and Camille probably would have made her feel better; Danica had already lessened the burden of it, after all. But Kaylie had never been the whiner in the group, and she wasn't going to tarnish her unrealistic happy Barbie reputation now.

"Yeah, I'm fine. I had so much fun with you guys. I started writing songs after everyone fell asleep."

"Really? Kaylie, that's great. It's good to have something to fill your days." Kaylie heard a longing in Camille's voice.

"Are you okay, Camille? We were so focused on my career that we didn't really catch up on you and Jeff."

"Me? Fine, yeah, we're perfect," Camille said too quickly. "Have you heard from Chaz?"

Kaylie heard the same feigned smile she had on her face. "He's going to Seattle for a few days. His partner's sick."

"Mm-hmm. And my baby?"

Kaylie touched her stomach and smiled. "You mean, *my* baby. It's kicking me like a champ. I'm wondering if it's a boy after all." Kaylie thought again about her mother and her baby things. She wondered if her mother knew she was having girls when she was pregnant. She'd have to remember to ask her the next time she spoke to her.

"No, no, you have to have a girl," Camille squealed. "We'll bring her up like a little spoiled princess with chutzpah! She'll be awesome."

"Yeah, about that. You do know that I can't control the sex of the baby, right?" Kaylie rolled her eyes, still glad that they had opted not to have more than one sonogram. With peer pressure, she might have given in and found out the baby's gender.

"No shit, but I can hope."

"Camille, I need a favor. I'm due in four weeks and we haven't had a baby shower yet." As selfish as she felt asking about it, she knew Camille would understand. A baby shower was like a rite of passage, and although she had a sneaking suspicion her sister and friends might have already been planning one, she didn't want to take a chance that they'd forget and she'd be left without ever having the experience.

Camille didn't respond.

"Camille?"

She remained silent.

"Oh no, I ruined it, didn't I?" Kaylie covered her mouth. "Shit. Shit, shit, shit."

"Did you really think we'd forget about your shower?" The hurt in Camille's voice was palpable.

"I'm an idiot. I'm sorry. Does Danica know, because if she does, she hasn't let on."

"My mouth is zipped. You aren't getting any info from me."

"Can you tell me when it is? I'm—"

"Can you hear this? It's me hanging up." The phone line went dead.

Kaylie's day went from bad to better. Now all she needed was to clear things up with Chaz. She left a message for him and another for Max. If she couldn't reach Chaz, then maybe Max could. She went back to work on her songs, humming to herself and feeling like things weren't so bleak after all.

An hour later, her heart jumped when Chaz's office phone rang. *Chaz.* She ran to the phone from the living room and picked it up. "Hello?"

"Chaz Crew, please." The woman's fierce, sexy tone struck Kaylie's curiosity.

"Uh, he's out of town. May I take a message?"

"Ah, yes, please. Tell him Lea called and that Hawaii was everything I dreamt it might be."

"Excuse me?" Kaylie thought she might pass out. Her legs weakened and she lowered herself into the leather chair.

"Yes, that's right. Tell him I'll be in touch."

Kaylie's confusion morphed to anger. "I'm sorry, who is this?"

"Lea Carmichael." The phone went dead. *Lea Carmichael. Lea Carmichael.* The name ran though her mind, sounding worse and worse with each iteration.

She picked up the phone and dialed Chaz's cell again, telling herself to calm down. Things weren't always what they appear to be, she reminded herself. *It's nothing. A client. A misunderstanding.* Chaz's voicemail picked up, and she stared at the phone, unable to come up with the right words. She was afraid she'd cry more than she already had, accuse him, and generally ruin any chance they might have at a civilized conversation. She hung up the phone and stewed while Lea Carmichael coursed through her mind.

Chapter Twenty-Six

The next day, Danica stayed late at the youth center, working with Sally and Gage to iron out the budget for the next quarter. Danica had spent most of their time together watching Sally get flustered every time Gage spoke and thinking about how awful it would be to start over after the death of a spouse. The minute they'd left for the night, she called Blake. Even the thought of losing him was too much to bear. She had to hear his voice.

She was exhausted from her narrow escape with Kaylie's relationship issues. If Kaylie hadn't come around, she would have been stuck counseling her sister for the next year, helping her navigate life as a single parent. Sometimes, Kaylie's insecurities took over, and while Danica was used to it, it was not something most men would understand for very long. She'd used the center's event as a pick-me-up, and it had worked. She only hoped it lasted long enough for Chaz to come home so the two of them could work things out. She prayed that Kaylie would settle down after she gave birth. Did all mothers get a little crazy before their baby was born?

Oh, God. Mom. Danica called her mother.

"Hi, honey," she answered.

"Hi, Mom. Sorry I forgot to call you back. I've been busy with Kaylie."

"How is she?"

Is that a man's voice in the background? "She's fine." *Definitely a man's voice.*

Her mother giggled.

"Mom? Am I interrupting something?" Danica looked up at the ceiling. *Please don't be in bed with him.*

"Oh, Patrick and I are with some friends, playing bridge."

"Bridge? You play bridge?"

She laughed again. "I do now. Listen, honey, I've got to go. I'm glad Kaylie's okay."

Danica stared at the phone long after her mother hung up. *Bridge?* She dove into her work, and was surprised that an hour had passed when her cell phone vibrated. She read the text from Blake. "Open the door?"

She texted back, "What door?"

"Front door."

Danica walked through the dark lobby to the entrance, where Blake stood holding a bag of Chinese takeout and two candlesticks. Danica pulled the doors open. "What's all this?"

"I missed you."

"I haven't been here that long. Maybe an hour or so later than usual." She laughed and took one of the bags from him.

"An hour, a week, what's the difference? I wanted to be with you. Eating dinner alone is no fun at all." He gave her a deep, sensuous kiss.

"Wow," she said when he pulled away. "You did miss me."

"With all this stuff going on between Kaylie and Chaz, I was just feeling thankful for what we have, and I never"—he kissed her again—"want to take you for granted."

Danica's lips met his. The taste of Blake, the feel of his hands on her body, transported her to some place far away from Kaylie's drama. Her body felt light, her mind happy, and she tingled all over. They kissed their way over to the lobby couch, where Blake laid her down beneath him, then gently pressed his fully clothed body on top of her.

He moved her thick curls from her face and stared into her eyes. Danica was hungry for more. She lifted her mouth to meet his lips, and he leaned back, out of reach. "If you won't move in with me, will you marry me?"

Danica laughed. "What?"

"I'm serious." His dark eyes softened, and his voice was just above a whisper, a sexy, soothing admission. "I love you, Danica. I love your wild hair and your sense of humor. I love the way you make sure you have everything organized the night before for the next morning. I love the way you pour more cereal to finish the milk in the bottom of your bowl."

Danica couldn't believe her ears. They'd never even talked about getting married. Hell, she hadn't even moved in with him yet—not officially, anyway.

"Baby." He kissed her again—a toe-curling, gut-wrenching, deliciously warm kiss, leaving her unable to think straight. "I will never love anyone the way I love you. You are the snow on my mountain, the wax on my skis."

"So romantic," she joked, resting her head back down on the couch. *Oh my God! Oh my God!* She didn't even know she wanted to hear the words, and when he said them—*marry me*—fireworks exploded in her head. Her heart screamed *Yes! Yes! Yes!* But her mind tethered her response to thoughts of Kaylie.

"Don't you see? You're everything to me. I adore you." He looked at her expectantly. His smile faded with her silent gaze. Blake lifted himself off her. "Danica?"

Marry him? Marry him. She blinked, then blinked again. Stunned didn't begin to cover the feelings that made her heart race and her mind reel. *Married?* Her mind went to thoughts she hadn't even realized she had—would they end up like her parents?

"I love you," she whispered. It was all she could manage.

He smiled. "Good?"

The confusion on his face brought Danica back to the moment. Blake was everything she could possibly want in a husband. He was courteous, empathetic, strong, and protective without being overly jealous. Sex with Blake set her world on fire—hell, kissing him set her world on fire. So, why was she hesitating?

"Kaylie," she said. *Oh, God! Did I say that out loud?*

"What?" Blake sat up, and Danica sat next to him.

"I can't get married unless I know Kaylie is okay."

Blake clasped his hands together, leaning his elbows on his thighs. "What does Kaylie have to do with us getting married? I'm not asking Kaylie to marry me. I'm asking you. You, Danica. Just you. You and me, a life together, you know how that works."

"Blake." She turned to him and reached for his hand. "Kaylie's life is in shambles. Can you imagine what would happen if I came to her and said I was engaged at the same time that she said they called off their engagement? She'd be devastated."

"Okay, then we won't tell her yet."

Love shone in his eyes, his voice, and in the warmth of his hand. His heart was on his sleeve, there for the taking, and she had no intention of breaking it. She just wasn't sure how to navigate her own happiness when Kaylie's was so fragile, and when hers and Blake's was on the line.

Chapter Twenty-Seven

Kaylie practiced with the band for two days. The songs sounded great, and the band knew just what to do to enhance the melodies. It had been two days since she'd heard from Chaz, and she was beginning to think that Lea Carmichael might have been the owner of the sock after all, even though Danica had spent an hour the evening before convincing her otherwise. All of Danica's comments made sense; Chaz had never given her reason to worry before. It could have been Max's brush and sock, or someone else's—it didn't mean he'd actually cheat on her. She knew Chaz loved her to pieces, and he wanted their baby as much as she did. But she had been really moody before he left, and that look in his eye when he said they had to talk had been a little unnerving. *Why am I doing this to myself? He loves me!*

She'd left messages for Chaz several times each day, and she'd finally given up. She wanted to believe that Danica was right. He was just busy. He'd come back and they'd figure it out, and their relationship would be just fine. But her heart broke a little more with each passing hour. She tried to take comfort knowing she was singing at the event in just a few days, and in her heart, she knew that no matter what came her way, she could handle it. But that didn't change the fact that she wanted Chaz, the way they were, with no woman coming between them.

She climbed into her car after band practice and answered her ringing cell phone.

"Max?"

"I can't talk long, but I wanted you to know that Chaz is miserable. He'd kill me if he knew I was calling you, but I can only imagine how hard this is for you, pregnant and all."

"Have you seen him?" Kaylie was caught off guard. She had forgotten she'd called Max and now, her mind raced with a million questions. The pain she'd been ignoring came rushing back, overwhelming her. She put her hand on her stomach and breathed in and out slowly, trying to calm her speeding pulse.

"We're in Seattle. We thought we'd only be gone one day, but Jansen's really not well."

"What happened?"

"We don't know. He's having some kind of heart issues. They're talking about all sorts of crazy things."

Kaylie took a deep breath and asked the question she'd been trying to forget. "Max, who is Lea Carmichael?"

Max didn't answer.

"Oh, God. I knew it," Kaylie said with a heavy heart.

"Kaylie, listen, it's over with them. She's just taking revenge or something, but don't worry. Chaz will make it all go away."

"Over?"

"Yes, it's over." She heard Max take a deep breath, then blow it out. "Kaylie, Chaz loves you. He's just overwhelmed right now. But he loves you more than life itself."

"But Lea—"

"He ended it with her in no uncertain terms."

Ended it. That means there was something to end.

Chapter Twenty-Eight

"Seattle sucks," Chaz said to Max. They were sitting in the waiting room at Seattle Hospital. It had been raining for two days straight, and Chaz was starting to feel the downward spiral of having not seen the sun for far too long, combined with every facet of his life being in turmoil.

"Hopefully, he'll wake up today and we'll be able to talk some sense into him." Max sat beside him with her laptop on her legs, using the hotspot from her cell phone for Internet service.

"Cooper said that I get first right of refusal, so obviously we'll stop this crap from going any further, but I really need to get all of this cleared up. I've gotta know what Jansen was thinking, but more important, what the hell is it that Lea wants?"

Max turned her dark, serious eyes toward him.

"What is it?" Whatever it was, it couldn't be anything worse than what was already going on in his life. The doctors were really worried about Jansen—and Cooper was working on the Lea issue. The whole thing sickened him. If Jansen died, it would be his fault.

Max crossed her arms.

"Max, you've got that look. What it is?" Chaz had seen that

I-don't-want-to-say-it look before. "Max," he coaxed, "just tell me. You look like you did when you told me about the mechanical failure on event day three years ago. We handled that. There's nothing we can't handle. Lay it out for me. What the hell happened now?"

"You know what she wants." Max's chest rose and fell with heavy breaths. "She wants you, and if she can't have you, then no one will."

Chaz laughed. "That's ridiculous. People don't really do that."

Max held his gaze.

"No way. She'd never take it this far."

"Chaz, I've done some digging, and I've uncovered some pretty unsavory dirt on her. She's crazier than we ever thought. Look at this." Max proceeded to show him several articles dating back seven and eight years, each of which documented affairs with wealthy, married men. "It seems as if she likes to break up marriages."

"I wasn't married when I met her, and she is far wealthier than I am."

"She was in and out of rehab in the early nineties, and ten years ago, she was accused of trying to *run over* an ex-boyfriend's girlfriend."

"Acquitted." Chaz ran his hand through his hair.

"You knew about that?"

"She told me when we were together. She said it was an accident."

"Chaz?"

He looked over.

"Don't you see the hint of a pattern here? She's getting all up in your business all of a sudden, now that you're having a baby and getting married?"

"Who would wait a year before trying to mess up someone's life?"

"Someone who does it for fun." Max turned back to her computer. She chewed on her fingernail.

"What else is bothering you?"

"Nothing."

"Max? You only chew your nails when you're really, really stressed. Like when you thought your dad was going to die type of stress. Spill it."

"You're gonna be really mad, so I'd rather not. When are you going to call Kaylie?"

"I told you, once I have this crap ironed out. Then I can focus on her."

"Aren't you worried it'll be too late?"

The thought had crossed Chaz's mind far too many times than he'd like to admit. But he was so hurt over her accusations that he'd almost convinced himself that they shouldn't be together after all.

"Chaz…" Max closed her eyes. When she opened them, he was staring at her, waiting, knowing she had something to say that he most likely didn't want to hear. "I called her."

"You what?" Chaz sprang to his feet. "How could you meddle in my business like that?"

"I was trying to help. She's pregnant and worried."

"Damn it, Max." Chaz went to the window and stared into the sheeting rain.

"I told her that you ended it with Lea. She deserved to know and not to have to worry about—"

Chaz spun around. "You did what?"

"I…I told her that it was over, that she had nothing to worry about. That you loved her."

"Max, she didn't know about Lea." Chaz paced, crossing

and uncrossing his arms.

Max rose to her feet. "Oh my God. Wait, she must have known. She asked me who Lea was. That's why I said that you'd ended it."

The doors to the ICU opened and all eyes turned toward the doctor who walked straight to Jansen's wife and children.

"I'm sorry. He had a massive heart attack. We did everything we could to save him."

Chapter Twenty-Nine

Chaz sat across from Max in a café down the street from the hospital, the loss of Jansen still sinking in. Max wiped tears from her puffy red eyes. He reached across the table and held her hand. "Max." He didn't know what else to say. A good man probably died because of something Lea did—because of him—and there was no way he could ever make that right.

"It's just…I didn't know him very well, a few phone calls here and there, but did you see his wife? His daughter? And it kills me just knowing that Lea was probably trying to break them up just to screw you over." Her eyes hardened. "Doesn't it bother you at all?"

"More than you'll ever know." His gut felt like one giant sinkhole filled with regret. "I really need to call Kaylie," he said quietly, "before I lose her, too."

Max nodded.

"Tell me again what she said."

Max took a deep breath and then a sip of water. "She asked me who Lea Carmichael was, like she knew about her. She knew her name, so I assumed…" She looked at him pleadingly. "You know I wouldn't have said anything if I'd known you never told her. I thought she knew and that was why she asked. The way she asked was like she thought something was going on with you and Lea, so I just assured her that it was over." Max wiped her eyes. "I never should have called her. I'm sorry."

"It's not your fault. I should have told her, but..." *I didn't want to deal with it.*

"I can call Kaylie and explain," Max offered.

"No, it's fine. I need to do this. I have no idea how Lea's name would have even come up." He stood and took his cell phone from his pocket.

"You were just so mad, and I knew you didn't mean it. I was trying to help," Max reiterated. "As for Lea, I wouldn't put anything past that crazy bitch."

Chaz put a hand on her shoulder and then walked out of the café to call Kaylie. The first call rang four times before going to voicemail, so he tried again. And again. And again until finally he heard her voice—and lost his.

"Hello?"

The chaos of the last few days whirred around him. Kaylie's voice was empty. Flat. His loving girl wasn't there. What had he done?

"Chaz? Are you there?"

A lump formed in his throat, and he pushed his strained voice through a whisper. "Kaylie."

"Chaz? Are you...are you all right?"

"I...no. Kaylie, I'm sorry." The realization that he'd somehow hurt her, lied to her, came rushing in and pushed the emotions he'd been holding in to the surface. "Kaylie, it's not what you think. I'm so sorry."

He listened to her breathing heavily, pictured her beautiful full lips quivering the way they did before tears fell down her soft cheeks, and he felt another fissure form across his heart.

"Kaylie, I only wanted you to be happy. I thought by telling you about..." He couldn't even bring himself to say the woman's name. He had to. He owed that much to Kaylie. "Lea. I was worried that if I told you about Lea, you'd worry every year if she sponsored our events."

"So you spent the night with Lea Carmichael to somehow save me?" she fumed.

"What? No. What are you talking about?" He looked up at the sky and willed the tears of shame and anger that burned at the edges of his eyes not to fall; he never should have kept this from Kaylie.

"I know, Chaz, okay? I found her sock on the couch and her brush in the bathroom. Damn it, Chaz, Max told me everything. She said you ended it, but it's too late. I can't marry someone who would cheat just because I forgot to call." She lowered her voice with her last words, and Chaz heard music in the background.

"Lea and I were together two years ago, not now." Anger stirred, and he tried to keep his voice calm and steady, but the woman he loved wasn't thinking straight, and he had to fix things. Now.

"I can't do this right now. I'm at band practice."

"Kaylie, I promise you. Lea and I were not together. I met her in Hawaii to talk about the sponsorship. That's it. You can ask Max. She came along. I wasn't leaving anything to chance." She had to understand.

"In other words, you didn't trust yourself so you brought Max with you? That's pathetic."

His voice rose despite his best efforts to tamp it down. "Damn it, Kaylie. That's not at all why I brought her. Lea's a bitch. She's trying to buy a percentage of ownership. Jansen's percentage. Now Jansen's dead, and—"

"Jansen's dead?"

Chaz closed his eyes and gathered his wits about him. Every

muscle in his body unclenched, and he sank against the wall of the building, beneath an awning. Rain splattered his shoes and the edges of his pants. "Yes, massive heart attack. It was awful. Kaylie, Lea's a nightmare. I swear to you on our baby's life that she and I ended things two years ago, before I met you. We were only together for a couple days. And it was Max's sock and hairbrush that you found. You can ask her."

Kaylie was silent, so Chaz continued. "It's you I love. You're the only person who matters to me. You and our baby."

She remained silent.

"Kaylie, honey, I adore you. Surely you know that. I'd never risk what we have for anyone, especially not her. But you have to trust me. We had one fight. You didn't call me, and you immediately jumped to the conclusion that I was with someone else? If we can't trust each other, how can we get married?"

"The sock," was all Kaylie said.

"It's Max's. When you didn't call, I went to Taylor's Cove for a drink. For several drinks, actually. I didn't know Max was there, but she was, and thank God; I was in no shape to drive. She drove me home and stayed on the couch, since we needed to be on the red-eye. Kaylie, there's no woman in the world who could replace you. The moment I found you, I knew I'd never look at another woman."

Kaylie sniffled. "I do trust you."

"Do you?" Chaz held his breath.

"Yes. I just...I'm so up and down all the time right now, and I came home and found those things...and"—he heard the strain in her voice—"I don't want to be my mom. I don't want to be home with kids while you're out living your life—or starting a new one—just to be left in the dust like some used up piece of trash." Someone yelled in the background. "Hold on, Alex," Kaylie called out.

Chaz lowered his hand to his eyes. "Is that what this is, Kay? You're worried that I'll do what your father did?" Relief swept through him. She didn't distrust just him. She probably didn't trust any man. Chaz knew three things about himself. When his father died, he learned that he had a hidden strength that he could call upon to get him through the toughest of times. He'd never let the festival perish because it was built by his father. And he was not *just any man*. "I will spend the rest of my life doing everything I can to prove to you that you can trust me. There is not, has never been, and will never be another woman in my life besides you."

Kaylie's voice softened, "And Max."

Chaz smiled. "And Max. And our daughter if we have one."

Alex yelled again. Kaylie let out a loud breath. "I have to go. I'm at practice. I'm writing songs. You were right. I can do more than sing, and I'm really, really good at it."

"I'm so proud of you," Chaz said.

"I love you."

He felt the noose around his neck loosen. "I love you, too, Kaylie, and I always will."

"Will you be back by the weekend? I'm singing at Danica's event this weekend."

"I will be back tomorrow, and, Kaylie…"

"Yeah?"

"I'm sorry, and can we promise never to jump to conclusions again? Either of us? This week was so hard."

"Promise."

Chaz felt the strangulation of the noose fall away, and for the first time in the last few days, he was finally able to breathe.

Chapter Thirty

The center bustled with energy. Teens were hanging out in the lobby, and adults mingled among themselves, discussing who was attending the weekend event and how excited they were for their kids to finally have a place to congregate. Danica followed a trail of laughter toward the basketball courts in search of Gage. She found him teaching a young boy how to dribble. She leaned against the doorway, listening to the thumping rhythm of the ball on the court floor and watching his easy, comfortable nature.

Gage caught sight of her. "Hey, buddy," he said to the boy. "Why don't you practice for a bit, and I'll be right back."

He watched the boy find a rhythm and then went to Danica. "What's up?"

"I'm just nervous. Do you have everything set for this weekend?"

"I've got it covered, and Sally and I met for coffee this morning before work and went over all the details for Kaylie's band, the tables for outside, the colorful lights you love. I think we have it all under control."

"Good."

"Danica, are you okay? You do remember talking to me earlier, right? I called, you answered, and I filled you in?"

Her mind had been like a sieve ever since Blake asked her to marry him. Every speck of her wanted to marry Blake, and yet she still held back because of Kaylie. "Yeah, I know," she lied. She'd forgotten until he'd just mentioned it. "I'm just making sure."

Gage put his strong hand on her shoulder and squeezed gently. "Danica, we've got your back. Really, it's gonna be great."

Danica turned and saw Sally standing at the end of the hall. Their eyes locked, and Sally turned and headed in the opposite direction. "Thank you. I'm gonna catch up with Sally."

She found Sally in her office, standing with her back against the wall. "What was that hasty retreat all about?" she asked.

Sally's face flushed.

"Sally? Is there something I should know?"

Sally licked her lips and reached for a chair. "We had coffee," she said.

"Yeah, okay."

Sally leaned forward. "It felt more like a date." She grabbed Danica's arm. "Is that weird? Lame? I mean, I haven't dated in years, and I work with him, and I don't even know if it was a date."

"Breathe, Sally. First of all, it was coffee. Before work. That could be a date, I guess, but it could be just an efficient way to cover the details of the event. How did he ask you? All flirty, like, *Hey, baby*, or normal? Like, *Hey, I've got an idea?*"

"Somewhere in between, maybe? Last night before we left he said, 'Let's go over the specs tomorrow before work. Café Duo.'"

"Okay, well, that doesn't really sound like a date. Do you want it to have been one?"

Sally groaned. "I don't know. I feel guilty. Dave isn't even dead a year yet, and my heart is fluttering every time I see this guy. Maybe I should quit."

"Oh, no you don't." Danica crossed her arms and sat back. "Just let it be. See what develops."

"I can't even think when he's around," Sally confessed.

"Then you're crushing something bad. You should have seen me when I met Blake."

"Really? Because I can't remember it being like that with Dave. We were so young, and it all happened so fast. Our lives just sort of became one, without any drama or butterflies, or anything."

Danica felt strangely like a therapist once again. "Sometimes love is like that, too. What you and Dave had was special. No one, and nothing, can take that away. And if this was a date, then maybe that's okay. I think Dave would want you to be happy."

Sally smirked. "Right."

"He would. Just be yourself, and see what happens. Maybe you misread it, maybe you didn't."

"What if this messes with our jobs?" Sally asked.

Danica thought about an office romance, and in the end, she went with her gut reaction. "You know, if this really is something strong between you two, or if it has the potential to be, then I would never stand in your way. We can deal with anything that comes up with work. You guys are adults. It's not like I'll find you going at it in the closet. Will I?"

"My goodness, no! But how can I keep from making a fool of myself?"

"Your heart controls the foolish button, and nothing I can say will make any difference." She thought of the night she and Blake first kissed and how her legs had felt numb. She'd thought she might fall down right then and there. And then they'd kissed, and in that instant, that shared heartbeat of a moment, her life had transformed.

"Okay, so I'll be a babbling idiot." Sally laughed.

Danica shrugged. "There are worse things than crushing on a guy." *Like not accepting a marriage proposal from the man you love.* She changed the subject to safer territory. "Gage said you have everything under control for Kaylie and the band."

"Yeah, I do, but I can't believe she's going to sing. She's three weeks from her due date. The strain of a big event can't be good for her."

"She needs it. She's been really down, and this will cheer her up. You're coming to the baby shower, right? The weekend after the event?"

"I wouldn't miss it for the world. Speaking of which, your mom called. She said she had a feeling that something was up with you but didn't want to be a pest."

"She called you?"

"She called the center to reach you. She said she didn't want to keep calling your cell because she didn't want to pressure you to call her back, so she said to just tell you she called and if you have time, to call her back. She's so sweet."

Danica would call her mother a lot of things—submissive, organized, loving—but sweet wasn't a word she would have chosen. Her mother was supportive in a strong way, not a syrupy sweet, coddling way. Realization dawned on Danica. "Oh my God. I'm turning into my mother."

"What?"

Danica hadn't realized she said it out loud. Kaylie was sweet, and God only knew where she learned it, but Danica was practical, efficient. She said things as she saw them, without sugarcoating them, as she'd done with Blake. The problem was, she didn't know if that was a good thing or a bad thing.

Sally stood to leave. "Listen, there are worse things than turning into your mother, trust me. Thanks for the sanity break," she said, and left Danica's office.

Danica picked up the phone and dialed her mother's number.

They sat outside at the Mountain Ridge Restaurant, midway between the town where her mother lived and Allure. The sun was warm, but a gentle breeze kept them comfortable beneath the table's umbrella. Danica watched her mother eat her salad. She'd never noticed how she patted her mouth with a napkin after every bite, or the way she chewed with her lips firmly closed. There were tiny lines around her mother's upper lip, and the veins in her hands were more prominent than Danica remembered. It occurred to her that she hadn't ever noticed much about her mother other than the insignificant things she'd noticed as a child and carried into adulthood; she could be annoying at times, was always supportive, and appeared to never be unavailable to her children. It saddened Danica to think that she'd almost made it to her thirtieth birthday without really getting to know her mother. She'd wasted years treating her like her mother, at worst an inconvenience, but at best, something far different from a friend.

"Mom, I miss you," Danica said honestly.

Her mother smiled. "Well, I miss you too, honey. Is everything okay?"

She was happy with the typical motherly response, but Danica wanted more. She wanted to *know* her mother. What made her happy and sad, what her new hopes and dreams were—if she had any. She did want to know all those things, but if she was honest with herself, what she really wanted to know was how her mother knew her father was the right person for her to marry—even if he turned out not to be.

"Yeah, it's fine. I just feel like I don't know you very well."

She put her fork down and cocked her head. "Honey, tell me what you want to know. I have nothing to hide."

"It's not that, Mom. It's just that I'm almost thirty, and I still see you as I did when I was a kid. There's so much about you that I don't know, and for so long, I thought you were just…"

"A taskmaster? Know-it-all? Busybody?"

"No," Danica lied.

"It's okay, Danica. I'm your mother, and I'm supposed to be all those things."

"But why didn't you ever correct me, or tell me it wasn't true. I mean we've spent months hardly ever seeing each other. I know it's my fault, but you're my mom. You should have pushed me, come into my life more. I'm not blaming you. It's my fault, but why did you just let it happen?"

"Oh, honey, you learn something when you have children. You learn a lot of things—about yourself, and about them. It was my place to raise you, and to make sure you turned out okay, or at least give you every opportunity to do so. But it's not your job to love me for it, or to even like me as a person."

"But I do like you," Danica said emphatically.

"Well, that's good, but you shouldn't feel guilty if you have moments when you don't. A mother knows her children love her, even when they claim they don't, but I don't think I need to force myself into your life. I'm here for you when you want to spend time with me, and I'm okay when you don't."

How can I not have seen that strength in my mother before?

She'd advised her clients of their roles as parents all the time. Why did she see her mother's role—or her own—as anything different? She sighed, then fiddled with her napkin. "Can you tell me something about yourself?"

Her mother smiled, as if Danica's question was silly. "I'm really not very interesting."

"Please?"

She looked up at the sky, the parking lot, then around at the patrons sitting at nearby tables. "I love wildflowers," she said finally. "I love the randomness of them, the vibrant colors and the way they grow without being planted each year."

"Me too. I love that!" *Baby steps*, Danica told herself. "What else?"

"I was surprised to find that I like bridge, and I don't like my red hair, and I love going to the gym, but not to exercise. I love the time with my girlfriends." Her mother looked thoughtfully at Danica. "That's something you should do, spend more time with girlfriends. I spent so many years taking care of everyone else that I lost all my friends and had to start over after—" Her unsaid words hung in the air.

"I'm sorry, Mom. We were a handful."

"Oh no, honey. You girls were perfect. Life just got busy and I didn't pay attention to the things that made *me* happy. I think that's one reason your father found someone else." She refolded the napkin on her lap. "I had lost myself. I didn't feed myself in ways that help people grow and feel alive. I gave all the time, but I never rejuvenated. I think he felt that. He'd come home and see how tired I was, or that I was helping with homework, and then cleaning, and none of it made for a very romantic marriage."

"But every marriage is like that." *Isn't it?*

Her mother shook her head. "I don't know. I've only been

married once, but if I have one bit of advice, it's to make sure you still do things with friends. Try not to get so wrapped up with Blake that you forget who you are."

Blake. I need to tell her.

Her mother reached across the table and touched her hand. "What is this really about? Is something wrong? Is something going on between you and Blake?"

"No, no, Mom. It's nothing like that. I just…Blake asked me to marry him."

Her mother's eyes lit up. "This is a wonderful thing, right?"

Danica didn't answer, couldn't answer. She was too torn.

Her smile faded. "Or, isn't it?"

"It's wonderful. He's wonderful. Our whole relationship is, but I didn't say yes yet."

"Well, that's okay. He can wait." She gave a little laugh. "I made your father wait two weeks before I said I'd marry him. He was a nervous wreck. He didn't want to keep asking, and I could see the question on his lips every time we got together. I could feel him holding it back, like he'd burst if I waited too long."

"Really? I can't imagine Daddy doing that."

"I know. Your father changed a lot after you girls were born. He became more work-oriented. I think he felt pressured to provide."

"Makes sense," Danica agreed.

"So, tell me what you're thinking, Danica. Do you love him?"

"More than anything in this world. I gave up being a therapist for him."

"And he obviously loves you."

Danica nodded.

Her mother took a sip of her iced tea, and Danica could see

the gears of her mind churning over the possibilities.

"It's Kaylie," she finally admitted, and she felt like a great weight had lifted from her chest. "God, Mom. I can't get married when Kaylie's so unhappy."

"Oh, Danica." She touched her hand again. "You've always been the best big sister. You've always looked out for Kaylie. You've guided her through the troubled times—too bad you didn't get through to her about sex when she was young. It might have been best if she'd slowed down a bit. But I guess no one could have gotten through to her. That girl had a hankering, and she'd be damned if she didn't sow those oats."

"You knew I used to talk to her about that stuff?" *What other secrets has she kept?*

"Of course. The sneaking out, the lying about who she was with so she could go make out with one boyfriend or another. Mothers know everything, and the truth is, Kaylie doesn't know how lucky she is to have you."

I know, and it sucks. I wish she'd grow up. I hate that I can't move on because of her. Guilt consumed Danica for the thoughts that were running through her head. Her mother must have read the guilt in her eyes because she took Danica's hand in hers and said just the right thing.

"Danica, Kaylie is not your responsibility. She's a big girl. She's a college graduate, and although she still comes across as impetuous and maybe even a little self-centered…"

Danica's eyes bloomed wide. "Mom!"

"Well, she can be." She laughed. "That's just Kaylie, but she's a big girl. She can, and will, figure out her life. You can't save her from herself. You can't fix her problems or make her be more like you."

"I'm not trying to make her like me," Danica snapped. *Am I?*

"I don't mean exactly like you. I just know how much it has frustrated you that she didn't always make the best choices."

Danica sighed. "I know she loves Chaz, and she wants this baby, but she's jumping to some pretty big conclusions. She's got herself all tied up in knots, and I'm not sure how well they're doing right now. He said something about how she could work or stay at home and not work."

"Oh no. God help the person who tells Kaylie what to do, or what not to do."

"Yeah, tell me about it. Kaylie took it to mean that he wanted her barefoot and pregnant."

Her mother shook her head. "Oh, Kaylie."

"I'm trying to talk to her, but I can't tell Blake I'll get married if Kaylie's life is in such shambles."

"Danica, you listen to me. Kaylie is who Kaylie is. I love her more than earth itself, but she does have a penchant for drama. You can't live your life to protect her. Let yourself be happy. You deserve it just as much as she does, and she'd be upset if she knew you were putting your life on hold because of her."

"No, she'd feel empowered. Kaylie likes to be the one calling the shots, the center of attention."

"No, that's where you have her wrong." Her mother sat back in her chair and gave Danica a matronly, stern look. "Your sister may be a lot of things, but she thinks the world of you. And she worries about you not having a life. I might not have seen her for a year, but those things don't change."

"Not having a life?" *I have a very nice life, thank you very much.* "Why would you think she worries about me? She's too busy having everyone else worry about her."

"Trust me. I know. Before your father and I separated, she'd call home from college almost every week, just to tell me that she worried that you were studying too much or not having enough fun. That I should talk to you about dating. She loves you, Danica, and she wants the best for you. She's just scared to allow it for herself."

Danica wanted to tell her mother that Kaylie's insecurities were driven by the divorce, but she didn't have the heart to. Instead, she just nodded, taking in what her mother had said and hoping that she was right.

"I think your father's leaving did a real job on her," her mother said. "I tried to keep the marriage together until you girls were old enough to understand, but Kaylie…" She shook her head. "She was so mad at me."

"She wasn't mad at you, Mom," Danica lied.

"She wasn't at first, but when she found out I'd stayed with your father even after I knew about the affair, she called me one night, stone drunk, and she told me exactly what she felt. In no uncertain terms."

"She did? She was drunk. She didn't mean it," Danica offered.

"When Kaylie is drunk, she tells the truth. I learned that when she was fifteen and she'd come home from a night out with Tommy Rose." She raised an eyebrow and nodded.

"I totally forgot about that night." Tommy Rose had been the first guy Kaylie had slept with, and she'd done it as a rebellious act against her father's punishment. Danica covered her eyes. She laughed and looked up at her mother, who was also laughing.

"Your poor father. Kaylie looked right at him and said, 'I'm not sorry, Daddy, and I liked it.' She was a spiteful little firecracker."

"She threw it in his face because Dad grounded her, remember?"

"I have no doubt that she also slept with Tommy *only* so she could throw it in his face. She showed him," her mother said with a shake of her head.

As they left the restaurant, Danica couldn't help but wonder if she was trying to show someone something now by not accepting Blake's proposal. Was she trying to prove something to herself? Her independence? Could she be trying to show her father that he ruined the idea of marriage for both of his daughters? Or was she just trapped in the same worries that Kaylie had about marriage and using taking care of Kaylie as an excuse?

Chapter Thirty-One

After band practice, Kaylie cleaned the house from top to bottom. She half expected to find more paraphernalia from Max, but she didn't. She pushed the little nagging voice that wondered if it was really Max's stuff from her mind. The nagging that she knew was driven by her father's affair brought her thoughts to her mother. She did want to make amends and move forward, and she was trying to figure it all out. It had been easy not to think about her anger toward her mother when she was just starting out with her career. Between marketing herself and actually working, she barely had time to think about the rift she was creating or the hurt it was causing. Now, after seeing her mother again, she realized how much she had missed her. Maybe the baby would be a good way to ease back into that relationship.

When she was satisfied that the house was spotless, she went out to the backyard, where she and Chaz had planted flowers beside a wooden swing built for two. She sat down and swung in the warm summer air, letting the breeze tingle her sweaty skin. The sun had begun its descent and the sky was a glorious mix of purples and pinks.

The baby moved, and Kaylie rubbed the crest of her belly where an elbow or knee elevated a little circular bump. She'd been thinking about Chaz all day, and she realized how childish she'd been to run out on him. She was going to have a baby. She was almost twenty-eight years old—an adult. She knew she could no longer pull the kind of crap she did with him, or he'd leave her for sure. Love and beauty took you only so far. She knew that. Even though everyone else thought she didn't, she did. Kaylie was well aware of the way others saw her. She was the pretty one, not the smart, dependable one, not the girl anyone would turn to in a crisis. And if there was one thing she wanted right now, as she felt her baby's life beneath her palm, it was to become that person. She wanted—no, she *needed*—to become that girl whom people could count on. And she didn't need to do it for her mother or father, or for her friends or acquaintances. She needed to be that person for herself, because she was going to be a mother, and that's the kind of mother she wanted to be. She'd be pretty and fun; that part was easy. The rest would take some help.

She picked a few flowers and took them inside, still thinking about the changes she wanted to make. She took a glass vase down from a shelf in the kitchen and arranged the flowers just so. As she took one last look around, a sense of pride took hold. She'd made a pretty home for Chaz. That was something, right? She grabbed her cell phone from the counter, her purse and keys, and headed out to her car.

Kaylie stood in the waiting room of the therapist that Danica had recommended to Sally. She didn't want to ask Danica for help this time. She had to take this step on her own. If she could become the person she wanted to be, and if she could find a way

to deal with her father's leaving and her mother's weakness…
no, not weakness… her mother's what? She wasn't sure what it
was, but if she could deal with it, then maybe, just maybe, she'd
have a chance at being a really great wife. She knew that Chaz
loved her as she was. He loved her personality and her looks—
and her body—and she knew he'd love her even if all those
things went away. Even if she lost her energetic personality to
some awful disease, she knew he'd still love her, and she knew
how rare that was. She had no doubt about any of that. But she
wanted to be a wife who was confident and wouldn't flee. She
wanted to be the kind of mother whom a child took for granted,
and how could she do that if she needed to be the center of
attention. Well, maybe not as much as she'd taken her mother
for granted over the past few years, but in the general way kids
take parents for granted.

Dr. Marsden came out of her office and she looked exactly
how Kaylie had imagined. She was not a tall or pretty woman.
Her short gray hair looked more like an old man's coif than a
woman's. Her face was stern, even with the smile plastered
across her thin lips. She wore a pantsuit that must have been
made in 1977, and she held her thick arm out to shake Kaylie's
hand, the same way Kaylie had seen her father do too many
times to count. The entire package made her feel safe, like she
was in the hands of a well-experienced teacher.

She shook Dr. Marsden's hand. "Thank you for seeing me
so quickly."

"You said it was urgent, and I had a cancellation. Danica's
family gets my full attention." She motioned for Kaylie to
follow her into a small, window-lined office. "Did you complete
the intake paperwork?"

"Yes, ma'am. I put the papers on the reception desk."

"Perfect. I'll take care of them later. Your sister was the best therapist in Allure. Next to me, of course." She let out a little laugh.

Confident. I love that.

"The profession could have used her, but she's doing good work at the youth center." Dr. Marsden settled herself into a leather chair and motioned for Kaylie to do the same.

"Thank you," Kaylie said, and she sank into the leather as she imagined hundreds of people had done before her.

"When is your baby due?"

"Three and a half weeks." *Can it be that soon?* Kaylie put her hand on her belly. "Wow, I haven't said that out loud lately. That's really soon."

"Are you happy about it?"

Dr. Marsden didn't have a pad of paper, a pen, or anything in her hands. *Doesn't she need to take notes? In the movies, therapists always take notes.* Kaylie imagined that she'd been doing this work for so long she'd trained herself to remember every little detail of her sessions. The question brought her nerves to the surface. She fiddled with the edge of her top. "Yes, very."

"And your husband?"

"We're not married yet. We're waiting until after the baby is born. But he's happy, too."

"Okay, so we've got a happy family welcoming a baby. Tell me what you're here for."

Kaylie tried out answers in her head. *I suck as a wife. I wanna be more like Danica. I'm afraid my fiancé will leave and I don't want to feel that way but I can't stop myself.* Before she could find the right words, Dr. Marsden spoke.

"Pretend I'm not here. What were you thinking when you were in the waiting room?"

Kaylie took a deep inhalation of breath and blew it out

slowly. The words tumbled from her lips. "I want to be a better person. I want to be stronger, less self-centered. I want to be counted on. I want to stop running when things get bad." There, she thought. *That's the hardest part.* She admitted the faults she'd been hiding her whole life. "Oh, and I don't want to be my mother."

"Okay, so we're looking at small changes?" Dr. Marsden's joke lightened the air that had become too thick for Kaylie to breathe. "Can you tell me a little about your mom?"

She promised herself to be honest. If Danica had taught her one thing, it was that honesty was the only way a person could really get help when they were in therapy. No matter how painful it might be. "She's a good mom. But I think she's weak, and I don't want to be weak." *I'm sorry, Mom.* "I feel really guilty saying that out loud."

"There will be a lot of things that you're uncomfortable saying out loud. Some will make you mad, some sad, some guilty. That's the only way to get to the heart of things. But as I'm sure you know, what you say in here stays within these walls." She motioned to the walls around them.

"Okay. Well, then, she's also never expected much from me, and I'm a smart girl. She should have. And I've always been second to..." *Crap.*

"Danica?"

Kaylie nodded.

Dr. Marsden motioned to the walls again.

"Second to Danica. We're very different, but I'm not any less...I don't know...capable than her. She's just smarter, more determined, more efficient at everything in her life." *Oh, God. I am less capable. Danica isn't the one in therapy.* She braced herself for Dr. Marsden to confirm her worries.

"What makes you think she's smarter?"

Really? She held back her expression of disbelief and said the obvious, "She was a therapist. I'm a singer. It doesn't take much to know there's a difference in intelligence."

"Did you want to be a therapist and fail?"

"What? No. I could never be a therapist. I'm more...I'd feel caged, being in an office all day."

"So, it's not that you failed, or you couldn't be a therapist. It's that you didn't want to be a therapist."

"Right. Yes. Danica and I both graduated from college with high honors, but her degree was in psychology and mine was in music." She felt the same feeling she'd felt—and hadn't put a name to—every time she mentioned their degrees in the same sentence. *Shame.* It was definitely *shame.*

"Do you enjoy what you do?"

Kaylie felt her cheeks spread with a familiar smile. "Immensely."

"So, why compare yourself to Danica?"

Why compare? Because everyone my whole life has compared us. I know no other way of life. She didn't answer.

"Have other people compared you? Has your fiancé? Have your friends? Family?"

"Yes, no, yes, yes." The truth hurt, and Kaylie wondered if she'd made a mistake by coming to see her.

"So, your friends and family compare you to Danica, and you feel like others do as well. That must hurt."

Kaylie nodded, feeling guilty for whining about being compared to Danica. Danica was a strong woman. There could be less flattering people to be compared to.

"Your fiancé doesn't compare you."

It surprised Kaylie that she wasn't asking a question, but stating a fact. It reiterated the pride she felt in who Chaz was as a person, and how he treated her. *Maybe therapy is good after all.*

"What is his name?"

"Chaz. Chaz Crew."

"Sexy name."

Kaylie smiled. "Sexy everything." She laughed. "He doesn't compare me to anyone."

"Does he demean you, or make you feel like you can't do things? Not outright comparing you, but making you feel the distinction without words?"

"Never. No." *Does he? No, never.* After the initial jolt of wonder, relief at the truth she'd just acknowledged swept through her. She'd always known it, but saying it to someone else somehow drove that knowledge home. "I know you're going to ask me how it makes me feel to be treated like Danica's shadow, but I really want to know how I can stop feeling like I do, and more important, not be the person who people want to compare to her, or anyone else."

"Okay, we have an uphill battle ahead of us."

Maybe you could tone down your straight shooterness a little. Kaylie's hopes deflated.

"Don't give up on me yet. All I meant was that you're her younger sister, and unfortunately, there's a pretty strong draw for connections among family and friends. I'm sure they compare her to you, too."

Kaylie laughed. "No way."

"I know Danica pretty well, and she's a very determined, headstrong, focused individual."

"Yup, that's her."

"And how might you describe yourself?"

"Now, or before I was pregnant?"

"In general," Dr. Marsden answered.

"Well, before I was pregnant, I was pretty, fun, spontaneous. Now I'm big, tired, and probably cranky is a good word to use sometimes."

"That's to be expected."

Kaylie shrugged. "I'm also a good singer, and it turns out I'm a good songwriter, too."

"Okay." Dr. Marsden looked at Kaylie expectantly, and when Kaylie said nothing more, Dr. Marsden added, "I didn't hear you say smart, efficient, organized, or any of the terms you might use to describe your sister."

Kaylie wondered where she was going with that comment.

"If you don't see yourself as those things, why would anyone else?"

"But—"

"Before you answer, I have a few more things for you to think about. When you sing, do you have to go out and find each singing job?"

"Yes."

"Is it easy to do? I mean, I'm not a singer, so I have no idea how difficult or easy it might be."

"It's vicious. There are fifty singers for every job."

Dr. Marsden nodded, leaving Kaylie in silence for a beat too long.

"And when you sing, do you have to coordinate anything? A band? Music?"

"Yes, I sing with a band and we have sets that we sing— different ones at each event, which we mix up. I take care of those. And we make these great flyers for each event so that the crowd knows who we are and can hire us in the future if they want. Oh, and I contact the media to make sure that the newspapers and radios knows where we're playing. We don't always get a mention, but mostly we do."

"Would you say that an unorganized, inefficient person could do all of that?"

Kaylie felt her heart swell with pride and her cheeks flush. "No, I guess I wouldn't."

Dr. Marsden nodded. "And do you think your mother might have been able to do those things?"

"Oh, goodness yes. She could bake with one hand, while talking on the phone and sewing a button on with the other. Well, not really, but you know what I mean."

"Do you think this could be more of a case of you not be-lieving in who you are?" She didn't wait for Kaylie to answer. "Maybe you should think about that." Dr. Marsden changed gears before Kaylie could even begin to process her thoughts. "Tell me how your mother is weak."

Kaylie dropped her eyes. A protective tug pulled at her heart and told her that she was about to expose something private, and she wasn't sure she should. The desire to be a better person was stronger than the concern over her parents' divorce. She blurted out how she felt about her mother staying with her father even after she knew about her father's affair.

"Kaylie, what would you have liked her to do?"

"Leave him. She didn't need to be second fiddle to some other woman."

"And where would that have left you and your sister?"

Kaylie thought about the timing. Her mother had admitted to knowing about the affair when Danica was fifteen and Kaylie was fourteen. "We were teenagers when she found out. We would have been…" She shrugged. "I don't know. We'd have been fine."

"Do you really think so? Maybe you would have, but many teenagers whose parents split up go on to rebel, angry with both parents. Some get into drugs and drinking, while others run away or lock themselves in their rooms. Some never graduate high school. And some do just fine."

Kaylie dropped her eyes.

"You could have been two who did just fine. But you'll never know, because your mom was weak enough to stay and protect you from all of that hurt. She protected you from knowing that who you thought your father was, wasn't really true."

"She never even let on. All those years, she supported him, and she'd tell us how wonderful he was. I remember." Kaylie closed her eyes against tears that had welled, then blinked them away. "She never let us think anything less of him. Even when he punished me and I said I hated him, she never let on. I wish she would have."

"Why?"

Kaylie didn't answer.

Dr. Marsden waited.

"Then I could have hated him," Kaylie admitted. "Instead, I thought she drove him away after we went away to school." *Is that really what I'm thinking? That's awful.* She looked up into Dr. Marsden's compassionate eyes. "I was so mad at him for leaving, and she still didn't tell me about him and the other woman until months later. She protected him."

"Why did she tell you about the affair?"

"I pushed and pushed. I was so angry about my dad that I started to blame her for his leaving, and I guess I pushed too hard one day, because she was crying and blurted it out." Kaylie paused to swallow the lump that was threatening to stop her from speaking altogether. "She blurted it out. I don't think she meant to."

"And then you thought she was weak, for having stayed."

Kaylie lowered her eyes to the floor, her heart heavy with the memories she wanted to push away.

"Kaylie, you have every right to feel that way. But let me

play devil's advocate here for just a moment. Have you ever thought that maybe it took courage and strength to stay for all those years? To protect you and your sister? And to take it a step further, by keeping that information from you after their divorce, she was allowing you to still adore your father for the man you thought he had always been until you gave her no choice but to stand up for herself."

"You sound like Danica," Kaylie huffed. She waved her hand like none of it mattered, but the truth was, it mattered too much. It was her fault that her mother had told her. "I'm sorry. I didn't mean that. But Danica says that all the time, that Mom was strong, not weak."

"I'm not conferring with Danica. I'm talking with you. I can see why you think she was weak. That's a natural inclination. You're protective of her. You don't like that she was hurt for all those years."

"I felt like she was blindsided."

Dr. Marsden nodded. "I'm sure you did. But your mother made a conscious decision that she thought was best for all involved, and you might never know why she made that decision. Have you asked her?"

"Yes," Kaylie answered quickly. Then she corrected herself. "No. I…we…I think I accused, but never really asked."

"Maybe you should."

Kaylie nodded. This was far harder than she'd thought it might be. She'd have to confront her mother after all. "Isn't there a magic something that you can give me—a mantra, a guidebook—something that will help me?"

Dr. Marsden laughed. "I wish there was. It sounds to me like you are every bit as smart as your sister, and there's no question about your efficiency or your ability to focus. And determination? You're here, and that takes determination.

Therapy is not easy."

"Thank you." Kaylie's voice didn't sound like her own. Her words came out as a whisper, hidden under an enormous heft of gratitude for telling her something she'd needed to hear for far too long.

"It sounds like you might need to work on your confidence a bit, but it also sounds like that might come from growing up in your sister's rather large shadow. And you know, Kaylie, you have the power to not only change what others think of you, but you have the power to change what you think of yourself, and that, my dear, is the place to start."

Chapter Thirty-Two

Max fell asleep on the plane with her head leaning on Chaz's shoulder. He was tired enough to sleep, but worry kept him awake. He hadn't heard back from Cooper yet about how to handle things with Lea, and he began to wonder if he would ever be rid of her once and for all. He hated that he'd ever allowed himself to get roped into her aggressive sexual manipulations in the first place.

He looked at his reflection in the window against the dark sky. The man he saw looking back at him was not one he was proud of. Lea was like a noose around his neck, and if he'd only been honest with Kaylie in the first place, she never would have worried. It dawned on him that Kaylie hadn't mentioned how she knew about Lea. Chalk up one more thing to worry about.

The captain came on the loudspeaker announcing their descent, startling Max awake.

"Sorry," she said sleepily. A few strands of hair had sprung free from their elastic band, giving her a messy librarian look.

"It's okay. I'm glad you slept."

"Didn't you?" She stifled a yawn.

He shook his head.

"Worried?"

"More than I care to admit." He tightened his seat belt.

Max did the same. "Max, I'm really glad you came with me. This would have been a much more painful trip had I been alone."

"I'd never send you to the wolves alone. I learned my lesson two years ago."

"You were at the festival two years ago," he reminded her.

"Yeah, but I left your side for just long enough for her to swoop in and sweep you off your feet. I'd seen the way she'd been looking at you. She made no effort to hide the fact that she wanted you." She smiled up at him. "Never again. I've learned my lesson."

The plane touched down and they followed the streetlights, heading toward the parking lot.

"I need to get my car from the Village," Max reminded him.

"Do you want to tell me why you had your bag in the trunk of your car?"

"I did that the night before. You asked me that the night I drove you home, but I guess you were a little drunk. Besides, don't you know by now that I'm a little neurotic about being prepared?"

"Or maybe you thought you'd meet a guy and get lucky at Taylor's Cove?" Chaz teased.

"Oh, yeah, 'cause I'm one of those girls, and because so many hot guys hang out at a bar that's known for hosting bikers and old men?" She smirked. "How many times have I hooked up with a guy in all the time you've known me?"

Chaz thought about it, and the more he thought, the more he was sure that he'd never heard her talk about a boyfriend. "I've never heard you even talk about a guy."

"Nope. Anyway, if my car's out of your way, I can take a cab."

"Right, after you saved me from the claws of Lea? No way.

Get in." Chaz was mindlessly running through his guy friends, wondering if any of them would be right for Max.

"Get that look off your face," Max said. "I don't need any introductions."

"I guess you do know me." He laughed. Driving back toward town picked up Chaz's spirits. He pulled out his phone and Max reached for it.

"No way am I gonna let you kill me in some crazy, fatigued, texting and driving accident. Tell me what to text."

"Okay, okay. I was just gonna tell Kaylie I was on my way. It can wait till we get to the Village."

Max was already texting.

He shook his head. *Little Miss Efficient.*

A moment later the phone vibrated. "She's quick." Max read the message. "Looks like you're in trouble."

"Why?" *What now?*

"She said she's got something to tell you. Didn't you already clear the air?"

Chaz sighed. "Yes. Shit. Did she tell you how she found out about Lea? I didn't ask her, and now I'm worried. Lea's going after a piece of the festival. I need to make sure Kaylie knows everything."

"I'd love to be a fly on the wall for that conversation."

"Not me," he said.

"Just be gentle, you know? Don't tell her about how I had to practically drag the two of you out of bed when you hooked up with the dragon lady. That's so embarrassing." She looked out the window.

"I'd never tell her that, and I'm sorry. You shouldn't have been put in that position. That was thoughtless of me." A sly smile crept across his lips. "It was fun, though."

"You're a pig."

When they pulled up beside Max's car, Chaz put the car in park and turned toward Max. "Listen, I haven't really been myself the last few days. I don't usually drink so much."

"I know. I knew when I saw you in Taylor's Cove that something wasn't right. You and Kaylie are usually glued at the hip. I can't remember the last time I saw you out on the town at all, much less without her."

Chaz nodded solemnly. "Thanks again, Max. You really are a great employee." He watched her climb from the car with a look of disappointment on her face. He grabbed her hand before she closed the door. "Friend, Max. You're the greatest friend, and I really do appreciate it."

Chaz opened the door to the chalet, feeling like he'd been gone a month instead of just a few days. He felt his shoulders relax. *Home.* So much had transpired that he could barely think straight. *Kaylie* was the only clear thought he had. He missed her more than he ever thought he could miss someone.

The smell of Kaylie filled the air. *Flowers. Happiness. Love.* He dropped his bags in the foyer. Candles shone brightly on the countertop that separated the dining room from the kitchen, and freshly picked flowers stood tall and beautiful on the dining room table. Kaylie was fast asleep on the couch, her belly arching across the wide base of cushions. His heart warmed as he knelt beside her and brushed her hair from her cheeks. He kissed her forehead, then slid onto the couch and wrapped his arms around her.

Kaylie nuzzled into him. The heady scent of her perfume drew his lips to her neck, and he felt her body respond. She opened her eyes and smiled, forehead to forehead, their baby between them.

"You're home," she said sleepily.

"I'm home."

"I'm sorry." She spoke fast, as if she desperately needed him to hear her. "I'm gonna figure out how to be better. I promise."

He touched her cheek. "Kaylie—"

She put her finger to his lips. "Not for you. For me. I'm going to a therapist. I'm going to figure out my own stuff, so our baby doesn't have to deal with my baggage."

Chaz had never felt love the way he did at that moment. Every inch of him ached to taste her, to swallow the talk he knew they needed to have and just make love to her until neither one could remember the pain of the last few days. But he'd done enough procrastinating. Kaylie was his fiancée, the woman he wanted to trust him, and in order to do so, he needed to know he'd done everything possible to make things right.

"I want you so badly," he admitted, "but I want to talk about what went on first."

Kaylie closed her eyes for a second, touching his chest. "We could fool around and then talk." She ran her finger down his shirt to the waist of his pants with a wanton look in her eye.

"I know we could, but it will be so much better after." He sat up, then took her hand and helped her get comfortable as well.

"Okay," she said with a sigh. "I guess I *was* really upset when that woman called. She made it sound like you two were together, and between Max's brush and her sock, I just lost it."

"I'm sure she did it on purpose, Kaylie. As I said on the phone, she was doing everything she could to drive a wedge between us."

"The way she spoke sent me—it sent me right back to the call from my mother about my dad and his affair, and all that hatred came rushing back. Hatred toward my father and anger toward Mom. I know I jumped to conclusions and I'm so sorry that I misdirected that anger at you. How could I have been so stupid?" She dropped her apologetic eyes to her lap.

He lifted her chin with his finger so they were eye to eye. "You are anything but stupid, Kaylie. You went into protective mode—protecting yourself and the baby. I could never fault you for that. I do wish you had let me explain first, but you had every right to be mad. I had kept something from you. It was me who was stupid. I should have told you about Lea when we first met, but I was afraid. I thought you'd worry every time the festival came around, and I swear to you, on everything on this earth that I cherish…" He touched her stomach. "And on our baby that has yet to be born, I would never, ever, cheat on you. Lea was a mistake, nothing more."

"But…why would she do that if it was…what was it? A fling, or were you in love with her?"

He watched her swallow hard and squeeze her thighs with her hands. He hated to see her readying herself for something hurtful. He took her hand in his.

"It was anything but love."

"But you told me that you were never really a one-night-stand guy."

"And I told you the truth. Lea was the only person I had ever done something like that with. She had been a sponsor for years, each year sponsoring a little bigger chunk of the festival, and through the years, she flirted, but I didn't pay much attention. That year, she was relentless, not that there is any excuse for any of it. But she pulled out all the stops and I just…" He paused to take a deep breath. "I gave in. And we had a weekend tryst—two days, that was it. I won't lie to you, Kaylie. It was all about sex. Nothing more. She wanted more, and on the second evening she started telling me how to do business and trying to weasel her way into how I ran the festival. She became clingy and aggressive, and when I noticed she was disrespectful to me, and then Max and the staff, I broke it off. I promise you, Kaylie, love was never even an option. Honestly, like wasn't really, either. It was just sex."

"Is that supposed to make me feel better?" Kaylie asked with tears in her eyes.

"No, but it is the truth." He closed his eyes, knowing he was digging a hole, but also understanding that honesty was the only way to heal their relationship and move forward. "Kaylie, you told me your background, and I know you get it, and I know it doesn't make it better. The one thing you can be certain of is that I will never make that mistake again. Look at me." He waited for her to look into his eyes. "When I met you, I knew my life was complete. You are the woman I love. You are the only woman I ever want to love."

"I do know that," she said. "You could have told me about her before, when we told each other about our pasts."

He nodded. "I know that now, and I'm truly sorry. I was so ashamed by what I'd done. I felt used and dirty. Never before had I shirked my responsibilities for something so meaningless, and I never have since."

"I still don't get why she's coming after you now."

"Because she wasn't over me, I guess. I don't really believe that's the whole story, though. I think she's just crazy. I mean, who pretends to buy a business and calls a man's wife pretending to having been intimate with him?" He shook his head. "Max thinks she's just obsessed and feels like if she can't have me no one will."

"Then do we have to worry?" She put her hand on her belly. Chaz shook his head. "No. Cooper is checking into things, but he said we can't get a restraining order because she's not outright harassing us. My mistake was taking the sponsorship and following her orders like a puppy. Her only connection to me was the festival, and now that's done. Max will never take another call from her. I was worried about the festival, and it was stupid. The festival is a job. You're my life." He took her hand again. "What we have is so strong, Kaylie. These last few days were a nightmare, and with your concerns about your job, it was a blip on the radar screen of the many years we'll have together. I can't imagine anyone or anything coming between the love we have."

Kaylie nodded, wiping a tear from her cheek. "I know. And I'm thankful for Max. She called me to make sure I was okay—and I know now that when she said you ended things with Lea, she meant two years earlier. That's something a sister would do. She's kind of like your work wife. She takes care of you when I'm not there."

"Yeah, she does, but not in the way you do." He kissed her on the lips, and when she pulled him into a deeper kiss he didn't want to let go, but he had more to say.

When he reluctantly pulled away, she was looking at him with desire in her eyes, and when she spoke, it was almost a whisper. "I get the idea that Max feels safe with us. Like she's been really hurt somewhere down the line, and she doesn't want anything to mess up the little family she has with us."

"Kaylie." God he wanted to kiss her again. He didn't want to talk about Max or Lea or anything else, but he had to finish, and then he'd let down that barrier and devour her. "I wanted to tell you before you went out with the girls, but you were running out and I thought we'd talk when you got back. It was my fault, the whole thing, and I'm so sorry that I hurt you." His words rushed from his mouth. The faster they were out, the faster he could allow her hand, which was inching up his thigh, to race forward. "And I'm so proud of what you have done. Even during such a stressful time, you kept your strength and your focus, and you found something more within yourself, while I barely made it through each day. I admire you so much, and I will spend the rest of my life showing you how much I adore you."

She tucked her hand between his thighs. Even without touching his most sensitive parts, the heat of her hand burned into him and the ache became a throb of need.

"It was you who pushed me, and I was so rude to you. I overreacted when you said that maybe I should write, and the truth is, I have no idea if I want to be barefoot and pregnant or build a career—but I want my options left open." Her last words left her breathless, and she leaned in closer, her breath on his chin.

"When I see that spark in your eyes, while you're talking about your career, I want that for you, too. I'd never push you to do anything you didn't want to. The only thing I want for you is happiness, Kaylie." He couldn't stand it. He kissed her hard and then pulled away fast. "I want you to wake up every day and know you're with a person who adores you and wants to protect you." He kissed her again and her hand slid up, cupping him through his pants. "I feel that way about you. I wake up and know you love me, and I want that for you."

She kissed his neck. "Okay, okay, shut up." Her kiss turned to a hard, tongue-pressing suck. How could he have kept anything from this sweet, delicious woman? He brought her lips to his and she arched in to him as he kissed her deeper, relishing the taste of her. He'd never let her go, and he'd be damned if he'd let someone like Lea come between them. His hand slid down her neck to the crest of her breast and she moaned, a hungry, desperate moan.

"Bedroom," she whispered as she came to her feet. She took his hand and led him down the hall and into their bedroom, closing the door behind them. "I missed you," she said as she unbuttoned his shirt, running her hands down his chest and sending a shiver up his spine.

"It's been too long," he whispered, guiding her to the bed. Chaz lifted her sundress from her body. Her heavy, full breasts were still confined within the black lace bra she wore. Even pregnant, Kaylie was the sexiest woman Chaz had ever known, and now, as he unhooked her bra and her breasts sprang free, he knew there would never be anyone else he'd rather be with. As she pressed into him, he said, "I'm so sorry."

"Shh. No more talking about that," she whispered as she dropped her hand and stroked him through is pants.

"I love these pregnancy urges." He took her breast in his mouth and she gasped and then lowered herself onto the bed, stroking the back of his head, pulling him closer, forcing his mouth harder around her nipple.

He drew down her lacy thong with one finger and gripped the supple skin of her hip. She shuddered beneath his touch, reaching for the button on his pants. He gently grabbed her wrist, stopping her from going any further.

"Kaylie," he said as he looked into her lustful eyes, "there is no one else on this earth for me. I don't care if you work, don't work, or what you do, as long as you're happy. I just need you to know that." He lowered his forehead to rest against hers. Her breath filled the space between them. "I don't want you ever worrying again. If you think something is going on, ask me. I'll always be honest."

"I think something is going on," she said.

He drew back.

She pulled him back to her and kissed him, exploring his mouth with her tongue as if it were the first time. "Something between us," she whispered, and teased him with a flick of her tongue along his lips. "I trust you, and I'm working on the rest." She kissed him again. "But I'll never..." Kaylie rolled him onto his back and unbuttoned his pants. "Ever..." She tried awkwardly to tug his pants off, and he took over, tossing them and his skivvies aside.

Kaylie watched his desire, growing stronger by the second. "Jump to conclusions again," she whispered as she licked her lips.

Just the sight of her sweet tongue on her lips made his adrenaline soar. He reached for her, just as she began to straddle him.

She slid down upon him and the shock of her warmth and the cool of her wetness stole his breath away. She drew his hands to her waist, letting him guide her slow, sensual movements, and in that moment, the worry of the past few days fell away.

Chapter Thirty-Three

Danica watched the sun ease into the bedroom, illuminating a path across Blake's legs. She'd been up for hours, thinking about her conversation with her mother, worried about Kaylie, and rubbing a knot of stress that had developed at the base of her skull.

She curled onto her side, watching Blake sleep. He wasn't a guy who carried his worries tucked away, and that was one of the many things she loved about him. She'd thought she was the same way, wearing her emotions on her sleeve; but lately, as she faced the biggest decisions of her life, she realized that she was the one who had been hiding her true concerns. In the predawn hours—as she lay next to Blake, listening to the rhythm of his contented breaths and the stillness of the condo—she tried to work through her emotions as she might have done with a client so many months ago, but she kept coming full circle. Her fears all started, and ended, with Kaylie. She'd always worried about Kaylie; that wasn't new. But had she always deferred her own happiness due to what was going on in Kaylie's life?

Blake stirred beside her. His eyes opened, then closed, as he reached his arm around her.

"You okay?" he asked sleepily.

"Yeah," she whispered. *No.* She felt the lie nipping at her nerves. It was unfair to Blake to let Kaylie's life have such a big impact on the life they were building together. She played a scene in her mind, telling Kaylie that she was getting married. She imagined Kaylie bursting into tears, too upset over her own broken relationship to be happy for Danica and then blaming Danica, somehow, for her and Chaz's issues.

No matter what Kaylie might or might not do, Danica realized, she wasn't willing to put her happiness on hold any longer. She cupped Blake's cheek and moved in closer, their knees touching, head to head, eye to eye. "I'm moving in," she whispered.

Blake's eyes sprang open. "I think I heard you wrong."

She kissed his lips. "I'm moving in. Here. With you. I'm doing it."

He pulled her body against his. "That's what I thought you said." He rolled on top of her and held down her hands. "Look me in the eye and say it again."

Wipe that silly grin off your face! His smile was infectious and he was so damned cute. Danica tried to keep a straight face, but her lips had other ideas. She felt her cheeks bloom. "I'm moving in."

"What about Kaylie?"

Danica shook her head. "I don't think I want her moving in with us," she teased.

Blake reached down and grabbed her ribs, sending her into a fit of giggles. She swiped at his arms as they rolled around on the bed, laughing. The weight of the world lifted from her shoulders.

He jumped off the bed and did a little dance, swaying his sexy, boxer-briefed hips from side to side, his fingers snapping, shoulders moving up and down.

"You're a fool." She laughed.

He sank to one knee.

Danica froze.

Blake took her hand. "And... is there more?"

She knew what he was asking. *Marry me. Say yes!* "Baby steps," she whispered, hoping he would understand.

His head fell into her hands. She ran her fingers through his thick hair. He lifted his eager eyes in her direction, and Danica knew they weren't eager with lust; they were eager with hope.

She loved him, and as she ran her hands over his muscular shoulders, she wanted nothing more than to be his wife. Kaylie's unhappiness still hovered like a bad dream, so she said nothing at all.

Blake rose to his feet, and Danica's heart cracked as the shine of hope left his eyes. She feared the loneliness she felt in that split second. Hers. His. Had she crushed him? Was she crushing herself? Was she running out of chances with the man she loved? She reached for his hand, and he looked at her with a mix of love and hurt.

"I want to marry you more than anything in this world. I want to be Mrs. Blake Carter, but not at the expense of hurting my sister. How can I be elated if she's so torn?"

Blake withdrew his hand and ran it through his messy bed-head hair. "I get it. I'm gonna shower. Alyssa needs my help with the inventory this morning."

If he got it, then why did Danica feel like she'd lost a piece of him?

Chapter Thirty-Four

"The chairs will go here, the table of refreshments, there." Sally pointed to the patio just outside the barn doors. "I still can't believe we got the barn."

Danica couldn't believe it either. The county owned the barn, which sat right at the edge of town. Generations earlier, the more than ten thousand acres of land surrounding the barn had belonged to the Allure family, for whom the town was named. Over the years, they'd divided the property, selling off acreage to developers and families. Finally, they donated the last thirteen acres to the county, along with the barn, placing it into a land trust. The county had restored the barn in recent years, an event that the entire town had celebrated.

As Danica stood in the center of the nearly three-thousand-square-foot structure, she marveled at the high ceiling. The substantial wooden rafters were exposed like bones of a fish, and the smell of cedar was artfully used throughout the building. She imagined her own wedding taking place there one day, and the thought brought sadness back to her heart for not being able to accept his proposal on the spot.

"Are you even listening to me?" Sally asked.

"What? Yeah, of course. Sorry. It's just so beautiful in here."

Get your head in the game, Danica.

"You're like a million miles away. Do you want to do this another time?"

"No, I'm good." They walked outside, and Sally showed Danica where they would place the tables and string the lights in the surrounding trees and along the rafters of the barn.

"The event is tomorrow. When are the lights going up?" She looked at her watch. "Didn't we specify this afternoon?"

"It's only ten, Danica. Wow, you really are stressed."

Danica sighed. "You're right. Sorry. Are we missing anything at all?"

"Nope. Gage is taking care of the programs, and Kaylie called and said she and her band will be here two hours early to set up. I still can't believe her doctor is letting her sing this close to her due date, but she said her doctor gave the okay." Sally shook her head and her shiny blond hair swung from side to side.

Danica noticed that she was wearing more jewelry than usual. "Necklace, earrings, *and* a bracelet. Mm-hmm."

Sally touched her necklace. "What?"

"Nothing." She began walking toward the car.

"It's just jewelry," Sally muttered.

"Would this jewelry have anything to do with Gage?"

Sally was silent.

Danica touched her arm and stopped walking. "Dish," she said with a smile.

"There was a moment."

"A moment?"

Sally blushed. "It wasn't really anything, and I probably overdramatized it."

"Overdramatized *what*?"

Sally looked around, as if someone might hear them among the empty acres of land. "We met for coffee again this morning to make sure we had everything covered."

Danica interrupted. "Who asked whom?"

"He asked me."

"Okay, go on." Danica was already picturing them as a couple.

"I'm such a lummox. I tripped on the way out of the coffee shop and he caught me, like this." She placed her hand on Danica's elbow. "And I was here." She moved in closer to Danica, their chests almost touching. "And our eyes met, and...I don't know. It sounds so stupid now." She released Danica's arm.

"No, it doesn't. So there wasn't a kiss?"

Sally shook her head. "But there was something. Our eyes didn't just meet; they held. You know that thing, that electricity that passes between two people?"

Danica thought of the instant attraction she'd felt with Blake outside of Bar None the night she'd twisted her ankle. The way her body had grown warm in places that had been asleep for too long. "Yeah, I know that feeling. When it's like the space between you is filled with desire but neither one moves on it? But then I usually feel stupid and *do* something stupid."

Sally clicked her seat belt as Danica started the engine.

"Oh, I did. I apologized, thanked him for catching me, made a stupid joke, but there was a *look* in his eyes."

"It's called lust."

"No, the more I think about it, the more I think he was petrified of me. Like I'd just made an inappropriate move on him or something. Thank God I didn't kiss him."

"You're being silly. He was probably just uncomfortable for the same reasons you were." She watched the worry creep across Sally's forehead. "Sally, you're beautiful, smart, and kind."

"A widow. The mom of a testosterone-laden teenager. I come with baggage. Major baggage."

Don't we all? Luckily, Blake loves me, baggage and all.

By the time Sally and Danica arrived at the center, Gage had already laid out stacks of information packets, signup sheets, and waivers for the next day's event. She could hardly believe the dance and gathering was coming together so well. If they pulled this off, and it was a success, Danica envisioned it becoming an annual event that members of the community could look forward to each year.

"Did you see the paper?" Gage stood beside Danica, showing her the announcement in the *Allure Times.*

"Front page! That's fantastic. We should get a big turnout." Danica looked at Sally, who was fiddling with her pencil. She stole a glance at Gage, and the way he kept his eyes trained on the newspaper told her that he was purposely not looking at Sally. *Oh, God. Had Sally been right?* Was she facing an employer's nightmare after all? She rescued Sally. "Why don't you take these out front and make sure the kids see them and take them home to their parents tonight."

Relief sent Sally hurrying toward her office with a nod.

"They were mailed to our community list, too, so most parents probably already received them. We've received eighty-nine back already," Gage said.

"Eighty-nine? Wow. I expected, I don't know, fifty kids. Tops," Danica said.

"This is gonna be huge. I can just feel it." Gage's smile, and the way he used his hands to demonstrate *huge,* told Danica that he was more relaxed now that Sally had left the room.

"So, you and Sally met this morning?" She didn't want to pry, but she needed to know if there was an issue between employees. Okay, maybe she did want to pry. Just a little.

Gage's face grew serious again. "Yeah, just to go over the details. I knew she'd be swamped today, and I have two basketball sessions this morning, so I thought it might save time."

Poor Sally. She's reading too much into this. "Sounds smart. Thanks. So are we missing anything? I feel like we're missing something."

Gage was looking out of Danica's office and into the lobby.

"Gage?"

"Huh? Oh, sorry."

Danica took a step toward her desk so she could better see the lobby. Sally was hovering over her desk, her backside pointed in their direction. Danica smiled to herself. *Maybe it's not poor Sally after all.* "I feel like we're missing something."

"Nope. We have refreshments covered. Nancy and Michelle are helping there. Sally and I will make sure things go smoothly, and you'll be there. We have a handful of parent volunteers who are chaperoning, so I think we're covered. You don't mind that I've been putting in extra hours, do you?"

What would I do without these people? "The door is open when you're ready for full-time. First aid? Who's got that station?"

Gage smiled, nodding and looking over his papers. "Mrs. Peck. She's one of the school nurses and volunteered."

"Perfect. Get a waiver."

"Already taken care of, and, Danica, thank you for the offer."

Danica leaned against her desk, thinking about what else she might have overlooked. Her cell phone rang. *Blake.*

Gage pointed at the door.

Danica nodded. "I'll get you if I think of anything else." She had a sinking feeling in the pit of her stomach. Blake hadn't stayed to talk over coffee, the way they usually did in the mornings, and when he'd kissed her goodbye, he'd brushed her cheek with his lips. He never brushed her cheek. He kissed her lips goodbye. Always. She grabbed her cell and answered. "Hi," she said in an overly perky voice, hoping it might be contagious and they could pretend she hadn't just broken his heart—and maybe her own.

"Hey, babe. Wanna meet at the café for lunch?"

Danica stood. "For lunch?" She ran through her phone calls and the last-minute confirmations she wanted to make regarding the lights and parking lot. Damn, she'd forgotten about parking lot attendants.

"Danica? Are you there? If you're too busy…"

"No, I can. I want to. Noonish?" She scribbled notes to herself so she wouldn't forget the parking attendants.

"Great. See you then."

See you then. Not, *I love you.* Not even, *Love you.* Danica moved around her desk and sank into her cushioned chair. It was ten forty-five. She had another hour and fifteen minutes until her life fell apart.

Chapter Thirty-Five

Kaylie walked up the steps to Dr. Marsden's office wondering if the previous night had been a dream. How could so much have taken place over a few short days? He'd forgiven her without hesitation, then proceeded to tell her how Lea had made him feel, and he'd been brutally honest. It was hard for her to hear the sordid details, but he didn't want any secrets and felt she needed to know what she was dealing with. No lies, no omissions. Much to her surprise, she felt better afterward. Instead of feeling jealous or cantankerous, she felt special. He'd trusted her enough to share something insanely intimate, and it turned out, so hurtful, too. Lea would probably always be a sore subject, but for now she took pleasure in the confidence of Chaz's love for her and in her ability to try to make the things that were in her control less dramatic so he could feel the same confidence in her.

Chaz was spending the day tracking down Cooper and getting things settled once and for all with Lea. And Kaylie was excited to see Dr. Marsden before band practice. She'd never really believed in the value of therapy, but maybe that was just because Danica was her sister. Now, as she opened the lobby door and sat in the deep cushions of the couch, Kaylie felt ready to take on the world. Talking to Dr. Marsden was already helping, and it gave her hope that maybe she wasn't too damaged by her parents' divorce to have a long, happy relationship with Chaz. She had a fleeting thought that maybe she didn't need therapy at all. Maybe she was happy because she and Chaz had made up. Danica's voice sailed through her mind. *Too many clients end therapy after their first big epiphany. You have to unearth the crap to find the fertile soil.* Maybe Kaylie was an exception. That's what she was thinking when Dr. Marsden opened the door, her steely gray hair swept to the side and her pantsuit a mirror image of the one she'd first seen her in, except for the color.

"You didn't skip out," Dr. Marsden said with a smile.

Kaylie stood, and before she knew it, tears were trailing down her cheeks. "I... I'm sorry." *I am definitely not the exception!*

Dr. Marsden guided her inside with practiced compassion. "I've seen tears before, Kaylie."

Kaylie settled into a chair and grabbed a tissue from a little wooden end table. She wiped her eyes and blew her nose. "Wow, I'm sorry. I don't know where that came from."

"Do you want to talk about it?"

Kaylie proceeded to spell out the events from the night before, stopping to wipe fresh tears and then starting again. She spoke fast and left no detail unexposed. She told her about their incredible lovemaking and how she felt closer to him than ever before. She told her about Lea and the craziness of the previous few days, and when she was done, she lifted her eyes, expecting to see Dr. Marsden's appalled face. Instead, she saw empathy and, she thought, some sense of pride in Dr. Marsden's eyes.

"Sounds like a whirlwind night."

Kaylie nodded, wiping the last of her tears from her eyes. "I haven't cried at all. I don't know why I'm crying now. I'm so embarrassed."

"No need to be embarrassed. Kaylie, you've had a very emotional time these last few months, with losing your singing jobs, the confusion with your fiancé, and you're unearthing emotions about your father that you have probably had tucked away for years. I'd expect you to feel something."

Kaylie let out a breath. "The problem is, I'm not sure why I'm crying. I mean, we talked through these things. None of it was problematic. He knows my entire past. Every person I've been with, every place I've gone, everything. And I know his. I feel good about all of this."

"Why do you think you cried?"

"You sound like my sister. She answers me with questions all the time."

"Career hazard," Dr. Marsden teased, but she didn't apologize. She waited for Kaylie to answer.

"I guess it was really hard to hear. There's something else, too. I was relieved that Chaz wasn't in love with Lea; he was showing me how badly he felt about the whole thing—and he left nothing out, which I hadn't really expected. And even though he was telling me all of these painful memories, I still told him I was relieved. Does that make me a bad person? Shouldn't I have been comforting him or something? Because I feel like maybe I was a total bitch."

"Did you hurt him or did Lea?"

"Lea, I just told you that."

"Would you have been relieved if they'd been in love when they'd had their tryst?"

Kaylie pondered the question. "No. I would have probably been angry, even though I know I'd have no right to be. His past is his past, just like my past is mine. I mean, I thought I was in love my senior year in high school, and it carried over to my freshman year in college, but I wasn't. And if he had gotten mad over that, I would've probably been angry with him for it."

"And it sounds like the talk you shared was a way to lay it all out on the table, right? No hidden agendas?" She looked at Kaylie expectantly.

"No. None. In fact, he's the one who started the discussion. I told him I didn't want to know, but he told me anyway. He said he didn't want to ever feel like we had anything to hide from each other."

"So you were honest. You said you were relieved. It doesn't sound to me like you did anything inappropriate—even if it felt like you did."

"I just don't want to hurt him," she admitted.

"Kaylie, you're obviously a passionate person with many things in your life. Sometimes passion comes out as sheer honesty, and sometimes it comes as anger, or pain. It's good that you care. You two have just removed the cap on your honesty jar. Chances are there's more to tell."

Kaylie fingered the damp tissue. "God, I hope not." She laughed.

"Don't fool yourself. You've known him how long?"

"About nine months." She blushed, touching her belly.

"That leaves about twenty-seven years of catching up for you to do."

"And twenty-eight for him." She looked at Dr. Marsden's calm demeanor and wondered how she pulled it off. Kaylie felt as though she were a living roller coaster ride, and Dr. Marsden never even flinched when she cried or cursed.

"There's a whole lot of living in twenty-seven or twenty-eight years. Don't be surprised if things come out along the way."

Dr. Marsden switched gears like a pro. "Have you given any

thought to your relationship with your mom?"

Kaylie groaned. "I know I have to. I've just been too busy."

"You have time," she assured her.

"I feel like I'm in a rush. Like I have maybe a month to get my head on straight before this baby's born."

"That's understandable, but it's not really necessary, and it might not be realistic. Change takes time. Once the baby is born, your priorities will change, and you'll probably take less time to work on yourself. That's only natural, so allow yourself to relish in your new baby."

"I really want to have things pretty well figured out before the baby is born for just that reason. I want Chaz to know he can trust me as a mother."

"Why wouldn't he?"

There's that directness again. Kaylie glanced at the clock and knew their time was coming to an end. She pondered not answering until next week, but she needed guidance if this was going to work.

"I've never even babysat. I was always too busy with boys to spend time babysitting. I have exactly zero experience with changing diapers, or even cradling a baby." *Cradling a baby. Craa-dling a baa-by.* Kaylie made a mental note for a future song and realized that, for the first time, she was actually thinking in terms of something creative again. She smiled at the thought.

"Many women don't have experience with babies before giving birth. Much of what you're describing will come naturally. Was your mother nurturing?"

"To me? Yes. Not so much to Danica. She put more pressure on her than me."

"So, do you think you had a good role model for the nurturing side of motherhood?"

Kaylie nodded, more to herself than to Dr. Marsden. "Yes. I do, actually."

"Kaylie, I'm not hearing what's really bothering you, and you don't have to tell me, but when you're ready, I'm here."

Kaylie felt the fingers of time tapping away. She finally blurted out, "What if I can't lose the weight, and then I get bitchy because of it? I do that, you know. When I don't look good, it's like I can't let anyone be happy."

Dr. Marsden opened her hands excitedly. "I think you've had a breakthrough. On that note, we have to end our session, but we'll have time during our next session to talk about things."

"But…How can you leave me hanging like that? Can't you tell me what to do?" Her annoyance pulled her words forcefully from her lips.

"Therapy isn't about giving you the answers. Therapy is about finding the answers within yourself. I just help you find the right path to them."

"I don't get it."

"It's okay, Kaylie." Dr. Marsden stood and patted her on the back. "There's nothing to 'get.' Go home. Think about it. Really allow yourself to think through the things you just told me. Then we'll talk."

"But tomorrow's Saturday." Panic prickled her limbs. How had she come to rely on her sessions so quickly?

"Yes, and since you requested weekly appointments until your baby is born, I've cleared Monday morning for you. We'll talk then."

Chapter Thirty-Six

Cooper sat behind his mahogany desk in his plush, downtown office. Before meeting him in person, Chaz had pictured Cooper Short as a stocky, cigar-smoking, balding man. His telephone manners were gruff and direct, his voice deep and raspy. Chaz laughed to himself now, as he remembered the first time he'd met the six-foot-three silver fox. His ski-boarding hobby had yet to diminish as he aged, and his green eyes glowed against his year-round tan.

"Chaz, my boy," Cooper said as he stood, his hand out-stretched.

"Cooper." Chaz shook his hand and sat in the chair on the other side of the desk. "Thanks for taking care of this mess." Chaz looked at the photographs of Cooper's wife, Belinda, and his three grown children. "Belinda looks beautiful. New photo?"

Cooper picked up the photograph and ran his hand over her image. "Yeah, took it when the boys were in town last month. She is beautiful, isn't she?"

The office door opened and a slim, big-busted woman entered the room donning a smile, tight skirt, and wicked high heels. The quintessential sexy secretary.

"Shirley, say hello to Chaz Crew."

She blinked several times and extended a dainty hand is his

direction. "Mr. Crew. Nice to meet you."

"Shirley is our new paralegal." Cooper held up one finger to Chaz and then took the files from Shirley, signing on each line that she pointed to with her perfectly manicured fingernails. "Thank you, my dear," Cooper said as she walked out.

Chaz shook his head. "Still playing those games?"

Cooper leaned forward, set his chiseled jaw, and pointed his pen at Chaz. "It's all for show. I'd never do a thing, and you know that. No harm in letting them feel good about themselves." He looked back at the photograph of his wife and shook his head. "I'll tell you one thing, Chaz, and it's something you should remember if you ever feel tempted to stray from your future wife. There's no one who will take care of you like a wife who's seen you through the good, the bad, and the ugly."

Chaz nodded. Cooper had given him that same advice several times in recent years.

"And I'll tell you something else that I haven't told you before, because now you're going to have a child, and God knows no one else will tell you this. Your wife will turn into a monster. It doesn't matter how sweet and sexual she might have started out. When a baby comes, those mama bear instincts take over, and you become second fiddle." He leaned back in his chair and crossed his leg over the opposite knee. "Wait it out. Let her make those baby decisions. Tell her she's beautiful, because you'll still think she is, even when she's all bloated with after-baby flab."

"Cooper—"

"I'm way older than you, and I like to think of myself as wise, so hear me out." He settled in his chair and leaned forward again. "Wait it out. Raising kids is painful as much as it's glorious. You'll fight over the things they do. You might even take sides over them, and then you and your wife are suddenly working against each other."

Chaz opened his mouth and Cooper held up his hand.

"Your old man isn't around to tell you this, so just quiet down a minute. When those times come, slow down and remind yourself that after those kids are grown, they'll have families of their own, and while women like Shirley might seem to hold all the answers to your momentary unhappiness, only your wife will ever fully understand what you've gone through, and only your wife can truly fulfill all those aching needs that you've stowed away for years of T-ball games and broken curfews."

"That's a lot to take in, Coop. Are you talking from experience here?"

Cooper let out a deep, throaty laugh. "Nah, my father told me that, and any time I've been tempted, I hoped to hell he was right. And you know what? He was. I've got nothing in common with that gorgeous leggy creature out there. She sees money and my handsome facade." He ran his hand down his chest with a laugh.

"You kinda make me want to call my wife right this very second." Chaz was only half kidding. "You're not kicking the bucket, are you?" he asked.

"No, but after what happened to Jansen, and with your impending nuptials, I figured it was time you heard it. Kids these days think relationships are disposable."

"Yeah, most do. I don't. You know my father."

"He's cut from respectable cloth," Cooper said with a nod.

"Okay, well, now that you've taught me not to cheat on my wife, maybe we can talk about Jansen's interest in the festival."

Cooper shuffled papers and pulled up a report. "Lea Carmichael. Owns several businesses in multiple states. Looks like everything from a large stake in Ralph's Sporting Goods to multiple music and arts companies, and a few restaurants overseas. Daddy's money paved the way for her. My associates tell me she's cutthroat and gets what she wants—even at the expense of others."

"Preferably at the expense of others."

"So I gather from past restraining orders." Cooper set down the papers and squinted at Chaz. "Is there anything you think I ought to know before we move forward?"

"God, Cooper. No. She and I had a tryst two years ago. She was clingy and demanding, and I broke it off. Hadn't heard from her again until this year, when Max told me that she'd put in a sponsorship donation, but she had requirements."

"My best advice is to cut her loose, Chaz. If you love your future wife, cut Lea Carmichael loose."

Chaz leaned forward, his elbows resting on his knees. He nodded. "That's the plan. Max is working her ass off trying to secure sponsors." He looked up at Cooper. The urgency in his voice could not be masked. "She said she was buying into the festival, and that cannot happen. She called Kaylie and tried to imply that we'd been together. The woman is cancer, and I want her out of my life before she destroys it."

"She was playing you, Chaz. She can't buy into the partnership. You have first right of refusal, and I assume you want to purchase Jansen's ownership? I already spoke to Jansen's family and I talked to Claude. He wants to phase out, too. I think Jansen's demise freaked him out a bit. So if you want to take over the whole festival, we can move in that direction."

Ownership of the whole festival? That would give Chaz full control of all legal decisions. He had no one to answer to now, but given the recent events, full ownership would alleviate the worry of future issues. But while Chaz had plenty of money besides his family trust, most of it was tied up in stocks and other investments. He had what he considered limited cash on hand, though to most people, two million wouldn't be considered limited. He'd have to discuss the matter with Kaylie, which meant that he'd have to let on to her about just how much money he really had. He'd never disclosed his monetary worth to any of his girlfriends—another golden piece of advice Cooper had given him—and Kaylie was no different. Chaz realized his mistake. When he came clean about Lea, he should have also come clean about the money. He scrubbed his face with his hand, wondering how he could be so stupid.

"You're thinking of your girl, right?" Cooper asked with a knowing smile.

Chaz nodded.

"See you took my advice. Good move. Why ruin it? You can do this without missing a beat. Seven hundred and thirty thousand will cover it. That's a drop in the hat for you after what your grandfather left you."

Chaz shook his head.

"I know. I know." Cooper held his hands up in surrender. "Listen, Chaz, you want to be a self-made man. I get it. And you are."

"Coop, I'm running my father's festival and living off of interest from my grandfather's estate."

"You can't pick your family. You know you're lucky, right? You come from great stock, Chaz. Your grandfather made his money honestly, as did your father. They invested rocks at the right times and came out with diamonds. Your grandfather built his fortune in real estate and your father, well, you know, software and investing in the entertainment field. Nothing like being in the right place at the right time." When Chaz remained silent, Cooper lightened his tone. "Chaz, you've earned a million in the last eighteen months alone off of investments and business negotiations that *you* chose. That's all you, Chaz. Your decisions, your intelligence."

It wasn't that Chaz was embarrassed by his wealth, but he was cautious of how he was seen. Ever since some asshole in prep school had called him a daddy's boy, he'd been careful not to expose where his initial wealth came from. He'd invested his trust fund wisely, and it had paid off. But still, it all started with a trust fund.

"Do it. Go ahead. I'll handle it with Kaylie."

"Be careful, there. Money does strange things to people." Cooper's warning did not fall on deaf ears.

Chapter Thirty-Seven

Danica's stomach twisted into knots as she opened the front door of the café where she and Blake had first met. Blake waved from a table in the corner.

Danica whispered, "Excuse me, as she wove around the too-close-together tables. She smoothed her shirt and fiddled with her hands on the way to the table. "Hi," she said in a thin voice.

Blake stood and kissed her. "How's your day going?" he asked as she sat down.

Danica told him about her morning, the whole time searching his eyes for a hint of what he had on his mind. "How did your inventory go?"

"That's kind of why I wanted to talk to you, but let me get our orders first. I got you a Caesar salad. I hope that's okay."

"Perfect." She tried to sound grateful, but there was no way food would stay down with butterflies taking on fight night in her stomach. She watched him cross the café. *Calm down.* Danica took several deep breaths. *You just told him you'd move in. He's not going to dump you for not marrying him.*

Blake set the tray on the table and set an iced tea in front of Danica. "One Sweet'N Low, two lemons, extra ice."

Oh, God, please don't break up with me! I love all these little things. Danica took a deep breath. *Shut up and think positive.*

"Remember when we met?" Blake took a bite of his grilled chicken.

Danica rubbed her nose. "How could I forget?" She still got the shivers when she recalled Blake's hand on her arm for the first time, the way her body had responded to his touch, his eyes, his voice, and the way the pain in her bloody nose—which he'd just elbowed—was silent until he'd stolen a glance at a blonde and she'd realized he was just like every other asshole out there. *Only he wasn't. He was so very different.* She pushed away that part of the memory and hung on to the rest. She reached for his hand. "Blake, I think we should talk."

"I know. We should," he said with a confident smile.

"I don't want you to end things with me just because I can't agree to get married right now."

Blake set his sandwich down. "End things? Danica, after all we went through to be together, do you really think I'd end things, just like that?"

"But you want to get married."

"No. I want to marry you. There's a difference. But I don't care if it's next month or ten years from now. I'm not going anywhere."

Her throat thickened.

He reached for both of her hands across the table and narrowed his serious eyes. "Danica Snow, stop worrying about silliness."

She nodded vehemently, unable to find her voice.

"Alyssa and I were doing inventory today and we came across all these boxes of old files. Nothing too interesting, but something that I had forgotten all about. When we'd first opened the business together, we signed a pact."

"A pact? This is about a pact with Dave?" Danica let out a breath she didn't realize she'd been holding.

"Yes, and I know it sounds like we were twelve or something, but it's not really that kind of pact. We didn't know how well the business would do, or if we'd even like running the store, so we made a pact that in five years, if we weren't having fun anymore, we'd sell the business."

"Sounds reasonable. It's been three years, right?" Danica had no idea what that had to do with her, though she was glad he was including her.

"Right, well, it got me thinking. I've been holding on to enough money to buy Dave out of the partnership, just in case he ever wanted out. And I finally got the courage to talk to Sally, because, you know, now that she's had some time to think, we had to figure out what she wanted to do with her half of the store. I could buy her out, or she could remain as fifty-percent owner."

Again, Danica wasn't sure where he was going with the conversation, but at least where it was, it was heading away from the subject of marriage.

"She wants to remain fifty-percent owner." Blake's eyes locked on Danica's. "So, now that I'm not buying her out, I thought maybe I'd hold on to it for a honeymoon. Whenever you're ready, of course. But I know honeymoons are important to women, so I can assure you, we can go anywhere you want." The gleam in Blake's eyes told Danica how much this meant to him.

"That's...wonderful," she said, and wondered if he meant to quietly apply pressure, or if it was really just coincidental. *Stop thinking like a therapist!*

"Yeah?" he asked.

"Yeah. You're so thoughtful. You just blow me away sometimes. Are you sure there isn't something else you want to buy? For yourself? For your store? I mean, I'm not like most women.

That's your money, Blake. You don't need my permission to spend it, and I won't be upset if you do."

"I knew you'd say that. In the therapist side of your mind, which you deny exists, you're wondering if I'm asking you about this so that if I do buy something else with it, you can't be upset about the money not being there for an elaborate honeymoon."

The more he accepted her little idiosyncrasies, the deeper she fell in love with him. He knew she wouldn't want an elaborate honeymoon, or an expensive wedding. Hell, she didn't even care if they lived in either his or her condominium for years to come. She only cared that they were together. *Where is he going with this?*

"That's not going to be an issue," he continued. "You see, I knew you would care about the bigger picture rather than the little picture, so I did buy something."

"Blake—" *Tell me you didn't buy a ring, or pay for a honeymoon!*

"Don't worry. It's not a honeymoon. But you did say you'd move in with me. One of the reasons I can always be honest with you is that you make sound decisions, and I trust your decisions."

She couldn't take her eyes off of him. His thick dark hair needed a trim. Its fullness made him look younger, more carefree. And when she shifted her gaze to his excited green eyes, she wanted to jump up and kiss him right then and there, before he even completed his thoughts.

"You think things through and always give me clear, honest answers. I can count on that, the same way you can count on me never leaving you."

The look Danica always dreamed of—the one where he looked at her like he couldn't imagine ever looking at anyone else, like she was his total focus—made Danica's stomach dip. *You're too good to be true.*

He reached for her hand. "Since you're obviously not going to eat, let's take these to go. I have something to show you."

Chapter Thirty-Eight

"This is great news!" Max jumped up from behind her desk and hugged Chaz. "You'll own it all? So no more worries about Lea sneaking in?"

"Not if I go through with it." Chaz had come into the office after meeting with Cooper, and as he looked around the small warehouse space, the walls stocked high with festival posters, yard signs, and other festival paraphernalia, he knew he was making the right decision.

"Can you afford to buy them both out? We're always scraping by to make ends meet with the festival, Chaz. Where will you get the money?"

"Max—"

Max paced in her jeans shorts and T-shirt. "No, no, you're right. This is none of my business." She spun around with an ear-to-ear grin. "I'm just so happy for you!"

Chaz had to laugh at her enthusiasm. She looked so young with her black Converse and ponytail that he had to remind himself she wasn't eighteen, but twentysomething. How could he not know how old she was? She'd worked with him long enough. He remembered her last birthday, but could not remember her age. *Strange.*

"How old are you Max?"

"Why, 'cause I act like a child?" She laughed.

"No. I just can't remember."

"That's because I never told you." She sat back down at her desk. "What about Lea?"

"Nice change of subject. What about her?"

"What happens now? She called you, so are you calling her back?"

Chaz sat across from her. "After everything we've been through, and what Cooper said? No way. You've got the sponsorships covered, right?"

"Almost," she said. "We're a little low, but I didn't want to say anything because I thought a few more might come through."

"Max."

"Don't worry. I'll get them. I went out on a limb and called some people and asked them to pull any strings they could." Max picked up the phone to call another potential sponsor. "Give me time. I'll get something."

He saw the doubt in Max's eyes, and as much as he hated it, if he had to dip into his trust fund, he'd do it to keep Lea out of their lives. He realized that he could have just used the money that he was using to buy out his partners to sponsor the festival, but that was money that he'd earmarked as a nest egg for security. With Kaylie in his life, he wanted that security, just in case the festival ever tumbled down around him. It gave him a bundle of cash that he'd earned and that wasn't tied up in investments. Using that money for the partnership made much more sense than using it on sponsorships. Ownership was security. *Max will figure this out.* She always took care of things.

Max left a message and when she hung up, the message light flashed on the console. She called voicemail and noted the message. "Chaz!" She jumped up from her seat and ran to him.

"Looks like we've got our sponsor!"

"Who is it? I thought I heard you leave a message."

"I did. It's not them. Take Enterprises? Do you know of them? I'm not sure who they are, but I'll research them and then call them back. They want a banner."

"A banner? That's twenty grand. An unknown is giving us twenty grand? Make sure Lea's not behind it."

Chapter Thirty-Nine

"Are you even going to give me a hint of where we're going?" Danica asked as Blake pulled out of town. "Oh, damn, I forgot to call Camille." She took out her cell phone and dialed Camille on speed dial. "Hey, sorry. I forgot to call back."

Danica listened as Camille filled her in on who was attending the baby shower. She still would have liked to see Kaylie extend an olive branch to her mother at least once before the shower, but she could push only so hard.

"No cancellations? Kaylie's going to be so surprised." She smiled at Blake.

"Nope. Your mom called and she said she was not only coming, but also baking cookies to bring along. She's so damn sweet. My mom would have brought the vodka."

Danica laughed and thought of her mother's recent advice. "Yeah, she's sweet all right. She's smart, too."

"Rub it in, why don't ya?" Camille joked.

"Sorry. What do we have left? What can I do?"

"Get her to the party on time. That's it. Just that one little thing."

"I can handle that. Hey, Camille, I really appreciate all you and the girls are doing. Please tell them I said thank you. I know I kinda left you guys hanging through all of this. I've been feeling so guilty because I've been too tied up with the No Limitz event to help out at all. I owe you big-time."

"No need to feel guilty, but paybacks are hell, so be prepared."

They said goodbye and Danica tucked her phone into her purse. "Hey, why are we headed toward Kaylie's?"

Blake drove up the long mountain road toward Kaylie's and Chaz's chalet. "I have to get something. Do me a favor? There's a file full of stuff I wanted to show you from the store. Can you grab it from the backseat?"

Danica turned around just as Blake turned down a narrow driveway, shaded on both sides by an umbrella of trees.

Danica reached to the floor behind her. "I can't reach it."

"Yes, you can. Just try." Blake couldn't stop grinning as the house came into view. A perfect stretch of lush green grass surrounded slate walkways leading around the little chalet-style home.

Danica threw her hands up and faced forward. "I can't reach—where are we? Whose house is this?"

"I've gotta take a look at a set of antique skis, so come on. No one's home. We'll go around back and use the back door."

"Blake, you can't just traipse into someone else's house. What do you have to look at?"

He was already halfway around the house. Danica looked up at the enormous windows. "Wow, someone loves nature." She followed him down a stone path and around to the back of the house, where the blue sky met the tops of the trees that cascaded away from the house at a slight incline; wildflowers peppered the grassy lawn which met an artistically laid slate patio. Danica gasped at the beauty of it, and her concerns of traipsing on someone else's property fell away. "It's so serene. Look at those blooms." She walked onto the lawn, her fingers trailing along a bed of wildflowers.

Blake stood back and watched her as she spun slowly around, her arms outstretched.

"Can you imagine what this would be like?" She pointed to two Adirondack chairs. "I can just see the owners sitting in those, looking out at the incredibly blue sky."

Blake walked over to one of the chairs and sat down, watching Danica marvel at the view.

Danica turned on him. "Blake, get up. What if they come home?"

"What if they do?"

"Look at those skis and let's go. I don't want the owners to think we're some sort of freaky squatters or something."

Blake took the key from his key chain and opened the back door. "You're such a goof. I have a key. Come on."

Danica followed him inside. "Would you look at those wide planked floors? They must have cost a fortune." She ran her finger along the smooth cherry wood of the bar to their right and then set her eyes upon the luxurious stone fireplace. "We shouldn't be here," she whispered. "Look." She pointed to a bottle of champagne on ice and two wineglasses. "We're interrupting something."

Blake walked over and picked up a glass, filled it with champagne.

"What are you doing?" Danica shot a look at the stairs that led from the basement to the first floor and then glanced back at the open glass doors.

Blake put the slim stemware in her hand and wrapped his hand around hers. "You're always worried about Kaylie, and now that she's having a baby—"

"What? Blake, can't we talk about this in your car?" She spotted antique skis hanging above the fireplace. "Are those the skis? Look, do what you have to do, and let's go."

Blake tried to quell his smile. "Danica, they're my skis. I had them at the shop."

Danica blinked as understanding set in. "Blake? Blake. What's going on?"

"Welcome home," he said.

"Home?" *He bought a house. A house. Blake bought a house. For us.* She didn't know whether to jump for joy or run for the hills.

Blake must have read her contemplation. "Don't get all freaked out. No pressure to get married. I'll wait forever, but with Kaylie having a baby, I know you'll be checking on her all the time, and why drive all the way back into town?"

"Wait, is this the house by Kaylie's?"

His Cheshire cat grin told her everything she needed to know.

"You'll be a mile away from Kaylie."

The trembling started in her legs and slithered like a snake up her middle, down her arms, and finally, up her neck, to her lower lip. "Blake," she whispered. *Can this even be possible? Is anyone really this romantic?*

"Do you like it? I know it's kind of impulsive, but we can afford it. It's the same monthly payment as your condo and my condo together."

"You want me to…"

"No, not sell your condo. Rent it. I know you need time for things, Danica. I know you like to process and mull things over, and selling your condo would mean a real commitment, bigger than a house even. It would leave you no escape route."

"I don't escape. That's Kaylie."

"Okay, that was unfair, but still. It makes it harder to leave if you give it up. You'd have no place to go if things didn't work out, and I know you like to have backup plans, so keep it. Keep the condo. I can afford the house payment on my own. I want us to have a place of our own. Not something filled with our pasts. Danica, I want to build a life with you." He took the stemware from her hands and pulled her in close. "If you hate it, we can stay in the condo. I just put a down payment on it. It's not really ours yet, and if you hate it, we won't buy it. But you'd be a mile from your sister, and you can decorate it however you want."

"However we want."

"However we want." He searched her eyes for an answer.

She took his face between her hands, the stubble on his cheeks tickling her palms. "Blake Carter." Words didn't feel big enough for what she felt. She felt full. Heart, mind, and soul completely one hundred percent, full. She lifted up on her toes and laid her lips on his, kissing him until he kissed her back. She felt herself opening up to him with new depth in a way she'd never before experienced. She didn't weigh the pros and cons. She didn't think about Kaylie or her reaction. She didn't think at all. She pulled back from him, and with the sweet taste of him still on her lips, she said, "Thank you. Thank you for our house."

Chapter Forty

Kaylie shot straight up in bed, her heart racing. She scooted off the mattress and hurried into the nursery. The white crib had been outfitted in delicate pastels of purple, pink, blue, yellow, and green. She ran her finger along the edge of the crib, taking in the gentle yellow on the walls and the soft white shag carpet beneath her bare feet. *Does it look too girly?* Although she and Chaz had chosen to be surprised by the gender of the baby, Kaylie was sure she was carrying a girl. She could just feel it. Every time she touched her stomach or felt the baby kick, she secretly heard the nickname Sassy. Surely, that counts as motherly instincts. She felt like she'd forgotten something. She searched the sweetly decorated room, trying to place what major item she might have missed. She knew they'd get smaller items during the shower, but something felt off.

She touched the Disney mobile above the bed, watching it sway back and forth. Chaz's hand landed warm and heavy on her shoulder.

"It's almost time," she said.

"Can you believe it?"

She went to the changing table and opened the drawers beneath. Empty. Empty! How could she have forgotten clothes, of all things? She had been so busy mourning her career and figuring out her life, she hadn't bought any baby clothes yet. Her baby would be naked!

"We need to go shopping." Anxiety rushed her words.

Chaz wiped the sleep haze from his eyes and sat in the rocker. "Sure. Now?"

Kaylie sat on his lap and kissed his forehead, then laid her cheek against it. "No, but the baby needs clothes."

"We've got a few more weeks. Don't worry." He ran his hand over her belly, then bent down and said, "Hear that baby? You can't come out till we have clothes for you."

Kaylie laughed. "I'm serious. Just a few things. Onesies, sleepers." She looked around and then said excitedly, "I forgot receiving blankets. And I know there are things we need, like the little sucker thing for when she gets a stuffy nose, a humidifier…"

"This must be what they call nesting, right? Isn't that what your Lamaze coach called it?"

"Maybe."

"Today's your big gig. Are you still excited to be singing at Danica's dance?"

Kaylie got up and reached for his hand. "I'm excited and nervous." They walked hand in hand through the living room, out the patio doors. The sun was already shining. Dew sparkled on the tips of the grass. Kaylie shivered with the morning chill, and then sat in the swing. "Wow, it's gonna be beautiful today."

Chaz sat beside her. "You asked Dr. Lasco about this, right? You're not going to go into labor while you're singing or anything, are you?"

"I called. She said it's fine. If I get tired or feel anything funny, then she said to stop. But I'll be fine. Tons of women are exercising all the way through their pregnancies, and look at Angelina Jolie. She piloted a plane! That had to be even more dangerous than something like singing."

"I can't wait to hear what you've written."

Kaylie brought his hand to her lips and kissed the back of it. "Every song I wrote was written for you and her." She laid their hands on her belly.

"Or him," Chaz said.

"Yeah, but we both know that's not going to happen. I mean, I'd love a boy or a girl, but I can tell it's a girl. I can feel it."

Chaz's head fell back as he let out a feigned sigh. "Two women in my house? Estrogen overload."

They headed inside, and Kaylie made pancakes while Chaz cut up cantaloupe and strawberries. It dawned on Kaylie that their mornings alone were coming to an end, and then she waited. She waited for that familiar feeling to encroach, the jealousy she'd been trying to ignore but couldn't deny. A tingle of worry that when the baby was born, she'd be thrust to the background of Chaz's life.

"Kay, they're gonna burn."

"Oh, sorry. I was off in space somewhere." She pushed away the worry and feigned a smile as she put the pancakes on the plate. Chaz made a face.

"Mickey Mouse pancakes?"

She hadn't even realized she'd done it. In the center of Chaz's plate were two big ears and the signature Mickey Mouse head.

He put his arm around her waist and pulled her close. "See? You're already the best mommy ever."

The gentle nag that had been haunting her appeared in the form of a tickle in her throat. *Damn it.* Did all women worry about being left behind when their baby arrived? She made a mental note to talk to Dr. Marsden about that.

"What did Cooper say about that woman?" She couldn't bring herself to even say her name.

"She can't touch the festival." He fiddled with the edges of his boxer shorts.

Kaylie saw in his eyes that he was holding something back. "That's good, right?"

Chaz nodded. "Yup."

She felt, more than saw, his body recoil. "Chaz, is there something else? It feels like there's more."

He lifted his eyes and met her gaze. Kaylie held her breath. "Just tell me."

He looked away, then down at his hands, which he'd clasped tightly together. His jaw clenched.

"Chaz." Her voice rose, and her body followed. She stood in front of him, arms crossed above her belly.

"It's not anything to worry about, Kaylie. It's just something that I have to figure out."

"Well, if you have to figure it out, and it has to do with *her*, then…" She turned away.

Chaz was on his feet and by her side, his hands on her shoulders. "It's not her. I promise. I have to tell you something, but I don't want it to change things, and I'm afraid it will."

Kaylie didn't want to overreact to things anymore. She tried to hide her worry, and she knew she'd failed when Chaz brushed her hair from her face with the most loving, caring, careful look in his eyes.

"You know how I said that I had…that I'm pretty well off?"

"Yeah? Why? You're not? Because I don't care one single bit about money. We could lose the house and the cars and live with Danica, for all I care." She put her hands on his strong hips and looked into his eyes. "Chaz, whatever it is, as long as you haven't been with another woman, I can take it. We can take it."

He leaned down and kissed her gently, then looked out over the mountains. The tension in his body dissipated beneath her palms. "I'm not broke. I'm actually just the opposite."

Kaylie shook her head. "I don't understand."

"Kaylie, we have more money than we could ever spend."

"More money than we can spend? Now, that's a problem I can deal with." The relief of there not being any more hidden issues—like that Carmichael woman—brought a smile to Kaylie's lips. Kaylie dropped her hands from his hips. "That's what you were worried about?"

He nodded. "Money changes people, and it's not just the money. It's where it originally came from."

"Hold on. I may need to sit for this. Can we go out to the swing? I think I need fresh air." Once outside, she lowered herself awkwardly onto the swing. "Did you rob a bank? Run a Ponzi scheme?" Her fingers clenched a wooden slat on the swing.

Chaz laughed. "I almost wish I did." He sat beside her and told her about the trust fund that had been left to him and of how hard he'd worked in the last ten years to create his own wealth and how he'd been successful.

"Wait. Let me get this straight. You're embarrassed to have been left a trust fund. You've worked your butt off to make something of yourself, separate from the fund…and?"

"Sounds stupid when you say it like that, but yeah." He'd told her about the teasing he endured at prep school.

Kaylie could feel her heart swell. "You poor thing. That must have been awful, especially since you already felt bad about it."

Chaz pulled his shoulders back and sat up straight. "Nah. Guys take that crap all the time."

Kaylie bit her lower lip and touched his arm, seeing something more behind his eyes. "You can tell me," she urged.

"Okay, yeah, it sucked. I hated it, but it made me push harder to become successful, and I've grown the festival to be three times as big as it was when I took it over. I invested well, and the money we live on is money that I earned based on those investments."

"So, what's the problem?" She understood that he was uncomfortable living off family money, but he still seemed to be holding something back.

"Money changes people, Kaylie. Suddenly we stop worrying about how we'll pay for things and we start spending money like it's water. Why do you think I hadn't bought out the festival partners in all these years?"

"I guess I thought things were fine, so why rock the boat?"

"Yeah, that's the real reason, but in the back of my head, I didn't want to do that until I had earned enough money to live on and buy out the festival. Me. Not my family."

"So, you didn't even really need Lea's sponsorship?" Her pulse quickened.

"I told you, we live on what I earn. We need the sponsorships or I'll have to dig into the family money."

"But you have money to buy out your partners, and that money could have been used instead of her sponsorship." Kaylie felt a lump tightening in her throat. "You chased her to Hawaii, and you didn't have to."

"Kaylie." His voice was stern, but his eyes were soft and pleading. "It was a choice, yes, to not use the money we live on for the sponsorship money. I made that choice so we would have security. It was a good choice. It was the right choice."

She didn't understand. "But...you're using that same money—our security money—to buy out the partners."

"Yes." He took her hand. "So that I can ensure that we are never, ever bothered by Lea again, and we'll never have to worry about anyone trying to buy it out from under us in the future." He scrubbed his hand over his face. "Maybe I should have used that money for sponsorships all along, but I didn't because I never thought that Lea would be as crazy as she was. Had I known, hell, it wouldn't have been a question."

"So, if you're using our nest egg, are we broke? I mean, I know we're not broke, but do we have enough money to live on, so you don't have to touch the trust fund money?" Kaylie had no patience for balance sheets and fine details, and because of that, Chaz handled their household finances.

"Yes, we'll just be careful while I rebuild that nest. What makes me nervous money-wise is much different from most people. We have more money—money that I have earned— than we'll need."

"Okay," she said, relieved, though moderately confused. "So why does the money have to change things?"

This time she saw the answer in the arch of his brow, the lifting of the corner of his mouth.

"You think I'll change. It's not that you're worried about you changing, but me." She turned away.

"Not just you, Kay. Anyone. It's a natural inclination to worry less and spend more when you know money isn't an issue."

He didn't trust her? Or maybe he didn't trust anyone. Kaylie spun around, shooting spears with her glare. How materialistic did he think she was? Then she thought of Dr. Marsden and having to relay the conversation to her. Then Danica's calm, serious eyes made an appearance, and Kaylie took a deep breath. What would Danica say? The anger momentarily ceased.

"Kaylie? Aren't you going to say something?"

Whatever she said, she had to be comfortable saying it to either Dr. Marsden or Danica, because whatever she said would either hurt or heal this moment. Kaylie wanted to start acting appropriately in all situations, and the way she was taking hold of her dramatic side was to remind herself that she'd have to answer to another person. Danica was a good reminder, because Danica called her on every little bit of drama she created. She just needed a minute to pull her thoughts together. She held up a finger to quiet Chaz, then stood and stared out at the mountain.

Kaylie tried to think of what questions Dr. Marsden might pose to her. Will the money change you? *I do love to shop.* Will it affect your decisions about strollers, baby clothes, cars, schools? She paced. *Would it make a difference? How could it not?*

She felt Chaz's eyes on her, and a fleeting panic coursed through her.

Of course the money mattered. It was stupid to assume it wouldn't play into their lives.

It was Danica's voice that rang through her mind, pulling her panic back down to a manageable flutter. Would she love Chaz if he had no money? If he was in a terrible accident and lost both legs? Would she care? Would all the money in the world make her leave him? Most important, if he cheated on her, would all the money in the world make her stay? Kaylie knew the answers. If she met a handsome Donald Trump tomorrow and Chaz was broke, she wouldn't stray, and if he cheated, nothing could make her stay. Maybe money didn't have to be anything more than what it had been for him all along—a safety net, of sorts. *Can't we just pretend it doesn't exist? Can I?* Obviously he could, and had.

He lied to me. She wondered what Danica might say to that.

He was protecting their relationship? He's telling her now, before they're married. That was worth something.

She turned back toward Chaz, his shoulders slumped forward and his head hung low. Kaylie walked over and sat beside him.

"I knew this would happen," he admitted.

"There's only one way I can honestly say this will not affect us."

Chaz looked up with hope in his eyes.

"You can't tell me how much money we have, and we have to promise to live how we have been living. The family money doesn't come into play."

"That's so much easier to say than to live by. Believe me. There have been a million times that I wanted to tap into that fountain."

"But you didn't." She took his hand.

"My pride held me back. And with a child, maybe everything changes. You've seen those spoiled kids with everything handed to them."

"I have, and you have my permission to kick me in the head if I raise a child with a silver spoon in her mouth." She relaxed into him. "I hated those girls when I was growing up, and that's enough to keep me from doing that to our child." She realized that she meant it. All of it. "You know, if I hadn't been forced to work my way through school, I'm not sure I would have become the person I am." She laughed. "Not the neurotic pregnant woman, but the prepregnant confident woman who wasn't afraid of going into dark places or following my heart. I know I lived a pretty wild life, but it's probably better than being a stuck-up snob, right?"

Chaz laughed. "I guess. But, Kaylie, when we're deciding on public schools or private—"

Kaylie held her hand up. "Don't even go there. No kid of mine is going to prep school. I know you went, and that's all well and good, but I didn't, and I'm not sure I would want that degree of separation from the—for a lack of a better word—normal kids around here."

"Okay, no prep schools."

"And no diamond earrings at three years old, either. She can wait till she's twelve, like I did."

"So now you're old-fashioned?" he teased.

"I don't know. I just know that I want this baby to be normal, whatever that is. She'll be spoiled enough with so many aunties hanging around. I want our baby to know that she can do anything in the world based on her own personality and abilities. I don't want to raise a selfish, self-absorbed child. I want to raise someone like you."

"I want the baby to be just like you."

"No, you don't. Trust me. I'm really insecure. I never thought I was, but I worry that once the baby comes, I'm gonna fall to the wayside, and that's totally not normal." She laughed, but inside, she'd said the hardest thing she'd ever said aloud.

"Is that what you worry about? Without you, there'd be no baby. I can live without this baby, Kaylie. But I'd never want to live without you."

"Does that mean you don't want the baby?"

"Oh my God. You're killing me."

She nudged him. "I'm kidding. I know what you meant." *Go away little naggy voice. Be gone.*

Chapter Forty-One

Danica sat at one of the picnic tables on the lawn of the barn, her hands wrapped around a half-empty large coffee. She'd left a voicemail at the center for Sally to arrange for some of the kids and/or parents to help direct parking. So many parents had offered to help, she knew it wouldn't be an issue. Then she'd headed to the site to make sure the lights had been hung and the tables set out. The lights were strung properly, but there weren't enough tables and, although her insides were clawing for her to call the rental company, she knew it was an overreaction. They had hours before the event. She lay back on the bench and stared up at the promising blue sky, reminding herself that it was okay to relax a little. The tables would show up, or they wouldn't, and if they didn't, the event could still go on.

She'd worked hard over the last few months to let go of the controlling side of her personality and allow herself to be more spontaneous and unwound. *Unwound.* That's exactly how she was starting to feel. It was one thing to be relaxed, but another altogether to let her fears go. She'd never admit it out loud—to anyone—but Blake was right. If she were to sell her condo, she'd have no place to go if things went bad. The fate of her parents' marriage kept poking its ugly head into her thoughts.

Blake's not Dad. She felt like she was talking to Kaylie. "And I'm not Mom," she said as she sat up. She wasn't her mother. She was headstrong and voiced her opinions, and Blake respected them. She was confident and had a career. Two, if she chose to! Danica paced the field, mentally ticking off the things that were different about her and Blake's relationship from that of her parents.

He adores me and considers my feelings when making major decisions (rent the condo!).

He is honest.

We have common interests.

We have helped each other grow, and aren't stagnated by each other either personally or in our careers. Oh, yes! That's a big one! Dad didn't help Mom grow. Ever.

The sound of tires on the gravel parking lot interrupted her thoughts. Danica walked back across the property as Blake opened the door of his SUV. She jogged over.

"Hey, what're you doing here?"

He kissed her and then twirled her around. "Did you think I'd let you stress out all by yourself? I went to the shop and Alyssa's going to handle things for a bit. She's got it covered tonight, too, so we're good."

He gives of himself for me and to me.

"Great!" she said with a little clap. Everything was falling into place, and Danica couldn't keep the smile from her lips or temper the racing of her excited heart. "Come on. I'll show you where things are taking place."

They walked toward the entrance to the barn.

"How are you going to get people not to just come around the back?"

"Some of the kids have volunteered to direct traffic in the lot, and they're putting up one of those ropes so people will come around to the front."

"And who's taking tickets, or whatever needs to be done?"

Danica stared at the enormous barn doors.

"Danica?"

She covered her mouth. "Crap. I forgot. The event runs on donations, so I just assumed that people would toss money into the box and come in. It's not like we're in some high-risk area where we have to worry about them taking the money. And Sally's got someone covering the waivers at a table just inside. I can ask that person to watch the front."

"I'll do it," Blake offered.

"No. Really?"

"Of course. What else would I do? Hang around and do nothing?"

Danica hadn't even thought of Blake helping. She was just glad he was going to attend. She stood on her tippy-toes and kissed him. "Thank you. That would be great."

They walked the property, and by the time they came back around to the front, the roar of trucks could be heard in the distance.

"Hey," Danica said as she spun around and faced Blake, stopping him in his tracks. "You..." She touched his chest. "Are buying *us* a house. And I'm not freaking out about it," she said proudly.

He kissed her nose. "I know. I'm so proud of you. My little girl found her big girl panties."

By the time the trucks showed up with the rest of the tables and chairs, Danica was ready for whatever the day held.

Back at the center, cars lined the street. *Damn.* She'd forgotten about the volunteers meeting. She rushed through the front doors carrying her purse in one hand and an empty coffee cup in the other.

"You must be Danica."

Danica didn't recognize the petite blonde with the beady eyes and perfectly matched blouse and slacks. "Yes."

"Trisha." She extended her hand.

Trisha? Trisha! Oh, God, Dave's other woman. "Trisha, hi." Danica fumbled with the empty coffee cup, dropping it on Sally's desk, and then caught it as it fell off the edge. "Sorry. Crazy morning." She shook her hand, stealing a look toward the back, wondering where Sally was.

"Thanks for letting me help out. Sally said you needed all the hands you could get, and with Michelle and Chase carrying on and all, it seemed the least I could do."

"Michelle and Chase?" *What on earth is going on?*

"Well, yeah. They're so cute. They text all the time, and I don't think they know that I know."

"Michelle and Chase?"

"Yeah, I know. What are the chances, right? I guess I hadn't remembered Allure being such a small town." She walked with a bounce in her step toward the front door. "I'll see you tonight. Thanks again. I'm really glad we've finally met."

A handful of adults and children came into the lobby from the hallway. She'd missed the entire meeting. The voices pulled Danica from her stunned state in the middle of the floor.

"Hey, Danica."

Danica waved at the teens. "Hi." She scanned the kids for Michelle, but she was nowhere to be found.

"Missed you at the meeting," Gage said as he came to her side.

Michelle and Chase? Then why did Rusty look so upset when Michelle was talking to Brad? "Sorry, I was at the barn. How'd it go?" She kept her eyes trained on the hallway.

"Great. As long as Kaylie doesn't go into labor, this should be a really fun night. I think the kids are really looking forward to it." Gage leaned over Danica and looked down the hall.

"Who are you looking for?"

"Michelle and Sally."

"They're in the game room. Is everything okay?"

Danica was already heading down the hall. She stood outside the game room watching Michelle and Sally putting the Ping-Pong paddles and pool cues away. Michelle had been wearing shorts instead of her black jeans lately, and Danica noticed, as she turned and smiled at Sally, that she'd done something different with her hair, too. It was still jet black and hung straight down to the middle of her back, but the bangs didn't fall in her face. She had them brushed back, and her smile reached all the way to the rosy puffs of her cheeks.

"Some people would call you a stalker."

Danica socked Gage in the arm. "I'm not stalking. I'm watching." She pointed at Michelle. "She was my Little Sister in the Big Sister program. Gosh, it's been a few weeks since we've done anything together."

"Michelle? She's great. Everyone really likes her. Her mom, too."

It wasn't Michelle whom Gage was watching. Danica noticed the way his eyes tracked Sally's every move. "Yeah, Sally's pretty great, too."

Gage handed Danica a piece of paper. "Uh, here. This is a list of the volunteers, phone numbers of the vendors, everything for tonight."

"I've got this already," she said, and watched his eyes return to Sally. "Hey, did you guys meet for breakfast again to go over the details?"

"What? No, not today."

No wonder you look like a lonely puppy. "Gage?"

"Yeah." His eyes were trained on Sally.

"Do you know if Michelle is dating anyone?"

He shrugged. "She hangs out with Rusty a lot, and Brad comes to see her. My money's on Brad, because Rusty sort of hangs back, you know? I'm not sure he's got what it takes to make a move."

"It's tough to be a teen." *Or an adult lusting after a coworker.* She eyed Gage as he practically drooled over Sally.

At three thirty, they locked the center doors and agreed to meet at the barn by five. The event started at seven thirty, leaving just enough time for Danica to stop by Kaylie's and see if she needed help. She considered calling her instead, but with everything Kaylie had been through, she thought it was best to see her in person.

Her cell phone rang, and she snagged it from the passenger seat.

"Hey, Mom."

"Hi, honey. I just thought I'd see how you and Kaylie were doing. She still hasn't returned my calls."

Danica sighed. "I'm sorry, Mom. You know how she gets when she's upset. I'm heading there now. I'll remind her to call you."

"Your event is tonight, right?"

"Yeah." It had been so long since Danica and her mother

had taken a real interest in each other's life that she had to remind herself that her mother might be vying for an invitation. The luncheon the other day had been a step, hadn't it? It was silly, really, the distance that had somehow formed between them all, like a cockeyed triangle where the angles didn't meet very well, and when they did, it was awkward and pokey.

"Hey, Mom, why don't you and Patrick come by tonight? We'll all be there, and Kaylie's singing, so it'll be a chance for you to see what it is that I'm doing and hang with me and Kaylie. Spend some time with Blake and Chaz."

"I'm not sure. It's a young event, isn't it?"

"Mom, come on. It'll be fun."

She imagined her mother creasing her brow, her finger on her lips as she thought through the potential scenarios.

"Mom?"

"Okay. I'll ask Patrick, and if he's free, we'll be there."

"Great!" When she hung up the phone, she knew she'd made the right decision. They were a family, and no matter how hard it might be for Kaylie, it was time to start moving forward.

Kaylie answered the door in a short yellow bathrobe that barely covered her thighs, her hair piled high on her head, secured with a rhinestone hair clip.

"Wow, aren't you the sexy mama?"

"More like the walking whale," Kaylie joked. "Come on in. What're you doing here?"

They went into the living room, where Danica studied the photos of Kaylie and Chaz on the mantel. She'd seen the photos dozens of times, but now, as she looked at their eager, excited faces, she wondered if they'd ever be those same carefree people after they had a baby to care for. "Are you nervous?" she asked.

"Not really nervous. I mean, I know how to sing in front of a group. More, I don't know. I think I feel out of practice. It's actually been a while."

Danica nodded. "I really appreciate you singing, and you'll be great."

Kaylie put her hand behind her and lowered herself onto the couch. Danica sat beside her and reached for her belly.

"How's the evil spawn?"

"You're not going to call her that when she's born, right? That could hurt a girl's ego."

"How about if it's a boy?" Danica joked.

Kaylie sneered at her.

"I just want to give you fair warning. Mom's coming tonight. Probably with Patrick."

"What? Danica, why would you do that?"

"Chill, would ya? It's time, Kaylie. We all have to move on, and you can't blame Mom for everything."

"I know I can't, and I'm trying not to. It takes me a while to get from knowing to acting on. You know that about me," Kaylie said honestly.

"Yeah, I guess I do." Danica heard Chaz talking in his office. "How're things?" she whispered, nodding in Chaz's direction.

"Great."

"Great, really? Or great, sarcastic? I have a hard time determining which sometimes."

"Great really." Kaylie pushed to her feet. "Wanna help me get ready?"

Danica followed her into the bedroom, where Kaylie had her clothes laid out on the king-sized bed. Spike heels lay on the pillow.

"Kaylie, really? You're almost ready to pop, and you're gonna wear those? What if you fall or something?" She touched her finger to the tip of the stiletto and pulled it back. "Dangerous."

"I'm not gonna wear them."

"Now you're thinking."

"I was going to, but then I realized, when else can I ever be comfortable while performing? Pregnancy is a great excuse not to wear killer heels." She bent down and when she stood back up, a pair of low-heeled black shoes swung from her index finger.

"Those look like mine."

"They are. I borrowed them when I stayed at your house. Who'd have ever thought I would be borrowing *these* from you?"

"You're such a snark," Danica teased, and flopped on the bed.

"Am I? A snark?" Kaylie asked as she slipped her dress over her head and tugged it down past her belly.

"Sort of."

Kaylie turned around for Danica to zip her dress.

"Where did you get that? You look like a pregnant model, Kay. My God, you really are stunning." The navy fabric clung to every curve of her life-affirming figure. The neckline scooped to the crest of her ample breasts, and her slim arms and fit legs gave her the appearance of a girl playing dress up with a fake baby bump.

"Maternity Road." She sat down next to Danica. "I don't want to be a snark," she said. "I hate snobby girls."

"You're not snobby. Snarky is different. It's…you. Fun, witty."

Kaylie smiled. "Good."

They went into the bathroom and Kaylie applied her makeup. "How's your licorice stash these days?"

Licorice—Danica's after-sex go-to snack. "Delicious," she gloated.

Kaylie's eyes lit up. "Yeah?"

"Oh, yeah," Danica said with a wiggle of her eyebrows. "Kay, how would you feel if I lived closer?"

"What do you mean?"

"Would you mind?"

Kaylie stopped applying her mascara and turned worried eyes on Danica. "Did something happen between you and Blake?"

"Nothing bad. Um. He…" Danica ran her finger in circles on the countertop. "He's sort of buying that house down the road."

Kaylie put the mascara brush down and leaned on the sink. "Shut up!"

Danica smiled, shrugged.

Kaylie squealed so loudly that Chaz came running into the room. Kaylie wrapped her arms around Danica. "We're gonna be neighbors!" she squealed.

"Great! Who?" Chaz asked, taking in his dancing wife and soon-to-be sister-in-law.

Danica pulled herself from Kaylie's grasp. "Us. Blake put in an offer on the house down the road."

"Fantastic!" Chaz hugged Danica. "Congratulations."

"Listen, you guys, if it's too close, or suffocates you, just tell me before he settles, please. I can take it."

"Nonsense. It's gonna be great," Chaz assured her.

"So great!" Kaylie confirmed.

Chaz excused himself so that he could get ready for the evening, and Kaylie finished putting on her makeup, already making plans for future barbeques and movie nights.

"I'm not really a movie night girl, Kay."

"I know, but you will be when our little one is born. You'll want to see her." Kaylie grabbed Danica's hand and led her to the nursery.

"You have such a knack for color. It looks amazing." Danica touched the soft stuffed bear in the corner of the crib.

"We're rich," Kaylie blurted out.

"Rich, like blessed?"

"Rich, Danica," she whispered. Then she grabbed Danica's arm and dragged her to the corner of the room. "Rich, as in more money than we could ever spend."

"What do you mean?"

"Chaz has a trust fund. He doesn't use it, but it's there."

"Kaylie, that's wonderful, right?" Danica eyes bounced across Kaylie's eyes. "Wait. You're not smiling. What's wrong?"

"We're not going to use it. Ever. We're going to live like we do now. Chaz makes plenty of money, and so do I, when I'm singing. He's sensitive about having money, so don't tell anyone."

Danica nodded. "Oh." Her jaw dropped as understanding shone in her eyes. "Kaylie, can you do that? You like to shop, and eat out, and…Oh, God, this is big, Kaylie. Can you do this?"

"Not only can I totally do this, but I will do this. I really don't care about money, and I'm just going to go on like I never knew it existed. I mean, I do like to shop and to go to nice restaurants, but we always had enough for that. I didn't miss it before. Why should it matter now? It's not like I'll change my behavior because of it." Kaylie paused.

Danica watched her intently. "Kaylie, money does weird things to people."

"That's what he said." Kaylie sighed. "I realized today that I don't care if he has money or not."

Danica took her by the shoulders. "Look at me, Kaylie, and tell me honestly what you are thinking."

Kaylie looked into her sister's eyes, and she felt as if she were on the edge of a precipice: twentysomething Kaylie on one side, grown-up Kaylie on the other. If she failed, she'd fall into an abyss of a lonely, meaningless life. "I'm thinking that I love him and that I hate snobby kids, and that I might need some reminding at times, when I long for something expensive. But overall, I'm thinking that I'm so thankful I didn't lose Chaz when I walked out, and no amount of money in the world could take his place."

Danica continued staring.

"Danica, I mean it."

She nodded. "I actually think you do."

Chaz popped his head in and Danica jumped away from Kaylie. "Did you tell her yet?" Chaz asked.

"No, what?" Kaylie muttered.

"Tell? No, we were talking—"

He looked from Kaylie to Danica, then back again. Chaz stepped into the room and crossed his arms as Kaylie dropped her eyes and Danica followed suit.

"Yes, we're rich. Incredibly, insanely rich."

The girls laughed.

"Sorry, she did tell me," Danica admitted.

"I'm sorry. I just wanted support." Kaylie bit her lower lip.

Chaz came to her side and put his arm around her shoulder. "Danica, she is going to need your support. I think Kaylie has every intention to ignore the money, but money has a way of sending out a scent that's hard to ignore. There'll be times when she needs you."

Danica shook her head. "You must really love her."

Chaz nodded, kissed the top of Kaylie's head.

"Why did you even tell her?"

"I didn't want to start our life together with a lie."

Kaylie watched Danica bring her hands together underneath her chin, and she knew that if Danica had ever doubted Chaz, he'd just won her over.

Chapter Forty-Two

Colorful lights glistened along the trees and the ridges and rafters of the barn, giving the evening a magical feel. Two adult volunteers worked the parking area and kept the kids from running past the ropes and into the back of the barn, where the refreshments were. Blake greeted the guests at the front of the barn, where a big banner hung from the high doorframe; "No Limitz" was written in funky letters, matching the center's logo.

Danica stood beside Sally, listening to Kaylie sing about a man who saved her from herself. She sang with such passion that, combined with the introspective and emotional words, it brought tears to Danica's eyes. Kaylie looked at Chaz as she hit the high notes and scanned the audience, pointing to different teen boys, as if every word was meant specifically for them, when her voice turned raspy in all the right places.

"She's incredible," Sally said, her shoulders moving in beat to the music.

"I know, right? It's easy to forget how talented she is, with all the drama that seems to follow her around." Pride filled Danica's heart.

"Your sister has some lungs on her," Gage said from behind them.

"Yeah, she does," Danica said, then made up an excuse and

left the two of them alone. She headed outside, where Nancy and Trisha were talking beside the refreshment table. She spotted Michelle standing beside Chase, each with a cup of punch; beside them were two groups of teenagers, each moving to the music, drinking punch, and laughing.

Danica went to the refreshment table and picked up a cookie. "How's it going?" she asked Michelle's mom, Nancy, and Trisha.

"Great. The kids are having a ball. That group of kids there must be the cool kids, because everyone seems to flock around them." Trisha wore white capris, a yellow tank top, and a set of matching flip-flops with big fabric flowers above the toes. On anyone else, they might have looked over-the-top, but the way Trisha carried her small frame, with her head held high and a ready smile on her lips, they looked smart.

Danica watched the kids and then turned back to Trisha. "I'm sorry if I seemed rude this morning."

Trisha swatted the air. "Don't be silly. I'm Dave's other woman, so to speak. I get it." She laughed a pleasant, sweet laugh.

Danica understood why Sally was comfortable with her. She wasn't threatening or intimidating in the least. She was quite pleasant. "Nancy, I'm so glad you came out to help. You look great."

"Thanks, I'm almost one year sober." Nancy crossed her fingers and held them up beside her smile.

"That's great news, and Michelle seems so happy. How's Nola? She couldn't come?" Danica would have to visit Michelle's grandmother sometime soon. She'd been so good to Michelle while her mother was in rehab.

"Nola's doing great. She wanted to be here, but it's her bridge night, and after Michelle and I moved back in together, I think she realized how much time she'd been missing out on with her own friends. I'll tell her you said hello."

Danica thought of her mother, who had texted her to say that she wasn't feeling very well, and she was sorry that she would miss the event. It made Danica happy to know her mother was creating a fulfilling life. "Thanks. I appreciate that." Danica watched Brad walk over to Michelle and talk with her. Rusty couldn't hide his dislike of the situation. He was practically breathing down the guy's neck. Chase, on the other hand, was happily drinking his punch and listening to the music while they talked.

Once she realized that everyone was taken care of, Danica went to find Blake. She couldn't help but feel good about how things were going. Everyone was smiling and having fun. She gave Kaylie a thumbs-up as she passed the makeshift stage. Kaylie was already on another song, something having to do with naughty and nice. Danica hoped none of the parents would complain about the lyrics. Could she be held responsible for inappropriate music? Another thing to put on her to-do list.

Blake leaned against the front wall of the barn, his long legs crossed at the ankle. Danica felt her breath hitch. *Damn, how long will his looks do this to me?* Her eyes dragged slowly from his dark, sensuous eyes, which were scanning the parking lot, unaware of her presence, to his slim waist and her favorite pair of Levi's—the dark ones that were tight in all the right places. He wore a pair of black boots, which only heightened his sexiness.

"Are you going to just drink me in, or are you going to come over here and actually talk to me?"

Jesus. He saw me? How the hell? Flustered, Danica shook off her embarrassment. She sidled up to him and whispered, "I was afraid you might elbow me again if I came too close."

In the next breath, his arms were around her waist and he was backing her up against the barn. "I'll elbow you, all right," he teased, lowering his lips to hers.

Danica scanned the entranceway. She realized they were tucked into a dark area and closed her eyes. Her limbs relaxed as they kissed the noise of the party away. When Blake pulled back, she felt like a teenager, kissed for the first time. Her mind was useless, a foggy mess of hormones and lust.

"Wanna sneak out into the woods?" Blake asked.

"Yes," she said, and then quickly added, "No."

The din of the party grew louder. Blake leaned down to kiss her again, and a shout pulled Danica from his arms.

"What the hell was that?" She and Blake ran into the barn. The crowd converged just beyond the back doors.

Gage's voice boomed above the music. "That's enough!"

The music came to an abrupt stop as Danica sped by, tearing past the open doors and through the crowd of murmuring kids and wide-eyed parents. In the center of the crowd, Brad lay on the ground with a bloody nose. Gage stood behind Rusty, his arms wrapped around Rusty's forearms, trapping him. Michelle reached for Rusty and he turned away. His chest rose and fell with each angry breath.

"What's going on?" Danica demanded. She fell to her knees beside Brad and asked him if he was okay.

He nodded silently, and Danica turned on Rusty. "What happened here?"

No one answered.

"Someone's gonna tell me what went on here," she said angrily. What a nightmare. Her first event and there was a fight? She felt hot, angry tears burn the corners of her eyes and the harsh stares of the crowd around her.

Sally's nervous, embarrassed voice broke through the silence.

"Rusty!" She said to Gage, "I'll take him home." Then she turned her mortified face to Danica. "I'm so sorry." She lifted her eyes to the rest of the crowd. "I'm so sorry." She took Rusty by the arm. He shrugged her off and stalked off toward the parking lot.

Gage helped Brad up, as he watched Sally and Rusty climb into their car. "Should I go with her? He seemed really angry."

Danica tried to think. What would Sally want? She had no idea how close she and Gage had become, or if Sally would be too embarrassed to even talk to him. She erred on the side of caution. "I think you'd better stick around. She'll call if she needs us."

"Okay, everyone, it's just a little tiff, that's all," Blake said to the crowd. "You know how kids are." He tried to lighten the mood, but parents were already guiding their kids toward the doors. He caught Chaz's attention and asked Kaylie to play if she was up to it.

Kaylie sang a slow tune laced with emotion. Two adults stopped by the exit and turned to watch her. Even the teenagers who had been huddled together were drawn closer by the husky voice that filled the barn. She sang of the weather, it seemed, something about hot and cold; then the band broke into an upbeat tune and Kaylie sang about dancing in the rain and riding on a train. Smiles came over the adults' faces. Kids began to dance to the beat of the music, and more guests filtered back into the barn from the parking lot. Danica let out a sigh of relief as she and Brad walked down the property.

"I'm really sorry, Danica. I didn't mean to cause any trouble." Brad's hands were shaking.

"I didn't see what happened. Why did he hit you? Did you provoke him?" She watched Brad's eyes for a hint of untruth. She had no idea what to expect. Rusty could be a bit of a hothead. She knew that from what Sally had said about how Rusty acted right after Dave had died, but she thought he'd moved past that.

She looked back at the barn and saw Michelle watching them. Chase and Trisha were off to the side, talking head-to-head. Danica assumed Trisha was also trying to figure out what had transpired.

Brad wiped the remaining blood from his nose. "I don't know. I was talking to Michelle and some other kids, and then someone said something, and the next thing I knew, I was being punched."

"Who said what?"

He shrugged. "I really have no idea."

"Brad, were you hitting on Michelle? I know she's really cute and really nice, but I think she's seeing Chase."

"Chase?" He looked back up at the barn.

"I don't really know. This is all kind of hearsay."

"Whatever. Look, I don't know what set him off, and I'm really sorry. All I did was ask Michelle if she was going to join the ski club this year. I told her it would be cool if we could ski down Little Hellion. My friends have done it and—"

Shit. "Brad, Rusty's father died there last year."

"Shit. Sorry," he said, then ran his hand through his hair. "I had no idea."

"He probably thought you were taking a cheap shot at him or something. I don't know." Danica was glad she hadn't told Gage to go with Sally. God only knew what she'd be dealing with tonight. "Listen, Little Hellion is named that for a reason. Please be careful. I'm not sure it's really safe for kids." She saw the creasing of his brow, and she knew she was overstepping her bounds. His parents could deal with the ski slope. She'd warned him, and he was a smart kid. Hopefully he'd think twice about going up there. Right now Danica had to deal with the issue at hand. She took another good, long look at Brad. He wasn't bruised or limping, which was a relief. "Are you hurt at all?"

"No."

"Okay, then you go ahead back and have fun. I'm really sorry this happened. I'll call your parents and let them know."

"You don't have to do that," he said.

"Yes, I do." Her first parental confrontation. *This should be fun.*

He headed back toward the barn. Danica watched Michelle come to his side and sling her arm around his shoulder. Chase wasn't far behind. She headed back toward the barn to talk with Trisha and Gage.

"How's the damage control going?" she asked them.

"Chase said Brad said something about Little Hellion and Rusty went off. Poor kid. He's carrying around his father's death like something he has to protect." Trisha's tone was fraught with empathy.

"Sally will take care of him."

"Tell me what I can do. We have to make some phone calls to the county. They'll hear about this, and it could have an impact on future events. I mean, I know you own the center, and the county generally keeps its nose out of these kinds of events, but if anyone complains, they might inquire." Gage's eyes were serious, dark. "Danica, I dealt with the county at my last job. It's better to be ahead of the game."

"I know. I'll call the director first thing tomorrow. I have his cell number. I want to talk to Sally and to Brad's parents first." She went looking for Blake, relieved to see him standing beside Chaz near the stage. Sentinels guarding Kaylie. She tucked her arm into Blake's as Kaylie switched to an unmistakable love song, looking right into Chaz's eyes with more love than even

Danica imagined she was capable of showing. *Good girl, Kaylie.* "She's beautiful," she said to Chaz.

"She sure is. I'm a lucky guy for more reasons than I can count." Chaz never took his eyes off Kaylie.

Danica pulled Blake into the center of the barn, rested her head on his chest, and swayed to the music.

"You okay?" he asked.

"I'll have shit to deal with tomorrow, but for now, I'm doing just fine."

Chapter Forty-Three

"You know, I always loved how you sang, but yesterday, Kaylie, something was different. It was like you weren't just singing, but you were living each word." Kaylie and Chaz had invited Danica and Blake over for brunch, and the four of them sat around a glass table on the rear patio. The sun warmed them like a spotlight against the mild mountain breeze, carrying the scent of fresh-baked croissants. Blake's hand on Danica's thigh sent goose bumps along her arms. They'd spent the morning making love, and Danica's body was still shuddering with tiny aftershocks. She crossed her legs beneath her long cotton skirt, and Blake lifted his hand. *Thank God.* Now maybe her lingering desire would settle down. She leaned back, focusing on Kaylie.

"She was amazing, wasn't she?" Chaz squeezed Kaylie's hand. He looked regal in his khaki shorts and white button-down shirt. He doled a few pieces of cantaloupe and honeydew melon onto his plate from the large decorative bowl in the center of the table, then went back for seconds of grapes, blueberries, and strawberries.

Kaylie reached over and snuck a blueberry from his plate, popping it in her mouth with a playful grin. "I felt different up there. I know that sounds weird, but I think it's because I wrote those songs." Kaylie tucked a strand of her golden hair behind her ear. "I meant every word of them, too, so they felt real to me, not just like empty lyrics that I needed to memorize."

"Crazy good, Kay. Seriously. I hate to say it, but I never knew you had it in you to be so deep." Danica realized how negative that sounded, and she quickly tried to remove the foot from her mouth. "I didn't mean that you're shallow. I meant—"

"Oh my God, sis, chill. I know what you meant." Kaylie had a serious look in her eye as she turned her focus to Chaz. "I think I'm changing. I honestly didn't know I had that in me either, but when Chaz suggested that I write, and I started writing just to show him that I could, I never thought I'd write anything worth singing." Her eyes lit up. "I was so wrong. So wrong!"

"See, sometimes it's good when boyfriends push a little," Blake said, nudging Danica.

"Speaking of nudging, I hear we're going to have neighbors. Good move, Blake." Chaz leaned his elbows on the table and said with a conspiratorial look in his eye, "You know what that means."

Blake raised an eyebrow. "More brunches?"

"These girls will be doing their girl things and we can go skiing all we want, do guy stuff—play golf, hit the clubs." He winked.

Kaylie punched his arm. "You hate golf."

"Yeah, golf? Not my thing either, Kaylie, don't worry. He's just playin' with you." Blake put his hand on Danica's. "And I can't even pretend to love clubs anymore. As far as they go, I've got no interest unless this pretty lady's on my arm. But I love hanging out with you, Chaz, so what about skiing and getting together for a drink and watching a game sometime?"

"That sounds even better," he answered.

Kaylie startled, knocking the table with her knee. Everyone

reached for their juice glasses to keep them from toppling over.

"What is it?" Chaz asked.

"The baby. She's going nuts in there." She rubbed her belly and leaned back. "It feels like my whole stomach is tightening."

"Braxton Hicks contractions," Chaz said. "Don't you remember? The Lamaze teacher said they could start three or four weeks before the baby came." He reached out and rubbed her belly.

"I'm impressed," Danica mused.

"Hey, I'm every bit as invested in this baby as she is."

"He is," Kaylie said, as she let out a long, slow breath. "Ah, that's better. Wow, that was weird." She filled her bowl with fruit and took a croissant from the tray. "We have some big news we wanted to share with you guys before anyone else found out."

Danica's ears perked up. "The sex of the evil spawn?"

Kaylie shook her head. "Can we please call her something cuter? Beautiful spawn maybe?"

"So it's a girl?"

Kaylie laughed. "No, that's not the news. We have no idea what we're having. I'll let Chaz tell you."

Chaz sat back and took Kaylie's hand. "We're buying out my partners. We'll be the full owners of the festival by the end of the month."

"Dude, that is huge." Blake stood and shook his hand. "What does that mean for the festival, exactly?"

"Nothing, really. I mean, it means more for the business. It means that I have full ownership instead of having two partners, so even though the other partners had no involvement in decision making before, now I don't have to worry about ever losing a piece of the ownership. I own the whole thing."

Kaylie looked at Danica and held her gaze. "And it means

that the freaky Lea Carmichael can't get her gaudy little claws into it."

"Why do I know that name?" Blake looked at Danica. She shrugged. "Wait, Lea Carmichael, I know who she is. She owns a ski shop—well, a ski mall, really—over in Vail. Why would she want to buy into the festival?"

"Because she's a freaky bitch who wants to ruin my future husband's life." Kaylie's smile had faded, replaced with an angry frown.

"We sort of had a thing for a few days a few years ago. It was a big mistake. She's a huge sponsor—well, she was. She turned all girl-gone-crazy on me and I ended it. After a few weeks, she stopped trying to get my attention, and I thought she was over it. I mean, it was a fling, you know." He looked at Blake.

"Sometimes flings can have the worst aftertaste," Blake said.

"I thought I'd heard the last of her, and then I met Kaylie." He paused, his gaze lingering on his fiancée. "Then she pulled this crazy scheme, told me she was buying Carl Jansen's percentage, and basically all hell broke loose."

"She even called me and tried to make it seem like she'd been with Chaz. *With* him, you know." Kaylie looked at Chaz and then shifted to Danica. "But I know better. She wasn't. She was trying to come between us."

"Anyway." Chaz stood to divert the conversation. "We'll be full owners, which is great."

"Hey, did Danica tell you guys that Sally is keeping her half of AcroSki?" Blake reached for a croissant as Chaz sat back down.

"Really? Why?" Kaylie picked a grape from Chaz's plate and fed it to him.

"She thinks that Rusty might want it when he's older."

Kaylie furrowed her brow. "I thought he hated skiing."

"He does," Danica answered. "But sometimes things

change, and Sally doesn't want to steal the chance that he'll grab on to something of Dave's."

"Not to bring up a sore subject, but what the hell was that about last night?" Chaz asked.

"What a nightmare." Danica sipped her orange juice. "I spoke to the director for the county earlier this morning. He didn't seem concerned at all about the fight. I wonder if I even should have bothered calling. It seems like I'm more worried about what they might think than they are about what's actually going on. Apparently, even though the county allows us to hold programs for them, they don't get involved with the rest of this stuff." She shrugged as Blake reached over and ran his palm along her back. "I talked to Brad's parents last night. They seemed to take it in stride, or at least as much as a parent can do that, I guess. So, I'm not going to stress over it too much. I'm calling Sally later today. I'll see what's going on with Rusty. As far as I could tell, Brad, the kid who was hit, said something about Little Hellion, and Rusty lost it."

"Maybe I should talk to him, just to make sure he's okay?" Blake offered.

Danica saw the memory of his friend's death shadowing his kind offer. "Let's just wait and see what Sally says."

"I can see a kid losing it over that," Chaz said.

"Hey, I don't want our children settling things that way," Kaylie said.

"I know, but hey, a guy's gotta be a guy. If someone said something bad about you or me, would you want our son to walk away?"

"No, but he won't have to punch the guy, either." Kaylie looked to Danica for support.

"Yeah, he won't have to hit. But the truth is, Kay, that boys that age have so much testosterone flowing through them that sometimes I think they can't help it. Besides, I'm not so sure it didn't have something to do with Michelle, too."

"Finally, some juicy gossip. It's been ages since I've heard any." Kaylie leaned forward, and Danica followed suit.

"I don't have any idea if what I heard is true or not, but there seems to be some sort of love triangle going on. Trisha says Chase is dating Michelle, but Sally says Rusty is. Throw into the mix that Brad comes into the center to talk to Michelle—alone—and I catch Rusty watching them through the glass." She sat back and crossed her arms.

"The plot thickens. God, I've missed this." Kaylie laughed.

Danica gave her a stern look and then cocked her head toward Chaz.

"What?" Kaylie's eyes grew wide. "All I'm saying is that we're all settled down now, and Camille is married, and I don't see the girls very often. Even Chelsea has been dating the same guy for two months. I'm not saying I want to live in that gossipy world again. I'm saying it's fun to hear about someone else's love life troubles instead of my own."

"That it is," Danica agreed. "Anyway, I have no idea what that's all about, but I'm hoping Sally can enlighten me."

Kaylie stood and stretched her legs. "Sometimes I just gotta stand or my legs go numb."

Danica jumped up. "Let's go for a walk." She looked back at Blake and Chaz. They were starting new lives, all of them, and she loved that they were starting their new chapters together.

Chapter Forty-Four

Later that afternoon, Blake went to AcroSki and Danica headed over to Camille's. The day was just as beautiful as the morning sun had promised. The meadows were in full bloom along the small but major road that led just outside of town to Camille and Jeffrey's house.

Camille answered the door with a ready smile, looking as cute as ever in a white cotton skirt and blouse. She had an unfamiliar emerald ring on her right hand.

Danica gasped. "What is it with the men around here? Are they all secret drug dealers or does money grow on trees out here—but only for the men?"

"Kaylie told you?" Camille asked tentatively.

Kaylie? Kaylie told her about Chaz's money? "What? She told you, too? So much for pretending the money isn't there." *Typical Kaylie.*

"Not really. Chaz and Jeff have gotten really close in the last year, but you know that. Anyway, Chaz's attorney is Jeff's family attorney. Small town and all. Jeff saw Chaz coming out of Cooper's office and I guess he told him. Kaylie hasn't said a word to me."

Not so typical Kaylie after all. "Well, don't tell her I said anything." Danica kicked off her sandals and set them next to

Camille's in an alcove by the door. "I was actually referring to your new sparkly ring."

"Oh, goodness. Jeff is so generous. He gave it to me because I said I didn't have any green jewelry. The man's a nut. Oh, and no worries. I'd never say anything to Kaylie about the money thing." Camille took her hand. "Slip your shoes back on. We're going out by the pool again, and it's so nice out, we might as well go around outside."

"Yay! Now the party can begin," Chelsea said when she saw Danica. She jumped up and gave her a hug, and Marie was right on her heels.

"We have almost everything planned. You'll be so happy!" Marie said right before hugging Danica.

They sat around the table with plates of crackers, cheese, finger sandwiches, and, of course, colorful drinks with little umbrellas.

"Do you ever forget to be such a good hostess?" Danica teased.

"Have you ever seen me forget?" Camille said with a wink.

"Today's all about things that are a little bit pink and blue, so we have…well, we have no blue, but we have pink covered. Strawberry daiquiris!"

Danica noticed a number of empty glasses on the cart behind Camille. "I guess I'm late to the party."

Camille handed her a drink. "That's okay when you're with your girlfriends, but don't ever be late to the party when you're with your man, if you know what I mean."

"Oh, I get it," Chelsea said with a laugh. She went into a litany of details about where they'd found the streamers and what kind of balloons and decorations they were having, but Danica's mind was now stuck on the memory of Blake's body on top of hers, as it had been just hours earlier. She rubbed her hands together, reminiscing over the smooth feel of his muscles beneath her hands. Goose bumps prickled her arms. *Jesus. Get a grip.* Danica shook the dirty thoughts from her mind and pulled her attention back to the group.

"We also have watermelon daiquiris," Chelsea said, taking a long sip through a straw.

"And they're delish." Marie giggled.

Danica took a drink, relishing in the icy liquid as it slid down her throat. Camille made her a fresh drink—*so you don't get too far behind*—as they filled her in on the rest of the details for the shower.

"So, we've extended the invitations, we've got the games, and we have ideas for how to get Kaylie to the party. Oh!" Chelsea's eyes lit up and she put both hands flat on the table and leaned in close. She lowered her voice and asked, "Do you guys think Kaylie's changed?"

Where did this come from?

All eyes turned in her direction. "In a good way," she continued, "but just a few weeks ago she was all, *I'm fat and ugly. Chaz won't want me after the baby's born,* and when I spoke to her yesterday morning, she was like on cloud nine, saying she was going to look hot in her dress for the event. Oh, Danica, how was it?"

She'd almost forgotten how Chelsea flitted from subject to subject.

"She hasn't changed. She's just realizing that her body is like a vessel for her baby, and she's owning it," Marie said eagerly.

"I think Marie's right," Danica said. "The event was great. We had a big turnout and people danced. The night was perfect, except for a little punching action between teens."

There was a collective gasp among the girls.

"No big deal, and Kaylie was amazing. I'd never seen her so

passionate before." Danica sipped her drink and pushed it away. Better not to drink too much. She still had to drive home. "Oh, and she looked incredibly hot. Only Kaylie could look like a sexy vixen while almost nine months pregnant."

They all agreed.

"It's good that she's changing. I was worried when she was saying all that stuff. I think she's finally accepting the whole motherhood thing and getting over the whole Kaylie-the-perky-girl thing," Chelsea said to the group.

What? "She's still Kaylie the perky girl," Danica said, a little annoyed.

"Yes!" Chelsea slammed her hand on the table. "But she's so much more! And damn if that girl ever has to worry about that man of hers thinking she's not gorgeous!"

"Flat out stunning," Marie added with an emphatic nod.

"No matter what size," Chelsea said.

They'd gone around the table complimenting Kaylie, and Camille turned expectant eyes toward Danica.

"Yes, right. She is, of course. But I never thought you guys saw her as so much more. I thought that was only me. I kinda thought everyone else saw her as, I don't know." Danica's annoyance was replaced with a flush that heated her chest and neck.

"Just another pretty face?" Chelsea asked. Her tank top had dipped to the right, exposing sharp ripples of bone.

"I think some people do see her like that." Danica handed Chelsea a cracker. "Here. Eat."

"Brainless Barbie?" Marie added.

"What? No." *Where is this coming from?*

"Sexy seductress who doesn't even need to speak to get attention?" Chelsea asked with a perky smile.

"I didn't mean that, really, but..." Danica scanned their

faces for understanding. Their harsh glares poked at her like needles on her skin.

Suddenly, Camille put both palms on the table and said, "I can't do this." She burst into laughter, and Marie and Chelsea followed.

"Jesus," Danica muttered.

"You should have seen your face," Chelsea squealed.

"That was just plain mean." Danica shook her head; then laughter bubbled up from deep within her chest, and she laughed with them, tears streaming from her eyes.

"Oh my God! You should have seen your face! You really bought it," Marie said through her laughter. "Kaylie likes everyone to think she's that flirty, pretty, no brainer, but she's not, and we, of all people, know that."

They went over the rest of the plans for the baby shower.

"So, we thought about where to hold the shower and figured we needed someplace where you could take her, Danica, so that she won't be suspicious the minute you drive up. That means any of our houses are out of the question. So, we decided on Bar None! It's where they met."

"A bar? Seriously? She's pregnant, you guys."

"Yeah, but Bar None has that little restaurant on the side, and you could take her there for lunch."

"True," Danica said. "Actually, I think that's perfect. I'll take her to lunch, and you all will be there, right? Did you book the tables already?"

"Danica, please. The moment Jeff heard about it, he booked all twelve of the tables in the restaurant," Camille said with a wave.

Danica fiddled with her straw. With the house and their condos, she knew that no matter what Blake said, she had to be careful with money. She prided herself on paying her own way and wasn't about to stop now. "What's the bottom line? What do I owe?"

Camille shook her head. "Danica, we're paying for this. Jeff wouldn't have it any other way. He loves Kaylie."

"Camille, I'm really not comfortable with that. She's my sister and I want to help. Really, I'll be upset. I didn't ask you guys to help so that you would pay."

Marie chimed in. "Camille, I want to help, too. This was from all of us, not just you guys, and it's really nice that Jeff offered, but I can pitch in. I want to."

Chelsea also chimed in, wanting to help cover the costs.

"Okay, whatever," Camille said. "Whatever you want to do is fine. I was just trying to help."

"Okay, it's settled then," Danica said, hoping they were all sober enough to remember when the bills came. "Let us know the total and we'll divvy it up."

Marie went over the list of party games she'd planned. Danica was already planning how to get Kaylie to the shower.

Her cell phone rang, and she snagged it from her purse. "It's Kaylie. Shh." She waited until the girls were quiet.

"Hey, it's me. I was just thinking. I know you're busy at the center and all, but do you want to go shopping with me this week?"

"Yeah, I'd love to. What's up?" Danica held a finger up.

"Nothing. I just need some things for the baby and thought it might be fun to hang out."

Danica listened intently for signs of distress in Kaylie's voice, but there was only happiness. "Sure. I have a ton on my plate this week, but I can do it Tuesday if you want. Lunchtime?"

"Perfect."

They said goodbye, and the girls let out a loud collective

sigh.

"Does she know you're here?" Chelsea asked.

"What did she want?" Marie asked. "Does she know about the shower?"

"I have no idea. She wanted to go shopping this week. I think it's fine." Danica put her purse away, but not before noticing a text from Sally. *Sorry I missed your call earlier. Will talk 2moro.*

"Kaylie called me this morning to go shopping today, but I said I had to do something with Jeff," Camille said.

"Oh no. Me too." Chelsea tucked a lock of her recently highlighted brownish hair behind her ear and frowned.

"Aw, poor Kaylie. She must think we're all ditching her." Marie ate a cracker, looking to Danica for guidance.

"It's fine. I'll make sure she's okay." *Of course I will.* She shook her head and realized that she wouldn't even recognize Kaylie if drama didn't follow her everywhere.

They wrapped up their discussion. Chelsea and Marie were staying at Camille's for the afternoon, hanging out by the pool. They asked Danica to join them, but she'd been repressing her sinful thoughts about Blake for too long, and she had no idea why, but she felt a little like a lovesick teenager. She called Blake on her way, and was thrilled when he said he'd been thinking the same thing. She had a feeling that they were in for a steamy afternoon.

Chapter Forty-Five

Kaylie bounced her leg up and down in Dr. Marsden's waiting room bright and early Monday morning. Between her honest talk with Chaz and discussing her worries with Dr. Marsden, she felt as if she was already starting to see things a little differently, and after this morning's call from Alex, she could barely sit still.

"Kaylie." Dr. Marsden entered the room looking just as comfortable and smart as she had during Kaylie's other visits. Her constant and dependable fashion choices, which Kaylie might have made fun of even as recently as a month ago, were now comfortably familiar.

"Hi," she said, pushing herself off the deep sofa.

"I think your baby grew over the weekend."

"That's for sure. I think she's having a party in my belly these days." She followed Dr. Marsden into her office and sat down.

"I have so much to tell you. I swear I never knew why people went to therapists—I mean, not why, but why they were so happy about it when they were working through problems—but now I get it. I was so excited to come and tell you about Danica's event and my writing, and I thought that was a lot, but there's more."

"You are excited. You're talking a mile a minute. Slow down and breathe. We have an hour."

Kaylie nodded. "I'm sorry, but this morning I got a call from our band manager. We had been taping our practices, and I had no idea, but I guess he and Trey, our drummer, sent some of our new stuff out, and they got a call. Benton Records, a small record label out of LA wants to sign us." She tried to keep the squealing excitement from her voice, but she couldn't control the jump in octave. Kaylie bounced her leg up and down and then tucked her hands under her legs to keep them from shaking.

"Is that what you want? Is that what you'd been working toward?" Dr. Marsden asked thoughtfully.

"Yes. Oh my God, it's a dream come true. A record label is like…golden. It makes it all real. I mean, we do well with our band and all, but they liked our songs. My songs. The songs I wrote. It's validation of my talent."

"That it is. Congratulations," she said calmly.

"I'm over the moon."

"Kaylie, that's wonderful. What does Chaz think?"

Kaylie looked down at her lap, then up again. "I haven't told him yet."

Dr. Marsden didn't push, accuse, or judge. She simply asked, "Why not?"

Those two words were more powerful than Kaylie had anticipated. She knew she'd have to answer. She'd thought about it the entire way over in the car, but she still wasn't sure herself about why she didn't have an answer.

"I don't know. There's a lot to work out."

"Like?"

Why are her questions so hard? "Logistics. I'd have to go to LA right after the baby is born. Travel back and forth while we're recording." Kaylie heard the unease in her own voice.

"Is that feasible with a new baby?"

"I think so. Parents travel all the time. We can get a nanny if we need to." *We can use Chaz's money.* Kaylie silently chided herself for already overstepping her bounds, even if only mentally.

"A nanny." Dr. Marsden nodded. "Yes, you could do that. Kaylie, tell me about the weekend. You and Chaz had made a big breakthrough last week. Honesty, remember? How will he react if you wait to tell him about this?"

She shrugged. "I think he'll be happy for me in general, but he'll be upset if I keep it from him."

"Then why are you? Do you want to risk your relationship? Are you having cold feet?"

Am I? Kaylie moved to the edge of her seat. "I've worked so hard, for so long, to get where I am right this very second. I have a record deal at my fingertips. Do you know what it's like to work your whole life toward something and then…"

"Then what? What are you worried about?"

"I've worked so hard." Kaylie set her hands on the sides of her belly. "What if after the baby's born I don't want to do it? What if I turn into one of those moms whose whole life *is* the baby? What if I'm just like my mom?"

Dr. Marsden waited while Kaylie thought through her feelings. When Kaylie said no more, Dr. Marsden asked, "Would that be so bad?"

Kaylie looked up with tears in her eyes. "I don't want to be the wife left behind because I didn't do anything to better myself while my husband grew—emotionally, mentally, career-wise." She played with the fringe of her blouse. "Did I tell you that we're terribly rich? Yeah, Chaz just told me this weekend. Oh, and he's buying out his partners in his festival business."

She looked around the office, uncomfortable with her own thoughts. "I should be thrilled, right? Wouldn't any normal person be happy about all of this? But how can I make a decision about the record deal when I have no idea how I'll feel when the baby comes? And what if I decide to just be a mom and then I resent the baby, or Chaz, or even myself, for not taking the record deal? It's a once-in-a-lifetime opportunity." Kaylie grabbed a tissue from the desk and dabbed at tears that welled her eyes. "And what if the money ruins us?"

"Those are all very viable concerns. Do you really believe this is a once-in-a-lifetime offer? What about your bandmates? How will they feel if you walk away?"

Kaylie hadn't even factored them into her decision. "I can't walk away, can I? It's their careers, too."

"Kaylie, you can—and you should—make whatever decision is right for you, your baby, and Chaz. Your family should come first with these things. Don't you think?"

She nodded. "I'll tell Chaz when I leave here. I guess we should make the decision together." She sighed. "I'm a mess of emotions right now, but I really did have a great weekend. The event was terrific. Well, except for two teenagers getting into a fight. But I sang like I've never sung before, and every breath felt like a new me was being born."

"And did you give any thought to your concerns about after the baby?"

Kaylie rubbed her belly again. "Yeah, I thought about it, and any way I cut it, I am that girl who will be cranky if I don't look good. I know that about myself, so that's just honesty."

"Good. Okay. That's the first step. What can you do to help yourself through it? How can you make yourself happy? Remember, you'll be moving on little sleep, and no matter how much you think you'll love this baby, when it's actually born, you'll love it ten times more than you ever thought you could."

"I can imagine a lot of love."

She smiled. "We all can."

Kaylie looked at the bookshelves, then at Dr. Marsden's desk. Both were void of photos. Kaylie wondered if she had children of her own, or a husband for that matter.

"I know I'll be tired, and over the moon with happiness, but I can still do all the things I always did to be healthy and to get my figure back. I'll eat right. And when the doctor says I can, I'll exercise." *What?* She crinkled her nose.

"You don't like to exercise?"

"I've never had to do it before. I guess I've just got good genes, but I can take walks, maybe go for a jog or something."

"That sounds reasonable. And what happens if the weight doesn't come off?"

Kaylie's jaw dropped. "I've only gained twenty-five pounds. I can lose it." *Can't I?* Panic prickled her nerves. "It can't be that hard. All the actresses lose weight fast. I'll do it. I know I can." Kaylie thought about dieting and exercising, and the thought was not appealing in the least. She wondered what she might look like with an extra few pounds on her body. Danica wasn't really skinny, but she always looked great, and she had to be at least ten pounds heavier than Kaylie. Kaylie tried to picture herself thicker around the middle. "I don't think I'd look bad if I were to have trouble losing the weight. Besides, I hear that nursing helps, and I planned on nursing anyway, so..."

"You're a pretty girl, Kaylie. You're used to being the pretty girl. Who will you be if you carry an extra few pounds?"

Ouch. "I'd still be pretty. And besides," she said indignantly, "I'm a fun, interesting person. I'll still be me, just a bit bigger."

"And how will Chaz react?"

"He loves me for me. He won't care if I never lose the

weight." *Will he? Of course not. He'd still love me.*

"So?" Dr. Marsden asked.

"Saying all this to you, out loud, seems really silly. I mean, I'll have a baby. A newborn baby. Even if the weight doesn't come off, it will have been worth it. And as for Chaz, if he were so lame not to love me because of my weight, then he's not really worth being with anyway, right? And I guess I would hope that I'd have made a better choice than that." The words settled around her, and Kaylie realized that she'd spoken the plain and simple truth.

She pictured Chaz as she'd left the house that morning in her maternity shorts and enormous tank top. He'd reached out and smacked her butt as she walked by, told her she looked hot. If she could look good pregnant, then she could look good no matter what.

"I'll put more pressure on myself than he ever would," she admitted.

"And why do you think that is?"

Kaylie shrugged, but a piece of her was thinking of her mother, how slim she'd been while Kaylie was growing up, and how her father's mistress had been even thinner and substantially younger.

"The only thing I'd say to you about that, Kaylie, is that I wonder what else you can discover about yourself. We know that you're a beautiful girl and that you are talented, but can you tell me what else you like about yourself?"

"I'm nice and funny. I'm a good friend. I love Chaz, and Danica, and Blake."

"I didn't mean to answer me now. Just think about it."

"More homework?"

Dr. Marsden laughed. "A little."

Kaylie drove straight from Dr. Marsden's office to Chaz' office. She breezed through the front door with an easy smile.

"Kaylie, wow, you're about ready to pop," Max teased from her perch behind her desk. She came around to give Kaylie a hug. "Listen, I'm really sorry if I caused any confusion about Lea."

Just hearing that woman's name sent a chill down Kaylie's back. That woman was trying to pull Chaz's strings in too many directions, but somehow, she had become bigger than life, and Kaylie was going to make sure that, in her mind, she became as small as a speck of dust.

Max continued. "That was ages ago, not when we were in Hawaii. And definitely not while he's been with you."

Her worry about Lea seemed like it was ages ago, too. "That's okay. I know. Chaz told me all about it, and I really did appreciate you calling me. Is he in?"

"I'm glad. I was so worried. Yeah, come on back. I need to tell him something anyway." Max popped her head into Chaz's door and said, "Excuse me. Chaz? I've got the four-one-one on that new sponsor. They're clean."

"Great. Sign 'em up."

Kaylie walked in after Max left and found Chaz sitting at a small table in his office, a stack of documents before him and his hand shielding his eyes. "Hey there," she said, and touched his shoulder.

Chaz smiled. "Kaylie. Hey, sit down. I'm just going over the partnership agreements." He pushed them away and focused on her. "How was Dr. Marsden?"

"Great," she said, fiddling with her keys.

"So, what's up? Did you want to grab lunch?" He looked at his watch.

"No, it's only eleven. I just…I need to talk to you about something. Alex got a call this morning. From a record label."

"Wow, really?"

"Yeah." She smiled, trying not to concentrate on her racing heart. Chaz's eyes drew her in, and she knew she had to tell him everything—her fears *and* her excitement. She took his hand, drawing strength from his touch. "They want to sign us," she said tentatively.

Chaz came around the table and hugged Kaylie. "That's great! See, all your worries were for nothing. Even they know how great you are."

She watched him settle back into his chair, his smile reaching all the way to his eyes. "Yeah, but it would mean traveling to LA after the baby is born and then going back and forth while we tape."

His smile faltered. "LA?"

"Yeah. I guess it's where their studio is."

"Kaylie, which label?"

"A small one. *Benton Records.* They heard me singing my songs. My lyrics! I can hardly believe it, but they loved them."

Chaz wrote down Benton Records on a piece of paper. "Honey, do you mind if I have Max check them out?"

"No, that would be great," Kaylie said.

Chaz called out the door to Max, "Max, can you check out Benton Records for me?"

"Sure," Max called down the hall.

"This is great news. I'm so proud of you."

Kaylie searched his eyes for something, anything that would tell her that he was feigning excitement, that he really did want her to stay home with the baby, but all she saw staring back at her in those gorgeous blue eyes of his was pride. She took her chances and laid it out on the line for him.

"I'm so excited, Chaz. I really want this. I've wanted it my whole life. So yes, I want to do it."

"Okay, then. That's an easy decision."

"No, it's not."

"Why? This is what you've been working so hard for, Kaylie. This has been your dream since the day I met you."

"What if after the baby comes, I don't want to go? What if I decide I just want to be with the baby? What if I don't take it, but then, a month, two months, six months after the baby's born, I'm resentful of the baby, or you, for not taking the offer?"

"Whoa—"

"Wait, let me finish. What if I go and I do terribly? What if I stay and all I can think about is how much I gave up to stay home? What if I stay home and you get bored with me? Then I've given up my career for you and the baby. I'm left in the cold."

"Like your mother," he said empathetically.

"Like my mother."

"I'm not your dad. You're not your mom."

Kaylie had heard that so often in the past week that she thought she'd hear it in her sleep. "I know, but anything is possible. Good or bad. It's a toss of a coin, really."

Chaz leaned forward, until Kaylie could smell the coffee on his breath and feel the love emanating from every inch of him. "Kaylie, I'll support whatever decision you make. If you want this, we'll make it work. If you want to stay home with the baby, we'll make that work. I can't promise that you'll be happy doing either, but what I can promise is to do everything I possibly can to make sure that you never feel like I don't appreciate you, all that you do for me, and all that I know you'll do for our baby."

"But how can I know what to do?"

He sat back and shook his head. "I don't understand the real dilemma here. You'll do whatever feels right. You haven't even met the company reps yet, so you have time."

"They're coming out Thursday."

"Thursday? That's fast. Okay, so you'll talk to them then and make a decision after you meet with them. I've heard the name before, but I don't know anything about them. I feel like I should for some reason."

"Probably because you love me and want to make sure they're on the up-and-up."

He smiled. "That must be it. So, tell me what they said."

"I don't know much, just what Alex told me. They loved my songs, my sound. They said they thought they could make me a big hit."

"Wait till they meet you. They'll know they've made the right decision." Chaz walked Kaylie to the front and kissed her goodbye, and she left feeling like a world of stress had been lifted from her shoulders. Her belly tightened as she climbed into her car. She leaned back and waited it out. "Settle down in there," she said to her belly.

Chapter Forty-Six

Danica spent the morning juggling phone calls. Between that, vendor payments, and the thank-you calls to the parents who had volunteered, she hadn't left her office since she'd arrived. She finally ventured out around noon, and found Gage at Sally's desk.

"Hey, where's Sally?"

Gage pointed toward the closed door to the little kitchenette. "She's on the phone."

"How's she doing? I didn't see her when I came in."

"Okay, I think. She didn't say anything, so I didn't ask. Did you talk to her this weekend?"

Danica shook her head. "Couldn't reach her."

The door to the kitchenette opened, and Gage and Danica snapped their heads in Sally's direction. Danica realized how obvious they were and scrambled for an alibi. "The county. Yeah, they're running an investigation."

"Can it. I know you're dying to know what happened." Sally pulled her hair back and secured it with an elastic band from around her wrist. She crossed her arms over her slim waist. "I don't know much, but here's what I could get from Rusty. I guess Brad has been hitting on Michelle, and at the dance, he asked her if she wanted to join the ski team this coming fall."

She had dark bags beneath her eyes, and when she spoke, it was as if all the air had left her words before they left her lips. "He said it would be cool if they could take Little Hellion, and Rusty said the way Brad looked at him made him feel provoked."

"The way he looked at him?" Danica asked. "When I talked to Brad, he didn't even seem to know Dave had died, much less died at Little Hellion."

Sally shook her head. "I don't know what to say. We're going back to Dr. Marsden again. Rusty said he'd go, so we'll see what she says."

"Good. That's probably smart." Danica wished she could help them more, but she knew not to mix too much business with too many personal issues, and lately, it seemed like everything in her life was a bit incestuous. "What about Michelle and Rusty?"

"I don't know. I tried to talk to him about it, and he doesn't really tell me anything."

"He's a teenage boy," Gage said. "He's not gonna tell you much, and honestly, you're lucky if he really does go see a therapist. I mean, at his age, no way would I have gone."

"He's right, you know." Danica saw defeat in Sally's eyes. "Do you want some time off?"

"Of being a parent?" Sally joked.

"From here?"

Sally shook her head. "No, I like to be here. It helps keep my mind off of things. I just thought he was doing so much better."

"He was," Danica assured her. "He hadn't seemed so angry or anything until recently, and if I know teenage boys, this has a lot more to do with Brad and Michelle than with Dave and Little Hellion."

Gage stood and Danica made a snap decision. "Why don't

you guys go down to the café and grab lunch. You could both use an hour out of the office, and I can handle things here."

"Sally?" Gage asked.

Danica pretended to look at a paper on Sally's desk, but gave total concentration to every word that passed between Gage and Sally.

"You don't have to," Sally said quietly.

"I want to. Come on. We don't have to talk about Rusty. We'll just eat." Gage put his hand on the small of Sally's back and guided her toward the door.

Danica pressed her lips together to suppress her smile.

Chapter Forty-Seven

"What should I do?" Kaylie asked Danica as they rifled through a rack of baby clothes.

"What do you want to do?"

"You know that's no help, right? You sound like Dr. Marsden." Kaylie lifted a pink jumper and showed it to Danica.

"How would you know what Dr. Marsden sounds like?" Danica's eyes grew wide with understanding. "You're seeing Dr. Marsden? Really?" Then she looked at the pink jumper and said, "Go neutral. You don't know if it's a girl or a boy. Do you?" she asked hopefully.

"No. I told you we weren't going to find out, and yes, I'm seeing her. I'm sorry I didn't tell you, but I really wanted to do this on my own."

"I'm so proud of you."

Kaylie rolled her eyes.

"Sorry, but Little Miss Therapy is for Losers is seeing a therapist? How is Rhonda?" Danica held up a light green onesie.

"Oh, I love that! Put it in the cart. Who's Rhonda?"

"Dr. Marsden."

Kaylie tossed a yellow jumper in the cart. "Rhonda? Really? I saw her more as a…Martha or Mildred, maybe. I really like her. She's kinda, I don't know, not very feminine, and she asks really direct questions, but I like her. Anyway, I figured that if I had a chance in hell of not becoming Mom that I had to do something pretty quickly."

Danica shook her head. "I never thought I'd see the day." She laughed.

"Yeah, yeah, so hell has now frozen over. What do you think of the blue one?" She held up a jumper with yellow flowers along the feet.

"That's cute. She's a great therapist, and she really helped me when I first started out. It's a shame what she's gone through."

Kaylie put the jumper in the cart and looked at Danica. "What?"

Danica shook her head. "Uh-uh. That just slipped out. I can't tell you her personal business. You know that."

Kaylie sighed. "Well, she has no photos in her office, so maybe she's gay."

"She's not."

"Well, she must not have kids, or a husband."

"Stop," Danica said sternly.

"Fine, whatever." Kaylie looped her arm into Danica's as Danica pushed the cart to the next circular rack of clothes. "I need some guidance, and I feel like I'm stuck."

"I can't tell you what to do. This is your career, your life. But I will just remind you that once you hold that cute little spawn in your arms, you may not want to leave it for anything in the world."

Kaylie sneered.

"What? I didn't say evil. You know I can't wait to meet it, whatever *it* is."

"I know. What if I don't sign with the record label? What if I don't go to LA? I could end up hating Chaz, or worse, the baby."

"You could, if you were a selfish bitch." Danica put two receiving blankets in the basket, obviously ignoring Kaylie's deadly stare. "Look, you're not a selfish bitch. That's the point. If you decide to stay home, then it'll be your decision, and you can't blame him later on down the line, or the sweet little evil spawn baby, either. If you decide to go, then you can only blame yourself. Whatever decision you make, you have to take responsibility for it."

Kaylie put her hand on her hip. "See, that's what I mean. How come Dr. Marsden or Chaz couldn't have said that? You're right. Whatever I decide, I can't use it against anyone else later. It will be my mistake—or not."

"Okay, now that that's settled. Blake got the house!" Danica closed her eyes and cringed.

Kaylie knew her sister was waiting for her to scream, or hug her, or do something, anything other than leaning on a rack, rubbing her stomach, and clenching her teeth, trying to breathe through another Braxton Hicks contraction.

Danica opened her eyes. "What? No reac—" Danica rushed to Kaylie's side. "Are you okay? What's wrong?" She put her arm around Kaylie and guided her to a chair by the cash register.

"I'm fine." Kaylie waved her off. "It's just those practice contractions. I get them a lot."

"Yeah, well, you need to see your doctor."

"I talked to her already. She said it's fine." She stood up when the pain passed. "Okay, see, I'm fine, and I'm so glad you're going to be my neighbor!" She hugged Danica before she could brace herself.

A quick trip to the doctor's office assured Kaylie that everything was fine with her baby and what she'd been feeling was indeed Braxton Hicks contractions. *Your baby is practicing for its big day*, the doctor had confirmed. *Try to stay off your feet a little more, and enjoy your last few weeks of freedom.*

Danica spent the rest of the afternoon working at the center. By the time she left No Limitz, the evening air had turned brisk. She pulled her sweater around her shoulders as she headed to the rear parking lot, where she found Rusty leaning against the driver's side door of her car.

"Hi, Rusty. You okay?"

Rusty wore a gray sweatshirt with the hood pulled down low over his eyes; his hands were tucked deeply into the front pockets. He lifted his eyes. "I'm all right."

"Do you need a ride? I think your mom's still inside."

"No, thanks." He took off his hood and Danica saw worry in his eyes. "Did something happen? Are you okay?"

"Nothin'. I wanted to tell you that I'm sorry about the other night. I shouldn't have hit Brad. He's a good guy."

Danica set her purse on the car and leaned against the side, next to Rusty. "Yeah, he seems to be." She looked at his eyes again and wondered what was weighing so heavily on him. "Did something happen that you want to talk about?"

He shrugged.

"Is there anything I can do?"

He shook his head. "I've never really had a brother before."

"Yeah, I know." Danica wondered where he was headed with the brother talk.

"So, when Brad was hitting on Michelle, well." He shrugged again.

She didn't want to ask too many questions for fear that he'd recoil and stop talking, but she wanted to know what Rusty was feeling, how he viewed his relationship with Michelle. "Are you and Michelle dating?"

He shook his head. "Naw. She's into Chase."

"Right."

"And he's kinda my brother, so—"

You've come a long way. Danica stifled the smile that threatened to break the mood of their talk. She hoped she'd read his intentions correctly. "So, you were keeping Brad from going after his girl."

Rusty nodded. "I can't tell my mom. Please don't tell her."

"She's worried about you." Danica looked at the building, stuck between her friendship with Sally and gaining Rusty's trust.

"I know, but it's all just weird, you know? She doesn't even really know how often Chase and I talk."

"I'm sure she'd be pleased that you two are friends."

Rusty looked at her and flipped his blond hair from his eyes with a quick snap of his chin. "Please don't tell her. She'd get all weird about it, and she'd offer to take us places and want him to come along, and…"

"I get it. She'd want it too much, and it would make it awkward. I won't say anything, but you know she's really worried that hitting Brad was all about your dad."

"I didn't know what else to tell her."

So, someone saying something about your dad is less of a threat than saying something about Chase?

Chapter Forty-Eight

Chaz felt his blood boil as he stared at the documents that Max had just handed to him. Two pieces of paper. That's all it took to bring his perfect morning to a screeching halt. He felt Max's eyes on him as she lowered herself into the chair across from him.

"I'm sorry," she said tentatively. "What are you gonna do?"

Kill Lea. Rip her to shreds. Chaz gritted his teeth as he lifted the pages off the desk and reread them.

"You're sure about this? One hundred percent?" He didn't look at Max. He couldn't. He was ready to blow up, and she would fall into his line of fire, even if she wasn't his target. Goddamned Lea had found another way to creep into his life.

"Unfortunately. I triple-checked."

"She's a partner at Benton Records. You realize what this means." How could he tell Kaylie that the offer of representation was little more than a ploy to tear them apart? He looked at Max and, for the first time ever, wished she'd never walked into his office. Chaz knew she was simply the bearer of bad news, but that didn't stop his overwhelming desire to start the day over and somehow skip this part altogether.

"Chaz, maybe she only owns the label, but she's not involved in the representation side. She owns so many businesses, she probably doesn't even realize she owns this one."

She was trying to placate him, and it just made him angrier. This was not a forgotten business any more than the trip to Hawaii had been necessary. She could have told him about Jansen over the phone—hell, she could have written an email. But that's not how Lea worked, and knowing what he did now, he realized that the whole thing had been a ruse, a way of thrusting herself in between him and Kaylie.

"I can't tell Kaylie. She'll be devastated. She wants this label more than anything she's ever wanted." He dropped his head back against his chair and scrubbed his face with his hand. "Jesus. She's never going to go away, is she?"

"We could hire a hit man," Max joked.

"Careful. I'm just about at that point." He had to figure this out. If he called Lea and told her to back off, it would only further engage her fantasies. Cooper was taking care of the festival, but there was no Cooper to take care of Kaylie. *Damn it!*

Max stood to leave and leaned over the desk, touching Chaz's hand thoughtfully. "I think you should tell her. She loves you, Chaz. She knows Lea is crazy, so this shouldn't come as a surprise."

"She's meeting with the company reps today. I'll see how that goes. Maybe she'll come to her own decision and decide not to take the offer anyway." Chaz sighed, putting the pieces together in his mind. "This explains why they said she'd need to go to LA right after the baby's born and travel heavily right after. Lea's just trying to drive a wedge between us. Goddamn it. Will she ever stop? There must be a way to stop this shit."

"Sorry, Chaz. Is there anything you want me to do?" Max stood in the doorway, the worry in her eyes only further fueled Chaz's anger.

He shook his head. "I gotta think." He reached for the phone and called Cooper.

Twenty minutes later, with all hopes of Cooper putting some sort of stop to his newest nightmare squashed, Chaz wondered how in the hell he was going to break Kaylie's heart.

Chapter Forty-Nine

Danica poured two mugs of coffee and then set a cup on the table in front of Blake, who was nose deep in the newspaper. His hair was still damp from the shower, and he smelled like Tommy Hilfiger cologne. She sat down at the table and ran her bare foot up the leg of his jeans, thinking about how she used to make fun of that exact same act when she'd seen women do it in the movies. She remembered wondering if women ever really did things like that. It had seemed so far removed from who she had been as a conservative therapist. *You've come a long way, baby.*

Blake scooted his chair closer, allowing her toes to touch his thigh. He lowered the paper and lifted his eyebrows.

She'd never known what she was missing back then. *Oh yeah, this is definitely fun.* She threw him a flirty smile.

"Careful there. You'll make us both late."

She heard the hesitation in his voice, the should we, or shouldn't we? He held her gaze as she used her foot to make his decision even more difficult. His eyes opened wide and then narrowed. She recognized the hitch in his breathing as the newspaper fell to the table.

"I was just thinking, we haven't really celebrated how well the first event went for No Limitz." *God, that's the lamest excuse for sex ever!*

"We haven't, have we?" he said playfully. "Don't you have...to talk to Sally today?" He ran one finger slowly up her leg, a whisper of hope unsaid.

Danica nodded, feeling her nerves clench. She ran her tongue across her lower lip, debating what a quickie might do to her schedule.

Blake grabbed her foot roughly and pulled hard enough to inch her chair closer. He ran his hand along the inside of her leg, then up her thigh, squeezing, ever so lightly, when he reached the sensitive skin along her panty line.

She held her breath and closed her eyes, willing him to keep going. He moved even closer, until the front edge of their chairs touched, his legs straddling the sides. He leaned forward and picked Danica up by the flesh of her thighs, wrapping her legs around his waist, and lifting her brown cotton skirt up, then letting it billow around them. She watched his hungry eyes as they roved from her mouth to her breasts, where they lingered. Her breathing quickened as her core pulled eagerly toward the firm bulge beneath her center. She reached down and fumbled with his zipper. He lifted up just slightly and set himself free, then wrapped his hand around the back of her neck and pulled her mouth to his while she mounted him quickly, gasping against his lips as he buried himself deeply inside of her.

They moved in unison. She clenched his shoulders, digging her nails into his hard muscles as his tongue probed her mouth, hard and passionately, in beat to the thrusts of his hips. Her desire heightened as he moved in quicker strokes, riding the crescendo, until she threw her head back just as he called out her name. Her body shuddered and clenched around him until every breath took too much energy, and she collapsed forward, panting against his cheek.

"You are definitely not the girl I met so many months ago," Blake said through heated breaths.

Danica settled her lips over his and kissed him until the aftershocks of their love rattled through her, sending goose bumps up her arms.

"No, I'm not," she whispered. "Shower?" She climbed off his lap and took his hand, leading him to the shower, wondering just how late for work they could get away with.

Danica was still riding the wave of their love when she walked into No Limitz. Sally was on the phone, a serious look on her face.

Her voice came through the intercom. "Michelle's on line three."

Danica picked up the phone in her office. "Michelle? Are you okay?"

"Yeah," Michelle said quietly.

"Why are you whispering?"

"Is there any chance you can meet me for a little bit?"

"Of course. Should I pick you up?" Danica listened as Michelle told her she was at home and her mom was at work, and suddenly Danica's pulse sped up. "Michelle, is it your mom?" She closed her eyes, praying Nancy wasn't drinking again.

"Yeah, but not because she's drinking. I just need to talk."

"It's okay. I'm on my way." Danica grabbed her purse and hurried out to the front.

"Got a minute?" Sally asked. The serious look still lingered in her eyes.

She needed to talk to Sally, but Michelle might give her additional insight into what Rusty was going through. "I've gotta meet Michelle right now. Can we talk when I get back?"

She hoped for a quick agreement.

Sally dropped her eyes to the desk. "Um, sure."

She could tell by the hunch of her shoulders and the missing gleam in her eyes that Sally was disappointed.

Gage came through the front door carrying two basketballs. "Hey! New balls today." He smiled, his eyes lingering on Sally for a beat too long.

Danica didn't miss Sally's silence. "Great," she said, filling the uncomfortable gap. "I'll be back soon. Meeting Michelle for a bit." Whatever was going on with Gage and Sally could wait.

Michelle hadn't said one word since they'd purchased sodas and began their stroll along Main Street. She kept her eyes trained on the ground. Questions were piling up like books in Danica's head, but she knew better than to jump right in with them. Michelle headed toward a bench in the courtyard, and Danica followed silently beside her, her patience wearing thinner by the minute. The flowers were in full bloom, and a gentle breeze swished through the trees. She lifted her chin to the sun and let her desire to rush things along fade away. If nothing else, Michelle might have just needed to know she was there. She let her mind drift to the house that Blake was buying. For her. For them. The more she thought about it all—the house, his proposal, the way they fit into each other's lives seamlessly, the decadent sex—the further she moved toward accepting his marriage proposal, regardless of what Kaylie might or might not be going through.

"Are you even listening?" Michelle asked, nudging Danica's shoulder.

"I'm sorry. I was—" She fluttered her hand toward the sky.

"I said your hair looks great. It's really grown this summer."

Danica reached up and touched her coarse curls, which now

fell past her shoulders. The extra few inches of growth added just enough weight to her curls, giving her less of an Afro look and more of a sexy, playful look, which at this point in her life suited her just fine.

"Thank you. Did you want me to come out so we could talk about my hair?" she teased, flipping her hair with an overexaggerated head toss.

"No," Michelle said with a hint of a laugh. She poked her straw in and out of the cup, sending a little sliding sound between them. Michelle's cheeks had thinned, giving her a more mature look. She'd be a sophomore in the fall, and shortly thereafter, she'd leave for college.

Danica realized how quickly life was moving along, and everyone seemed to be evolving with it. Maybe she should accept his proposal. Maybe this was her turn to evolve even further.

"Okay, so here it is," Michelle said, and then closed her mouth tight.

Danica waited.

"I'm kinda sorta seeing Chase."

Relief swept through her. *Not Brad.*

"But I kinda sorta like Rusty."

Uh-oh.

"And Brad."

Shit. She patted Michelle's leg. "Could you have picked a more difficult love triangle?" she teased.

"Oh, God. I know." Michelle covered her face and shook her head. "I'm not a slut. I promise I'm not. I'm not do-ing…that or anything."

"Michelle, I'm not judging you. Your body is your body, and you can do with it whatever you feel is right." She turned on her serious voice. "Just be sure you are doing what you really want, and not what some boy tells you to do because he wants it."

"I know that," she said with a roll of her eyes. "I met Chase through friends, and you know I met Rusty through No Limitz, but I had no idea they were brothers, well, half brothers, but whatever."

"Okay, I get it."

"And Brad, well, you know. I knew him in school, but I didn't think he liked me. But he keeps coming around, and I kinda think he does, and every time he comes around, I get butterflies in my stomach."

The innocence in Michelle's eyes pulled Danica right into therapist mode—just long enough to figure out the right strategy to walk through Michelle's dilemma. She took Michelle's hand, and when she spoke, she was back to being just Danica, Big Sister, friend, confidant.

"You're not the first girl to be in this situation. My sister has weaved her way through men triangles so many times I could help you navigate this in my sleep."

"Really?" Michelle looked hopeful.

"Really. Let's run through this. Tell me what you like about each boy and what you don't like. We can do the pros and cons."

Michelle rattled off her lists, which she'd obviously thought about for quite some time. It included everything from the way Chase really listened to her and didn't expect anything physical from her, to the way Brad made her knees weak with little more than his voice and how he included her in the places he went and things he did—even if she turned him down. And then, finally, Rusty's badboy image, which she found hard to turn away from, and how he reminded her of a hurt puppy some-times, and she just wanted to take care of him and make him laugh.

Danica was impressed with her less-than-typical teenage responses. She'd expected to hear about how hot the boys were. "Those were really pros. How about cons?"

"That's the problem. They don't really have any. I mean, Rusty is protective of me, but that's not really a con."

"It could be. He could become possessive."

"Yeah, I guess. Every girl wants to date Brad." She rolled her eyes.

"That could also be a con. A lot of competition can be bad for your ego. You might always feel like you have to measure up to someone else."

Michelle nodded. "And Chase, well, he's Rusty's brother. So…there's that."

Danica chewed on her answers, knowing she couldn't make the decision for her. If it were her decision to make, she might just go with Brad because he was the least complicated of the three.

Michelle cocked her head and then stood with a bounce. "Can we walk some more? Blake's store is right around the corner. We can stop in."

Danica felt a flush run up her cheeks. "We don't have to do that."

"I want to. I really like Alyssa. Besides, then you can see him."

Why did her mind immediately go to the seclusion of his office in the back? *Get a grip.* "We didn't really resolve your dilemma."

Michelle headed for the corner. "I know, but it feels better to at least say it all out loud. I didn't expect you to figure it out for me. I just wanted to talk. And you're such a good listener."

Danica accepted the compliment with a sense of pride as

they walked in silence, watching the cars pass and sipping their sodas.

AcroSki had just opened for the day and wasn't yet busy. Michelle headed for Alyssa while Danica found Blake at the back of the store, organizing a display of running shoes.

"Hey, babe," he said as he took her into his arms and kissed her cheek. "I thought about you all morning." He ran his hand along her hip.

"I was out with Michelle and she wanted to stop by."

"Everything okay?"

There he goes again, caring about my life. "Yeah, more than okay." She looked for Michelle and Alyssa and found them deep in conversation by the summer sportswear.

Blake went back to work on his display and asked her if she'd spoken to Sally yet.

"No, but I will. There's something weird between her and Gage, too. I can't tell if they're playing cat and mouse because they really like each other, or if they don't."

"He does like her," Blake said.

"What?" Danica knelt beside him. "How do you know that?"

Blake shrugged. "Guys talk." He touched her cheek. "I am the one who introduced the two of you, remember?"

"Yes, so tell me. Wow, having a spy around could make my life so much easier. So he likes her?"

"I can't break my man's confidence." A sly smile spread across his lips.

Danica pressed her body against his with a coy smile.

"That's really unfair," he said.

Danica put her hands on his hips, feeling like a lusty teenager. She could drag him right into the office, or the dressing room. The dressing room was closer. She was pondering the two when he touched her chin and moved it in his direction.

"Put away that dirty little mind of yours. You're with Michelle, remember?"

She stepped away from him and put her hands behind her back. *Jesus, what is wrong with me?* "Sorry."

"Don't be. I'd take you into the office and ravish you in a heartbeat if I thought we could get away with it." He nodded toward Michelle and Alyssa, heading their way.

"Tell me quickly."

"Not much to tell. He likes her. He's worried about dipping the pen in the company ink, but besides that, he seems to really like her. And Rusty, which is a big plus."

Danica smiled as Michelle approached.

"Ready?" Michelle asked as she sidled up to Danica. "Hi, Blake."

"Hey there. Having a good summer?" he asked.

"Yeah." She blushed and then said, "I'm really sorry about everything that happened at the dance."

"No sweat," he replied. "Really, as far as teenage fights go, that falls on the tame side." She noticed Alyssa tapping Michelle, giving her an I-told-you-so look. Once again, Danica was comforted by how close Alyssa and Michelle had become.

Blake put his hand on the small of Danica's back. "See you later."

Michelle talked a mile a minute as they headed for the parking lot. "Alyssa said I didn't really need to decide, that I should just be good friends with all of them until I definitely want to be more with one of them."

"How do you think they'll feel about that?"

Michelle shrugged. "I'm not sure, but Alyssa said that guys like when girls are hard to get, and not to act snotty or anything, just to keep being nice to all of them."

She watched Michelle process her own words. She turned her head one way, then the other, and shuffled her feet. Then she lifted her trusting eyes toward Danica.

"That might work, right? I mean, I have kissed Chase, but that's all I did."

"Michelle, take them out of the equation altogether. Does it feel like the right thing to do? To you, I mean, not to Alyssa or the boys."

"Kinda. I feel bad for Chase, but I also feel bad every time I see Rusty or Brad, so I guess it doesn't feel any worse than it does now."

They climbed into the car. Danica knew such a scenario wouldn't work with adult men, and she had her doubts about it working with teenagers. "Will you tell them that you're just friends with all of them?"

"I haven't gotten that far yet. But I can tell you this. When I saw you with Blake, in the store, I knew that *that* was what I wanted." She smiled, her eyes full of hope. "He looks at you like he can't breathe without you. You do the same with him."

Danica felt a flush of color heat her cheeks. *Is it that obvious?*

"I don't have that with any of those boys yet. I want that."

Chapter Fifty

Danica avoided talking to Sally for most of the day. She had to tell her about Rusty's motivation being chivalrous rather than being driven by his father's honor. She didn't want to break his confidence if she didn't have to, and she still held out hope that Rusty might come clean to his mother himself.

Right before closing time, Danica visited the basketball courts, which she found empty, the balls all stacked nicely in the bin. She headed to the game room, stopping cold at the sight of Gage's enormous body flat against the wall as he peered into the game room. She stifled a laugh as she sidled up next to him.

"Who are we spying on?"

"Rusty and Sally."

"Rusty's here?"

He nodded toward the game room. She peeked around him and saw mother and son, sitting side by side on the floor next to the pool table.

"Oh, thank goodness," she mumbled.

Gage shot her a questioning look.

"What? Why are you spying anyway?"

Gage smiled. "Just wanna make sure they're okay."

She nudged herself against him to get a better look. "Me too."

Sally looked up and they both jumped back, then hurried back down the hall.

The door clicked open behind them. Thinking fast, Danica pretended to talk about next week's schedule. "So, what do you think? Two basketball classes or one?"

At first Gage looked at her like she'd lost her mind; then he saw Sally heading toward them, Rusty right behind, hands in his pockets, eyes trained on the ground. "Oh, yeah. I'm not sure."

"Meeting? In the hallway? Uh-huh," Sally snipped as she passed, though the smile on her face told them she was onto their eavesdropping ways.

"I'm gonna talk to her." Danica watched as Gage met Rusty halfway down the hallway, put his arm around him, and the two of them headed out the back doors.

"Sally, wait." Danica hurried to her side and cornered her in the break room. "What's going on?"

Sally poured out the coffeepot and began scrubbing it like it had ground-in coffee stains—which it didn't.

"Sally?"

Sally shook her head. Her eyes welled with tears.

"Oh, God. What happened? What can I do?" She took the pot from Sally's hands and set it in the sink, then led Sally to one of the two metal chairs beside a small round table.

Sally tried not to cry. Her lower lip trembled, and every time she opened her mouth to speak, she cried harder. Danica passed her a handful of napkins.

"It's okay. Take as long as you need."

Sally shook her head, dabbing her tears with the napkins. "It's just. Rusty. And Gage." She brought her fisted hands to her eyes, elbows resting on the table. "Oh, God."

"Sally, what is it? What happened with Gage and Rusty?"

Danica's mind went all sorts of places it wouldn't normally go. Had Gage hurt Rusty? Did they have an argument? She couldn't fathom the thought.

She shook her head again. "Rusty likes Michelle. But Chase likes Michelle. And Rusty punched Brad because of Chase liking Michelle. To protect his friend, you know?"

I should have told her.

"And Gage. Goddamned Gage," Sally continued.

"What did he do? Sally, I'll get rid of him. If it's a choice between you or him, there's no question."

"It's not that. I like him, Danica. I mean, I really like him."

Now she was really confused. "So, what's the issue?"

"I can't date Gage. Rusty likes him. Can you just imagine if Gage and I started dating and Rusty got pissed off about it? The one person he trusted would be gone from his life. He talks to him. He and Gage are like this." She crossed her fingers.

Why did every relationship have to be so complicated? Sally'd already gone through the torture of losing her spouse. She'd finally allowed herself to feel something for someone else, and her happiness was hamstrung by her son's recovery from his father's death. *Like me. I'm finally happy, and I'm afraid of rocking the boat with Kaylie.*

"As right as it is to protect those we love, we have to look out for our own happiness. No one else will do it for us." Danica should be giving herself the same advice.

Sally's jaw dropped. "So, I should forgo Rusty's happiness for my own? What kind of therapist were you?"

"That's not really what I meant. Have you talked to Rusty about Gage?"

"Not in so many words. He said he really likes him, and that he trusts him. Trusts him." Her eyes implored Danica to understand.

"I know. I get it. What did he say about Michelle?"

Sally explained again what Danica already knew. "I feel so bad. It wasn't Michelle he was texting. It was Chase. He didn't want to tell me."

"But he did. He told you, Sally, and you know how big that is."

Sally nodded. "I can't help him with the whole Michelle thing, but I can stay away from Gage."

"Gage," Danica said with a sigh. "Give it time and space. It will probably work itself out one way or another. If you're drawn together, then you are. That's how it goes. And I think Michelle will fix that whole mess. She kinda likes them all."

"All three?" Sally laughed a little despite her tears.

Danica nodded.

"Can you imagine being a teenager again? I wouldn't want it for anything in the world." Sally wiped her tears.

"Me either." Danica was glad that Rusty had told his mother about why he'd hit Brad, but she hated knowing that Sally felt as if she couldn't act on her feelings with Gage. "Give the thing with Gage some time. Kids are fickle. Maybe next week Rusty will have another person he trusts."

Sally rolled her eyes. "Do you even know my testosterone-laden, nonverbal son? He grunts. He doesn't talk. But apparently he talks to Gage."

"Give it time. That's all I'm saying." Danica heard Gage and Rusty in the hallway outside the break room. "Speak of the devil."

Sally wiped her eyes, and Danica reached over and brushed her hair away from her face. "Beautiful," she whispered with a wink. She hugged Sally and, together, they walked into the lobby, where they found Gage and Rusty standing side by side, eyes on Sally.

"Mom, is it okay if I head over to Michelle's? Can I take the car?"

"I can drive you home," Gage offered Sally.

Sally looked at Danica, and Danica recognized a plea for rescue when she saw one.

"I can take her," Danica offered. "I need to head that way anyway." She watched Gage's brows draw together. Sally dropped her eyes and went to her desk to grab her purse and turn on the answering machine.

"Uh, okay." Gage turned away, but not before Danica saw the disappointment in his eyes.

"Give her a little time," she urged when she caught up to him.

Chapter Fifty-One

Kaylie set candles on the patio table, atop her favorite summer tablecloth, the white one, speckled with flowers and bees. She hummed one of her songs and moved her hips to the music, thinking of the meeting she'd had with Mr. Thompkins, the rep from Benton Records. He'd been more interested in the songs she'd written than in the band itself. She'd watched Alex's jaw drop when he mentioned Kaylie also considering a solo career. She'd been quick to nip that idea in the bud, but now, hours later, the idea buzzed around inside her head like a humming-bird, strong and undeniable.

She went inside and took the roast and potatoes from the oven. A rush of pride ran through her at the beautiful meal she'd prepared. She felt like a real wife, whatever that was. A pain seared through her lower back. Kaylie dropped the pan on the stove and leaned on the edge of the counter, rubbing her stomach and breathing in long, low breaths, as she'd been taught. If the Braxton Hicks contractions were only a prelude to labor, she'd definitely opt for an epidural.

"Kaylie?" Chaz called as he came in the front door.

The contractions subsided as he entered the kitchen, look-ing as fresh in his khaki pants and powder-blue shirt as he had that morning, though the brightness had left his blue eyes.

"Is something wrong?" Kaylie reached for the roast.

"I've got it," he said and took it from her hands. "I'm fine. Where are we eating?"

"Outside." She carried the salad and potatoes out to the porch. "Just set the roast there." She pointed to a hot plate she'd set in the middle of the table. "I've got to get the salad dressings and glasses."

"I've got it. You sit." He pulled out her chair and she settled into it, thinking maybe she'd misread whatever she thought she'd seen in his eyes.

Chaz set the glasses on the table beside the salad. "This looks amazing. You must've had a great day. I have to admit, I was worried when you didn't call after the meeting."

"I was going to call you, but then I thought I'd just tell you in person instead." She searched his eyes again. Kaylie lifted her water glass. "A toast."

He lifted his glass. "Good news?"

"To us," she said, and clinked his glass. Kaylie took a gulp of water. "Chaz, they want me. I mean, they really want me. But I don't think they really want the band."

He squeezed her hand. "They'd be crazy not to." He pulled his hand from hers and put a piece of roast on his plate. "So, you're taking it, then?"

The way he asked, not quite short or clipped, but something in his voice gave her pause. "I haven't decided." She really hadn't, but she'd expected a little more excitement from him—maybe even a gushing compliment or two—and the disappointment stole a bit of her thrill. She put salad on her plate and continued to explain how bad she felt for Alex and Trey. "I didn't really know what to do, so I just said that I wanted to hear about representation for the group. Poor Alex. If you could have seen him. I mean, Trey didn't look too happy either, but

Alex." She shook her head. "I kinda felt like he blamed me, which I know is silly. I mean, he did all the work. He sent out the inquiries and everything. It wasn't like I went looking for Benton Records."

"Kaylie."

She saw in his eyes that he had something to say, and the drawn-out silence had her thinking that maybe she'd done something wrong by not calling him after the meeting. She'd wrestled all afternoon with her feelings about the opportunity, and she'd wanted to figure out where she stood before seeing where he stood on it, even though she knew it would be a joint decision. She'd spoken to Danica, but Danica was completely neutral, just as Kaylie had counted on. Now that she was about to find out exactly what he thought, she wished she could plug her ears and make childish noises so she didn't have to hear it. She could tell by his tone that he wasn't exactly overjoyed, but wasn't it her turn? He had a career. She supported him, no matter how often he had to travel. Couldn't he do the same for her? She felt herself getting revved up and told herself to calm down. She rubbed her belly, and her confusion returned. *Do I really want to do this?*

"What is it that you want? Not Alex or Trey. Not what Benton Records wants. What does Kaylie Snow want?"

Why did she feel like she was about to cry? Damn hormones, screwing with her again. Was he really asking what she wanted, or was she missing some hidden way of telling her that he didn't want her to do it?

"Honestly?" she asked.

He nodded, smiled. "Of course."

"I know it's a once-in-a-lifetime thing. I'm excited to finally realize my dreams, so I think I want to do it." She watched him nod and reach for her hand. She had promised honesty. She had to deliver. "But there's another side of me that doesn't want to make a decision until after the baby's born."

She saw relief in his eyes and wondered what it meant. Did he not want her to take the job? She knew he would never tell her not to take it. This had to be her decision.

"Will they let you wait?" he asked.

Goddamn it! Why was he so damn supportive? Why were his eyes so emotive? He was making her decision even more difficult. Kaylie felt a knot form in her lower back, and she rubbed it while she answered. "Yes. They'll wait for another couple of weeks."

He nodded.

"I kind of think that you don't want me to take it," she admitted.

"It's not that. I'm happy for you. This is what you've worked so hard for."

"Then what is it? You were relieved when I said I hadn't made a decision."

Chaz nodded, poked at his food, then turned back to her. "Yeah, I was, but not because I didn't want you to take it. I just think you made a smart decision by waiting until you see how you feel after the baby is born, that's all."

Kaylie saw something else, some untold thing in his eyes, and she felt it like a bubble between them. "Chaz, just tell me."

"There's nothing to tell." He wrinkled his nose, the way he always did when he was keeping something from her. The slightest little wrinkle, like he had an itch.

Kaylie supposed it would be understandable that he didn't want her to take the opportunity, but she just wished he'd tell her already.

They finished dinner in silence, and Chaz retreated to his office.

Chapter Fifty-Two

Danica answered her cell phone on the second ring. "Chaz?"

"Hey, Danica."

"Did you dial my number by mistake? Blake's on his way home."

"No, I wanted to talk to you."

Danica sat down on the living room sofa. "What's wrong?" Chaz had never sought her out before, not even when he and Kaylie were having such a rough time over that Carmichael woman.

"I need to bend your therapist ear, but before I do, I need to know that you won't rat me out."

What now? "Chaz, I'm Kaylie's sister, so if you're going to tell me that you cheated on her, or unload some other guilt that's just as bad, please don't, because I can't keep that secret."

"It's nothing like that."

She listened to him breathe deeply.

"If you knew something that would really hurt Kaylie, but you also knew she should know, then would you tell her?"

"I gotta tell you, Chaz, you're scaring me." Danica clenched the phone tightly. Whatever he had to say, she'd better find out so she could be there to catch Kaylie when she fell. "Okay, I guess the answer is yes, I'd tell her if she needed to know."

"You know how she got that record label offer?"

"Yeah, she met with them today. It went really well."

"I know. She didn't call me after, and I knew that was because she was still really wrestling with it. Well, it turns out that Lea Carmichael owns Benton Records."

"Yeah, and…" Danica shot to her feet. "Oh, shit. Shit. Really? Are you sure?"

"Yes, and I'm not sure what to do. If I tell Kaylie, she'll think I'm saying that her songwriting and singing isn't good enough for Benton Records to want her, or something like that."

"No, she won't. She'll understand." Danica wanted to believe her sister would understand, but she knew better. Kaylie'd had one thing on her mind this afternoon when she'd called after the meeting. Pride laced her every word. She'd finally accomplished what she'd been striving for, and it was vindication for all the years she'd felt like she'd been living in Danica's shadow. Before Chaz could say a word, she stopped him. "Wait, she will. You're right. I mean, after a while she'll see it clearly, but at first she'll blame you." She paced.

"She's worked so hard for this, and I really, really wanted it to come true for her. We could make it work, with the baby and all, but now? With Lea involved? It's not even real anymore. She's not making a decision until after the baby is born, so that buys me some time, at least." Chaz paused. "I was thinking that I'd contact Lea, tell her to back off."

"Because that did so much good before?" Danica sat back down, thinking about the awful situation he and Kaylie were in, and it pained her to think of Kaylie's hopes dashed by that other woman. She was using Kaylie. That much was obvious. "What do you think her thing is? Why's she doing this?"

"I don't friggin' know. I mean, she's a nut. She wants to

break us up, but it's not like I'd go back to her, so I have no idea what she's even thinking."

"Does she know that? In no uncertain terms?" Danica trusted Chaz and already loved him like a brother, and she knew how much he loved Kaylie. But if it came down to it, there was no choice to make. She'd push and make him as uncomfortable as necessary to ensure that Kaylie was protected.

"Of course. She's a nut. Max found all this dirt on her trying to break up people, basically stalking them. Cooper is doing what he can, but she's not physically stalking me or Kaylie, so he can't do anything about it."

"Okay, let's think."

"I think I have to talk to her, tell her to back off." The pain in Chaz's voice was palpable.

"What if she doesn't? What if she somehow makes it seem like you were going after *her*?"

"She's crazy enough to do that," Chaz admitted.

"Well, if she's waiting until the baby is born, that gives you at least a couple weeks to figure this out. Until then, I don't think I'd say anything to Kaylie. No need to get her all riled up before she's even made a decision."

"All right. I hope you're right. I feel horrible. This is all my fault. I should have never hooked up with that woman."

Danica thought of all the strange guys Kaylie had dated over the years. "We all make mistakes, Chaz. It just sucks that this one came back to haunt you."

"Tell me about it. Hey, can you tell Blake thanks for the sponsorship?"

"What sponsorship?"

"Take Enterprises? That's his company, right? He bought a sponsorship for the festival."

Blake walked in the front door as Danica hung up the

phone, still reeling from her conversation with Chaz. He sat beside her on the couch, and she nuzzled into him. "Chaz said thanks for the sponsorship."

"Hmm."

She touched his chest. "You didn't tell me that you sponsored the festival."

"It was a quick decision. He was having all that trouble with that psycho woman, and I had a few extra bucks. I had a banner made with No Limitz on it."

"What? Blake." She kissed him on the cheek, but was distracted by the looming issue with Kaylie's offer of representation. "That was sweet. Thank you."

"No big deal. Hey, are you okay? You seem a little edgy."

"I'm just really mad. Chaz called, and that record label that offered Kaylie representation is partially owned by that Lea Carmichael woman. He doesn't want to tell Kaylie yet. He wants to wait until she makes her decision, in case she decides not to take the offer. He's so worried about crushing her dreams. You know, she did just find her footing again. As much as I hate keeping anything like this from her, maybe he's right?"

Blake leaned against the counter and crossed his arms. "That's crazy. He's sure?"

"Seems to be."

"Well, I can't even begin to figure out what's right or wrong in not telling her, but I do think that after everything your sister has been through, maybe it is best if he waits to tell her. I mean, if she turns it down, then the problem's solved, right?"

"I guess, but the whole thing just stinks. I really wanted this for her. You should have heard how excited she was when she called today. It was like she finally got the validation that she'd been looking for all these years." Danica let out a frustrated sigh.

Blake approached her and her heart swelled. When he wrapped her in his arms and she lay her head on his chest, she was able to close her eyes for a second and just breathe him in. She knew the whole thing with Kaylie would eventually blow over—either with drama or without—but this…being with Blake…feeling safe and loved…this was her *now*. This was the present, and it was all she really wanted to think about.

Blake kissed the side of her head. "How did things go with Sally?"

How many other men would remember what else their girlfriend had going on after the heavy discussion we just had? I'm so lucky. Danica was ashamed to admit that she'd danced around talking to Sally for most of the day. "It turned out that while I was worried she'd want to talk about Rusty, she was fretting over Gage *and* Rusty."

"Is that good or bad?"

"I'm not sure."

Chapter Fifty-Three

"Are we still on for this afternoon? Lunch and shopping for evil spawn?" Danica had a job to do today—get Kaylie to her baby shower. She was enjoying teasing Kaylie about the niece or nephew she'd already fallen in love with, and when the baby was finally born and given a real name, she knew she'd miss seeing the little annoyance on her sister's face.

Kaylie sighed. "Yes."

"What? Too much teasing?"

"No, I know you're kidding. Something's up with Chaz and I don't know what it is. I told him that I was waiting to make a decision about the record label, and I swear he reminds me of a balloon about to burst."

"He's probably stressed about the baby." Danica hated lying to Kaylie, but saying anything now would only make it worse. Besides, they had a baby shower to attend.

"Maybe. I guess. But it feels like he's not telling me something, and if it's that he doesn't want me to take the contract, he should just tell me that."

"I'm sure that's not it. He's so proud of you, Kay. You could see it in his eyes when you were singing."

"Yeah," Kaylie said in a dreamy voice. "That's true. Maybe it is just the baby. Ow, ow, ow."

"What? You okay?"

Kaylie breathed hard into the phone. "Yeah, it's those damn Braxton Hicks contractions. I swear they really do suck."

Danica waited for Kaylie to breath normally again.

Kaylie let out a little *whoop!* "Okay, where are we meeting again?"

"I'm almost there. I'm picking you up." Danica slowed as she passed the house Blake was buying. *Our house.* "Can you believe I'm moving in a mile away?"

"I know. I can't wait!"

They hung up the phone just as Danica pulled up the long driveway.

Kaylie stood in the open doorway in a beautiful pink sundress. Her hair shone bright and full.

"Your belly looks lower," Danica noticed.

"Tell me about it. I swear this baby is sitting right on my bladder, and it hurts. Whoever said pregnancy is wonderful lied. Between the Braxton Hicks contractions and my bladder, I'm sure it's some sort of punishment."

Danica laughed. "A few more weeks and it'll be over and you'll be all googly-eyed at your tiny evil spawn."

"At least she's moved down past my diaphragm, so I can breathe again."

Danica pulled down the driveway and headed toward town. "Atta girl. Way to see the bright side." She watched Kaylie's hand resting on her belly and reached over and touched her softly. "I'm kinda jealous, you know. I mean, you're about to have a baby, Kay. A baby!"

"Jealous? Really?"

Danica took her hand back. "Don't get too full of yourself."

"I'm scared shitless. What do I know about raising a baby?" The look in her eyes spelled P-A-N-I-C to Danica, and she knew just how to talk her sister off the ledge.

"Remember how you used to worry about when you finally had sex? You kept worrying about if you would measure up and all that bullshit?"

"Yeah, you laughed at me and told me to keep my pants on."

Danica smiled at the memory. "Yeah, well, remember how you figured it all out?"

Kaylie looked at her newly manicured fingernails. "I was damn good at it. Still am." She shot a smirk in Danica's direction.

"This is the same thing. You just go with your gut on it. I mean, you do have Mom to fall back on."

Kaylie groaned. "Mom was a natural. I'm not at all like her. Besides, we haven't really talked much since lunch that day."

"So, call her."

Kaylie looked at her sideways.

"Kaylie, she's your mother. Time to move on." Danica dug her phone out of her console and handed it to Kaylie. "Do it. She's pound three on speed dial."

Kaylie stared at the phone.

"Do you even know why you're mad at her anymore?"

Kaylie shrugged. "She stayed with Dad."

"For us," Danica reminded her.

"Yeah, I know." Kaylie ran her fingers over the numbers. "I feel stupid. I mean, I haven't exactly been nice to her. What if she doesn't want to talk to me?"

"She's a mom. It's her job to unconditionally love us. You should take a few notes along the way," she teased. "These are all things you need to learn before evil spawn comes around."

"Sassy."

"What?"

"Evil spawn. I nicknamed her Sassy."

"Sassy spawn. I like it. Now, call Mom before we get to town." She watched Kaylie dial her mother's number and then pretended not to eavesdrop as Kaylie said the two most important words in any relationship.

"Mom, I'm sorry. I shouldn't have shut you out of my life for so lo—" Kaylie listened to her mother speak. "But I shouldn't have—" She blinked away wetness from her eyes. "Okay. I know. I love you, too." She listened again and turned toward Danica and mouthed, *Thank you*, then listened again to her mother on the other end of the phone. "Mom, I know you were strong to stay with Dad. It was him I was pissed at, but since I wasn't talking to him, well, I'm sorry." She paused. "No, I haven't talked to him. I know, Mom. Okay, whatever." She mouthed, *Dad*, to Danica and rolled her eyes. "I love you too Mom."

After she hung up the phone, Danica remained silent. Her sister was growing up, and Danica was relishing in the amazement of it all.

They walked into the dimly lit restaurant at Bar None. Jimmy Buffet played softly in the background.

"Why's it so dark in here?" Kaylie asked. "Do you think I really need to call Dad? I don't feel like I need to. I mean, it's been a few years since we've actually spoken to each other."

"I don't know, Kaylie. He is our father."

Kaylie bit her lower lip, then took Danica's hand and said, "Before the wedding I promise to talk to him, okay?"

The last thing they needed was more drama right now. She

told the hostess that they needed a table for two and winked when Kaylie looked away. They followed her to the back of the restaurant, where Kaylie immediately buried her nose in the menu.

"I'm starved. I swear this baby steals my food the second I swallow it." She pored over the entrees.

"Hi, I'm Camille, and I'll be your waitress today."

Kaylie spun her head around. "Camille?"

The kitchen doors swung open and Chelsea, Marie, Michelle, Sally, Nancy, and Chaz's mother, grandmother, and two sisters streamed out carrying pink and blue balloons, laughing, all heading directly for Kaylie. Danica saw their mother trailing quietly behind, pride beaming from her eyes.

Kaylie's jaw hung open. She stood and hugged each of her friends. "I can't believe it." She shot a look at Danica. "You little sneak!"

Camille stood behind her, and Kaylie mocked, "And you! This is why you wouldn't talk to me about a shower!"

"What kind of friend would I be if I spilled the beans? Besides, you know you can count on us with any reason for a party! And your baby? That's the best reason of all!"

Kaylie hugged Maria. Chelsea couldn't keep her hands off of Kaylie's belly. "Don't worry. Sassy will know Auntie Chelsea!" Kaylie joked.

Danica watched Kaylie's and their mother's eyes meet across the table, where she stood beside Chaz's sisters Abby, the baby of the family, and Astrid, the eldest. Their mother smiled and nodded, giving Kaylie the space to greet her visitors before tending to her. Danica was surprised when Kaylie made a beeline for her mother. She wrapped her arms around her neck, gently touching their mother's hair, and said with a smile, "Still red? I guess I can deal with red."

"I know you like it blond," her mother answered.

"I love it red. I love you, Mom, and if you love it red, then I love it red. I'm sorry I wasted so much time figuring that out."

Her mother held Kaylie tight, then whispered in her ear, "I hate the red, too."

Just when Danica saw Kaylie's eyes dampen, her mother released her and said, "Go. You've got more guests to welcome."

Danica wanted to run over and hug Kaylie, but she remained where she was and gave her sister space to swallow past the lump she was sure had formed in her throat.

Kaylie hugged Abby. "Thank you for coming."

"I wouldn't miss it for the world." Abby looked the most like Chaz. She was tall, with thick blond hair and warm blue eyes.

Astrid put her hand on Kaylie's belly. "I can't believe my baby brother is having a baby." She hugged Kaylie and told her that she couldn't wait to meet the baby.

Kaylie approached Chaz's mother with a nervous gait. "Elise."

Danica watched Elise Crew look Kaylie up and down. Her mother touched her shoulder.

"Let them be," she said calmly. "She's a big girl."

Elise took a step toward Kaylie. Danica saw the way Elise's body went rigid in Kaylie's arm. Elise stepped back and put a hand up to pat her hair. Danica knew that Elise had been cold and not very accepting of her sister in Chaz's life, but seeing the interaction between them was a whole different ball game, and Danica didn't like it one bit.

"Well, you look…" she said, her gray eyes scanning Kaylie from head to toe.

The hope in Kaylie's eyes nearly crushed Danica's heart. She took a step forward and her mother tightened her grip on

Danica's shoulder. Then she stepped forward.

"She looks beautiful, doesn't she?" Their mother looked at Elise in a way that spoke volumes of protection. A look that Danica read as, *If you know what's good for you, you'll wipe that judgmental smirk off of your face and admit that you see the beauty that is my daughter.* And it made her proud.

Elise nodded. "Yes, she is glowing, isn't she?"

"Thank you," Kaylie said, and kissed her soon-to-be mother-in-law on the cheek, then quickly escaped to the safety of Max, Sally, Michelle, and Nancy.

By the time they'd each settled into their seats, the staff had tied pink and blue balloons to the chairs, hung pastel streamers along the walls, and set pink and blue centerpieces on each table. Danica saw the surprise in Kaylie's eyes.

"Isn't it pretty?" she asked.

Kaylie put her hand over her heart. "The beauty of it takes my breath away."

Danica watched Kaylie chatting with Camille and Chelsea and sharing her news about the record deal. Danica knew that when Chaz shared the knowledge that Lea was an owner, it would definitely crush her spirit.

Her mother whispered, "Thank you."

"For what?" Danica said, turning to her and seeing the love in her eyes.

"I know you pushed her to call me, and I appreciate that."

Danica smiled. "She'd have called...eventually."

"I know. But thank you. Boy, that Elise is something else, isn't she?"

Danica watched Elise as she looked in her compact mirror, applying fresh lipstick to her wrinkled lips. She patted her short gray hair again, took one last smug look in the mirror, and snapped it shut. "She thinks Kaylie trapped Chaz, and she's obviously making her disapproval of the situation known."

"Please don't let me ever get that way," her mother teased.

"No way. Chaz's sisters seem nice, though."

Astrid laughed at something, and Abby looked at Kaylie with admiration. "I think Abby is really taken with her," her mother noticed.

"Yeah, she's only twenty-two. I think she admires the rascally side of Kaylie that everyone loves so much."

Her mother squeezed her hand. "You have that side, too, you know."

Danica nodded. Lately, with all the changes that both Danica and Kaylie had made in their lives, the dividing line between the type of person Kaylie had become and the type of person Danica had become was starting to blur. She found herself looking up to Kaylie for all the attributes she possessed that Danica simply didn't. She no longer saw Kaylie as her wild little sister. Kaylie was becoming a mature woman. She was handling her issues head-on, and thinking through her decisions and the ramifications to both Chaz and her baby. Danica was so proud of Kaylie that her heart physically ached. Kaylie would always be Barbie doll pretty, effervescent, and flirty—God help Chaz when she got her figure back. But she was becoming a mother right before Danica's eyes, and that was a transition Danica would never forget.

Chapter Fifty-Four

They'd been playing silly baby shower games for an hour, and everyone was getting a bit punchy. Kaylie was bent over a tub of baby bottle nipples bobbing up and down in water.

"Come on, Kaylie!" Abby cheered as Kaylie tried to pick up as many nipples in her mouth as she could.

Chelsea whispered in Danica's ear, "That girl can do wonders with her mouth. She's got this."

They both laughed.

Marie heard them and added, "That's what he said!" Sending them all into fits of laughter.

Michelle touched Danica's sleeve. "Thanks for letting me and my mom come to the shower."

"I wouldn't have it any other way. Neither would Kaylie."

Danica looked back at Max, who had been a quiet calm amidst the excitement. "You're next Max."

Max shook her head. "I have better things to do with these lips than sink them in a tub of water."

"Aw, come on. It'll be fun," Danica urged.

"It's okay. I like to watch more than take part in this stuff. I'm just not a giggly girly girl."

Danica put her arm around her. "That's what we love about you!"

Kaylie came up for air with three nipples in her mouth. She threw her hands up in the air and shouted, "Yes!"

Everyone clapped and cheered.

"That's my sister!" Danica yelled.

"Look out, Chaz!" Chelsea teased.

Kaylie gasped and the room grew quiet. All eyes turned to her as she shifted her hands to her lower back, her tummy protruding heavily before her. She looked down and gasped another breath. Danica's eyes followed, settling on the water that was now soaking Kaylie's sandals—and it wasn't water from the tub of bobbing nipples.

"Danica?" Kaylie said with a trembling voice.

Danica ran to her side. "I'm right here, Kay."

"My water broke."

"I see that. Let's get you to the hospital."

Kaylie clung to Danica's hand. "Max, call Chaz please?"

"What's happened?" Abby asked.

"I think her water broke," Camille said.

"She's in labor?" Chelsea asked excitedly.

"Oh, my goodness! It's time!" her mother yelled.

Suddenly, Chelsea, Camille, and Marie screamed in unison, "It's time!"

Max was on her cell phone calling Chaz. She left a message.

"Mom, call Blake. My cell's in my purse," Danica ordered.

Her mother scrambled for their purses and followed them outside to Danica's car.

"I can't sit down. It'll ruin your seats." Kaylie clenched her sister's hand.

"Kaylie, like I care?" Danica said.

"Take mine. Leather seats." Camille started the car and opened all the doors to her Lincoln Navigator. "Sorry, Kay. It's a big step," she said as she and Danica helped lift her into the backseat.

"I've climbed bigger things than this." Kaylie winked, then winced as she settled into the seat.

"I'll sit with her." Danica climbed in and Camille started the car. The others piled into their respective cars.

"Mom!" Kaylie yelled before they shut her door. "Mom, come with me. Please."

Her mother climbed in on her other side. Kaylie reached out and took Danica's hand in one hand and her mother's in the other just as a contraction hit and Camille sped out of the parking lot.

Kaylie moaned. "Mom, it hurts. It hurts."

"I know, baby. This is just the beginning."

Kaylie shot a stunned look at her. "Thanks! That's reassuring."

"Kaylie, look at me."

Kaylie looked at Danica.

"Breathe, just like they showed you in Lamaze. In and out. Focus on evil…sassy spawn. You'll meet her—or him—soon. That's a girl. Breathe."

Sweat beaded Kaylie's forehead, and her mother dabbed at it with a tissue as the contraction subsided. "You know, first babies are supposed to come late, not early," she said.

"What can I say? She's impatient."

"Just like her mama. You know, Danica was two weeks late, but you"—she poked Kaylie playfully in the arm—"You were three weeks early, and you came out ready to tell the world what they were doing wrong."

"Really?" Kaylie's eyes gleamed.

"Really."

Kaylie gritted her teeth against another contraction.

"Jesus, they're coming quick," Danica said. *Please don't have the baby in the car.*

Her mother shot her a stern look. *Relax*, she mouthed.

Danica nodded.

"Mom, she's not going to relax for my sake. This is our first baby!" Kaylie arched her back against the pain.

"Breathe, Kay, breathe." Danica mouthed, *Sorry* to her mother.

"Did Max reach Chaz?" Panic laced Kaylie's words, and then the contraction eased.

"Shoot. I forgot to ask her before we left." Her mother fished for Kaylie's phone in her purse, then searched for Chaz's number.

"Call Max. See if she got him," Danica said. Then, realizing that her mother never called Blake, she took the phone from her mother's hand. "Sorry, Mom. It's just easier." Danica called Max, and she hadn't been able to reach Chaz either. She dialed Blake's number. "Do you know where Chaz is?"

"Yeah, he's right here."

"Oh, thank God. Get to the hospital. Kaylie's in labor. We're pulling in now. Come quickly, because her contractions are really close together." She heard him repeat her words to Chaz.

No sooner had she hung up than Kaylie's cell phone rang.

Danica handed it to Kaylie. "Chaz."

"Where are you?" Kaylie said, breathless. "Yeah, fine. I'm…hold on…shit." She slammed the phone into her mother's hand and groaned as Camille pulled up in front of the Emergency entrance. Kaylie stretched backward, arching against the contraction. "Ugh! I wish I could just climb out of my constricting body and let someone else birth the baby. Jesus. Get me inside. I want that epidural!"

"Chaz, she's having another contraction. How far away are you?" her mother asked. "Okay, good. Hurry, but be safe."

Danica helped Kaylie from the car, recognizing the fear in Kaylie's eyes. She wrapped Kaylie's arm around her, then put her own arm around Kaylie's waist, taking the weight of her while they moved slowly toward the entrance. Danica did the only thing she knew would take Kaylie's mind off of the pain. "Just think, at least you're dressed for the occasion."

Kaylie's scowl morphed into an attempted smile. "True."

Her mother ran up and put her arm around Kaylie's other side while Camille parked the car. "You can do this, honey. You're almost there."

"Mom, it hurts," Kaylie whined. "It feels like the baby's gonna drop right out."

"That'd save you on hospital bills," Danica joked.

Both Kaylie and her mother glared at her. "Sorry, trying to lighten the mood." Danica laughed, but they didn't. "Kay, you're doing great. Just think, soon you'll meet sassy spawn."

"You said sassy. Didn't you mean evil?"

"No. I can't imagine you ever giving birth to anything evil."

Another contraction gripped Kaylie, and she stopped, grasping at her belly. "Ow, ow, ow, ow."

"Breathe, just breathe through it," her mother said.

Tears sprang to Kaylie's eyes. "I'm trying!" She looked around frantically. "Where's Chaz. He's coming, right?"

"He'll be here any minute," her mother assured her.

"You can do this, Kaylie," Danica urged.

Marie, Camille, and Chelsea ran up the walkway toward them. Danica felt her body relax just a bit.

"You came!" Kaylie walked through the doors with an entourage, tailed by Max, Sally, Nancy, and Michelle.

"I'll get her signed in," Danica said. She yelled to the woman behind the desk, "Wheelchair? We're in labor."

Someone in scrubs ran out with a wheelchair while Danica gathered the paperwork. Kaylie, safely secure in the wheelchair, took Camille's hand. "I can't believe it's time."

Camille dug in her purse and withdrew a brush and a hair clip. She quickly brushed Kaylie's hair back and fastened it in a decorative clip. "Gotta look good when you meet your baby."

"Definitely," Marie added.

"She's always beautiful," Chelsea said, touching Kaylie's shoulder.

The attendant who brought the wheelchair out said, "We should get her into a room so that we can examine her."

The girls agreed and followed on his heels, chattering excitedly. The attendant stopped, giving Kaylie a disapproving stare.

"Don't even try. They're coming with me," she said, reaching for Chelsea's hand.

Max, Sally, and Nancy sat in the waiting room. "You can come, too," Kaylie offered.

"That's okay. We'll wait until the baby's born," Sally said. "Trust me on this. Too many people and you'll want to rip your hair out—or theirs."

"I need Kaylie's purse with her insurance information," Danica said to Camille.

"I already preregistered. It's done," Kaylie said.

"Wow, really?" Danica never would have expected Kaylie to be so organized.

Kaylie changed into a gown with the help of the girls while her mother and Danica peppered the nurse with questions.

After answering, she turned her focus to Kaylie. "I'm Gail, and I'll be your nurse today. Dr. Lasco will be here shortly. She's just wrapping up a delivery." She spoke sweetly while she hooked up the fetal monitor. "This will let us keep an eye on that baby of yours," she said. Her touch was gentle and her brown eyes soothing. "Do you know what you're having?"

"No," Kaylie said as the nurse checked her blood pressure.

"That's exciting. It's rare that we get to deliver a baby who doesn't yet have an entire wardrobe." She pushed her dark hair from her shoulders as she watched the monitor.

The girls were whispering to one another. Kaylie caught every other word—*Excited! Auntie! So brave!*

Gail leaned down and whispered in Kaylie's ear, "Let me know when you want some privacy and I'll clear the room."

"Oh, no, it's okay. I want them all here," Kaylie said. "But can you please check and see if my fiancé is here yet? Chaz Crew? Tall, blond, incredibly sexy."

"Not that she's biased or anything," Danica added.

"Sure. I'll go check."

Gail left the room and mayhem exploded. All of them spoke at once.

"Are you okay?" Camille asked.

"Want ice chips? I hear ice chips help," Marie offered.

"She doesn't want ice chips. She needs a back rub," Chelsea said.

Kaylie grabbed her belly as another contraction took hold.

"Breathe, honey. That's a girl. I'm so proud of you," her mother said, as she rubbed Kaylie's forearm lightly.

"Ouch, that's gotta hurt," Chelsea said.

Kaylie shot an annoyed look in her direction as she breathed through the pain.

Dr. Lasco breezed into the room donning light blue scrubs, her long brown hair secured on the top of her head. "Hello, Kaylie. I hear your baby wants out."

"Yes! Please!" Kaylie blew out slow breaths as the contractions subsided.

"They're coming every two or three minutes," her mother said.

"Are they, now?" Dr. Lasco proceeded calmly to the foot of the bed.

Gail came into the room and put a pair of hospital socks on Kaylie's feet, then set Kaylie's feet gently in the stirrups.

Dr. Lasco sat on a small round stool and put on a pair of latex gloves. "Let's just take a look." She lifted Kaylie's gown.

Camille and Marie held each other's hands beside Chelsea, who watched every move the doctor made. Danica and their mother stood to Kaylie's right. Danica held her hand, while her mother rested her hand on Kaylie's shoulder, as if they both could protect her from pain and provide the strength she'd likely need.

"Everything looks great." Dr. Lasco stood and removed the gloves. "You're about seven centimeters dilated."

"Is that good?" Kaylie asked impatiently.

"It's very good, Kaylie. And if you really want that epidural, now's the time to get it."

Chaz burst through the door, "Kaylie?"

Danica and her mother moved aside. Chaz took Kaylie's hand. "Are you okay? What can I do?" Sweat glistened on his forehead. "Dr. Lasco, is everything okay?"

Dr. Lasco moved with practice ease. "Yes, she's fine." She patted his back. "She's got some time yet. She's doing great."

Chaz let out a breath, then rested his forehead on Kaylie's.

"Epidural, please?" Kaylie said as another contraction ripped through her, squeezing her belly so tightly she thought the baby might eject right out of her body. A dull pain spread across her back, and she groaned.

"Breathe, two, three, in two, three," Chaz said calmly. "You can do this, Kaylie. I know you can."

"I'll go get the anesthesiologist. Gail." Dr. Lasco nodded toward the door.

Gail followed Dr. Lasco out of the room.

"What…what's she"—huff, huff—"saying? Why'd she"—huff, huff—"call her out? What's"—huff, huff, huff—"wrong?" She squeezed Chaz's hand.

Danica went out the door to eavesdrop.

"She's a doctor, Kaylie. She was just in a delivery. She's got more patients than just you. I'm sure it's nothing. She told you everything was fine," her mother said.

Danica came back into the room and looked at the girls with apologetic eyes. "She's worried about having so many people in the delivery room."

"What? No!" Kaylie whined.

"It's up to you, Kaylie," Danica said.

Kaylie reached for Camille's hand. "It's our first baby. You guys are staying."

"Are you sure?" Camille asked.

"Of course." Another contraction took hold, and Kaylie gritted her teeth.

Danica turned to her mother. "That wasn't two minutes," she whispered.

Her mother raised her brows. "Babies have a mind of their own."

"And any baby of Kaylie's won't be told when it can be born," Danica added.

"Hey, I'm in pain over here," Kaylie said. "Where is that epidural?"

"What can we do, Kay?" Chelsea asked.

"Nothing. Just be here."

"Oh, I know! Names!" Marie exclaimed.

"Whew, that was a long one." Kaylie looked at Chaz, whose

face had lost some of its color. "Are you okay?"

"Yeah, I'm just a little nervous. I'm fine. This is about you, not me. I'm good."

Kaylie's mom put her hand on his back. "Do you want to sit down? First babies are known to take their time." She lifted an eyebrow. "Although this one does seem to be in a rush."

Chaz shot a look at Danica, catching her eye with a silent plea. "Danica, Blake's here. Let's let him know we'll be a while."

"Kay, do you mind?" Danica asked, taking her cue that Chaz needed to talk.

"No, I'm good." She released Chaz's hand and replaced it with her mother's. Camille held her other hand. "But hurry. Just in case."

Chaz kissed her head, and he and Danica went to find Blake.

"What the hell, Chaz?" Danica asked. Was he too nervous to be in the room? If so, she had to be there. Kaylie needed one of them.

"It just hit me. The baby's coming, and I haven't said anything to Kaylie about Lea and Benton Records. I feel like I'm lying to her, and I promised I wouldn't lie. I can't start our family with a lie."

Jesus, really? Now? Danica and Chaz hurried into the waiting area, where her eyes were drawn to Blake, a dozen red roses across his lap. His eyes lit up, and he stood. Danica melted into his strong embrace. If Kaylie hadn't been in labor, she'd have stayed within the safety of his embrace until she was pried away. Chaz wanted to do the right thing, and she couldn't fault him for that. She regretfully pushed back.

"They said we had some time, but I don't know," Danica said.

Chaz stood with his arms crossed, his right hand on his chin.

"Dude, you okay?" Blake asked.

Chaz shook his head, looking at Danica.

"It's the offer from Benton," Danica said. "It's vying to be revealed, and Chaz feels like he needs to do it now, before the baby is born."

"Yeah, he told me," Blake said. "Smart move. You know that if you don't, this day will forever be remembered as the day you kept the truth from her instead of the day your baby was born."

"He's right." Danica knew Chaz was right, but the timing couldn't have been worse. "You might want to just wait until she's had the epidural."

The girls came charging down the hall.

"Chaz!" Marie yelled. "Get in there. She's having the epidural and needs you."

"She kicked us out. Said it hurt too much to be nice," Camille said with a wave of her hand.

"Does she want me?" Danica asked, watching with jealousy as Chaz headed toward Kaylie's room.

Chelsea pushed Danica lightly. "If you don't go, she'll eat him alive," she teased.

Chapter Fifty-Five

Kaylie sat on the edge of the bed, her head bent forward, her back to the door. The IV line in her arm pinched, but she was too busy listening for Chaz's return to complain. Fear riddled her nerves. She hadn't meant to snap at the girls, but the last contraction was mountainous. The rush of noise from the hall filtered in with the opening of the door.

"Chaz? Danica?" she called out.

Her mother squeezed her hand. "Both, honey. They're here."

Chaz came around and took their mother's place. "I'm here, and I won't leave again. I promise."

The anesthesiologist wiped Kaylie's back and said, "Okay, now, it's really important that you stay completely still."

"Wait!" Kaylie cried. "What if I have a contraction?"

"Just try to stay still. You'll feel a little pressure now."

"Ow, ow, ow," Kaylie cried, squeezing Chaz's hand.

Her mother held her arm, and Danica reassured her. "You're doing great, Kay. He's almost done; then you'll feel so much better."

Kaylie squeezed her eyes closed. "Oh, no. Oh, no. A contraction."

Her mother held tight to her arm, anchoring her in place,

and in her best matronly tone, she said, "Kaylie, you stay still now. He's almost done. You're almost there."

"Breathe, two, three," Chaz said, and Danica breathed right along with them.

"Okay, you did great, Kaylie." The anesthesiologist worked with Gail to tape the epidural catheter up Kaylie's back to her shoulder. "Are you okay, Kaylie? How do you feel?"

"I'm good. Thank you."

He stood by the bed as Gail helped Kaylie lie back. Then he touched Kaylie's legs and torso with something she couldn't see between his fingers. "Can you feel that?"

"No. That's good, right?"

His dark skin contrasted with her fair complexion like chocolate against milk. When he spoke, he spoke with tenderness, as if he hadn't a worry in the world, which instilled confidence in Kaylie. "That's great. You shouldn't feel much during the delivery. A bit of tugging and pressure, but no more of those all-consuming contractions. You'll feel sensations, but you'll do fine."

Kaylie breathed a sigh of relief. "Thank you."

"Thank you," Chaz said, and turned his attention back to Kaylie as the anesthesiologist gave directions to Gail, then left the room.

Chaz looked at Danica, and Danica touched her mother's arm. "Mom, let's give them a minute."

How did she know? Kaylie had been dying to get Chaz alone. She'd made a decision about the offer from Benton, and she wanted him to know before the baby was born. As soon as they were out the door, she said, "I need to talk to you."

"Me, too. Oh, God, Kaylie. Can you believe our baby's coming? Today?"

Kaylie wanted to spend the next ten hours gushing about

how excited she was to be a mom and to finally meet their baby, but she'd been thinking about the record label ever since her water broke, and holding in her excitement was too much.

"Chaz," she said in a serious tone. She knew by his fading smile that he expected bad news. "Don't worry. It's not about the baby." When his worry lines didn't disappear, she reassessed telling him. Maybe it would be too much for him. Maybe he didn't really want her to go, and he really was just being supportive, with the hopes she wouldn't go.

A contraction gripped her belly, and she watched with discomfort as her belly contracted, then eased. She breathed, clenching Chaz's hand, feeling strangely detached from the contractions that had been racking her body just minutes before.

"Are you okay?" he asked.

"Yeah, fine. It doesn't really hurt very much now. It's just pretty uncomfortable." She breathed through the contraction. When it subsided, she said, "I've made a decision about the label."

His Adam's apple bobbled as he swallowed.

"I've worked really hard, and I just can't see myself stopping now. I know I said I would wait until the baby was born to make the decision, but, Chaz, I can't. I just can't give up what I've worked so hard to achieve."

Chaz nodded. "Okay," he said in a flat, emotionless tone.

"Okay?" She hoped he'd say something more.

"Okay. I support your decision." He sat back and ran his hand through his hair. It fell from his fingertips in a playful fashion.

He needed a trim, and Kaylie reached for his hair. She wanted to touch it, to touch him. To make sure he was okay with her decision. He leaned into her, and she took his head in her arms, held his forehead against her shoulder. "I know it won't be easy," she said.

"We'll make it work," he said, then pulled back and rested his hand on her cheek.

If Kaylie had ever doubted his commitment, the doubt was gone. Washed away like waves rolling back into the sea. She took comfort in his touch and relaxed into his warm palm.

"I need to tell you something, too," he said. "It's not easy, and it might not even be important, but—"

Another contraction crawled across her back and whispered across her belly. The mild discomfort turned to pain and pressure in her groin that she'd never felt before. Kaylie lifted her head from Chaz's palm and grabbed the sides of the bed with a cry.

"Breathe, Kaylie. Breathe through the pain."

She knew Chaz saw the panic in her eyes when he raced out the door to get the doctor. In the next thirty seconds, Kaylie had never felt so alone—or so scared. Pain ripped through her belly, and pressure built along her pelvis floor. *Breathe, two, three.* She tried to calm her raging anxiety, staring at the closed door, willing Chaz to return. The pain subsided as Dr. Lasco entered, followed by Chaz, Gail, Danica, and her mother. "Oh, God," she cried, as another contraction hit.

Gail checked the monitors and reported the findings to Dr. Lasco.

"This baby must be anxious to meet you," Dr. Lasco said as she slipped on another pair of gloves and situated herself at the foot of the bed.

Kaylie grabbed Chaz's hand and watched as Danica allowed her mother to go to the other side of the bed. "Danica," she cried. She didn't mean to. She wanted her mother, too, but she needed Danica in a way she didn't need her mother at that very moment. Danica had been her one constant throughout her life—through her parents' divorce, through her year without contact with their mother. Danica stepped behind her mother and put her hand securely on Kaylie's shoulder.

"I'm right here. You're doing great. Sassy spawn will be here soon."

Kaylie knew, without a shadow of a doubt, that no matter what happened, or how much the birth hurt, she was surrounded by love, and their baby would be born into that same safe cocoon.

She closed her eyes as the next contraction tore across her belly.

"Don't push, Kaylie. You're almost there, but fight the urge."

"I...have to," Kaylie huffed through gritted teeth.

Danica squeezed her shoulder. "Look at me, Kaylie. Look up here."

Kaylie did.

"Breathe, that's a girl. Just breathe. You've carried this baby for this long. You're not going to disappoint her now. You can do this, and you will."

Kaylie nodded.

"A little harsh, don't you think?" her mother said to Danica.

"She can take it. Besides if I say something softer, she'll fight me on it," Danica said with a wink.

"Danica! Mom!" Kaylie snapped as the next contraction hit and she blew for the millionth time through pursed lips. "This hurts like a son of a"—huff, huff—"gun."

"You're doing great," Danica encouraged.

"Kaylie, you're almost there," Chaz assured her.

Kaylie suddenly remembered that Chaz had been telling her something. "Chaz," she said breathlessly. "What did you want to tell me?"

Danica caught his eye and shook her head.

Chaz looked down at the doctor preparing to deliver their child, and the look in his eyes when he looked back at Kaylie pulled at her heart.

"Whatever it is, you can tell me," she assured him.

"It's about the label. I had Max check it out."

"Chaz," Danica whispered harshly.

"It's okay. Go on," Kaylie said, but when Chaz started to speak, it felt like someone had kicked her in her lower back. She cried out and sat up, bearing down with the pain.

"Kaylie, don't push," Dr. Lasco commanded.

"Ugh!" Kaylie whined.

"You can do it, Kaylie. Lean back." Her mother gently pressed Kaylie's shoulders back toward the pillow.

Her belly contracted, and she bolted upright again. "I can't. I can't wait. I gotta push."

Dr. Lasco spoke calmly and sternly. "Kaylie, I can see your baby's beautiful head. Go ahead and push, but if I tell you to stop, you stop." She lifted her eyes and nodded.

Kaylie rode the crescendo of the next contraction until she thought her body might tear apart. She bore down and pushed, gritting her teeth; the encouragement of her mother, Danica, and Chaz became white noise behind the rushing of blood in her ears. "Get it out!" she yelled.

"Stop pushing, Kaylie. Stop."

She felt fingers on her shoulder, pushing her back toward the pillow. Her eyes fluttered closed, then open, as she tried to catch her breath. Before she did, another contraction gripped her and sent her reeling forward, bearing down hard. *Who's screaming? Make them stop!* She opened her eyes and found the wails coming from her own throat. Suddenly, she felt an enormous pressure, then release.

"Kaylie, stop pushing. Your baby's head is out, but the cord is wrapped around its neck."

Kaylie looked frantically down at the doctor. "Oh, God. Fix it. Fix it, please. Please!"

"Shh," her mother urged. "She's doing all she can."

"Danica!" Kaylie cried.

Danica moved swiftly to the end of the bed. She covered her mouth and lifted her gaze to meet Kaylie's, as tears of joy spilled down her cheeks.

A high-pitched cry filled the air, and Kaylie fell back, laughing, as another contraction took control and sent her upright once again. This time she pushed with all her might and felt the pressure of the baby as it slithered out of her body. She lay panting, waiting for the doctor to say something. Anything. Finally, Dr. Lasco rose to her feet and held the baby up so Kaylie could see.

"Say hello to your bouncing baby girl."

"A girl! It's a girl!" Chaz said, and leaned down to hug Kaylie.

"Sassy spawn!" Danica cheered and hugged her mother.

Kaylie looked at her baby, covered with blood and goo, her wrinkled face a mask of wailing cuteness, her impossibly tiny arms and legs flailing in the air. She was her baby. Their baby. She looked from the baby to Chaz as another contraction stole her thoughts.

"Kaylie, I need you to focus," Dr. Lasco said in a serious voice.

"What?" Kaylie gritted her teeth. This couldn't be right. Something was wrong. Her belly contracted and she had to push again. She bore down hard.

"Kaylie, listen to me."

A nurse that Kaylie hadn't noticed earlier took the baby and hovered over it beneath a light.

"What is it?" she cried.

"Ultrasounds are not always right," Dr. Lasco said. "I need you to push again, Kaylie. Push until I tell you to stop."

Kaylie pushed until her face hurt and she had no breath left in her lungs.

"Good, good. Hold on now." Dr. Lasco glanced up at Kaylie. "Looks like you're going to have another member of the family."

"Twins?" Chaz and Kaylie said at once.

"You insisted on having only the one sonogram because you didn't want to know the sex of the baby." Dr. Lasco lifted her smiling eyes to Kaylie, then continued. "It was so early on that we just didn't pick up on the second heartbeat. That happens with twins sometimes. The beats are the sa—"

"I gotta push!" Kaylie cried.

"Okay, push, Kaylie."

She bore down again and felt the same relief when her second baby slipped from her body. She fell back, out of breath, exhausted, clenching Chaz's hand.

"Twins?" Tears of joy streamed down her mother's cheeks. "We have no twin genes in our family history."

A distinct cry, different from the first baby's, filled the room. "And now you do. May I present to you your son," Dr. Lasco said as she stood with their second baby.

Kaylie lay holding Chaz's hand, her eyes on the nurses who hovered over the babies. She turned toward her mother, who was wiping joyful tears from her eyes as she bent down and hugged Kaylie.

"I get it," Kaylie whispered.

"I always knew you would," she said.

Danica stood by the table where the nurse cleaned and checked out the babies. "Kaylie, she's the most gorgeous sassy spawn I've ever seen, and he's, well, he's just going to be a lady killer." She wiped her tears and watched as the nurses brought the swaddled babies to Kaylie.

Holding her babies for the first time was like nothing Kaylie had ever experienced before. Something inside her changed, a switch flipped, a door opened, and she knew she would never be the same again. She kissed their foreheads and tried to listen as the doctor told her what to expect with regard to recovery. Kaylie didn't register a word of it. She couldn't take her eyes off of their beautiful daughter and son.

She looked up at Chaz and knew she'd made the wrong decision.

Chapter Fifty-Six

"Chaz." He lowered himself beside her. "I can't do it," Kaylie said. She looked at the babies and got lost in the beauty of them, oblivious to the fact that all the blood had drained from Chaz's face. When she looked back at him, she saw the unbridled fear in his blue eyes.

"Kaylie, I won't work as much. I'll change however you think I need to." Chaz shot a look at Danica.

Kaylie caught the worried glance and pulled his chin, locking eyes with him. "Oh, goodness, Chaz. Not us. I can't take the job with the label. I can't do it. I can't leave them. I don't want to."

Chaz's eyes darted to Danica. Kaylie looked at her sister. Her dark curls stuck out at all angles. She looked from Kaylie to Chaz and back again.

"What is it?" Kaylie asked. They both had a guilty look in their eyes. "Danica Joy, tell me what's going on."

Danica bit her lower lip and moved closer to the bed. "Look how beautiful she is," she said, touching the baby's cheek.

"Can it," Kaylie said sharply. "Chaz, why do I feel like you guys aren't telling me something? Is something wrong with the babies?"

"No," they said in unison.

Kaylie watched Chaz clench his jaw. He looked up at her mother, then back down at Kaylie again.

"Whatever it is, just tell me," Kaylie said, on the verge of tears.

"I had the label checked out. Remember I asked Max to check it out?"

"Yeah, so?" Kaylie asked, her eyes darting back and forth from Danica to Chaz.

"It's—"

Danica jumped in. "Kaylie, let's focus on the babies. Everything is so good right now. You're so happy. Let's just focus on them for a while. Right, Mom?" She turned to her mother for support.

"I can't...Here. Can I hold one of them?" Her mother took the baby boy in her arms.

The nurse removed the tape and catheter from Kaylie, and Kaylie waited as Dr. Lasco and the nurses left the room.

"We'll come get them shortly," Gail said before closing the door behind her.

Chaz took Kaylie's hand and said, "I have to tell you something, and Danica, please don't cut me off." He didn't give Danica a harsh look, but rather a gentle smile. Then he mouthed, *Please?* When Danica nodded, he said, "I wanted to tell you earlier, but I was afraid to ruin things for you. Benton Records is owned, partially, at least, by Lea Carmichael."

Kaylie nodded. "I know," she said, matter-of-factly.

"You knew?" he asked.

"Yeah. I knew."

"Why didn't you say something?" he asked. "Why'd you keep it from me?"

"I figured you knew, and I was waiting for you to say something. I was there that day you asked Max to check it out.

Remember?"

"Then how could you take the offer? Why would you?" Chaz asked.

"I'm not a stupid person. I know that crazy woman is capable of all sorts of stuff. You're not the only one who knows how to Google someone, you know." She looked at Danica, then back at Chaz, and realized that they both were looking at her incredulously. "Look, I just figured that this was my one chance to make it, and if you and I know what she's capable of, then we know what to watch out for. She can't come between us if we're both aware of how she is. So..." She shrugged. "Why not use her for her connections?"

"Kaylie, she's so much crazier than you know."

"Chaz, I think I know how crazy she is. I'm sorry. I should have told you sooner, and maybe you should have told me, but the day I had the meeting, I asked all the right questions: who owns the company, what's expected of me, who will oversee my musical career, my travel, my gigs. They were very up-front about it all. They said she was the one who had found me and she'd practically demanded that they rep me, but Mr. Thompkins said he'd have total control over my career and that they'd even put it in writing and make sure it was stipulated that she had no say in any of that end of things. I never had a chance to tell you about it. Everything happened so fast, and the night after I met with them, you seemed a little bothered by something, and I still hadn't made up my mind about if I wanted to sign with them or not—regardless of Lea's role in it all. With all of their assurances, it seemed like I could still have this great career regardless of her."

She watched understanding dawn on Chaz and Danica, and she reveled in the pride that gleamed in her mother's eyes as she cooed over the baby.

"I should have told you sooner," Chaz apologized.

"And I should have told you. I guess we both have to work on the whole *tell each other everything thing*. But at least neither of us withheld it for the wrong reasons. When you said you'd support my decision to take the job, I knew how much you loved me. That woman's a psycho, no doubt, and who knows, maybe she would have tried to tear us apart." Kaylie kissed her little boy's head, then said confidently, "I would never have let that happen, but once I heard their cries"—she nuzzled the baby—"I knew I couldn't leave. I can't leave them and I can't leave you."

"Kaylie," Chaz said. "We can make it work."

"Free babysitter." Danica waved from behind Chaz.

"Maybe in a few years," Kaylie said. "Right now, there's nothing that will take me away from you, or from them."

Chapter Fifty-Seven

"Can you believe it's been three weeks since Kaylie had the babies, and she still hasn't named them? Who does that?" Danica and Blake were driving toward Kaylie's house for a barbeque that Kaylie swore she was ready for.

"You know Kaylie. Decisions aren't her forte," Blake said with a laugh.

"Seriously? They keep calling them him and her."

"Actually, Kaylie calls her Sassy and him Buddy." He shrugged.

"Yeah, but those aren't real names."

Blake pulled into the driveway of their home.

"Why are we stopping here? We haven't settled yet."

He smiled at her as he parked in front of the house. Danica recognized Kaylie's and her mother's cars. Sally's car pulled in behind them.

"Blake?" Her eyes grew wide.

He smiled and got out of the car before she could ask more questions. Danica was surprised to see Gage stepping out of Sally's car. Rusty, Michelle, and Chase piled out of the backseat.

"Oh, my," Danica said as she stood beside Blake. "This should be fun."

"I hear it's all very friendly."

"Sally never mentioned a thing to me." She met Blake in front of the car. "So, why are we here?"

"It's ours. I settled three days ago."

Danica punched him in the arm. "How could you not tell me?"

"Because then I wouldn't get a reaction like his." He laughed. "There are so few surprises in life. I figured I'd take full advantage."

"Congratulations?" she said with an arched brow.

He took her in his arms. "Congratulations!" He swung her around just as Gage and Sally walked by.

"Get a room," Gage teased.

Danica kissed Blake, then fell in stride with Sally. "You kept this from me?"

Sally blushed. "Nothing to keep."

"And Gage? You kept *that* from me?"

"We're friends. Very good friends." A sly smile worked its way across her lips. "Maybe one day we'll be more, but for now, at least, we're spending more time together and getting to know each other better. You know what? It's perfect for now."

"And them?" Danica pointed to Rusty, Michelle, and Chase.

"Them, too. Seems friends is the way to go."

They headed inside, where Chaz and Kaylie stood beside their mother, who was swaying back and forth with a very sleepy baby in her arms.

Kaylie shrieked and hugged Danica.

"I just saw you last week!" Danica said, looking Kaylie up and down. "Good God, girl. How are you turning back into Barbie so quickly?"

"Oh, stop," Kaylie said with a swat. "I still have a lot to lose, and check these babies out." She shimmied her maternal breasts with a laugh. "Come on. Say hi to Sassy and Buddy."

"Seriously, Kay, you've got to give them names. What do their birth certificates say? Female and Male Crew?"

Kaylie, obviously ignoring Danica's question, waved her arm, presenting the house to Danica. "Are you surprised?"

"Yeah, I am. But I think Blake is going to be even more surprised," she said with a wink.

"You haven't told him yet?" Kaylie whispered conspiratorially.

Danica shook her head.

"What about Mom?"

Danica nodded.

"What are we whispering about?" Sally asked, squeezing in between the two sisters.

"Danica's secret."

Sally crossed her arms and looked at her expectantly. "So, we're keeping secrets now?"

Danica pretended to zip her mouth closed and throw away the key. She *ooh*ed and *aah*ed over the babies, and she watched her man from across the room. She waited for the old Danica to return, to chide her for not making a formal list of pros and cons, or for not talking things through with a professional, or at least someone she trusted, but that little voice never came. Danica trusted her own judgment, and the nudge from her mother had given her the clarity to act on her decision, even if it had taken her a little while to come to one.

She watched Blake make kissy faces at her nephew. Her own McDreamy, she mused. As she ticked off all of the things about him that she'd fallen in love with, he moved toward her, with a warm, interested smile in his eyes.

"Hey, there. Wanna go someplace quiet?" he teased, nuzzling her neck.

"Actually, I want to be right here." Danica held his hand. "You haven't pressured me about marrying you."

"I know better than to badger. I've learned." Blake moved in closer.

Danica could practically taste the desire on his breath. "You've learned, have you?"

"Yeah, and I've learned that life is way too short to let things bring us down." He glanced at Sally, then back at Danica. "I'd live in sin with you until we're old and gray. I don't need a marriage certificate."

Danica lowered her eyes. "Thinking of Dave?"

Blake nodded. "Things happen, babe. The last thing I want is to not spend every second with you that I can, and if that means living together, well"—he put his hands around her waist and pulled her in close—"I hear living in sin can be pretty great."

Danica reeled in her racing heart. "What if we didn't have to?"

"Hmm?" he said into her neck, planting gentle kisses along her collarbone.

"What if we didn't have to live in sin?"

He stopped kissing her and raised his eyes.

"I've been thinking. Maybe sin isn't so great. Maybe we should live in legal splendor instead."

"Are you saying what I think you're saying?" Blake couldn't hide his enthusiasm; it came out with every hopeful word.

She beamed. "Yes."

"Yes, what? I want to be one hundred percent certain that I understand what you're saying."

The room grew quiet, and Danica felt the others' hopeful eyes on them. She looked into Blake's beautiful green eyes, tiny flecks of yellow dancing against the light, and she said, "Yes, I will marry you, Blake Carter. If the offer is still—"

Blake picked Danica up and spun her around. "Yes! Yes! She said yes!" He laughed.

"Woo-hoo!" Kaylie cheered.

"Double wedding!" Chaz added.

When Blake finally set Danica down on the hardwood floor, she was dizzy with happiness. She was passed from Sally to her mother, to Kaylie, to Chaz, and even Michelle, Chase, and Rusty got in on the congratulatory hugs.

She'd done it.

She'd said yes!

She watched Blake receive the same enthusiastic welcome to the family, and she leaned against the wall, taking it all in. She wanted to remember every second of this day.

Kaylie came and stood beside her and took Danica's hand in her own.

"Wanna know my secret?" Kaylie asked, watching Chaz give Blake a heavy pat on the back.

"Yeah," Danica answered, still reeling from her own life-changing decision.

Kaylie guided her to the babies in their double stroller, each swaddled in blankets, their tiny eyes closed. Kaylie looked down at them and smiled, then drew her eyes up to Danica.

"Auntie Danica, meet Alexandra Ellison Crew. Lexi for short." She touched her son's cheek. "And Trevor Michael Crew. Trev for short, Michael for Chaz's dad." Kaylie looked at Lexi the way their own mother looked at her—even now, so many years since she'd been a tiny baby.

"Alexandra and Trevor. You used Mom's maiden name, Ellison." Danica rolled the names over in her mind. They were such big names for such tiny babies, but if Danica believed one thing, it was that any child of Kaylie's would not have a tiny personality. *Alexandra Crew. Trevor Crew.* She liked the feel of them. *Lexi and Trev.* Even better. "They're perfect."

The End

Please enjoy the first chapter of the next *Love in Bloom* novel

Sisters in White

Snow Sisters, Book Three
Love in Bloom Series

Melissa Foster

LOVE IN BLOOM SERIES

SISTERS IN WHITE

Snow Sisters - Book 3

NEW YORK TIMES BESTSELLING AUTHOR
MELISSA FOSTER

Chapter One

"I thought they were going to do a cavity search," Danica joked as she and her fiancé, Blake Carter, finally passed through security at the Nassau Airport. After six hours on an airplane, she felt like she'd been folded, packed tight, boxed, and shipped. The sooner she stepped out those glass doors and into the sunshine, the better. "Maybe we should go walk around a bit."

"Don't you want to wait for your sister?" Blake asked, holding the doors open for Danica to pass through. Her sister, Kaylie, and Kaylie's fiancé, Chaz, were not far behind. His consideration of Kaylie and his gentlemanlike manners were just two of the many reasons Danica had fallen in love with—and finally agreed to marry—Blake.

"I guess. Then maybe we can take a walk after we get to the hotel."

Blake set their bags down and pulled Danica in close. He lowered his voice to a sexy, sleepy drawl. "If you think I'm gonna let you out of our room any longer than to attend our wedding, you're wrong."

She playfully pushed him away as he made a show of nibbling on her neck.

A few minutes later, Kaylie breezed through the doors with Chaz, who was weighed down by two enormous suitcases. Her hair blew in the warm breeze like thick, shimmering strands of gold. "That took for-e-ver!" She took a deep breath and drew her arms open wide. "So this is what freedom feels like."

"If you call six hours on a plane freedom," Chaz joked. His blond hair was slightly disheveled, and still, in his ever-present khaki shorts and smart linen shirt, he and Kaylie looked like Ken and Barbie.

Kaylie shot him a flirty smile.

"Oh, you mean as in no-children freedom," he said.

Kaylie and Chaz had met three years earlier, and Kaylie's unexpected pregnancy, and the surprise birth of their twins, had kept them running at a frenetic pace ever since. Chaz Crew had proven himself as not only a loving and involved father, but he was the calm to Kaylie's dramatic storms.

"I love my babies, but after two years of chasing the twins nonstop, I need this little break. Three whole days before they come with Mom. Three. Whole. Days. And two whole nights. It feels so decadent to be here in the middle of the week."

It had taken Kaylie two years after Lexi and Trevor were born to feel like herself again, and as Danica watched her sister's face light up at the prospect of time alone with her soon-to-be husband, she was glad they'd waited to have the wedding. At first, a double wedding had seemed like a bad idea. Danica had been sure Kaylie would want to be the star of the show, and wasn't it just as much Danica's day as Kaylie's? But Kaylie had proven her wrong time and time again; from choosing flowers to bridesmaid dresses, Kaylie was agreeable, and even deferred to Danica on several occasions. At times, Danica still had trouble processing just how much Kaylie had changed since she'd met Chaz. She was no longer a party girl, but a mature mother of two…who just so happened to have a flair for drama at times.

"Two whole nights," Chaz repeated.

"Now, that's what I'm talkin' about." Blake picked up their bags and hailed a cab.

Although the others thought he was teasing, Danica saw the gleam in his eye and recognized the hunger that had yet to abate between them. She felt a flush rush up her neck and ducked into the cab so no one would notice. Each time they made love, it left her wanting more, like a hormone-infused teenager. *Or a sex addict*, she mused. Lately, in the darkest hours of the night, when Blake lay sleeping beside her ravished and sated body, she found herself wanting more, thinking about new and different things she and Blake might try. Things that, in her pre-Blake years, she'd never have even entertained. But she'd never— ever—say such things out loud. Not even to him. She'd learned that from her parents' divorce a few years earlier. Danica knew that no matter how much she loved, and how much she trusted, sometimes life kicked you to the curb, and all that love—and all those promises in the dark—could be forgotten just as quickly as they'd slipped from her lips. A partner could walk away at any moment, taking the dirty scenes of their intimate moments with them and sharing them with God knew whom. She wasn't having cold feet, and she trusted Blake explicitly, but some lessons were engrained too deeply to simply forget.

"Oh no. I'm talking about sleep, my friend." Kaylie linked her arm through Chaz's as they climbed into the cab. "My man needs to rest."

After Chaz had taken over full ownership of the Indie Film Festival his father had started, he'd planned on taking the business to a whole new level. He'd been working night and day to ensure that he would never be desperate for sponsors again, and he'd succeeded. The bags under his eyes, and his slow pace, revealed the stress of working twelve-hour days and then coming home to late nights with the toddlers.

Danica and Kaylie both gasped as they entered the elaborately decorated hotel. The incredibly high ceilings, and the widely sculpted, artistically weathered pillars, were highlighted by salmon-colored granite floors speckled with flecks of black, white, and gold, dramatically reflecting the crystal of the chandeliers.

Kaylie took Danica's hand. "Oh my God. This belongs to Blake's cousin?"

"Yeah. Treat Braden," Danica said in a breathy voice. "This is too much."

Blake put his hand on the small of her back. "He was happy to comp us the venue. It's his wedding gift to us."

"He must be loaded," Kaylie said.

"Kaylie!" *Maybe Kaylie hasn't changed that much after all.*

Kaylie smiled, and covered her mouth with her hand. "Oops. Sorry."

Blake took it in stride. "He is loaded. His entire family is well off, but you'd never know it. All five brothers, and his sister, too. But they're good people. Very humble, generous to a fault."

"And from what Blake told me, each one is more handsome than the next, and yet they're all single. Even Savannah, their sister."

Kaylie furrowed her brow. "Are they all gay? I mean, women must flock to them, and guys to her."

Blake shook his head as he checked in at the registration desk.

"They're not gay; trust me, they all play the field. A lot," he said as they headed to their separate rooms, agreeing to meet for a quick bite once they were settled in.

Danica brought her wedding checklist to the café to go over it
one last time.

"Everyone arrives Friday. Sally and Max are bringing our
dresses with them; the flowers and food are all set, and Treat has
reserved an entire island for the ceremony. Oh, and of course a
boat, too, to get to the island." Danica let out a relieved sigh,
wondering what she might have forgotten. She still couldn't
believe that they were really getting married. She grabbed
Blake's hand, and when he turned his green eyes toward her, the
yellow specks that had always intrigued her were dancing in the
light.

He put his other hand on her cheek and said, "Yes, we're
really doing this."

He'd been reminding her every chance he got that she
would soon be his wife. Danica found it funny. He'd been the
player when they'd met, not her, and yet he was the one afraid
she'd leave him at the altar. "Yes, we are," she assured him.

"Oh, please. Get a room." Kaylie set the menu down as the
waitress arrived and took their orders.

The waitress's pearl-white teeth contrasted against her deeply tanned skin, and colorful beads were weaved through tiny
braids in her long dark hair. Danica expected some sort of island
accent, but when the summer beauty spoke, she was as Ameri-
can as apple pie. "I'll be y'all's waitress today. What can I get
ya?"

They ordered tropical drinks, salads, and sandwiches, and
Danica watched Kaylie survey the young waitress as she
sauntered away, her hourglass figure expertly defined beneath
the long, tight skirt and slinky tank top. She waited for Kaylie's
snarky remark.

Kaylie moved her chair closer to Chaz and said, "Wow, she is gorgeous. If that's what the tropical sun does to a girl, then I'm never leaving."

"Who are you and what have you done with my sister?" Danica was only half joking.

Kaylie swatted the air. "I'm old now, sis. I'm almost thirty, with two kids to boot."

"If that's old, then what does it say about me?" Danica asked.

"You're right. At almost thirty-two, you are old. I'm still a spring chicken."

The waitress brought their drinks and meals, and Blake raised his glass. "To two marriages. May they last forever." They all clinked glasses.

Chaz took a drink, then asked, "What time does your father get in?"

Kaylie groaned.

"Play nice, Kaylie," Danica said. Kaylie hadn't seen their father since right after she graduated from college, when she'd found out about his long-term affair and he'd moved away and married his mistress. "He, Madeline, and Lacy get in today around six."

"Madeline is coming, too?" Kaylie asked with a long sigh.

Of course, Kaylie already knew their father's wife was coming. Danica shook her head at her sister's penchant for drama.

"Please tell me why he's coming on Wednesday when our wedding isn't until Sunday," Kaylie said. "I'll need more of these, please." Kaylie sucked down her drink and held up the glass, indicating to the waitress that she wanted a refill.

"Slow down, girl. You should at least be coherent when he arrives," Danica said. "He wants time with us, and he knows we'll be busy the day of the wedding. I told you all of this, and you agreed."

"I didn't agree," Kaylie said with a vehement shake of her head. "You just didn't listen to me when I said it would ruin my week. And that girl is coming, too. At least I don't have to be nice to *her*," Kaylie said.

Blake and Danica exchanged a worried glance. They'd anticipated how Kaylie might react to meeting their half sister, Lacy—their father's love child—who was born just a few years after Kaylie, while their parents were still married.

When the twins were born, Kaylie had refused to call her father. Danica had taken it upon herself to give him the news about his grandchildren, and through her father, she'd made contact with Lacy. Although Danica had yet to meet her in person, they'd been exchanging emails, phone calls, and even a few handwritten letters over the past year and a half. Kaylie had been livid at her for weeks about contacting their father, so Danica decided to keep her relationship with Lacy a secret...just until Kaylie settled down. And by her reaction, it appeared that the subject of their father was still an open wound.

"Kaylie, I let you make most of the decisions, and you won on the dress decision. You were worried about Chelsea and Camille forgetting the dresses, or something happening to them, and practically demanded that Max be in charge."

"She's Chaz's work wife. She gets everything done perfectly," Kaylie said with a wave of her hand.

"Work wife? Whatever. Listen, whether you like it or not, Lacy is our blood relative," Danica said carefully.

Kaylie pointed at Danica. "Half. If even that. I mean, how do we know she's really his? We don't know this Madeline woman. Maybe she's a slut. I mean, she has to be to break up a marriage, right?"

Chaz had heard this from Kaylie dozens of times. He

pushed back from the table. "Do you mind if I go lie down for a bit? I'm beat."

Kaylie touched his thigh. "Do you want me to come with you?"

"No, babe. I'm fine. I'm just gonna rest a bit so that I'm awake when your family arrives."

So, Chaz has learned the art of escape.

They kissed, and Kaylie turned back to Danica and Blake. "Sorry. He's been working a lot."

Danica had given up her therapy license almost three years earlier, when she'd realized her feelings for her new client— Blake—were not therapist-client appropriate. Even now, so many years later, she still could not ignore the therapist's voice inside her head. Danica tried to hold back the worry that nipped at her nerves, but as she watched Kaylie suck down another drink, the words tumbled out.

"Kaylie, is something wrong between you and Chaz?"

"What? No, of course not. Why?"

Danica shrugged, trying to downplay her concern. "He just seemed to take off awfully fast when we started talking about Dad."

Kaylie rolled her eyes.

There's the old Kaylie.

"He thinks I'm being childish about the girl."

Danica saw the pleading in her eyes; *Support me. Tell me I'm right.* She'd decided, after almost turning down Blake's proposal because of her sister's relationship drama, that she would play things straight from then on. She was done putting her own feelings aside in order to save Kaylie's from being hurt. Danica was sticking to her guns and allowing her true feelings to be known; she was determined to no longer placate Kaylie's needy side—*too much.* Her relationship with Lacy, however, was excluded from that straightforward deal. That subject had to be handled with kid gloves.

"Well…" Danica said.

Blake kissed her cheek and stood. "I'm gonna check out the gift shop. I'll meet you back at the hotel?"

"Sure." She watched him lazily, sexily saunter away, his thick, muscular back swaying with each step, and her favorite pair of jeans hugging his—

"What are you, fifteen?"

Danica hadn't realized she was licking her lips until Kaylie's voice interrupted her thoughts. She snapped her attention back to Kaylie. "What?" *Oh God. I've turned into one of those sex-crazed girls.* She made a mental note to tame her libido. At least in public.

"You look at him like he's a Chippendales dancer and you're made of one-dollar bills." Kaylie crinkled her nose, like she was disgusted at the thought.

"Don't you look at Chaz like that sometimes?"

Kaylie shrugged. "I guess. But once you have kids, you kind of put all that stuff aside."

Uh-oh. "Kaylie, now that the guys are gone, can we talk about Dad and Lacy? Just you and me?" She'd tried to bring up her father at least once each month since the twins were born, and each time, Kaylie had refused to discuss him. Danica had to try, just one last time.

"Why do you do this? Why do you feel the need to ruin a perfectly beautiful day? Isn't it bad enough that he's coming to the wedding?"

No need to beat me over the head with a stick. Lesson learned.

To continue reading, be sure to pick up the next
LOVE IN BLOOM release:

SISTERS IN WHITE, *Snow Sisters, Book Three*

More Books By Melissa

LOVE IN BLOOM SERIES

SNOW SISTERS
Sisters in Love
Sisters in Bloom
Sisters in White

THE BRADENS at Weston
Lovers at Heart
Destined for Love
Friendship on Fire
Sea of Love
Bursting with Love
Hearts at Play

THE BRADENS at Trusty
Taken by Love
Fated for Love
Romancing My Love
Flirting with Love
Dreaming of Love
Crashing into Love

THE BRADENS at Peaceful Harbor
Healed by Love
Surrender My Love
River of Love
Crushing on Love
Whisper of Love
Thrill of Love

SEXY STANDALONE ROMANCE
Tru Blue
Truly, Madly, Whiskey

THE MONTGOMERYS
Embracing Her Heart
Our Wicked Hearts
Wild, Crazy, Heart
Sweet, Sexy, Heart

BILLIONAIRES AFTER DARK SERIES

WILD BOYS AFTER DARK
Logan
Heath
Jackson
Cooper

BAD BOYS AFTER DARK
Mick
Dylan
Carson
Brett

HARBORSIDE NIGHTS SERIES
Includes characters from the Love in Bloom series
Catching Cassidy
Discovering Delilah
Tempting Tristan

More Books by Melissa
Chasing Amanda (mystery/suspense)
Come Back to Me (mystery/suspense)
Have No Shame (historical fiction/romance)
Love, Lies & Mystery (3-book bundle)
Megan's Way (literary fiction)
Traces of Kara (psychological thriller)
Where Petals Fall (suspense)

Acknowledgments

As I wrote *Sisters in Bloom* and lived with Kaylie, Danica, and each of their friends and family members (even if only in my mind), I realized that the number of people I would need and want to thank has grown significantly, reaching far back into my childhood and extending through my forty-something years. If you have interacted with me in any way, you've touched my life and inspired me. Since that would take too many pages to print, I would like to send a worldwide, heartfelt thank you and virtual hug to those who have touched my life, and if you have interacted with me in any way—via email, telephone, social media, or in person—you have touched my life.

To all of the generous bloggers, authors, readers, and reviewers who have supported my efforts, I toss you virtual chocolate kisses. Your time, energy, and enthusiasm are greatly appreciated.

My editorial staff deserves a gold medal for their patience, keen eyes, and inspiration. Kristen Weber, Penina Lopez, and Colleen Albert, I am indebted to you for helping me to refine my writing and giving my readers the quality they deserve. No one likes to be caught "peaking" when they should be "peeking."

A special thank you goes to Melissa Ann Rich, who came up with the name of Danica's youth center, No Limitz. It's perfect, and I hope you feel that my writing did the name justice.

Writing would not be possible if not for the incredible support of my family (nuclear and extended). I love you to the moon and back—and you'd better send Jess with me or I might lose my way.

www.MelissaFoster.com

Melissa Foster is a *New York Times* and *USA Today* bestselling and award-winning author. Her books have been recommended by *USA Today's* book blog, *Hagerstown* magazine, *The Patriot*, and several other print venues. Melissa has painted and donated several murals to the Hospital for Sick Children in Washington, DC.

Visit Melissa on her website or chat with her on social media. Melissa enjoys discussing her books with book clubs and reader groups and welcomes an invitation to your event. facebook.com/MelissaFosterAuthor

Free Reader Goodies
www.melissafoster.com/reader-goodies

Reader Group
facebook.com/groups/MelissaFosterFans

72321302R00224

Made in the
USA
Middletown, DE